OF THE DIVINE

Also by Amelia Atwater-Rhodes

Mancer Trilogy
Of the Abyss
Of the Divine

Young Adult Novels

Den of Shadows
In the Forests of the Night
Demon in My View
Shattered Mirror
Midnight Predator
Persistence of Memory
Token of Darkness
All Just Glass
Poison Tree
Promises to Keep

The Kiesha'ra
Hawksong
Snakecharm
Falcondance
Wolfcry
Wyvernhail

The Maeve'ra
Bloodwitch
Bloodkin
Bloodtraitor

OF THE DIVINE

Mancer: Book Two

AMELIA ATWATER-RHODES

HARPER
VOYAGER
IMPULSE
An Imprint of HarperCollins*Publishers*

This is a work of fiction. Names, characters, places, and incidents are products of the author's imagination or are used fictitiously and are not to be construed as real. Any resemblance to actual events, locales, organizations, or persons, living or dead, is entirely coincidental.

OF THE DIVINE. Copyright © 2017 by Amelia Atwater-Rhodes. Printed in the United States of America. No part of this book may be used or reproduced in any manner whatsoever without written permission except in the case of brief quotations embodied in critical articles and reviews. For more information, address HarperCollins Publishers, 195 Broadway, New York, NY 10007.

Digital Edition August 2017 ISBN: 978-0-06-256215-9
Print Edition ISBN: 978-0-06-256216-6

Cover design by Guido Caroti
Cover photographs: © Getty Images; © Shutterstock

Harper Voyager, the Harper Voyager logo, and Harper Voyager Impulse are trademarks of HarperCollins Publishers.
HarperCollins is a registered trademark of HarperCollins Publishers in the United States of America and other countries.

FIRST EDITION

17 18 19 20 21 OPM 10 9 8 7 6 5 4 3 2 1

Of the Divine is dedicted to Chivas, 2007–2017,
and to the bluest pair of eyes I have ever seen.
Chivvy, you have been part of my life, part of my work,
and part of my heart since you came to me as a tiny
kitten, and nothing is quite the same without you.

OF THE DIVINE

PROLOGUE

The ocean that covered most of the Numen's first level was clear and sweet. It lapped against diamond sand where tiny long-legged birds spread wings the color of honey as they raced back and forth, plucking drifting seeds from the air. The Numini—those perfect, beautiful sentinels who ruled the divine realm by might and decree—watched the birds' antics with gentle amusement.

One Numini looked past the white sands and crystal waters below to a realm where the ocean was cold and tasted of salt, where verdant green cascaded across rich earth, and where the mortal creatures lived.

Soon, she thought. She was one of the three arbiters who ruled the Numen, second only to the high justice of her kind.

"I am concerned about the Abyssi," remarked one of her brothers, a lesser judge. "We have worked for generations to nurture these lines of power, and now they could all be—"

"Have faith," she assured him. "Abyssi scrabble at the mortal realm like dogs at a closed door. They always have. They lack the wisdom or discipline to do more than that."

"But do the mortals have the wisdom to keep the door closed?" he challenged.

"Faith," the arbiter said again. This time it was a clear chastisement.

She knew their children in the mortal world were defenseless. Humans had minds barely capable of comprehending their own existence, and as a consequence lived short and brutal lives. They needed their divine guardians to guide and nurture them. The Abyssi—vicious, mindless beasts of the infernal realm—could fight for sovereignty all they wanted. In the end, it wouldn't matter.

In the mortal realm, all things served the divine.

PART 1

Spring, Year 3917 in the Age of the Realms

Seventy-One Years Before
The Events of Book I: Of the Abyss

CHAPTER 1

VERTE

"Back up," Verte whispered. Tealyn was following too closely, her presence disrupting his ability to read the currents of magic in the area.

"Sir, are you sure that is wise?"

Verte paused, drawing air slowly into his lungs and then letting it out again so his impatience with the situation wouldn't spill out in his words. Then he asked, "What exactly is your plan if we open this door and find a cabal of hostile sorcerers?"

The door in question hung slightly crooked on the front of a run-down home at the outer edge of the docks district. It was one of the last places Verte had wanted to be that afternoon, but on the long list of responsibilities that came with the title Terre, responding immediately to reports of malevolent sorcery was near the top. The fact that his original plans had included an intimate dinner with the witty, powerful and beautiful sorceress whom he was courting, and *not* a criminal who might or might not be in command of potentially murderous magic, was not a sufficient excuse to neglect his duty.

Tealyn reluctantly moved back a pace. "My plan is to stay behind you, sir, allow you to address the magical threat in the way you consider best, and only engage the subject if you signal me to do so."

She sounded as if she was reciting, which she might have been. Tealyn had only been promoted a week ago, elevated from the ranks of city soldiers to one of the prince's personal bodyguards. She took her job seriously, and clearly wasn't comfortable with the expectation that she should step back and let him face the danger head-on.

If this had been a mundane situation, Verte would have trusted her blade to protect him, but Tealyn wasn't a sorcerer. Like any citizen of Kavet, her primary defense against magical maleficence was *him*.

Verte put his palm flat on the splintery wooden door and closed his eyes, blocking out visual distractions—and mental ones, like thoughts of how Henna would react when a messenger told her he would be late—so he could examine the power seething inside. He heard Tealyn shift behind him so she could protect his back. Certain she would be more than enough to warn off any would-be pickpockets, Verte gave himself over entirely to his magical sight.

What he discovered was a chaotic soup of spells, old magic mingled with cold.

As the name implied, old magic had existed in Kavet for centuries; its practitioners displaying skills ranging from healing to the ability to speak to plants and, rarely, even power over the dead.

Cold magic, which was Verte's specialty, had appeared in Kavet more recently; Verte's great-grandfather had written of it as a strange new phenomenon in his journals. Some cold magic users used it to create light, or to sculpt stone or metal. Almost all could use it to manipulate and persuade.

"Wenge," Verte called, pushing with his power as well as his voice, "come to the door."

Verte's magic struck the haze of half-formed spells inside. They writhed in response, trying to thrust him away from the sorcerer who was most likely equal parts their master and their prisoner.

Wenge had been accused of maleficence—specifically, of committing fraud through a combination of spirit work and cold magic, which allowed him to manipulate the recently bereaved into paying him ridiculous amounts of money to speak to their lost loved ones. Few people really could speak to the dead; Verte had never met anyone who could do so with the regularity and reliability that Wenge claimed. Even if his séances were legitimate, using power to manipulate customers into agreeing to his price was itself illegal.

This was the second time Wenge had been accused. The first time, he had gone to court, paid the fine, repaid his duped customers, and agreed to cease the illegal practices. This time, if he were found guilty, the penalty would be harsher.

"Who's there?" a voice finally rasped.

Wenge was supposed to be in his mid-thirties, but the voice sounded like a frail old man's. Working with the dead could suck the moisture from a person, leaving him hoarse and trembling.

"Terre Verte."

Silence answered him, and stillness.

"Sir?" Tealyn asked softly. "Do you want me to go around—"

"Hush," Verte snapped softly. He would need to apologize for the sharpness later, but just then he needed all his concentration in case Wenge wasn't as docile as he seemed.

He heard the *snick* of a bolt pulling back, and then the door opened slowly. Verte wasn't surprised to see that Wenge appeared gaunt and pale. His lips were chapped, he had bags under his eyes, and his body trembled as if he was recovering from the flu.

It wasn't the flu. It was power exhaustion—maybe even addiction.

"Do you know why I'm here?" Verte asked.

"You're here to help me," Wenge answered. "Aren't you?"

"Do you need help?"

"They talk to me all the time," Wenge whispered, his eyes wide. "I can't get them to be quiet. I just want them to go away. I want them all to go away."

He looked up with watery gray eyes, bleached of all color by the time he had spent staring past the mortal veil.

Verte shuddered inwardly. Though a child of magic users tended to inherit at least some form of power, most sorcerers in Kavet were born from otherwise mundane families, their power unbidden, its strength and type decided, as far as anyone knew, by a random toss of divine dice.

Supposedly, many of the Terre ancestors had claimed incredible power over the dead, but Verte was glad to have little of that skill. He had seen what it could do to a person.

"You've been accused of maleficence," Verte said formally. "You have the right to a trial, but it is also your right to forego a trial and take the brand, at which point all charges will be dropped." More gently, he added, "It will make the ghosts go away."

The brand, crafted on a spell-imbued forge deep under the palace, severed a sorcerer from his magic absolutely and permanently. Most practitioners saw it as a mutilation; even without the stigma, the long-term effects of stripping all magic from a body used to wielding power were unpredictable, potentially including long-term physical or mental damage.

Wenge, however, appeared overjoyed at the suggestion. "It will? You're sure?"

"I swear it." Verte's heart went out to the poor, desperate man. According to Verte's sources, Wenge had refused three offers from the Order of Napthol to help him study and control his power. Verte didn't know why, only that the evidence was irrefutable. If he insisted on going to trial, he would be found guilty, branded anyway, and face additional criminal penalties.

"Can we do it now?"

"Creating the brand takes some time, but we can start now. Will you come with me?"

Wenge nodded. Verte tried to show only assurance and compassion on his face, and keep his relief hidden. There was always a potential for violence during a visit like this.

They crossed through the docks district, drawing only moderate attention. Tealyn wisely kept back, keeping a wary eye on the crowd without drawing Wenge's attention to her.

At this late-afternoon hour, the busy shipping port bustled with people trying to get their work done for the day so they could enjoy the evening, so no one paid much attention to Verte. His fair, fawn-colored skin—at its palest this time of year, after the long, bitter winter—marked him as a local, unlike the tawny-gold skins of the Tamari and the deeper brown and ebony skins of the Silmari, but there were enough Kavetans around that he didn't seem out of place in the crowd. The sharper-eyed merchants would notice that the cut and fabric of his clothes were a bit finer than average, but there was nothing that obviously identified him as the prince of the land. The few people who might have intercepted Verte paused when they saw Tealyn, whose tan and white regalia made her stand out in a crowd even before she was close enough for her sword to be visible.

Uninterrupted, Verte ushered Wenge past sailors, hucksters, craftsmen, bards, musicians, and the rest of humanity that continually filled this area. As they headed uphill to the city center, the smells of salt water, fresh and old fish, liquor, sweat, and perfume faded in favor of occasional wisps of smoke from wood stoves and forges.

Verte skirted the central market and approached the palace from the side, where the guard barracks were attached.

Wenge's steps started to drag. He whispered, barely loud enough for Verte to hear, "They say this is a bad idea."

"You cannot live your life as a slave to those who have gone before," Verte replied. "You need to let the living and dead alike move on."

Wenge glared up at him. Verte paused, keeping

his stance and expression neutral as he raised magical shields against a possible attack. His gaze flickered briefly to Tealyn, just long enough to signal her to move closer and be ready if she needed to step in.

"You don't know where the dead go," Wenge accused. "We talk of the realms beyond, of the Abyss and the Numen, but no one really knows for sure what happens once our shades pass out of the mortal realm. What if we just go screaming into the void? What if—"

Verte took the man's frail, trembling hand in his own. He wished he could use his magic to urge him to keep moving, but Wenge's decision whether to demand a trial or to take the brand willingly needed to be made without magical coercion.

"Even the royal house, with all our strength and training and resources, does not practice death sorcery. Maleficence or not," Verte said, hoping the words would pierce the man's sudden anxiety, "if you continue to let your power use you this way, it will kill you before the year is out. Of that I am certain."

Wenge's body sagged. He waved a hand next to his face as if to chase away a buzzing fly—or in this case, a whispering spirit. He flinched at whatever the ghost said, then muttered, "I do not know what to be without it."

"We will help you," Verte said again. "Counselors at the Order of Napthol will help you learn how to cope with the side-effects of giving up your power.

Once you're ready, an agent from the Ministry of Health and Prosperity can help you find mundane employment."

This time, Wenge allowed Verte to lead him the rest of the way inside, through a side door into the palace and downstairs into the row of cells kept for those accused of sorcery-based crimes.

The place wasn't quite a prison. The rooms had sturdy doors with good locks on them, and wards cast upon them to dampen power, but they also had clean, serviceable bedding and an alcove for the necessary. Guards on the hall monitored movement and controlled who came and went, but those who came willingly, like Wenge, were allowed a reasonable amount of freedom, provided with sufficient food, and given access to reading material and other simple pastimes.

It would take at least two days to craft the brand that would strip Wenge's power from him, and in the meantime, he would be treated as a respected though potentially fractious guest.

Verte took leave of Wenge, gave the information he had to the sorcerer-smith who would craft the brand, sent a messenger to the Cobalt Hall to request a counselor for Wenge, and instructed Tealyn to update the other guards.

Then he took winding back hallways from the barracks to his private quarters on the second floor, hoping to make the trip without interruption no matter how much it scandalized the servants to see him skulking back there. The formal areas of the palace were packed with visiting aristocrats from Tamar and Silmat who had come for the impending Apple Blossom Festival, and they tended to stop him to chat any time he passed. But he had spent all day looking forward to his rendezvous with Henna, and he had just barely enough time to clean up and still meet her at a vaguely reasonable dinner hour. He wasn't about to let another matter of "utmost importance" that would "only take a moment" delay him.

Nobles from Tamar and Silmat, who tracked their bloodlines back generations, thought it odd and quaint that Kavet's only prince would court a woman with no known family background, but Kavet's monarchy had never cared much about lineage—only magic. Verte's mother had been a refugee from the distant country of Ilban before she came to Kavet. She had brought with her a new kind of sorcery, generally referred to as hot magic. Henna was a sorceress of the same ilk.

Unfortunately, though he could safely avoid the thronging nobles, he couldn't ignore the page sitting in front of his door. The boy looked like he had been half dozing, but as Verte approached he came to attention and stood with a start, biting his lip as if chagrined at his drowsiness.

"Terre," he said, greeting Verte respectfully by title and with the half-bow appropriate for a longtime servant at home. "The emissary from the Osei requests your time tonight."

The word *emissary* was elevating Kegan's station quite a lot, Terre thought. He suspected the word *request* was also an embellishment. Though clearly a slave to the Osei, relaying their words and carefully refraining from any mention of his own thoughts or opinions, Kegan spoke with all the authority his masters believed they had.

"I will see him," Verte sighed. It couldn't be helped. His parents had other obligations that evening, which meant it was up to him to coddle the Osei *emissary*, even if Verte was quite certain it would be nothing but a reiteration of the arrangements they had already made in preparation for the Osei's actual arrival in another three days.

Like any Kavet native, Verte had seen the Osei in flight off Kavet's shores, and marveled at the way their massive, serpentine bodies and immense wings sparkled in the light of sun or moon, but he had only ever spoken with their human messengers. This would be the first time the creatures themselves had visited Kavet since the last treaties had been signed almost seven centuries ago, and their slave was insistent that preparations be made exactly as his masters commanded.

The last "urgent" summons had been about the formal dinner, and the fact that the flatware must be sterling silver made of a copper alloy and not an iron one. Verte had assured the slave it would be done despite not knowing the first thing about how the forks had been made. Sepia, the head housekeeper, had been livid that, weeks after they had been told that there must be *absolutely no iron* at the dinner or ball, the slave would think she was be stupid enough to set the table with it—if there even were such a thing as sterling silver made with iron.

Verte could think of better uses of his time than being a middle-man between a pretentious Osei slave and the highly qualified housekeeper, but the last time he had tried to dismiss Kegan—over a matter of whether the ball would include fiddle music or a woodwind quintet—the slave had warned that the Osei might call the entire visit off if they felt insulted.

They couldn't afford that.

In their natural forms, the Osei were large enough to lift a merchant vessel clean out of the ocean—or sink it in the blink of an eye. As if that wasn't enough, the beasts were also shapeshifters, capable of taking the forms of humans. It was rumored they could read minds. All that made them uncomfortable allies and potentially deadly enemies.

Kavet was an island. They could not rightly take their place in the wider world when crossing seas the Osei claimed as territory exacted strangling penalties. But the old treaties had been fashioned in a time when Kavet had been a handful of city-states allied under the Terre line. They had possessed some of what was now called old magic, but it hadn't been enough to give the young nation an advantage against the Osei, who claimed dominion over all the world's waterways.

Times had changed. Kavet had changed, and it was time to renegotiate.

CHAPTER 2

DAHLIA

Dahlia peered into the half-empty canvas sack that held all she had to show for five years of teaching: a few personal notes from her students and their parents, a scattering of trinkets, and several pens and bottles of ink.

Is that really all?

Over the years, she had collected books, samplers, examples, lesson plans, and supplies she could have claimed as her own, but she planned to leave them for the next teacher who used this room. She wouldn't need them. She was done teaching.

Her heart gave a little thump.

"Dahlia?"

The concerned query came from Maimeri, a fellow teacher and good friend who had come to help Dahlia pack away the remnants of one life in preparation for another.

"I'm sorry," Dahlia replied. "My mind was a million miles away."

Breathing past her anxiety and trying not to let her hands shake, Dahlia took down the decorative quilt, which had been embroidered with one of the sixteen key tenets of the Quin faith: *Holy are the teachers and the students, for study and learning are the heart of faith.*

She had almost left it because it had been intended as a gift for a teacher, and that wasn't what she planned to be. However, the quilt spoke to teachers *and* students, and once she left this small, tightly knit Quin community, she intended to be a student once again. She would learn everything there was to learn in the city. If it truly was as rife with sorcery and corruption as everyone warned her, maybe she would come home, or maybe she would find a place there working to improve the situation.

She was making the right decision; she knew it. She just needed her stinging eyes and pounding heart to believe her.

"Just fifty miles, I suspect," Maimeri corrected, reaching over to squeeze Dahlia's hand. "You already know I think you're mad, and *I* already know I'll never talk you out of leaving, so I'm not going to give another lecture. I just—" She paused, eyes widening as if something just occurred to her. "Has anyone warned you not to look for or accept any employment near the harbor?"

"Why would I go looking for a job at the docks?"

Everyone Dahlia knew had warned her of the dangers of Kavet's capital city, Mars, but this was the first time anyone had suggested she might consider work at the busy shipyard. All she had ever heard of being down at the docks, aside from the obvious ships, were taverns and brothels.

Maimeri sighed. "I *know* you. I know you're better suited to a farm than a classroom—oh, I don't mean it that way," she said, her freckled face flushing as she worried she had given offense, though Dahlia hadn't taken any. "You're a fine teacher, but you don't love it. You'd rather be driving a plow through rocky fields in pounding rain than give one more grammar lesson. There are jobs at the docks that call for education like yours, scribes and tariff secretaries and the like. I can imagine you thinking it would be exciting to work there, where you could see the ships come and go and interact with captains from far away . . . oh, dear. You had no idea, did you?"

Dahlia hadn't.

"You think I could get a job like that?" she asked, intrigued.

"*No!*" Maimeri gasped. "I didn't mean—*oooh*, well, someone in the city would have mentioned it, impressionable girl like you, so it's good I brought it up."

We're almost the same age, Dahlia resisted the urge to say.

Maimeri said, "You know my mother came from the city."

Oh, this was going to be one of *those* stories. Dahlia perked up. Maimeri started all stories about her mother the same way, as if Dahlia might have forgotten her mother's origins since the last hundred times she was reminded, but that was fine—the stories were usually worth hearing. Maimeri's mother had been born a child of A'hknet, an amoral sect condoning all sorts of scandalous behavior, ranging from theft and lying to witchcraft and prostitution. The path that had finally resulted in her giving up her wild ways and swearing fealty to the Followers of the Quinacridone out of love for Maimeri's father always reminded Dahlia of a fairy tale.

Maimeri continued. "She says girls and ladies who live or work down at the docks are taught to always carry a knife. Anyone who looks like she won't be missed is liable to be picked up by slavers."

"Slavers?" Dahlia echoed skeptically.

"To the *Osei*," Maimeri hissed, dropping her voice as if afraid the creatures in question would overhear her. Dahlia instinctively flicked her gaze toward the window, beyond which she could sometimes see the Osei gliding on their immense, jewel-colored wings. Today she saw only a shepherd sitting on a rock, watching his charges. "A ship captain who's in debt to the

Osei and can't pay in coin can pay in people. I've heard the Osei eat them." Maimeri shuddered. "You're going to be alone in the city, no longer surrounded by people who know you and will protect you. If you're working down at the docks, sooner or later someone is going to decide you won't be missed, and well, you're a pretty girl. You might be valuable."

If the Osei would just eat me anyway, why does it matter what I look like? It seemed like a logical flaw to Dahlia, and besides, it wasn't true. With enough effort, she could pass as moderately attractive, but that kind of vanity was frowned upon. Most days she was acceptably bland, with her straw-blond hair tied back to keep it out of the way, her hazel eyes unpainted, and her strong fingers tanned by sun, hardened by labor, and frequently stained with ink.

Whether or not Maimeri was right about what the Osei did with their slaves, Dahlia had heard they kept them. *Everyone* knew that, though she had never stopped to consider how they got them.

"I'll avoid the docks," she assured Maimeri. Her eyes fell on the clock and she jumped. She had dawdled in the classroom far too long. "Oh, goodness! I have to go! Mister Cremnitz is going to be here tonight and I promised Mother I would help prepare dinner."

Maimeri's eyes widened. *"Celadon* Cremnitz?"

Dahlia nodded distractedly, hoisting the canvas sack and taking one last look around the tidy room.

"I saw him speak when I visited the city for market day last year," Maimeri whispered. If her voice became any lower and more dramatic, Dahlia wouldn't be able to hear her. "He's—he's—" She stammered, and Dahlia fought a grin at the ever-loquacious Maimeri brought to speechlessness by a city boy. In a few moments, she gulped audibly, then went on. "You know he goes before the Terre himself to protest unjust laws? He spoke at trial for a Quin boy who was jailed for refusing to greet Terra Sarcelle by title."

"I've heard." Celadon's famed virtue was why Dahlia's father trusted him to be her chaperone on her three-day journey, and his aunt to be her host until she was independently settled in the city. Dahlia had heard enough Celadon Cremnitz stories in the last month that she could only hope they were exaggerated.

"Maimeri, I need to go. I'll write to you when I'm settled."

She hugged the other woman, and discovered there were tears in her eyes.

"You don't *need* to go," Maimeri said.

"I do. Thank you for—" She broke off, thinking of the all the days they had spent curled up in front of the hearth at either Dahlia's house or Maimeri's, planning lessons, grading papers, and debating pedagogy, politics, religion, or even just town gossip. "For everything."

They separated reluctantly, but there wasn't time for a longer goodbye.

Dahlia dashed home, bordering on unseemly as she swung a leg over her horse's saddle too quickly to arrange her skirts properly and thus flashed a great deal of leg at anyone who happened to be looking. Her mother kept trying to convince her to buy a pair of riding pants, but the ride to and from work wasn't long enough to justify an entirely different outfit when a saddle blanket did the job well enough.

At home, she was immediately greeted by a gaggle of unruly ducks, who were barely bright enough to avoid being trampled by the horse as they demanded acknowledgement and begged for handouts.

Maimeri had been half right earlier. When sitting in a classroom teaching the same lesson for what felt like the hundredth time, answering the same questions, and making the same corrections on papers, Dahlia *had* daydreamed about being home, tending the ducks, horses, and goats, and helping to turn and plant the fields alongside her father. When this was all her life had been, though, she had craved opportunities to challenge her mind.

Like most Quin, Dahlia's father believed that everyone benefited from education, so he had supported her interest in continuing her studies even when that meant his only child became a teacher instead of taking over management of their vast holdings. He and Mother were both hale and healthy; they had faith that Dahlia would find her calling, then eventually settle down with a good man who could help care for the lands as she followed more academic pursuits.

"You could still change your mind," her father said as she passed him in front of the henhouse. This was the first day that had been warm and clear enough to send the ducks and chickens outside, allowing for a thorough spring cleaning. "How could you walk away from all this?" He lifted a shovelful of straw and excrement with a forced smile.

He didn't *want* her to leave the farm, and he wanted even less for her to go to the city, but—Numen bless him—he supported her decision despite that. Celadon Cremnitz's father served on the Quin leadership council with Dahlia's father; when it had become clear that Dahlia's restlessness wasn't going to subside as the seasons changed, her father had used his connections to arrange for her escort and support in the city.

"Maybe I'll bring a duck with me." Dahlia smiled back.

"Celadon is here," he said. "He arrived about midday, says the roads are better than he expected. I didn't realize he was so . . ." He trailed off.

Dahlia tried to fill in the blanks based on what she had heard about the famous preacher, who had left his home and moved to the heart of the wicked city to support the Quin movement there. "Severe?" she suggested. "Eloquent?" People who had seen him or heard of him raved about his charismatic sermons.

"*Pretty*," he huffed, the crease between his brows deepening. "This is the man I'm sending my daughter off with."

"From everything I've heard," Dahlia said around a chuckle, "he would die of shock if I dared do something as improper as *flirt*. I think you're safe." Belatedly, she processed more of what her father had said. "He's *here*? Already? Oooh, Mother is going to *kill* me for being late!"

She hurried inside, trying to rush without *looking* rushed. She wanted to make a good first impression, not only because Celadon was such a well-respected figure in the community, but also because she was going to be living with his family for an indeterminate length of time, and possibly working with them as well if she struggled to find other employment.

The image she confronted when she entered the room was the last she had expected, and she burst out laughing.

A young man who could be no other than the famous Celadon was sitting cross-legged in front of the hearth with a duck upside-down in his lap as Dahlia's indomitable mother hovered over him, apparently instructing him on the finer points of petting the molting feathers from its belly.

Her laugh startled Celadon, who jumped and lifted his blond head, revealing blue eyes that widened farther when the duck in his lap panicked, squawked, flipped itself over and pecked at him, sending the small pile of down Celadon had gathered floating into the air.

Dahlia's mother tended to the fleeing duck and Celadon stood hastily, brushing feathers from his clothes as he regained his composure.

He had a soft face, a bit of what Maimeri called "city plumpness," and lacked the deep tan common in farming communities. Combined with his blond hair, which had just enough curl for the tips of strands to twist away from its otherwise neat, short style, the result was indeed "pretty," in a cloth doll kind of way.

Dahlia tried to be kind and cease her chuckling as Celadon approached, clearing his throat and offering his hand. "You must be Dahlia?" When she nodded, not trusting herself to open her mouth yet, he added, "I'm Celadon Cremnitz. It's an honor to meet you at last. My father speaks quite highly of your family." He glanced out the door where the duck and Dahlia's mother had escaped. "It will be all right, won't it? I don't have much experience with ducks."

He had a nice voice, deeper and more resonant than Dahlia would have imagined based on his looks.

She managed to compose herself enough to say, "It will be fine. I'm sorry I startled you. I couldn't believe my mother had a guest . . ." There were the giggles again, partly prompted by the memory of Celadon's horrified expression when the duck flailed away from him, but more so the result of weeks of anxious planning and waiting. She took a breath. "I'm sorry. I don't mean to be rude. I just . . ." *From everyone's stories, I pictured someone sharp-chinned and hard-eyed, skinny and severe like the preacher at the town meeting hall, who would never deign to do something as mundane as help pet down from a duck.* "I'm pleased to meet you as well."

The rest of the evening passed less eventfully; Celadon was complimentary of everything served for dinner, stood whenever one of the ladies stood, and seemed to win over even Dahlia's father. He wasn't as rigid and intimidating as Dahlia had expected based on rumor, just calmly, politely proper, in a way that made Dahlia sit a little straighter at the dinner table.

No one would ever say Dahlia Indathrone's parents hadn't raised her right.

CHAPTER 3

NAPLES

Naples sprawled at the back of the Cobalt Hall temple, flipping idly through his notes on the creation of warm foxfire.

He had been quite proud of the globes he had made for the central fountain, which had kept the water from freezing all through Kavet's frigid winter. He had made four last fall; one had lasted all the way until this spring before finally guttering out. The others, he had replaced as they failed, each new one a bit stronger, brighter, and warmer than the last, but making foxfire, while exceptionally useful, nicely lucrative for the Order, and certainly the latest fad, was getting tedious. He was glad Henna had taken the commission for the city stables.

If he had to spend another week building one of those itty magical flames to strength, like a mother bird tending to a runty chick, just so it could keep some horses from shivering for a few months, he was going to lose his mind.

He wanted to do something *new*. Something big. Something no one had ever done before. The desire was like kitten claws drawn down his spine, an itch so sharp it bordered on pain which he simply couldn't find a way to scratch. He was so restless he had actually accepted a job—a stupid, mundane assignment to serve in the palace during the festival ball—just for a break in the tedium. Hopefully he would earn a little pocket money while he was at it. Maybe someday he could travel, and seek rare and foreign magic to bring back to Kavet.

"Naples?"

He tilted his head to see Dove, an expert at old magic, who had spent many long hours trying to teach him to harness the Order's oldest and most respected forms of sorcery. Naples' complete lack of ability with that power was unusual in their order, and more and more as he came of age he caught Dove looking at him with dismissive pity.

"Yes?" he asked.

"There's a visitor for you," she said. "I'm on my way

out, so I can tell him you aren't available if you're in the middle of a project."

Naples looked at his books dismissively. He wasn't busy exactly, but he was in a lousy mood, and unsure if he was fit for company. "You're working?" he asked, taking in Dove's somber attire. At home in the Hall, she dressed as casually as any of them did. The modest blue-gray dress she wore currently, buttoned up the back with a row of onyx beads and embellished only with swirls of darker blue embroidery at the cuffs and high collar, was one he only ever saw her wear on vigil visits, when she went to comfort the bereaved who were having trouble recovering from the loss of a loved one. Her strength with old magic gave her insight into grief and the kind of healing that needed to follow both expected and unexpected death.

Unlike his hot sorcery, which, she had once remarked when she thought he was out of earshot, was, "Very good at producing impressive baubles and luxuries, but not essentially useful on a day-to-day basis."

Her mouth set in a grim line. "A messenger from the palace just informed me that Wenge is taking the brand. I've volunteered to serve as his counselor."

Naples winced, sucking in a breath. He knew the name. Dove had been trying to convince Wenge to accept help with his power for years, hoping he could avoid this fate.

"I'm sorry," Naples said. She had to be devastated

that someone she had tried so hard to help had fallen so far. "If you want to . . . talk . . ." The offer was awkward and halting, because they had never been close friends, but he knew he had to say *something*.

She gave him a small smile, thankful but dismissive. "You have a guest," she reminded him. "Cyan, of the *Blue Canary*."

Naples' heart skipped a beat. "Cyan? Really?"

The clash of conflicting emotions from the two pieces of information—Wenge and the brand, and Cyan at the door—made his head spin. He tried not to let the excitement show too obviously on his face, because it was inappropriate in Dove's presence just then, but he couldn't help it.

"I need to gather my tools," Dove said, stepping past him toward the rows of shelves.

He nodded, and kept his pace sedate as he put his books away and exited the temple.

The moment he had passed the doors, though, he hurried down the long, winding staircase, past the second floor living quarters, and to the common rooms. If he hadn't grown up in this place, he probably would have broken his neck dashing down the well-worn, slightly irregular stone stairs, but his feet knew the way too well.

He skidded to a halt just before he reached the main foyer, where his guest would be waiting, as he realized he was half dressed and more than a little rumpled. His feet were bare against the chilly stone floor and his long black hair had been tied back hastily a few hours ago with the intention of keeping it away from his eyes and the fire he worked with, not of looking neat.

He glanced back the way he had come, wondering if it would make sense to have Cyan wait a few minutes while he cleaned up. This wasn't the impression he—

"Naples?"

He spun toward the doorway to the foyer, which was now filled by a broad-shouldered man dressed in the simple shirt, jerkin, breeches, and boots favored by Silmari sailors. Sun and sea air had given a bronze glow to his deep brown skin, which stood out against the ivory of his linen shirt—and even more so, Naples knew, against the milky undertones of his own skin, which by the end of summer would still look like it had never seen the sun.

Any Kavet native would have heeded Dove's instruction to wait, as would any foreign noble, the former because of the awe they tended to hold toward the Order of Napthol and the latter because aristocrats were used to the layers of formality and etiquette that made up court life. Cyan of course was neither; that was one of the things Naples loved about him.

Not love, he chastised his errant thoughts. *Don't be foolish. You only see him a few days each year.*

"You're early," Naples said, the first words that came to mind. "I didn't expect you for another week."

Of course, that had stopped him from going down to the docks each afternoon to see which new ships had come in.

"Captain skipped part of our regular route to bring in a large shipment for some local festival. I thought I'd take the chance to see you in your natural habitat." Cyan touched Naples' cheek with a teasing grin that was explained when his fingertips came away ashy. "It's a treat to catch you without your armor."

Naples raised a questioning brow. Cyan had seen him naked. How much less armor could a man have?

His confusion seemed to amuse the sailor, who tugged on Naples' tangled ponytail, then wrapped a hand around the back of his neck to pull him forward for a kiss. Naples' eyes closed instinctively, then opened again when he heard footsteps.

His gaze met Dove's accidentally as she came down the stairs, then hers slid away. Naples felt heat rise in his face as she quietly slipped past them and out the door.

"You're *shy* suddenly," Cyan murmured, smiling, as Naples pulled back. "Is this the same hussy who fearlessly prowls the Mars docks?"

My mother *lives here*, Naples had the sense not to say. He had grown up in the Cobalt Hall; except for the youngest novices, most of the people here saw and treated him like a son. Like a child. The only time Naples had tried to flirt with one of the new novices, it had elicited so many sidelong glances and patronizing remarks he had decided never to try it again, and to turn down any overtures they made.

He glanced away from Cyan to try to regain his equilibrium and his gaze fell on the hall clock.

"Shit," he whispered. "It's late. I mean, *I'm* late. I—oh, of all the Abyss damned luck. I'm working during the Apple Blossom Ball, too. If I'd had any idea you would be in town . . ." He trailed off, miserably, realizing he'd missed his chance to actually have a *date* for Kavet's largest holiday, which was three days away.

"A man has to work," Cyan said, understandingly— and completely failing to understand.

Naples didn't need to work, beyond what he already did at the Cobalt Hall. All his needs were met by the royal house in exchange for his help giving instruction to those who came to the Hall with uncontrolled power and his occasional work on commissions like the fountains' foxfire. He had committed to work at the palace, though, so he would. Not doing so would damage his reputation, and that of the entire Order of Napthol.

"Before you go, I have something for you." Cyan reached into his vest pocket and pulled out a small, parchment-wrapped packet. "We stopped in the Forgotten Islands last winter and this made me think of you."

A gift. As Cyan had hinted, Naples was well known down at the Mars docks. He wasn't short on lovers—or at least, on meaningless liaisons—but he tried to be realistic, and he would have been shocked to learn any of them spared a thought for him when he wasn't there. Naples knew Cyan was different to *him*, but he hadn't expected the regard to go both ways.

"I only have a few minutes and I need to get cleaned up and dressed, but you're welcome to come upstairs if you want?" Naples offered belatedly.

He hadn't realized how obviously nervous he was about Cyan's presence until the sailor paused, looked him up and down, and asked, "Is that all right with you?"

Yes.

No.

He pictured the sailor walking into his quarters, which weren't large or lavish but were luxurious compared to a hammock strung in the cramped forecastle of the *Blue Canary*. Naples' space was decorated with a Tamari tapestry he had seen at the market and bought on impulse, a small collection of carved jade animals from Silmat inherited from his father, and lately a warm foxfire sphere the brilliant orange of the setting sun. The stone floor was softened by a woven rug so thick his toes sank into it, and the linens on his bed were combed wool and goose down.

Briefly, the thought of Cyan sprawled out on that plush, luxurious bed pushed his discomfort aside, and then he imagined how Cyan would react to seeing it. Unlike many sailors, Cyan had never assumed Naples was soft and spoiled and useless just because he was a sorcerer. That could change.

"I really should hurry," Naples said, telling the truth but evading the obvious question. "Can I come find you at the *Canary* later?"

"If you don't wait too long," Cyan said, the warning lightened by the teasing lilt in his tone. "And if you open that before you go."

He nodded to the gift in Naples' hands. Naples couldn't remember accepting it; he had been too startled by its offer.

He peeled back the parchment wrapping to reveal a scrimshaw carving of a hunting cat about the size of his palm. Its flank had been painted with symbols in purple and black ink.

"Shamans in the Forgotten Islands carve these and claim to enchant them," Cyan explained. "This one is supposed to bring pleasant dreams, but I have no idea if it's actually magic or not. Either way the cat reminded me of you, and if it is magic, I thought you might have fun doing . . . whatever it is you people do." Cyan idly flicked the silver charm dangling from Naples' left earlobe, stamped with the symbol of the Order of Napthol, three stylized waves inscribed in a circle.

"Thank you," Naples breathed.

Don't be stupid, he told himself. *He came here looking for you. No one's ever done that before. If you send him away, he won't assume you're embarrassed by what he might think of you. He'll assume you're ashamed to be seen with a simple sailor. He won't come back.*

Naples planted his feet, straightened his spine,

and drew in a slow grounding breath as if preparing to raise power. Instead, he lifted his gaze to Cyan's, knowing that in this dim light his irises were thin bands of molten copper.

The sailor's breath caught for a moment, and then he smiled slowly. "There's the Naples I know."

"I have a few minutes," Naples decided aloud. "Come on upstairs."

Naples had intended to be early, to make a good impression, and as a result was only a bit late. The head housekeeper, Sepia, seemed surprised that he had come at all; he wasn't sure if he should be frustrated by the low expectations, disappointed that he had apparently *met* those expectations, or relieved that it worked out in his favor.

The others hired as temporary help during Festival were mostly professional stewards and butlers borrowed from well-off families, mixed with adult children of shopkeepers and craftsmen. They all gathered in the vast palace kitchens to receive instructions.

Sepia explained their presence while evaluating their appearance as a group.

"As you all know, the palace is hosting a delegation of Osei for the first time in centuries." She frowned at a boy younger than Naples, who was gazing wide-eyed around the room. "What you probably do not know is that an Osei pride—that's what they call their nuclear group—consists of a queen and several mates, called princes." Naples did know that, but his education as a member of the Order of Napthol had probably focused more on those magical beasts than the average citizen of Kavet. "Princes never speak to or interact with any woman other than their queen. Unfortunately, half the regular staff of the palace are women, so—*Your Majesty.*"

She broke off, dropping into a brief curtsey. Naples turned, following Sepia's gaze, to find a woman in a luxurious emerald velvet dressing gown, worn casually and untied to reveal the simple cotton dress—barely more than a frock—beneath.

Even if he hadn't heard Sepia's greeting, Naples could have identified Terra Sarcelle. It wasn't her porcelain-fair skin he knew, or her mahogany hair, which had half fallen from its pins. It was her magic. Henna was the strongest hot magic user at the Cobalt Hall—after Naples—but even after a week of elaborate ritual, she never exuded this level of pure, magnificent *power.*

"*Naples,*" Sepia hissed, chastising him for his inappropriate staring.

Terra Sarcelle laughed, a throaty sound carried on a wave of honey-sweet magic. "Don't worry, Sepia," she assured her head servant. "He's given no offense. In fact, I believe his assistance may be useful to me. Can you manage without him?"

The words were asked as a courtesy. Sepia replied,

"Of course, Terra," with only the faintest note of disapproval in her tone.

The Terra waved informally for Naples to follow her, then spoke with her back to him as she led him up the hall. "I don't believe you're new to the Cobalt Hall. That means they have done a very good job of hiding you away. Why is that?"

Naples frowned, about to object that no one had been "hiding" him, but then an awkward truth crossed his mind. Inside the Cobalt Hall, it was no secret that the king and queen had been estranged almost since the birth of their only son, or that Naples' mother was the king's longtime mistress. Naples' younger brother, Clay, was the king's bastard son. Considering all of that, it was quite possible that a deliberate effort had been made to keep Naples from crossing this woman's path.

"I don't do much work in the palace," he answered, trying to be politic.

"That is going to change."

As Terra Sarcelle pushed open a door, Naples realized they were leaving the servants' areas of the palace and entering what had to be the wing containing the royal family's private quarters. "As it happens, I am in the midst of a very complicated, very difficult and exceptionally important piece of work. My husband and son do what they can, but they favor cold magic, which is useless for my side of the spell. Your power is similar enough to mine that I can use it."

The phrasing felt vaguely threatening to Naples, and he noticed that she didn't try and pretend he had a choice in the matter. Any member of the royal house had the right to demand service from any member of the Order of Napthol, but such requisitions were usually made politely, through messengers and paperwork—not through an autocratic draft.

You wanted to do something different, Naples thought, remembering his boredom. *Here's your chance.* Besides, the Terra was credited with bringing hot magic to the country when she had come to Kavet and married Terre Jaune just a handful of years before Naples was born. He wanted to see this project of hers.

CHAPTER 4

HENNA

Henna trailed her fingers through the rune stones without feeling them.

The letters etched on the stones were meaningless to her. It was the stones themselves—irregular, slightly translucent pieces of black volcanic glass kissed with white blooms—that focused her power and allowed her brief glimpses into other times and places. In this case . . .

Pounding waves, howling wind, flashes of lightning before growls of thunder, and the slick boards of the ship lurching beneath her feet. A little girl laughed, tossing long, tangled hair out of her bright hazel eyes as she scrambled to help secure the deck. Rain cascaded down her tawny-brown skin, but it was summer rain, warm like—

Warm like blood.

Blood splashed across stone. Gray cobbles stained scarlet. So much blood. Was this the old nightmare, or a new one? The little girl on the ship was Henna from long ago, but the blood . . .

Too late to make sense of it. Another vision subsumed the first.

A woman in a cinnamon-colored dress danced briefly before Henna's inner eye, then twirled away. Words came to Henna without her consciously seeking them. "Trouble in your path," she murmured. "Don't trust her." The woman smiled with painted lips. "She will cherish your heart but devour your security. You need to decide."

In the world outside the visions—the real world, the *current* world—a man standing nearby said something. But all Henna could hear was the click of the rune stones as she ran her fingers through them.

The visions didn't always come just because she sat here and offered to give prophecy for a coin. Thankfully, her usual customers didn't care if she spoke the truth or made up a story. They came for entertainment, and most days, her prophecies were nothing but wish-fulfilling inventions.

Other days, true visions came to her like storm

waves over the deck of a ship, threatening to drown the woman who had once been a little girl who laughed at the lightning.

The moment her customer left, Henna tried to turn her mind back to the blood on the cobblestones.

It was gone.

As soon as she tried to direct the visions instead of letting them drift the way they wanted, the trance broke. All Henna saw were the snowflake obsidian stones, which had been polished smooth, then carved with letters of an ancient language once spoken by an unremembered tribe.

"*Damn*," she whispered, blinking as the sounds, smells, and sights of the city square washed over her.

The cobbled plaza extended one hundred paces in each direction, packed with the carts, tables, and sprawled mats and blankets that delineated each merchant's claimed—and jealously guarded—space. The scents of roasting dainties, pastries, and perfumes mingled with the salt air that drifted up from the harbor. Conversation competed with street musicians and mongers touting their wares.

Henna looked up to gauge the time, then squeezed her eyes shut, momentarily blinded by the setting sun as it bounced off the mirror-polished marble decorations and pristine, sparkling windows of the palace that delineated the northern boundary of the square.

The time didn't matter, she remembered belatedly. Verte's messenger had said he would be late.

Other magic users who plied their wares here were just coming outside at this hour, transforming the city square from a place that sold luxury goods to one ringed with examples of Kavet's famous sorcery. Members of the Order of Napthol didn't need the money for survival, but the marketplace was a way to earn personal income, and for Henna it was a way to practice a gift that was hard to exercise in the predictable confines of the Cobalt Hall. It was also one of the novelties that brought a steady stream of foreign visitors and trade to the otherwise isolated island of Kavet, so the royal house encouraged it.

Henna had intended to stay a few hours, or until Verte arrived, but the vision had left her feeling shadowed and hunched, as if someone would suddenly look at her and say, *she doesn't belong here.*

It had happened before. Her Kavetan and Silmari customers didn't know any better, but she had seen the horror in more than one Tamari sailor's eyes when they got a good look at her and realized she wasn't some unusually dark-skinned Kavetan, but one of their own.

It was her hazel eyes, which were only found among the seafaring *boucan* caste, which gave her away. While working, Henna favored vivid scarlet and violet blouses and dark charcoal and mahogany eyeliner and shadow, which drew the attention away from her eyes and made her just one of the crowd of performers, but she was still careful to avoid meeting anyone's gaze directly. Many of the magic users who practiced "show trade" adopted similar garb, so no one in the Order of Napthol questioned her chosen style, or realized that the games they played to make themselves appear dramatic and mysterious for their customers were indispensable camouflage for her.

"*Uugh!*" Her frustrated exhalation startled a young girl who had been tentatively approaching. She darted back behind a man who appeared to be her father. Henna gave an apologetic smile, shook her head, and began to sweep the rune stones into a pile and transfer them into a pouch.

The brief flash of sparkling waters along a faraway beach did not make her pause. Those waters weren't from her own memories, but associated with the voice that now inquired, "Are you clearing already?"

Helio had taken the opposite approach to show magic. Dressed in the simple slacks, loose shirt and brightly colored vest-style doublet currently fashionable among Kavet's young men—a demographic he was clearly beyond, as his first gray hairs indicated—he could have been anyone. The only thing marking him as a sorcerer was a discreet silver bracelet engraved with the Napthol's symbol.

"Take it," Henna said, anticipating his next question and gesturing to the well-worn carpet.

Helio smiled and carefully set his bag down to unpack. His specialties were potions and charms, which meant that like Henna, he was sometimes mistaken for one of the small magic users who plied their wares down at the docks. Unlike them, his work was more than bluster, snake oil, and a basic knowledge of herbs. He had been hauled before the royal house and almost charged with magical malfeasance the year before when a potion meant to catch a lover's eye accidentally turned out to be what could only be called a true love potion. He had done brisk business with the charm, unaware of how dangerous it was until after it caused several nasty enough altercations that the Terre became involved.

"What's that smile about?" Helio asked.

"Apple blossoms," she admitted, naming one of the key ingredients in the potion that went awry.

He scowled good-naturedly, then went back to setting out his wares. In addition to the vials of potion, he had a few glass containers that flickered with magical light.

Helio was one of only a half-dozen members of their order powerful enough to create foxfire, a magical light that burned for days, weeks or even months depending on the strength of the creator with no need for additional fuel and no danger of setting anything else ablaze. Most of Helio's were a clear, silvery blue that reminded Henna of sunlight streaming through water. Cold magic like his couldn't produce heat, but they would still be good for evening reading. They would fetch a good price. More importantly, their presence made it clear to his customers that he was more than a simple witch.

Henna started to turn away, then hesitated. Henna's skill for prophecy was unique among Kavet's sorcerers, but even without second sight, Helio often had insight beyond the mundane.

"I keep seeing visions of violence in this place." She pitched her voice so it wouldn't carry farther than the other sorcerer. "They aren't clear, but they're enough to disturb my work."

Helio never paused in positioning his wares, but the exercise of setting them out seemed to occupy his hands in much the same way her rune stones did. His gaze went distant as he consulted his knowledge and his power.

"It's only three days until the Apple Blossom Festival," he speculated, referring to the upcoming spring celebration. "I've heard rumors the Quin intend to protest again. There are also more faces in the city than usual, not only sightseers but men and women of power, here to meet with the Terre. There is always the potential for violence when so many people from such different backgrounds stand in the same place, but I've heard nothing of blood."

She had *said* nothing of blood, but Helio had heard the word she hadn't spoken aloud. He wasn't a mind reader; he simply read between the lines, or more accurately, saw more lines on a page than most others.

"Have you asked Maddy?" he suggested. In addition to being a leader of the Order of Napthol, and

Henna's dearest friend, Maddy had been Terre Jaune's mistress for more than five years. If something was happening with the royal house, she generally knew of it. "Or Terre Verte?" Helio added.

"Hush, you," she snapped. Her relationship with Verte was still young and, while she was sure there was gossip, it wasn't public knowledge.

"I won't say anything. At least *he* isn't married." Given Helio's knack for knowing things others tried to keep private, Henna appreciated that his discretion was as well developed as his power. "Though marriage is going to be a question, isn't it? Sorry. I'll drop it."

He finished artfully arranging the last of his potions as if he hadn't had an entire conversation based mostly on facial expressions he hadn't even bothered to look up to see. Verte hadn't said a thing about marriage yet, but he was the only child of the royal house—and the only one likely to be born, given the reigning Terre and Terra hadn't shared a bed or even had a civil conversation in almost a decade. Any woman seen in the twenty-five-year-old prince's company was inevitably evaluated by his parents and advisors as a potential spouse.

At least Helio had taken Henna's mind off *blood*.

When Verte had first approached her in the market, Henna had been flattered by his attention and intrigued by his magic. She had expected that they would have a brief, meaningless affair; Verte was known for those. When Henna had decided sleeping with him would only lead to unwanted complications, she had assumed he would lose interest.

Instead, her declining his sexual advances meant they had more time for conversation, debate, and exploration. She got to know the man and, damn it, discovered she liked his company. Worse, he seemed to enjoy hers.

Most people would consider that a good thing, but it left her needing to make a decision: If this became more than a spring fling, could she stand to be the partner of a prince?

Given the close relationship between the Order of Napthol and the royal house, there was no option for them to be strangers—this vision, and her need to follow up with one of the Terre about it, was only one example of the kind of thing that would take her across the market frequently for the rest of her life. If she already knew she had no interest in sitting on that throne, it was time to say, "It's been fun, but we should both move on," before they became too emotionally entangled and threatened the peace of their future business relationship.

As she ducked back into the Cobalt Hall to wash up and eat, she was no closer to a conclusion than before.

Compared to the glistening palace across the city square, the home of the Order of Napthol was modest, made of native granite with none of the imported marble décor, gadrooning, and cornices of the more ostentatious building. On a clear day, dawn light brought out the blue and purple mineral swirls in the outer walls that gave the Cobalt Hall its name, but that was the only marvel of its architecture.

Inside, it felt like home. The entry hall was vast, as if in another day and age it had been intended for grand balls, but the other rooms were cozy and welcoming. The kitchen had always been Henna's favorite spot, with its long, low-slung stone hearth and stove where the more culinary-inclined initiates kept a constant revolution of stews, bread, and "experiments" going.

Today, a vat on the stove held a dense venison, buckwheat, and apple stew, and several loaves of crusty dark bread waited beside the hearth. It was good, simple food that fed the belly and comforted the soul.

Henna was mopping the last bit of stew from her bowl when an anxious-looking novice peeked in to say Terre Verte was asking for her. The young man was clearly uncomfortable leaving the prince waiting on the doorstep, but even a Terre didn't enter the Cobalt Hall without an invitation from a full initiate.

Henna left her rune stones in her room and traded her light day cloak for a heavier one in deference to the cold she knew would sneak in behind the departing sun. Spring in Kavet was a tricky season, capable of vaulting ahead to days that felt like summer or slinking back to the chill and snowy flurries of winter without warning.

She smiled as she saw him waiting on the front step, occasionally exchanging a nod of acknowledgement with a passer-by who caught his eye or called a greeting.

It was technically correct to say Verte's garb and appearance were the height of fashion. His dove-gray shirt, which she knew would have been buttoned to his throat and completed with a cravat during visiting hours, was now left informally open at the collar. Instead of a full, formal jacket, he wore a green and blue patchwork-style doublet that comfortably hugged his lean form and brought out the flecks of sea color in his otherwise charcoal eyes. His cinnamon-brown hair was long enough to hang to the bottom of his shoulder blades, and it, too, had been released from its braid—probably because he knew she loved to twine her fingers in its silky length.

It took a moment too long to realize Verte's attention had turned from the market crowd to her, and he was watching her stare with quirked lips. "Approve?" he asked.

She smiled, unashamed of her frank assessment of this lovely man. "I think I saw Helio wearing that same vest today," she teased. Helio's hadn't been hand tailored.

"If not, he will be tomorrow." The reason it was only *technically* correct to call Verte fashionable was that his style created many of the trends.

Verte offered his arm. "Would you care to join me for a walk in the gardens?"

"I would love to." The Terre gardens were miraculous, filled with species that grew nowhere else in the world. Some speculated the most exotic plants and animals were, perhaps, not from this world at all, but had actually come through tiny cracks between the mortal realm and the ones after. Having seen the gardens up close now, Henna suspected there was some truth to the rumor.

At that moment, though, the place's magic was of secondary interest. The garden was also blessedly *private*. Here on the front steps of the Cobalt Hall, she and Verte maintained a formal, awkward distance, wary of all the eyes that followed him. Once they were alone, Henna looked forward to accepting the promise implied by that partially unbuttoned shirt.

Wings in the sky.

The image slapped her the moment she put a foot down on the city square's cobbles. Verte's arm under her hand was no longer warm and firm and tantalizing. Instead, her fingers felt the slickness of Osei scales and the heat of their immense reptilian bodies. Ignorant people called the Osei *dragons*, but someone who used the term where one of the Osei could hear would regret it; a true dragon, or lesser wyrm, was a smaller, dumber, mundane creature—as much like an Osei as a crow was like a hawk.

"Why do I keep seeing the Osei?" she asked, her

voice barely a whisper. Verte probably thought she was being discreet. He didn't know why her throat would tighten and try to choke back those words. Her history with those beasts was one of the many things she needed to tell him if they were going to continue seeing each other.

Tonight, she thought. *I really will tell him tonight. I'll tell him all of it, and he will agree this relationship is a bad idea.*

He shot her a startled look, then shook his head ruefully. "This is what I get for courting a seer. I'll tell you what I can once we're alone, but my parents have agreed we should keep the news quiet, so I can't share everything."

My parents have agreed was, for Verte, a powerful statement. Terre Jaune and his queen Terra Sarcelle rarely agreed on anything, often out of principle instead of opinion. If they had agreed on silence, Verte would want to honor that.

Henna intended to convince him otherwise. She needed this answer.

CHAPTER 5

VERTE

Despite his having come here almost daily for years, to Verte, the twining of nature and magic that defined the royal gardens was still awe-inspiring. Some of the plants, such as a dwarf weeping lemon tree, had been transplanted from distant countries in the last decade, since Verte's mother had started creating warm foxfire spheres to keep them alive through the winter. Others grew nowhere else in this world; they were products of magic, and if they had peers anywhere, it was in the divine realm, not the mortal one. The power they exuded was enough to give even a mundane individual a sense of tingling expectation; for a sorcerer, it was exhilarating, like a sweet champagne massage.

All day long, Verte had looked forward to drawing Henna into his arms, and breathing in her spicy scent mingled with the heady aroma of the honeycreepers. He wanted to feel her body against his, and hear her heart in time with the pulse of magic.

Instead, he didn't dare reach for her. Tealyn was on guard by the garden gate, and Verte nodded a greeting as they passed, but Henna remained distant and introspective.

When she passed the graceful, fernlike bellflowers, whose blades sang like wind chimes when they rustled in a breeze, she did not reach out to set them dancing as she had before. Tiny nocturnal hummingbirds with sparkling, gemstone wings fluttered around the silver-leafed plants, and one trumpeted a challenge at Henna as she passed, but Henna didn't seem to notice.

"Are you all right?" Verte asked.

He expected her to ask about the Osei again. He didn't share her gift of prophecy, but he had seen the moment a vision had crossed her mind, and suspected it had prompted her earlier question.

Instead, she turned to him, green-brown eyes direct and challenging as she asked, "Do you know why we haven't made love?"

He opened his mouth, then shut it, aware of how treacherous the conversation had just become without knowing how or why. He waited, hoping it was a rhetorical question, but when Henna provided nothing else he ventured the only response that seemed safe: "You said to stop."

That *stop* had been disappointing—especially the most recent one, which had come while they were sprawled full length along the garden path, after she had deftly removed his shirt, at the moment he attempted to return the favor—but he had respected it. He could think of a dozen reasons she might have made such a choice, ranging from not liking casual sex to not wanting to jump into a physical relationship with royalty. Not all women saw his title as an advantage.

"It's not that I'm not interested," Henna continued. Her lips curled up as her gaze traveled down. "I didn't want to have to tell the whole long story in the hopes of having a little fun."

He bit back the teasing query, *"Just a little?"* and took the more appropriate cue. "Long story?"

With a few quick tugs, she loosened the ties on her bodice and used the slack to pull her blouse down on one side. For a moment, his gaze was riveted on the expanse of smooth skin he longed to touch and the soft, round breast she had almost entirely bared. But then she shifted so he saw the back of her shoulder instead.

The first thing he noticed was a coin-shaped tattoo of the three-wave symbol of the Order of Napthol. Most sorcerers chose to wear their symbol on a piece of jewelry, not their skin, but a tattoo wasn't shocking enough to warrant such a dramatic reveal.

Verte stepped closer, since it was clear there was more she wanted him to see. At the edge of the bared skin, he spotted the pulled white flesh of old scars. Just the tips of what he imagined were longer lines were visible before the marks disappeared under her clothes. His breath caught. Had she been whipped? He had heard of sailors being flogged. Such brutal treatment might explain why she had left her previous seafaring life, and if the marks of that cruelty were numerous, it could explain why she hesitated to bare her body to him.

Then he saw it. The tattoo had been inked over another character. He squinted, but couldn't quite make it out. "What was the first tattoo?" he asked, confident that was what she was waiting for.

"It was the symbol of the Ninth Royal House of the Osei," she said. "Not all Osei mark their property, but the Ninth House is so close to Tamar's coast that slaves who flee the island can sometimes swim ashore. Marking them ensures they can be identified and returned."

Henna had never been coy, but the dispassionate bluntness with which she shared the fact caught him off guard. It implied a history Verte could imagine all too well, and wished he couldn't.

"The Osei marked you as a slave?" He couldn't keep his voice as neutral as hers. He only hoped she would understand that the horror in his tone was in response to what had been done *to* her, not how he felt *about* her.

"I *was* a slave," she said. "The ship I was on hit poor weather. We were damaged, drifting and out of fresh water for two days before the Osei spotted us. In exchange for saving us, they claimed all surviving hands. I managed to escape and made my way to Kavet four years later. I was sixteen by then."

He wanted to reach for her, pull her close, and swear no one would ever dare hurt her again. It was a chauvinistic response Henna would not have appreciated, both because her tight shoulders and crossed arms suggested she didn't want to be touched at all in that moment, and because she wasn't the kind of person who wanted pity and coddling. She wanted what she had asked for—an explanation about her visions of the Osei—and she had offered this demonstration as the only argument she needed for why she deserved that explanation.

As a compromise, Verte offered his hand. After a moment, Henna took it and squeezed it like a lifeline, edging closer to him.

He said, "Kavet has more freedom than most other countries, but the situation with the Osei remains intolerable. Over the next two weeks, we'll be hosting delegations from Silmat, Tamar, and the Osei to renegotiate current treaties."

"That's why I keep seeing them here." He hated to hear her voice so hollow. How had she survived, coming of age amid such monsters? How had she freed herself? Another time, when Henna wasn't clearly more concerned about the future, he would ask. "They *are* here . . . or will be. Which ones?"

"The Third Noble house." The Third Noble House and the eighteenth common house were almost as close to Kavet as the Ninth House was to Tamar. "If it goes well and we are able to come to an accord, the First Queen will attend the final days of the negotiations to give her consent and seal."

There was more he wished he could tell her, but he had to watch his words. He trusted Henna not to do anything stupid, but the fewer people who knew the whole plan, the better.

She shook her head, shrugging her blouse back onto her shoulder as she demanded, "You think you can negotiate with them? Osei aren't *people*, Verte. They can look like humans if they want, but they don't think like us. Some people say they are deliberately cruel, that they can be so feral they will eat humans when other prey is lacking, but that's like saying a cat is being deliberately cruel when it crushes a bug. They cannot comprehend why we object when they claim us."

"They see us as animals who can be bought or sold like chattel," Verte agreed. "We're hoping to change that impression."

Henna started to pace as she ranted, her tone raised but her words clear and logical. "It isn't how they see *us* that's the problem. It's how they see *themselves*. Osei don't possess a notion of freedom. They don't have aspirations beyond those set for them by their Queen or their House. You can try to explain to them that humans cherish independence and self-determination, but you might as well preach individuality to an ant or a bee. They don't understand. They *can't* understand."

Without knowing her history, Verte hadn't realized how unique a perspective Henna might have on the creatures. To his knowledge, there wasn't anyone else in Kavet who had ever lived among the Osei. The potential value of her wisdom outweighed the risks of telling her. He was certain his parents would agree.

"We haven't had Osei on Kavet soil in centuries," he said, "but we have discussed the issue with leaders from Tamar—" Henna scoffed dismissively "—and Silmat. We understand the difficulty of communicating with—"

"If you discussed the issues with the so-called leaders of Tamar, you spoke to someone in the *Lasable* caste." Her accent, which had previously been local with just a hint of the rolling Tamari tongue, became stronger as she talked about her homeland. "What do they know? They live in the city. Those who live on the water know the Osei cannot be regulated. They are seen in the same way as a tempest, a natural disaster that—"

He interrupted her rising tirade with a soft voice. "Sorcery can mitigate the worst effects of nature."

Henna's mouth snapped shut and her eyes widened as she caught the implication of his words.

"You intend . . . to *enchant* . . . the Osei?" she asked. "You can do that?"

"We believe so." Verte looked around the garden, which was already a demonstration of Terre power doing what most sorcerers considered impossible. "My parents and I have been working on the spell for months. It needs to be done carefully, though. We need to lull them into believing that acquiescing to our demands is their own decision, based on respect and fondness." Again, she scoffed, but it was softer this time. She was listening. "If you have any insight that could help the negotiations go well, I would be grateful. We need to avoid giving any offense during the days they are here."

She dropped to sit comfortably on the ground and idly warmed her hands on the gold foxfire, which cast ghostly shadows across her face as she moved her fingers in front of it.

"The next few days," she repeated. "You mean they'll be here for the festival." It wasn't a question, so he didn't answer it. "You will want a woman beside you. The Osei won't speak to an unattached prince, since they have no status except as . . . I don't know how it works, really, except that a prince seems to be considered no one until a queen chooses him. If the Osei see you and acknowledge you at all, they're more likely to assume you've been presented as a valuable trade good than to deal with you as a man who has authority in his own land."

Verte nodded. "My mother will do most of the face-to-face negotiation with the Osei queen. My father and I, and the other men in the Silmari and Tamari delegations, have been warned to only speak to the princes. I had hoped to have you with me."

Henna shook her head at once, a tinge of regret in her expression. "I cannot guard my thoughts well enough to mingle with Osei for an evening. They would sense my hatred, and they might give you trouble for harboring an escaped slave. Find someone else." She tilted her head thoughtfully. "Do you want recommendations? I know two or three ladies here at the hall who have the comportment to manage a royal event but no interest in a longer relationship. My first would be Dove. She loves lavish parties, but rather wishes you had a sister."

The frank words and the implication—that she would happily hand him to another woman for the night, as long as she could ensure that woman had no interest in him—made him laugh aloud despite the seriousness of the topic.

"I'll find someone," he assured her.

"Can you do anything about the Quin? If you're casting a delicate spell, the last thing you want is those fanatics holding their annual protest in front of the palace."

Verte sat beside her, close enough to feel her warmth like foxfire next to him, and her heart pounding hard enough to make her skin vibrate. Despite her calm voice and careful poise, she was fighting panic. She leaned toward him, and he put an arm around her shoulders, hugging her close.

"When have I *ever* been able to do anything about the Quin?" he grumbled. "There's no reasoning with them. If I give them any hint their efforts might cause the royal house trouble, they'll only redouble them. If I tell them the *truth* . . ." Even Henna laughed at that. The Quin blamed every evil imaginable on sorcery. Numini only knew what they would do if they learned the royal house was preparing such a powerful and delicate spell. "Short of rewriting the country's laws to make peaceful protest illegal, I can't stop them from gathering in public places to share their ideas."

"*Phah*," Henna sighed. "What good is royalty if you won't abuse your power?"

"The Quin would say I abuse it plenty already."

She shook her head and reached out to caress one of the heart-shaped aquamarine flowers on the honey-creeper vine, triggering a waft of perfume like sweet whiskey. "There seem to be more of them every year. How can such a dismal sect attract such interest?"

"If I succeed with the Osei, I'll have time to deal with the Quin." And if he failed with the Osei, the Quin would be the least of his problems.

"The scars cross most of my back," Henna said suddenly. "I've said all I plan to say to you about how I got them. The other thing you should know is that some of the Tamari won't like what they see if they get a good look at me on your arm. I'll have to tell you more about that at some point, but . . . not today. Not today. Are either of those things a problem for you?"

Tamari culture was complex, and Verte didn't understand all of it despite many interactions with the sailors, politicians, and aristocrats on holiday who frequently came to Kavet's shores. He did know they had a strict caste system, which he imagined didn't have much leniency when it came to allowing a woman to abandon her native traditions and resettle as a sorcerer in a faraway country.

If Henna's warning meant more than that, there was time to learn the details another day.

"No, it's not a problem."

"Good. That means there's no reason I shouldn't do this." The hand that had been tickling the honey-creeper bloom reached up to stroke his cheek, then settled firmly on his shoulder to stabilize her as she turned and swung a leg over his. "You answered all my questions," she murmured. This close, her skin smelled of incense and wood smoke from her ritual workings, and her warm breath held a hint of citrus and spice. "Now I'm ready to change the subject."

Her lips met his, and all thoughts of the Osei and politics fled from Verte's mind.

CHAPTER 6

NAPLES

The palace temple was behind a door in the middle of an apparently empty stretch of wall, which only appeared when Terra Sarcelle put her hand on it.

"How—"

"Simplicity itself, once the portal has been established," the Terra crooned as Naples followed her through the dim passage into what appeared to be a small, private library.

The room was lit by spheres of pure white foxfire—clearly the work of cold magic, but more steady and brilliant than any Naples had seen his mother or Helio make. Most foxfire was dim and flickered like a candle flame. This made Naples look around, expecting to see a window streaming sunlight.

There were no windows, only shelves of books in all shapes and sizes, and rows of magical paraphernalia, most of which Naples recognized but some of which was a mystery. Instead of an altar, a sturdy, oblong table filled the center of the room, currently occupied by a man Naples had to assume was Terre Jaune, King of Kavet. He was dressed as casually as his wife, with his shirt collar untied and his sleeves pushed up to his elbows.

When they entered, the king had four books open in front of him; he was taking furious notes in one while referring intermittently to the others. At first Naples didn't think he was going to acknowledge his wife or her guest as they crossed to a blank section of wall at the back of the room, but just as the Terra raised a hand as if to summon another doorway Terre Jaune inquired, "A little young even for you, isn't he?"

Naples stiffened, unsure how to respond.

The Terra didn't hesitate. As she called the door, she murmured back acidly, "Oh, but he's from such a *wonderful* bloodline."

Well, that answered *that* question. She knew who his mother was.

Naples was almost certain the Terra hadn't brought him there for the reason Terre Jaune was implying, but . . .

He cleared his throat. "Er, what kind of work did you want me for?"

As they passed into the Terra's private ritual space, the air heated and became dense and smoky. The light in here was dimmer, provided by a row of tiny yellow foxfire orbs, each no larger than an apple seed, strung on a golden chain draped carelessly on the corner of a bookcase. Distracted from his question, Naples approached it, and discovered the strand was hot to the touch—not just warm, but scalding, like metal that had been left baking in the sun.

"Not what my *husband* thinks," she said. "Sex *is* a delightful way to raise our power, as I'm sure you've learned for yourself, but I'm rather particular in my partners. And if I've heard right about you, I'm not your type, either."

He cleared his throat again, determined not to let her drive him to speechlessness a third time in a row. "You didn't seem to know who I was, downstairs."

"One must dissemble in front of servants," she replied. "It wouldn't do for gossip to say the Terra sought out her husband's mistress's son. The entire Cobalt Hall would be up in arms, convinced I meant to sacrifice you in some obscene blood ritual." As she spoke, she began to gather materials, moving through the dimly lit space with confidence and grace. "That said, it would be a criminal waste of your potential to let you stay at the Cobalt Hall, and since my son favors his father when it comes to sorcery, I am in need of an assistant and apprentice. Or do you still feel you have more to learn from the Order of Napthol?"

Naples' gaze was already traveling over the bindings of the books within his sight. He had studied and mastered every tome of sorcery at the Cobalt Hall by the time he was fifteen—which wasn't saying much, since hot magic was so new to Kavet that there were few resources on its use, and unlike his mother, he seemed utterly devoid of cold power. Henna's power was similar to his own in type and strength, but hot power was so new that even she spent more time experimenting with him than instructing him.

"You have more you could teach me?"

"Oh, yes." There was a purr in the Terra's voice as she placed the items she had chosen on a sturdy but unremarkable hardwood table—oak or ebony, Naples thought, though it was hard to tell in this light. The surface seemed to be irregular, scarred by time or use, but otherwise there was nothing noteworthy about it.

"You don't use an altar?" he asked.

The Terra shook her head. "Cold magic is finicky. It wants sanctity and respect and therefore is best focused by white silk and pure silver and other elaborate and pretty claptrap. My husband and son both have altars with those things in their private ritual spaces. The old magics want a tie to the land, and as the Cobalt Hall temple is on the highest floor, it's useful to have an altar of clay or wood or stone. We on the other hand carry our magic in our veins. This is the only altar I need."

With that, she drove the tip of a knife into the already pitted wooden surface, next to a pile of fine metal chains—jewelry of some sort. She seemed to be waiting for Naples' response, so he examined both more closely.

Looking at magic was like trying to see two faces instead of a vase in the old optical illusion; if one had power, it took only a mental shift to see another version of the world on top of the mundane. The knife seeped with potential power, but it was clearly a tool, not enchanted itself. The chain . . .

"Oh, lovely," he breathed. The magic woven into the simple jewelry blazed so brilliantly it should have scalded the table beneath. The spell seemed to hum and whisper just beyond his ability to understand. "What is it?"

He leaned closer, trying to listen to the undercurrents of magic and make out what they had to say to him.

"A trap," the Terra replied, with all the pride of a new mother. "My husband and son are working on the other half. Blending cold magic and hot is—oh, you trusting fool."

He heard a sharp *crack* and pain shot up his arm from his hand. He jerked back and realized the Terra had just slapped the back of his hand with one of the wooden sticks he had taken for kindling, hard enough to make his fingers tingle.

Then, a moment later, he realized he was on his

knees next to the table, and had been reaching for the jewelry with trembling fingers.

Trusting fool, indeed. He refocused his thoughts, this time warding himself against outside power, and hugged his throbbing hand to his chest. He would have a nasty bruise there later, but the shock of pain had snapped him out of her spell.

"What do you need my help with?" His voice was hoarse, breathy. "You could have any man in Kavet with that."

"I don't *want* any man in Kavet," she answered. "I need to snare an Osei queen."

He blinked up at her, trying to imagine the scope and danger of such a charm. If Terra Sarcelle had put those baubles on and deliberately focused the spell inside on him, he probably would have thrown himself at her and let her have him on the table, insensible of the fact that he had never been attracted to any woman, much less one over twice his age. Deliberately invoking such an impulse in an Osei, a creature known to disdain human opinions or preferences, could only result in disaster.

"What possible benefit could come from having an Osei queen want you that way?" he asked, keeping his gaze anywhere but on the charmed jewelry as he unsteadily rose to his feet.

"My side of the spell is designed to intrigue and fascinate," the Terra said. "It is the first lure, a blaze of desire meant to draw the Osei near and hold them close. Jaune and Verte are creating the more subtle persuasive elements, since cold magic is needed for that work, but they will never be able to get their spells around the Osei unless I can snare them first."

"I'll help if I can, if you tell me how," he said. How long had it been since he had genuinely had to ask someone to *teach* him something? Though she may have already limited his efficacy; he experimentally flexed his hand, and winced. Nothing was broken, but it was swelling. "Do you have some ice I can put on this?"

She made a *tsk* noise and said, "I have something better."

She reached out and he offered his throbbing hand. He expected a salve of some sort. Instead, she grasped his wrist firmly. He only realized she had pulled the knife out of the table when its blade cut a fine, swift line across the back of his bruised, swelling flesh, raising a thick line of blood.

The noise that came from his throat was somewhere between a shriek and a gasp, the choked noise of a terrified animal. He was no healer, but he had studied enough anatomy to know how delicate the tendons in the back of the hand were. If she had cut them—

The Terra dropped the knife with an indifferent clatter and slapped her palm over the wound. New pain, fierce and dizzying, stole his breath as her power danced between them. His knees weakened and he had to balance himself by grabbing a nearby bookcase.

A cold draft enveloped him when she let go. He shivered at the absence of her magic, and looked despondently at his abused hand.

No bruise. No swelling. No cut. No blood.

"What . . ."

Historically, one of the primary responsibilities of those in the Order of Napthol was to act as healers, because old magic was excellent for repairing damage to both body and mind. Cold magic was excellent for curing disease and repairing damage done to the body by poison or infection, so sorcerers powerful with both of those types were especially versatile in the realm of medicine—Naples' mother, Maddy, and Terre Jaune were both renowned for their healing abilities, which was how they had first become so close.

One of the greatest criticisms of hot magic was that it was helpless in the face of illness or injury, which was why people like Dove saw Naples as exceptionally powerful—there was no denying that—but in an utterly useless way.

Even if her methods were uncomfortable, the Terra had just done something most of the Cobalt Hall believed impossible.

"There is so much you need to learn about our power," she said, rather fondly for someone who had just taken a knife to him. "First, I need you to forget the Cobalt Hall's mandates against the use of blood in sorcery. It has crippled you. If you wish to stay on as my assistant, and my student, you must accept that my ways are not the ways you're used to. You must also understand that I am not gentle, or particularly patient. I will push you to your limits and maybe past them. We'll see."

Naples looked away from his hand and stared instead into her intent green eyes. He'd had his share of generous, patient, cautious education at the Cobalt Hall, and he hadn't tested his limits in what felt like years.

"That sounds wonderful."

"Then let us begin. We'll start with this." She picked the knife back up from the table. Naples flinched instinctively, but she merely flipped it around and offered it to him with the same casual air as a Napthol novice handing out clean bed linens.

"It's Silmari made," she said, as Naples took the knife from her and looked it over. It wasn't long—not much bigger than a fruit knife—but the razor edge of the blade shone in the faint foxfire light. The handle was dark and slightly irregular; he thought it was bone. "You may keep it."

Naples raised his brows at that. Even he knew the Silmari made the best steel in the world, but the Osei strictly regulated the trade of any iron-based material across the ocean. Cyan claimed iron could repel Osei, and maybe even poison them; many Silmari wore an iron ring in order to differentiate themselves from the shapeshifting wyrm. That was easier to do in Silmat, which had vast iron mines, than it was in Kavet, which had exhausted its meager iron veins centuries ago.

In short, this little blade was probably even more valuable than one of Naples' hot foxfire spheres.

"Thank you," he managed to say, past his nerves and surprise.

"We don't need as many tools and accoutrements as the old magic and cold magic users, but a good blade is indispensable. Now, it's time to work."

And work they did.

The Terra wasn't much of a teacher; she rarely bothered to explain her actions in words, but instead demonstrated a technique and impatiently waited for him to replicate it, or simply threw power at him and sat back to see if he would drown. The only time she was cautious was with the spell for the Osei, where she took charge, ruthlessly using his power to supplement her own instead of letting him anywhere near the delicate strands of the enchantment itself.

At one point, she stepped out to consult with Terre Jaune and left Naples alone in the ritual room, saying on her way through the door, "Look around if you wish. I may be a while."

The door disappeared behind her, leaving him to realize she hadn't yet explained how to open it. He wondered how hard it would be to figure out if she didn't come back, but decided not to worry yet—not when he was surrounded by so many fascinating tools and tomes.

He immediately went to the bookshelf, where he found the Terra's work journal. He shook his head as he flipped through it; the notes were irregular, full of half thoughts, ellipses, and questions. Naples would have been ordered to sit down and rewrite the entire thing if it were his journal.

He grinned, realizing he might never be forced to revise another ritual report for his mother's discerning editorial eye. Then the smile slipped, as he considered how he would tell her he had found other instruction and was going to leave the Cobalt Hall.

More protests from the Quin, the Terra had written at one point. *They accuse us of stealing our power from the dead . . . from the divine and infernal realms. Fools. No one claims it's evil or even theft when a flower uses energy from the sun or a mill uses energy from a river. The sun and the water are not lessened and the flower and mill benefit. What does the source of the power matter?*

Naples snickered. He too was tired of that debate. No one knew where a sorcerer's power came from, why cold power had appeared a few decades ago or why yet another form of magic had accompanied the Terra to Kavet. The surge of new talents had, unfortunately, been matched by an exponential increase in the number of ignorant and judgmental non–magic users in the population.

Naples hesitated again on a scrap of prose near the beginning of the bulky leather-bound journal that had nothing to do with sorcery: *Weeks of false labor . . .*

finally rewarded with such a tiny creature. My Verte. We nearly lost him so many times. The midwife says he never turned, that he was born with the cord around his neck. I don't remember it. If not for Antioch, I would have bled to death on the birthing table while Jaune struggled to keep our son alive. I would not have blamed him. I will battle the Abyss itself to keep this frail child—

Naples snapped the journal shut hastily. He had only been looking for the Terra's notes on her sorcery experiments, not to snoop on such a personal memory.

"Thank you, Antioch," he murmured as he put the journal back on the shelf, wondering who he or she had been. The name sounded familiar. A healer from Cobalt Hall, perhaps?

No, that wasn't right. He was strangely certain it wasn't a name he had heard spoken about at the Hall as a well-respected older member, or someone he had known as a young child who had passed away or moved on. In fact, the more he focused on the name, the more he noticed creeping tension tightening his back and shoulders.

Nothing conscious. Nothing he could explain. As if it were a name he had heard whispered in a dream—or a nightmare.

"It's nothing," he said aloud, his own voice seeming loud in the Terra's study. He was jumping at shadows.

CHAPTER 7

DAHLIA

After two days of travel, and most of an afternoon riding uphill, Dahlia watched the sun sink into the far horizon with alarm. She didn't want to be caught on these isolated roads after dark.

"When do you expect to camp for the night?" she asked, trying to keep the doubt from her voice. She wasn't sure if they were traveling as fast as Celadon had expected. Dahlia was confident on horseback, but hadn't ever spent an entire day on one. Celadon sat comfortably in the saddle, like a man who traveled long distances often. If many of the breaks they took were for her benefit alone, it may have affected his timing.

"We'll reach the Overlook Inn soon, just over the

crest of this hill," he promised. "They're expecting us. With weather this clear, you'll be able to see the city from there," he added.

At the top of the promised hill Dahlia paused, reins slack in one hand as she idly patted her horse's mane and drank in the sight before her with unquenchable thirst.

Her hometown of Eiderlee was a large, sprawling village in acreage, but it was small in population. Even the "busy" town center held few imposing buildings; the school where Dahlia had worked and the attached chapel were the largest structure, though they lost in a size competition with the great silos and barns in the surrounding farmland.

The city of Mars was still hours away, but Dahlia could see it now stretched out beneath her, at the heart of a spider-web of converging roads that wound out from the darkness of dense trees. The rusty sunset painted the city's tangled streets and crowded buildings in sharp angles and shadows.

Farthest away, Dahlia could see the misty edge where the land ended and the sea began. Fog obscured the ships in the Mars harbor from her eyes, but she could see them in her mind.

She scanned the skies instinctively, expecting to see winged figures—but that was silly. The Osei could often be spotted from the south and west banks of Kavet because those bordered territory that belonged to the giant wyrm, but there was no reason they would be flying here off the north bank. These waters belonged to human sailors.

"The Overlook Inn has a sign in the lobby that claims this is the highest point in Kavet," Celadon said. "After this, the land falls away until the city itself is just above sea level. If it weren't for the tree farms and natural forests between here and there, one good storm could wash half of Kavet down this slope to bury the city, royal house and all." The quirk of his mouth suggested that wasn't an entirely unattractive notion.

I won't let him ruin this for me. "We'll be there tomorrow?"

"Late morning, most likely."

From here, the great city looked like a toy she could reach out and play with. Dahlia wished they could push on until they reached it, but trusted Celadon that it was farther away than it seemed.

The Overlook Inn was inviting, squat and square except for sloped roofs designed to shed the snow, ice, and rain. Its door was painted a white so pure and crisp it was startling against the rest of the sedate, red-brown exterior. Its side yard boasted a trio of apple trees, their newly opened blossoms an explosion of pink against the sunset.

Anywhere in Kavet, a white door indicated welcome and a safe place to stay. There was no formal inn in Eiderlee, but farmers with extra space they were willing to rent to travelers often painted their doors or doorframes. Out of habit, Dahlia looked for the nearest window and saw an oyster shell, turned with its iridescent side up, on the inside sill. That more discreet sign, hidden by the curtain once inside and thus easy to miss unless one looked for it, indicated the inn had a Quin owner, or at least was welcoming to Quin guests.

Despite those signs of safety, anxiety made her jittery and restless at the Inn the way she hadn't been the night before, when their first long day of travel had ended with them still surrounded by farmland and they had stayed overnight with a shepherd who knew both Dahlia and Celadon. Surrounded by the shepherd's large, rambunctious family during dinner and then by his sleeping eight-, nine-, and twelve-year-old daughters that evening, there had been no space for nerves.

The inn was comfortable and clean, Dahlia supposed, but she awoke the next morning feeling less rested than when she had gone to bed. She met Celadon downstairs and hated him a bit for the brightness in his step.

"I'll admit, I'm looking forward to being home," Celadon sighed, once they had saddled their beasts, mounted up, and started on the final, downhill path to the city. "I've been away too long this time."

"How long have you been traveling?" She should have known he hadn't made the three-day journey from Mars to Eiderlee just to escort her to the city, but she had been too focused on her own plans to consider what else might have brought him to the area.

"Six, almost seven weeks now," Celadon answered. "I spent the end of winter in Wyrm's Shadow, or what used to be Wyrm's Shadow. I'm bringing a petition to the city from the residents asking to change the town's name to Quin Towers, in honor of the completion of the monastery there."

Dahlia was familiar with the town, and had even been there once. Wyrm's Shadow, so named because it was situated a stone's throw from territory owned by the Third Noble House of the Osei, was on the far southern tip of Kavet. It offered poor anchorage for ships even if the Osei hadn't controlled the waters off the coast, and the land wasn't as fertile as places like Eiderlee, but it was the birthplace of the Followers of the Quinacridone—perhaps because it was so far away from the capital city, and thus received little attention from the royal house.

"Have you visited since they've started working on the monastery?" Celadon asked. "It's an incredible building, an architectural wonder. I know you said you're sick of teaching, but with your credentials, you would be an incredible asset. You could create your own curriculum, and teach advanced topics that might interest you more."

"Mmm." Dahlia had already been invited— *repeatedly*—to join the newly rising monastic order, so she could dedicate her life to teaching good Quin children while also helping manage the flocks and fields the order kept. Her parents had considered it an opportunity and an honor, and had encouraged her to accept despite how far away it would take her. Realizing her noncommittal response was hardly polite, she added, "I've been once, but at that point they only had plans and part of the foundation laid. Is that why you were visiting?"

"Partly," Celadon said. "I also had a meeting with one of the princes from the Third Noble House of the Osei. He wanted to confirm that we did not intend to create docks that would trespass on their waters."

"You spoke with . . ." She trailed off as she imagined standing before one of the Osei and trying to hold a conversation with a creature that massive. One lash of a long, serpentine tail could surely throw a horse and cart across the square, and those talons could rip a man in half like a soggy biscuit. *"How?"*

"They're creatures of pure magic," Celadon explained, his tone surprised, as if everyone knew this fact. "When they want to communicate with humans, they take human form."

That made Maimeri's outlandish theory of their eating humans even more unlikely.

Dahlia hoped.

"Why did he speak to you and not the Terre?"

"The Terre don't pay any attention to that place as long as they get their taxes paid," Celadon scoffed. "The Osei would never have waited for one of that line to drag themselves away from their parties and politics to meet with them."

If her incredulity hadn't put Dahlia so off-balance, she never would have brought up the Terre. She knew better. Celadon, who normally seemed so affable and relaxed, tensed and practically snarled whenever the royal house was mentioned.

"You were born there, weren't you?" she asked, recalling one of the many stories she had heard about Celadon and trying to return the conversation to safer waters. "Why did you move to Mars?" *If you hate the royal house and all it stands for so much, why do you choose to live in the capital city?*

"I can accomplish more in the city," Celadon said. "Besides, my youngest sister, Ginger, is apprenticed to one of the best chandlers in the country, who unfortunately keeps his workshop and storefront in Mars. She needs someone to keep an eye on her, and my aunt is too busy minding her own store to manage." He frowned, as if imagining the trouble the girl might have found or created while he was away.

"Do they bother with Festival here?" she asked as the city gradually became larger, trying to keep the ambivalence from her tone. In Eiderlee, the spring agricultural celebration was a light-hearted, jovial time, full of games for the children, the unearthing and exhibition of every craft and odd talent possessed in theirs and the surrounding villages, and late-night barn dances. Dahlia had been grateful to dodge it this year, since it was also a time famous for meddling matchmakers, but now she felt a nostalgic pang. It was hard to imagine a city with no green places celebrating the blooming fruit trees, the birth of spring lambs, the return of the eider ducks for whom Eider-lee was named, or new growth in the fields.

Celadon's mouth pinched into a disapproving line. "Yes," he answered, each word measured, "but it isn't the same. The city fills with foreigners and locals alike carousing. For a young lady like yourself, it's a good time to stay inside."

Young lady.

She only realized she had scoffed aloud when Celadon shot her a sidelong look. She said mildly, "I'm twenty-four." *And you're not much older, mister!*

"I'm aware," Celadon replied. "And if you pardon my bluntness, a celebration where any sailor in port can buy an enchantment to make him irresistible is not one where a pretty woman is safe."

The warning—and compliment—both would have been easier to accept if they hadn't been spoken in such a patronizing tone.

Perhaps seeing the pique on her face, Celadon continued, "If you want to see for yourself, you're welcome to come with me. I lead a group from the local parish that goes each year to try to educate people, and protest the dangerous use of sorcery inside city limits."

"I'll consider it." She could start the evening with them. If it looked as dangerous as Celadon described, she could stay with their group or ask someone to escort her home. If this was just a matter of the same kind of Quin overprotectiveness she had occasionally encountered at home—well, she was a free woman and had the right to leave to explore on her own any time.

She was so deep in thought, sifting through all she had heard from people at home and all Celadon had told her, she almost didn't notice where they were until he said, "We'll leave the horses here. They aren't allowed inside city limits."

She started, lifting her gaze to discover they were at a large, well-maintained stable at the edge of the city. Two grooms approached; one politely took the reins of Celadon's horse while he dismounted, and the other offered a hand to Dahlia, which she declined. The day she couldn't get on and off a horse on her own was the day she would decide she had been in the city too long.

"Isn't Ash usually working this time of day?" Celadon asked, one hand lingering on his horse's neck possessively.

The groom in front of Celadon shook his head, and shot a concerned look to the other, who dismissed him with a wave. "Ash quit about a month ago," he answered, voice clipped. "Would you like to hire a porter to deliver your bags to your residence?"

When Celadon didn't answer, but continued looking around as if hunting for something, Dahlia said, "Yes, please." Celadon had explained earlier that they would probably hire someone with a cart after they gave up the horses, so she knew it was an expected expense and not an extravagance. She didn't fancy carrying everything on her back, no matter what bee had found its way into Celadon's bonnet.

The groom—head groom, Dahlia decided, based on the way he had dismissed the other—looked at her and gave a strained smile, then summoned another groom to start undressing Dahlia's horse.

"Is that all, sir?" he asked Celadon, who still had his hands on the reins as if he might refuse to turn the horse over. "If you would prefer to see to your own horse's care, that is of course your right."

Celadon looked at Dahlia as if evaluating his options. Now that they were finally at the city, she was anxious to be off and explore, but courtesy made her say, "I don't mind tending the horses, if you want to. I always have before." She knew people who were adamant that a rider should always perform all pre-and post-riding care himself, even when given the option of professional help, but hadn't expected Celadon to be one of them.

As if her permission had unfrozen him, Celadon said gruffly to the head groom, "I'd like them in the old stable. Is there space?"

"Plenty," the groom said, the expression on his face blandly controlled, "and the monthly fee is less. Would I be presumptive to assume you would also prefer not to make use of the other upgraded facilities?"

"Not presumptive. Thank you."

For a moment, Dahlia thought he was being cheap—*frugal*, she told herself. Then she spotted the sign on the barn door, only half visible from where they stood, announcing the stable had been upgraded to include the new warming foxfire to help maintain a steady and comfortable temperature for the livestock. Once she knew to look for it, it was easy to see the enchantment's tell-tale glow from within the building.

Sorcery.

It was such a mundane, unexpected place to see evidence of the practice that it left Dahlia feeling torn between habitual revulsion and natural curiosity.

All fire burns something, Dahlia remembered her father saying gravely, when she asked about the possibility of investing in the new foxfire to create a warm room for the ducks. It would have allowed them to breed all winter long, but he had adamantly refused. *Ask yourself, where does the fuel for foxfire come from? Not wood or coal or oil, or any other natural source. Sorcery draws its power not from this world, but the next. Is it worth disturbing the dead to save the effort of keeping the hearth coals warm?*

Dahlia wasn't stupid enough to express her interest or ask questions with Celadon around. Quin teachings said sorcery was unnatural, that sorcerers stole from the realms of the dead and the vitality of the living to create pretty tricks, but if it was so dangerous, why would someone risk using it for a task as silly as warming a stable?

Later, when Celadon wasn't around, she would try to get that answer.

After all, she was in the city to learn new things.

CHAPTER 8

NAPLES

Seated in front of the low, round table he always used as an altar in the Cobalt Hall's temple, Naples clasped a circlet of metal between his palms. The Terra might be right that he didn't need an altar for his magic, but he was still used to these trappings, and wanted the support of familiarity for this project.

Mentally and magically, he tied off the strands of magic he had braided into the iron and tiger's eye. He used his power to sculpt and smooth, until he opened his hands to observe his creation: a man's ring, a bit too large for his own hand.

At first glance the design was simple. He had modeled it after the basic iron rings many Silmari wore, which weren't intended to be ornamental. The last thing a sailor wanted was a clumsy bauble that was likely to snag or get in the way while he worked.

A closer look revealed that the metal had orange and black swirls, as if the tiger's eye crystal Naples had used in its creation had been folded into the metal. Such a thing would have been impossible with any forge, but was exactly what he had done with his magic. By inverting the principles the Terra had used for her net to trap the Osei, he had also imbued the ring with a spell of aversion, designed to make any of the major wyrms instinctively want to avoid the individual who wore it.

At least, he thought he had. He hoped. There wasn't any good way to test it.

He stretched, rolled his shoulders, and touched the fragment of shell he had used as a focus for the spell. The inside was creamy white, and the outside a hypnotic, iridescent gray-blue. The egg it had come from had been large enough that the curve of the shell was barely noticeable in the palm-sized piece the Terra had given him. Many years ago, an Osei queen had been born from it. The Terra had acquired it, and a few other fragments, at great effort and expense.

Naples sensed familiar power behind him before a voice asked, "What is that?"

A twinge in his neck chastised him for being still and focused for so long as he tried to twist to greet Henna. He winced and said, "It's a gift for a . . . a friend."

"A date for the festival?"

The words were asked politely, not from real interest. Henna didn't want to know about his "dates" any more than he wanted details of what she had been doing with Terre Verte that made her power glow like a midsummer sun.

Fortunately, Naples' mother used almost entirely cold magic, which meant she was essentially blind to the way a hot magic user's power sparked and sang in reaction to sex. *Un*fortunately, Naples hadn't known about that particular aspect of his power until he had returned from one of his first successful trysts and Henna had cornered him with a diatribe about being *careful*.

Their ensuing argument had covered everything from Kavet's age of consent laws to the value a healthy, attractive, fourteen-year-old boy could fetch if sold as a slave in any of a half-dozen ports where the Tamari traded. Naples still wasn't sure if Henna had been more horrified to learn her young student had had sex, or that he had done so on a Tamari ship, without any knowledge of the danger.

After that, Henna had left the rules to Naples' mother, and done her best to keep her lectures focused on safety. From her, Naples had learned things like how to identify the drugs would-be slavers sometimes slipped potential victims, how to avoid disease, and the quickest way to use his power to sap the fury from an ornery sailor bent on beating the shit out of him when he misjudged a situation. He had scoffed through the lessons with a petulance he had later regretted; he'd had enough occasions to use the skills since that he had long ago apologized and thanked her.

Henna had used the word *date* ironically, but Naples answered, "Actually, yes. Well, somewhat. I won't be available in the evening, but Sepia assures me I will have some free time during the day."

He would still be working nominally as a servant during the ball, but only so he would be available to help support the spell to ensorcell the Osei. He wished he could discuss the spell and his role in it with Henna, but the Terra had forbidden him from doing so, even if Henna already knew of the spell's existence.

Henna's brows lifted in surprise. She had seen him turn down a half-dozen Napthol novices in the past year alone—not that that was much of an accomplishment, given the limited selection among sorcerers his age.

"Anyone I know?" she asked.

"Probably not."

Henna didn't pursue the question. Naples was used to most of the Order's members dismissing sailors as somehow less than human, but Henna's reaction to them always seemed more personal. Since the only thing he knew of her experiences before she came to Kavet was that she had been from a seafaring family, he never challenged her aversion to those who still sailed.

"I was going to do some work," Henna said, changing the subject as one of them inevitably did whenever they discussed relationships. "Are you done with your project, or should I set up in another spot?"

There were half a dozen altars in the temple at the highest level of the Cobalt Hall, of different sizes, shapes, and materials. Novices worked at all of them during their education, eventually discovering which materials called to them most, which rituals would respond to them, and which would fade into nothing. Most sorcerers found two or three they liked, depending on the type of magic they were using, but Naples always used the same one, which was made of precious cast iron. The surface was covered with three layers, the first being soft leather, then a circle of black-and-white rabbit's fur, and a disc of polished obsidian glass to make the surface smooth and slick.

"I'm done," he assured her, gathering his materials to put them away. He tucked the Osei egg shell into the trunk where he kept his personal projects and made sure the Terra's knife was sheathed securely at his waist, then returned the rest of his tools to their shelves. A glance at Henna showed that she had already given herself over to her magic, and was focused on the whispers of power that guided her to choose the tools she needed.

Naples returned to his room to clean up and wrap Cyan's gift. He was just about to head out when he heard fussing from nearby, a distressed voice announcing, "Abibi! Gi gabba gimme! No! No!"

He recognized Clay's two favorite words: *abibi*, which they all thought meant "banana biscuit," referring to the toddler's beloved snack, and *no*, which he had recently learned and liked to use at the least sensible times.

Naples sighed and went to check on the toddler, who was supposed to be napping. Their mother would hear him in a moment through a pair of crystals she had bespelled to carry his cries to her, but she was currently working downstairs and three flights of stairs were a lot for her to take if her younger son was just tossing restlessly before falling back asleep.

Clay was standing defiantly in his crib and jumped with an excited gurgle when he saw Naples, clearly expecting that the sight of his big half brother meant rescue from his imprisonment.

"Nana! Nana!" Clay shouted, the closest he had been able to come to Naples' name.

Henna breezed in behind Naples just as he caught the eye-watering stench from Clay's diaper, and he was exceptionally grateful when she said, "I've got him. You were on your way out."

Naples wasn't going to argue. He had changed plenty of diapers since Clay was born and was willing and able to handle another if necessary, but he *was* supposed to meet Cyan soon, and would far rather do that than deal with the hygiene needs of a tiny person. As he walked out, he shook his head at Henna's conversation with Clay, which sounded perfectly earnest as they "discussed" topics like whether or not the toddler's clothing would need to be changed and how he felt about having porridge with roasted apples for a snack.

Focused on his own plans for the day, Naples opened the front door too abruptly and nearly hit the man standing there, one hand raised toward the brass knocker and the other holding a bouquet of flowers.

Terre Verte. Naples' breath caught for a moment and he felt his shoulders straighten.

"Can I help you?" he asked, grateful his voice didn't crack. Something about Kavet's prince always made him feel like he was an awkward fourteen-year-old again.

"Is Henna available?" the Terre asked. "We don't have plans until later, but I have some unexpected free time. I'm hoping she might, too," he added.

"I can—"

"Honey, who is—oh!" His mother's voice interrupted his response, followed almost immediately by her looping an arm around his waist to pull him out of the way—not unlike how she might have moved Clay. "Terre, do pardon my son. Are you looking for Henna?"

"Is she available?"

"Naples, go see if Henna wants to come down." Only a slight rise at the end of his mother's order made it seem like a request.

Naples nodded, suppressing an inappropriate sigh of irritation. What exactly did she think he was doing, that she needed to apologize for him?

"You're . . . Madder, right?" the prince asked as Naples turned toward the stairs.

"Yes, that's right, but you're welcome to call me Maddy. Everyone else does."

Including your father, probably, Naples thought, with an ironic smile. He wondered idly what Terre Verte thought of finally meeting his father's mistress. Was his parents' feuding and infidelity such a fact of his life that it didn't bother him anymore, or was he concealing his awkwardness behind a well-practiced political veneer?

As Naples stepped out of the room, he heard his mother add, "That was my oldest son, Naples."

"Is his father part of your order?"

Naples hesitated, and heard his mother do the same. They rarely spoke of his father these days.

"My husband worked in the paper mill before the fire," Maddy replied, her voice soft as she referenced a tragedy that had taken over twenty lives a decade before. "Henna tried to warn him to stay home that day, but she was new to our order then, and we didn't understand how powerful her gift was. When I ignored her, she convinced Naples to play sick. Otherwise he would have been with his father that day."

Naples' jaw tightened. Henna had kept him home by offering to teach him to juggle candlelight, which had interested him even more than his father's promise to show him how the machinery at the mill worked. He wondered for a moment why his mother felt the need to share the whole story—a simple *no* would have sufficed—and then he realized she wasn't talking about his *father* at all. She was warning Terre Verte that the woman he was courting was part of their family, and they expected him to treat her well.

"How accurate are Henna's prophecies?" Verte asked. "She always downplays her second sight whenever we speak of it."

"They tend to be accurate," Maddy answered, "but she can't always call them. The ones she tells in the square are often more fabricated than true. Most of the time, people are just looking for a moment of entertainment."

"Maddy!" Henna's voice carried well down the stairs, startling Naples into remembering he was supposed to be fetching her, not eavesdropping. She shot him a distracted smile as she brushed past. "Clay was fussing, so I—"

As much as Naples would have enjoyed seeing how the prince responded to meeting his own bastard little brother, he had places to be. Instead of risking more distractions in the front hall, he ducked out a side door.

He skipped the bustling marketplace and took familiar back alleys, tracing a path he had first discovered when trying to find a route to the docks that didn't pass anyone likely to report his movements to his mother. These days secrecy wasn't as necessary, but he still took it out of habit, especially on days when he was running late and didn't want to run into anyone who might consider it rude if he refused to stop to talk.

Oh, perfect.

He sighed as he turned a corner and discovered a group of young men clustered together, speaking in low, entitled grumbles outside the door of a chandlery. Their austere clothes, deep frowns and choice of meeting place warned him they were Quin even before a familiar blond man turned around to regard Naples with singular distaste.

"What are you doing here, witch?" Celadon demanded, as if Naples were the one acting strangely. They had met soon after the preacher had moved to the city, and their relationship had become increasingly antagonistic since, as Celadon had evolved from trying to rescue the poor, innocent child raised in the Cobalt Hall—even going so far as to file an accusation of abuse with the king to try to get Naples removed from his mother's custody—to deciding he was a lost cause. Naples had rather hoped Celadon's recent long absence meant he had finally been eaten by one of the Osei who haunted his beloved Wyrm's Shadow.

"Walking down a public path," Naples replied. There were five of them, and though Celadon clearly avoided heavy labor, the others had the hard look of men employed in physical work. The hostility in their eyes could have been frightening if Naples hadn't trusted his ability to teach them a scalding lesson if they attempted violence. "I'm not the one who spends my time whining in back alleys about how the Terre are ruining the country by using their wicked magic to do deplorable things like . . . what is it today? Fund schools and feed orphans?"

"*Fund schools*," one of the Quin scoffed. "I had to pull my daughter out of the city school so she wouldn't be indoctrinated with—"

"Don't bother." Celadon's voice was soft and resigned as he cut off his follower's rant. "This one would rather spend *his* time in back alleys in the valuable pursuit of another trick."

Naples wasn't sure if he was being called a common witch who performed silly magic stunts, or if he was being called a whore. Celadon had slung both slurs at him in the past. Naples had occasionally responded by trying to educate him about the difference between a sorcerer and a witch—the latter were usually Tamari or Ilbanese, and though their power was different than a Kavetan sorcerer's, it wasn't safe to insult them. Naples had also pointed out that he wasn't pretty or skilled enough to compete with the Order of A'hknet prostitutes, who considered their vocation an art form.

But such verbal sparring had long since lost its entertainment value. These days, the only thing Naples really wondered was how the Quin could swing between claiming sorcery was useless chicanery to suggesting it was powerful enough to accidentally destroy this world and the next.

"Unfortunately, the tenets of your so-called faith mean I'm unlikely to find one *here*," Naples drawled. Of course Celadon had resurfaced in time for his favorite holiday; he and his closest followers always protested Festival, and Naples and the other younger novices always gave him a hard time about it.

Like counting apple seeds to tell fortunes and kissing your sweetheart under the moon, it was a tradition.

Naples moved forward, trying to ignore the creeping sensation along his spine that warned that each of these men would like nothing more than to put a knife in him. He didn't think they would dare try, not so close to the Cobalt Hall, but they also didn't move out of the way. He had to push past them, roughly planting a shoulder in one man's chest and using a burst of power to supplement his own strength as he shoved the Quin back a pace to clear a path.

They get bolder every day, Naples thought, unnerved despite himself as he hurried on his way. *It's getting ridiculous.*

It was worse than ridiculous. It was, almost, starting to get a little scary.

CHAPTER 9

DAHLIA

It was getting late. Celadon had warned Dahlia to avoid the central market square come evening, and she knew she should heed his words, but she didn't have the heart to return to his house yet.

It wasn't that she felt unwelcome there. Celadon's aunt Willow was as quiet and reserved as his sister, Ginger, was exuberant and gregarious, but both had been friendly and glad to have her. But it didn't feel like *home*.

She hadn't imagined she would stay there long. She was well educated and a hard worker. She carried with her a letter of recommendation from the Eiderlee school dean, another from the parent of a particularly challenging young boy she had tutored one-on-one, and one from the town mayor. The *mayor*! Of a small town, yes, but he spoke of her accomplishments, her invaluable help in organizing civic events, and her talent for coordinating volunteer groups to manage community tasks. With credentials like that, how hard could it be to find a job in the busiest city in Kavet?

Very hard, apparently, which was what made it so difficult to face returning to the Cremnitz household.

For two days now, she had chased promising leads for jobs only to be told the vacancy had just been filled—usually right after she told her prospective employer where she was staying, or where she had grown up.

Dahlia couldn't help but recall the scene at the stables in a new light. She wondered if Celadon's associate Ash had quit entirely of his own volition, or if he had been encouraged to do so. No wonder Maimeri had thought Dahlia might get desperate enough to look for a job at the docks!

She plodded into the market square, thinking she would buy something to eat before turning tired feet back toward the Cremnitz house. There had been a pie seller there earlier whose venison pasties had smelled delicious.

Lost in thought, it took her longer than it should have to realize the character of the market had changed.

Where previously there were merchants selling luxuries like fancy sweets, fine jewelry, and hand-carved cherry wood boxes with mother-of-pearl inlay, she now saw the distinctive glow of multicolored fox-fire, individuals with elaborate costumes surrounded by strange implements, and—oh, goodness, it was too cold for those people to be wearing so little!

She had heard people say there were Order of A'hknet prostitutes who blatantly advertised their profession in the city square at night, but she hadn't believed it. She decided she didn't want to know if it was true. She carefully avoided meeting the gaze of the scantily clad men and women lounging near the fountain.

"Careful."

The soft warning from nearby made her jump, realizing she had nearly trampled the wares of a merchant set up on a brightly colored carpet.

"I'm sorry," she said, taking a deep breath to steady herself. Doing so brought a sweet, ashy scent to her nose. It was reminiscent of the smoke released in midsummer brush-burnings, and caused a pulse of nostalgia to briefly tighten her throat.

The merchant gave a kindly smile, revealing fine lines at the corners of his brown eyes. "Can I help you?" he asked.

"I'm sorry," she admitted, "I don't have any spending money with me." Despite her better judgment, she couldn't help gawking at the wares fanned out around him. The small glass bottles looked similar to those Celadon's aunt made for perfumes, but these were full, sealed with wax, and decorated with brightly colored ribbons. Some appeared to hold liquid or sand. Some glowed. There were also satchels of various colors and sizes, embroidered with symbols Dahlia didn't recognize.

"Looking is free."

"What are they?" she asked. She could recognize the small foxfire globes; these were mostly white and yellow. One, located closest to the merchant and probably therefore most expensive, was baby pink. Otherwise, she had no idea what the paraphernalia was, though she imagined it all fell under the category of sorcery—so why was she still standing here?

Because everyone else is, she thought. *Because, if sorcery is so dangerous, why are they allowed to practice it a stone's throw from the palace?* There were other young women in the square, looking perfectly happy and unafraid, unintimidated by the crowd. There were even *children*, laughing and playing while their indulgent guardians shopped or chatted in the twilight. The scene did not match what Dahlia had been prepared to encounter.

"These here," the merchant said, gesturing to the glass containers, "are prepared enchants. Foxfire is the one most people are familiar with, but there are others. Here, smell this." He opened one of the vials and held it out to her, but she drew back. She was curious, but not stupid enough to take a whiff of something someone had just told her was magic. He gave a little smile. "It won't hurt you. It's a perfume, designed to enhance the grace and allure of the wearer. It doesn't do anything mystical unless it's actually applied."

Tentatively, she leaned forward to smell the supposed perfume. Its scent was subtle, a little lemony.

"This one is for energy," the merchant added, opening another and holding it out. The smell of this one reminded her of burned cloves. "It's most commonly used in the shipyard, and other places where people find themselves working dangerous jobs without enough sleep, but it's been popular this week as young men and women prepare for tomorrow's festivities."

"Are they herbals?" she asked, wondering if this man had a mundane answer to her father's question about what made the magic work. She tried to sound only curious, but the sorcerer frowned, as if he heard her anxiety.

"I can't answer your questions until you open your mind enough to hear the answers," he said, tone flat.

She bristled. After yet another day of being dismissed as soon as would-be employers learned she was Quin, having this sorcerer loftily accuse *her* of being close-minded was infuriating. "Do you *know* how they work?" she challenged. "Do you have any idea where your power comes from?"

"Do you?" he returned.

"Do I . . . what?"

"Never mind." He sighed. "You should speak to Henna. She knows more about the theories of power than anyone else in our order. She can do a better job answering your questions than I can."

Dahlia wanted to storm away indignantly, but that would confirm his accusation that she wasn't willing to hear the answers she claimed to want.

"Who's Henna?" she asked reluctantly.

"The seer over there," the merchant said, gesturing to a garishly costumed Tamari woman lounging not far from the palace doors, the bright crimson and yellow of her dress sparkling with metallic embroidery. Her face was tilted up as she spoke to a man not much older than Dahlia, whose flirtatious smile implied he was attempting to distract the woman from her task.

"I . . . I will ask her," Dahlia said. "Thank you."

The sorcerer smiled, once again appearing the kindly father.

Dahlia shook her head, but resolutely started toward the future-seer, whose fingers were idly trailing through a pile of black and white stones. As Dahlia drew near, the rattling of those stones reached her ears like waves hissing over the pebbles that lined the coast of Eiderlee, though surely it was impossible to hear anything so quiet above the market din.

"Your future for a coin?" the woman offered when Dahlia neared.

"Excuse me?"

"Your future. A prophecy, a telling," the woman elaborated. "A single copper coin is sufficient."

"I'm sorry, your . . . *colleague* told me—"

"You have questions," the woman said, interrupting before Dahlia could explain that the other sorcerer had suggested she come over. "Questions about loyalty and truth. Questions about . . . power. Of which you have none. As yet. I can perhaps answer some of those questions for you."

"That's what I was hoping," Dahlia mumbled, a chill running down her spine. The woman hadn't looked up at her yet, and her voice had an unnerving, melodic lilt.

She didn't realize she had recoiled until she bumped into the man who had been flirting with the fortune-teller. She jumped away from him so quickly that she stumbled, and he caught her shoulders to help her regain her balance, saying, "Steady."

"Sorry. Thank you." Dahlia found her footing, cleared her throat, straightened her spine, and stepped forward again. It was one thing to ask a question and decide she didn't like the answer. She refused to be the kind of coward who couldn't stand to *ask*. "I spoke to your colleague over there. He told me you might be able to answer some questions I have about sorcery."

"Did he?" Henna finally looked up, amusement in her eyes. Dahlia was startled by the bright complexity of their hazel depths, nearly lost amid overly dark eyeliner and shadow. "I will answer your questions if I can. But first, let me read your future for you."

Fortune-telling was just a performance, wasn't it? Even most Quin who railed against sorcery laughed at those who claimed to see the future. Dahlia hesitated, then realized this wasn't a curiosity she could justify indulging, anyway.

"I'm sure your fortunes are . . . helpful," she said, trying to be polite, "but I haven't found work in the city yet, and I don't have much spending money."

"Here." The man who had steadied Dahlia earlier stepped forward and tossed a coin toward Henna. The sorcerer caught it deftly, and then it was gone. Magic, or sleight-of-hand?

"I couldn't accept—"

"Nonsense." The man dismissed her protest before she could complete it.

"I . . . thank you, then." Dahlia's heart sped with anxiety. This woman was a sorceress, not just a roving entertainer. What if her prophecies were real? Did Dahlia *want* to know her future? "Do you need to know anything about me?"

Henna shook her head, trailing her hands through the runes.

"I was right." Her voice was distant, breathy. "You have no power in the traditional sense, the sense of magic, but you have a strong destiny. You are . . ." Her breath hitched. "Your thirst is insatiable. You aren't meant for the Order, but you will walk its halls. You fear others like yourself because they are not like you. Oh!" She sighed, an almost sad sound. "You need a guide. Helio was right about that. But I am not the guide you need."

As Henna's hands fell away from the stones, Dahlia saw that they were trembling. She looked up, not at Dahlia, but at the man standing nearby, whose lips were quirked with amusement.

"This is the man who can answer your questions," Henna declared.

His smile faded. "Excuse me?" he asked.

"You need to . . . to keep her, teach her," Henna said. She looked frustrated, as if her vague, incoherent declarations were as irritating to her as they were to Dahlia. What did *any* of that mean? Was she making excuses to foist Dahlia off on someone else, as the other sorcerer perhaps had? Or were they all playing a game at Dahlia's expense?

"Well, thank you for your time," Dahlia said stiffly, deciding it was time to take her leave of the situation. "I should be getting home."

"You need a partner for the Apple Blossom Festival," Henna said to the man, her tone urgent.

He snorted laughter, obviously finding the suggestion ludicrous. Dahlia agreed, though she saw less amusement in the situation.

"You *need* her," Henna insisted. "I don't know why,

but she matters. She needs a teacher, and you *don't* want it to be someone else. And you . . ." She looked at Dahlia. "You're clearly new to the city, so you probably don't have an escort."

"I wasn't planning to go," Dahlia said, unable to keep the wistfulness from her voice. "My hosts don't approve."

"Your hosts don't . . ." The man stifled another laugh. "Henna, I do believe you're trying to set me up with a rebel *Quin*."

"All the better," Henna said smoothly. "You keep saying you don't understand their movement. She can tell you everything you want to know about the Quin, and you can answer her questions about sorcery." With a wicked smile, she added, "And a good Quin girl would never put her hands on a man she just met, so you're safe from unwanted advances." Dahlia blushed at the implication, and took another step back from the strange pair. "Do you dance?" Henna asked her.

"Only some country steps," Dahlia demurred, feeling no need to trot out her dancing resume for these strangers. She cleared her throat and said firmly, "I think you're both mistaking me for someone else. I'm flattered by the invitation, but I'm not going to the festival with a total stranger."

The man let out a half laugh, half cough.

Henna dealt with the statement matter-of-factly. "Then I should introduce you. My name is Henna, as you know. I'm a full initiate in the Order of Napthol. You can usually find me here or in the Hall. And this is Terre Verte. Do you need a lengthier introduction?"

Dahlia felt her flushing face go cold. Her stomach rolled.

Of course she knew the name.

Had she really been talking to—

He couldn't be!

She stared at the man, waiting for him to deny it while frantically trying to remember everything she had said to him and how much of it was probably completely inappropriate to say to a prince. Was it *legal* to turn him down? Briefly, she imagined the look on Celadon's face if she told him some random sorcerer in the market had set her up with Terre Verte for the Apple Blossom Festival, and that almost made her smile again. *Almost.*

Even picturing Celadon's horror wasn't enough to overcome the sudden, uneasy knot in her chest. It seemed she was standing blindfolded on a precipice, aware she was one step from disaster, but unable to tell in which direction the fall awaited her.

CHAPTER 10

HENNA

Watching the series of expressions that crossed the girl's face might have been amusing any other time—almost as amusing as watching Verte go from mildly entertained, to intrigued, to incredulous, and now resigned.

"Terre," the girl said, her voice tight, but still with more poise than Henna would have expected. She gave a clumsy half curtsey, as if she weren't at all sure how one was performed or if this was the right situation to perform one.

It wasn't. No one curtsied or bowed out here in the market, when the Terre was in his street clothes and walking among the people, his personal guard a discreet distance away. Still, the girl's confusion and anxiety were understandable even before she stammered, "I'm—I'm so sorry. I'm not from the city. I didn't recognize you."

"Evidently," Verte said.

Verte didn't look like he was taking this seriously yet, but Henna wanted to kiss him for the fact that he hadn't casually dismissed her words, either. He was playing along, willing to let her have her game.

Only it wasn't a game. She could barely speak past the chest-constricting panic.

Why couldn't her visions be clearer? If she could have told Verte, "On this day, such-and-such will happen unless you do so-and-so," he would have listened.

The girl, on the other hand, looked ready to bolt, only held in place by her sense of loyalty to the Terre. Or perhaps her terror at displeasing him. The Quin probably taught their disciples that the Terre sacrificed people who offended them, or some such nonsense.

Henna shut her eyes, both to recall any details of the vision that had overpowered her when she read for the girl and to steady herself so she could speak more plainly. She considered trying again to communicate how dire the image had been, but the girl looked close to panic already.

"My visions sometimes overwhelm me," Henna said, with a measure of calm she did not feel. "I apologize if I frightened you. But I believe what I've said to you is true. You've come to the city to learn, haven't you?"

The girl hesitated, as if considering the truth of those words, but finally nodded.

"The Terre regulate sorcery in the city, and have access to more records and manuscripts on the subject than even the Order of Napthol. If anyone can answer your questions, a Terre can, and you can trust his words to be true. And if you want to advocate for your own people, Verte has expressed frustration to me in the past that it is so hard to understand the . . . the Followers of the Quinacridone, you call yourselves, right? It is hard for those of us with power to understand you, because most of you won't even speak to us."

"You're serious about this," Verte murmured.

Henna stayed focused on the girl. Verte would trust her. A young Quin woman had no reason to.

"I am unable to attend tomorrow's festivities," Henna continued, "which means Verte needs a partner. A well-bred, educated partner who is capable of behaving properly at a formal dinner, with no romantic designs or desire for the throne. I believe you fit that description?"

The girl nodded slowly, acknowledging the point with a proud tilt of her head, but not yet ready to agree.

Henna shifted her gaze toward Verte, silently pleading with him to support her.

Verte spent long seconds studying Henna's expression, and then his posture and expression shifted. He was no longer the amused, idling man who flirted and teased; he now wore the polite, engaged expression Henna had seen on him as he held court.

"If Henna is right that you are willing to speak for the Followers of the Quinacridone, I would be honored to escort you to the festival and answer any questions you might have about sorcery, or the city or country in general." Verte cleared his throat gently. "I have been trying to open civil dialogue with the Quin for a while now, but their leaders tend to be . . . unenthusiastic about such conversations."

The girl laughed at Verte's understatement, then bit her lip as if unsure laughter was appropriate. When Verte didn't strike her down, she ventured, "I've been told that Celadon Cremnitz talks to you."

Verte's lips thinned. "I'm not sure *talking* is the right word for how Celadon approaches a conversation. You know him?"

"His aunt is my host in the city."

Verte winced. "Of course. Was he expecting you to join his group of protestors in the market?" He shot Henna a look that she couldn't read. Concern?

"He offered, but I never accepted."

Now that her immediate shock was passing, the girl was becoming more confident. She spoke formally, politely, but no longer cringed in response to every change in Verte's expression. That was good. Henna knew she needed to put this girl in Verte's path, but even if Verte trusted Henna for now, he would set her aside if he didn't think she could manage to behave appropriately for the formal events of the evening.

As her confidence rose, the girl's expression became more assessing. Speaking respectfully but not cowering, she explained, "I have not yet made up my mind about sorcery, or the Terre line. I have heard many things from my parents, friends, and the Cremnitz family, but I want more information before I come to a conclusion. If you feel it is necessary—" she looked briefly at Henna before returning her gaze politely to Verte "—and appropriate and useful, I will gladly accompany the prince of my country to the festival."

Verte raised a brow, now clearly intrigued by this country girl who had managed in the last few minutes to find her poise and courage.

She's not a girl. Henna had to stop thinking of her that way. She wasn't much younger than Verte and Henna, if at all. All her apologizing and hesitation earlier had made Henna think of her as a girl, but her direct, articulate response to Verte—no, to her Terre, since her careful phrasing made it clear she was accepting out of respect for the title, not interest in the man—now made her seem older. Girl she might be, due to her sheltered upbringing in a movement where females were increasingly protected and controlled by their male relatives, but she was on the cusp of becoming her own woman.

A powerful woman. That much was for sure. *Why? What power?* And why was Henna so certain this one, apparently open-minded Quin would be dangerous if left to her own devices, in a way radical preachers like Celadon never had been?

"Thank you," Verte said. "Would it be acceptable if I sent someone to the Cremnitz house to pick you up at, say, eight tomorrow morning? I know it's early, but attending with a Terre means a certain level of pomp and formality, and I want to make sure you have a chance to review what you need to know."

His brow tightened. Henna suspected he was doubting the wisdom of this decision as he imagined all he would need to do to prepare this woman for her responsibilities during such an event.

"I grew up on a farm. Eight is not too early."

"And may I ask your name?" Verte asked.

"Dahlia Indathrone." She gave another brief curtsey, this one slightly more graceful, as if it were something she had learned once long ago but never had reason to practice.

"A pleasure to meet you."

They shook hands. Henna felt a shudder run through her, as if the contact had completed some kind of circuit. She tried to follow the almost-vision, but couldn't, and before she had refocused on the conversation Dahlia was excusing herself and Verte was saying goodbyes on their behalf.

The moment Dahlia was gone, Verte's polite smile faded. "What was *that* about?" he asked.

Henna wished she had a better answer for him. "I don't know," she said. "You need to keep her. Protect her. You do *not* want her going to someone else to learn. Of that I am certain."

He opened his mouth. Closed it. Opened it again. Hesitated. Then said, "Maddy told me about her husband. Is this like that?"

A wash of relief, like salt-water spray. "Yes," Henna whispered. *Thank you, Maddy.*

Verte nodded. "Then I'll trust you. My parents will be horrified, but I'll make it work." His mouth twisted half up, as if the prospect was at least a little enjoyable, but the expression didn't have a chance to fully form before he sobered again. "It isn't just me this is likely to cause trouble for, you know. Celadon thinks I am womanizing, grave-robbing, elitist scum. He will be horrified, and he is in a position to make her life miserable."

"He'll make her life miserable anyway, as soon as he realizes her curiosity puts her at odds with his doctrines."

"True," Verte conceded. "I suppose at least this way she'll know she has other allies in the city. Unfortunately, this means I should cut tonight short. I need to find someone to prepare her for tomorrow. Oh, and I need to ask Sepia's help to get her outfitted. I can't imagine our little farmer packed attire appropriate for a formal ball." He looked more anxious about telling the palace's head servant about the additional work than he had about telling his parents about his Quin partner. "I should also set up a meeting with Mistress Rose of the trade guild. I was supposed to escort her daughter tonight. I'll have to see what kind of groveling and concessions she'll expect in response for the slight. And . . ." He winced in anticipation. "I should ready myself for a very *long* talk with Celadon Cremnitz tomorrow morning. Can I have him arrested if he pounds on the palace door before I've had my coffee?"

"That would solve your problem about how to keep his group from protesting tomorrow," Henna said wryly, trying not to let her lingering uneasiness show. She wasn't sure she succeeded; their kiss goodbye was brief and felt awkward, both of them clearly lost in thoughts of the past and the future instead of the present moment.

When she returned to the temple, Henna found Helio and Maddy both there, Helio working with an apprentice Henna barely knew and Maddy sitting with Clay at a carved wooden altar favored by old magic users. The child was batting at something, probably remnants of cold or old power that Henna would need to strain her senses to see, while his mother mixed ingredients for what looked like a healing salve.

Helio and his student worked at another altar, one made of silver and glass with a pure white silk cover. The girl kneeling at the altar had all her attention focused on spinning rainwater into thread. In addition to being an early cold magic exercise, the thread could be used by healers as incredibly fine sutures, which kept most wounds from scarring.

Helio murmured something to his student, probably an encouragement or word of advice, then stood and met Henna at the door.

"Were you able to accomplish what you needed to?" he asked without preamble, pitching his voice low to avoid disturbing the others working.

Henna frowned, still unable to shake her sense of unease. "I'm not sure."

"Who was that girl?"

"*No one,*" Henna sighed, exasperated. "A Quin farmer recently come to town and staying with the Cremnitz family."

Helio shook his head emphatically. "She isn't *no one*. She has disaster all around her."

Maddy had noticed their conversation and rose to join them, brows raised in question. Henna briefly tried to summarize her strange vision, hoping Maddy or Helio had some words of advice.

"Is it possible you're sensing the general, ongoing

conflict with the Quin?" Maddy asked, concerned. "Or something that might—"

"Nanana!" Clay interrupted in his emphatic way. "Abibi! No gimme!"

"Maybe," Henna admitted, "but—"

"Nana nana abibi!"

The child's voice rose, soon joined by a discordant noise, like bells tumbling to the ground. Helio glanced apologetically toward his student; the sound had been her hard-worked thread snapping.

"Just . . . *watch* her," Helio said. "I feel like she has had the potential to do something wonderful, but also something very dark. I don't—"

"Mine!" Clay shouted, grabbing restlessly at Henna's earrings. "Dis mine! Gimme no gimme abibi!"

"I'll take him out," Maddy said. "The temple usually calms him when he's fighting sleep, but not tonight apparently. I'm sorry we disturbed your lesson, Helio. Henna, we should talk more about this later."

Helio nodded distractedly. "Let me finish this exercise with Lassia, then I'll meditate on your mystery girl. I'll let you know if I see anything."

"Thank you. Will it distract Lassia if I try to work as well?"

"I don't think so. She has traces of hot power, but not enough to see someone else's magic unless she—"

The bowl of rainwater abruptly froze and exploded, sending icy shrapnel flying in all directions. Lassia, who had apparently run out of patience and attempted to restart the spell without Helio's guidance, let out a string of curses as she wiped frost from her face and hands. Clay let out a delighted whoop, followed by a rising wail as his mother carried him from the room.

Helio returned to his chagrined student. "Well, that's something I haven't seen before. Do you know how it happened?"

Henna sighed and opened her personal supply trunk, where she had the pieces of a spell she had been working on to deter foxes and fisher cats from attacking chicken coops. It was dull work now that she had mastered it, but just then, dull was what she wanted.

She had an unsettling feeling that boredom was a luxury she should cherish while she could.

CHAPTER 11

VERTE

Closer.

Closer.

Verte held his breath and wished he could still the distracting beating of his own heart. Slowly, he nudged one last drop of power into position in the complex web of spellwork surrounding and saturating the palace, as if placing the final Numini on the head of a pin.

His mother muttered a curse as she pushed back with equally exacting precision, balancing her magic to his.

"That has to be enough," Sarcelle said. Her voice was husky from tension and hours spent in the smoky interior of her private ritual space. She had knocked on Verte's door to ask him for help just before dawn, after her new apprentice had apparently passed out from exhaustion from working through much of the night. "If we push any more, we'll bring the whole thing down."

She arched back and rolled her shoulders, making Verte aware of the aches and stiffness in his own body. They hadn't been here more than an hour or two at most, but each new breath of power was harder than the last.

So much for so little, he thought, touching the fine metal chains piled haphazardly on top of his mother's altar. His father would have spread them out lovingly, displaying the gold and silver netting with reverence, but his mother didn't bother with such niceties. A tool was a tool to her.

These tools appeared to be jewelry—a hairnet for the Terra that shone with rubies and diamonds in addition to the finely crafted metal, and belts and wristbands for the two Terre men. They looked exquisitely crafted and expensive, fit for royalty. They did not look magical.

A net to represent a net, as Verte's father said.

When Verte stood, spots danced in front of his eyes, sparkling like shooting stars.

"You're pushing too hard," his mother warned as she saw him wobble on his feet. "Get yourself something to eat, and maybe take a nap before—oh, you have to deal with that Quin now, don't you?" She glanced at the clock. "There should still be time for you to make it, if you're so insistent on going yourself."

Once the dizziness had passed, Verte lifted his head. He had left directions with the housekeeper to dispatch a groom to pick up Dahlia if Verte's last-minute assistance to his mother took too long, but he would rather not subject the servants to Celadon Cremnitz if he could avoid it.

He left the spelled accessories behind, trusting his mother to store them properly. If Verte had been with his father this morning, some sharp parting words about Dahlia probably would have followed him out the door, but Sarcelle had been sanguine when Verte had explained that a vague vision meant he needed to take a complete stranger to Festival this year.

Her acceptance, of course, had begun an argument that had ended only when each of Verte's parents left for their own private ritual spaces to complete last-minute preparations for greeting the Osei.

It always created a bit of a flurry when Verte stopped in the kitchens, as if he hadn't been dropping in to swipe food at odd hours since he was a young boy. His schedule had never been regular, and he liked to avoid formal meals with his parents whenever he could.

Today as he slipped in through the door, one of the kitchen staff looked up, handed him a bag, and said in a tentative voice, "Miss Sepia says she has packed you breakfast, since she knows you will not have time to eat before leaving to pick up your companion, and—" The servant, a slip of a boy Verte thought was the cook's son, gnawed on his knuckle a moment, then realized what he was doing, clasped his hands and went gamely on with Sepia's words. "And that I should tell you to keep out of the kitchen today, because she is far too busy preparing for Festival to deal with your antics. Um, sir. They were her words."

Verte laughed, shaking his head as he accepted a basket of still-warm fruit pastries. Sepia had worked for the Terre line for longer than Verte had been alive, but not all the staff were as comfortable with her informality.

"Apple tart?" he offered Tealyn, as the guard fell into step behind him on his way out the front door.

"No, thank you, sir," she replied.

"You're familiar with Celadon Cremnitz?" Verte asked, as he led the way toward the Cremnitz residence, a little over a mile north of the palace in an area of the city Verte rarely visited.

"I'm aware of him and his movement," Tealyn confirmed. "I haven't dealt with him directly, but I've had interactions with other Quin. They tend to have a lot of bluster and brag, and they'll fight back if attacked, but they don't usually start physical altercations." Respectfully but firmly, she added, "I know the difference between posturing and threatening. I won't get in your way as long as it's all talk, but Celadon isn't a sorcerer. If I feel he is a threat, it is my duty to respond."

Verte nodded, accepting the guard's confident assertion of her responsibilities, and her frank acknowledgement of the difference between this meeting and their last potentially hostile confrontation. He wasn't particularly worried about violence from the Quin preacher—today—but the fact that the royal guards had been discussing the Quin enough for Tealyn to know how they "usually" acted boded ill.

"With any luck, this visit will be as uneventful as the last," Verte said, thinking of Wenge.

"Uneventful," Tealyn echoed skeptically. "I've never seen a person look that close to death while still walking. Will he be all right?"

"He takes the brand today," Verte answered. "Once his magic isn't overwhelming him, he will have a chance to recover. Nothing is certain, but his chances are better now than they were before."

"The Quin position on sorcery starts to make a little more sense after something like that." Hastily, Tealyn added, "That doesn't mean I agree with their other tenets, or that I approve of their disrespect toward yourself and your line, sir. I'm loyal to the Terre, not Celadon Cremnitz."

I should have followed up with her sooner, Verte thought, mentally kicking himself for neglecting that duty to his new guard. As it was, now wasn't the time to get into a conversation about the risks and benefits of sorcery.

"You might find it useful to speak to Dove, the counselor working with Wenge," Verte suggested, as they turned the corner to the block where Celadon's home was. "She could offer perspective on your concerns, and update you on Wenge's condition." Verte would check in with him as well, though it would probably take Wenge a day or so to recover from the brand itself enough to want visitors.

Tealyn nodded. "Thank you, sir."

The tenements and townhomes on the Cremnitzes' block were well maintained, their paint crisp and shutters straight as the occupants opened them to greet the warm spring morning. By contrast, the cobbled street looked loose and shabby, clearly neglected.

I should talk to the district manager, Verte noted absently, as he moved to avoid tripping on a cobble. Ice and snow always heaved some cobbles out of the road each winter, but this seemed particularly bad, as if the public maintenance crews had been neglecting this area for some time.

Or they've been refusing aid from the crown. How many of the homes in this area belonged to Quin families?

When Verte and Tealyn reached their destination, the first person they saw was neither Dahlia nor Celadon, but a teenage girl with curly blond hair. She was tending a small garden grown in containers around the front door with a level of violence not normally required to pull weeds and deadhead flowers.

"Is everything all right?" Verte asked her, alarmed by her vehemence.

She looked up with a start. Her blue eyes widened, and she wiped dirty hands on her apron before giving a half curtsey, stopping, and saying with less fluster than her manner suggested, "I'm not sure how I am supposed to greet you."

Verte had heard that Celadon had a younger sister, but had never expected to meet her.

"You could say good morning," he suggested.

She glared at him. "Oh, do you think it is?" she asked acidly. She waved a hand in the direction of the house. "Because I think it is a terrible morning, and I think that is your . . . fault." She hesitated only once in this pronouncement, when raised voices from inside interrupted her.

Verte winced. He couldn't make out the words from here, but he recognized Celadon's furious voice.

"Have they been fighting long?"

"Oh, only since Dahlia said you invited her to the festival," the girl replied. "Celadon told her the only reason you would invite a naïve country girl to the ball is because you think she'll be too awed and provincial to object when you decide to spread her legs. Dahlia called him a close-minded fool and said if anyone was naïve it was him, since he clearly wasn't willing to educate himself or listen to any point of view different from his own. Then Celadon realized I was listening and ordered me outside." She spat each word at him defiantly, and at the end tossed her head. "*I* have a date, too, but I'm not foolish enough to tell Celadon about it."

It was not Verte's responsibility to help Celadon manage his little sister, even if he had wanted to. It *was* his responsibility to rescue Dahlia from the mess he had caused for her. "I should get in there."

Conflict was clear on Tealyn's face, in the pinch of her lips and the narrowing of her eyes. Verte had a feeling she would love it if he said, *Go in and get Dahlia and don't let Celadon get in your way.* Instead, she said, "I will wait at the door unless you call me or I hear threats, sir. The presence of an armed guard is more likely to escalate the situation."

Verte nodded at her wisdom, then reached for the door with no solid idea just *how* he intended to defuse the argument. As he pulled it open, he heard Celadon bark, "I will not have a royal slut staying under the same roof as my aunt and sister."

"In what wild dream did you think I would *want* to stay here, after this morning?" Dahlia retorted. "I'll grab my belongings and be on my way."

"I'll have Ginger pack them for you. You can—"

At that moment, they both saw Verte. Each, Verte noted, had a blotch of reddening flesh on their face.

Who had hit whom first? Either way was intolerable, given Celadon's larger size and Dahlia's position as his guest.

Before Verte could speak a word, Dahlia said flatly, "Oh. You're here. Well, I'm ready to go, as you can see."

She turned her back on Celadon and stormed through the front door.

"Your line poisons everything it touches," Celadon declared.

Verte had heard it all before. "I assume I will see you at the festival," he sighed.

"You know you will."

Without bothering with pleasantries, Verte followed Dahlia. She had paused to say goodbye to Celadon's sister, who threw herself forward to hug Dahlia fiercely. "My brother is *stupid*," she declared. "I know you're not a . . . what he called you." She glared at Verte, eyes flashing, and added, "But that doesn't mean you know what *he* wants from you. Be careful."

As Dahlia murmured her last goodbyes, Verte stepped back to give her privacy and to plan his next words. When Dahlia took her leave of the younger girl and approached him, her back was straight, her eyes were dry, and her expression was set in lines of determination. No weeping for her, at least not here, not now. Instead, she led the way back toward the market square and the palace with long, confident steps. Tealyn, apparently comfortable that Dahlia wasn't a threat, dropped discreetly behind, though the fury at what she had seen and heard remained on her face.

Apologies and explanations wouldn't be sufficient. Verte said, "This rift between you and your guardians is my fault. I will see that you are taken care of."

Dahlia looked at him sharply, and Verte realized his words had been badly spoken. He had meant that he would ensure she had a place to stay and resources to get back on her feet, but Dahlia Indathrone clearly wasn't a woman who wanted anyone to "take care" of her.

"I would appreciate your help, but only until I can find my own way," she replied, flawlessly polite. "I have job prospects."

He didn't want to upset her more, but she needed to be honest about her situation.

"I doubt that," he said, as gently as he could. "I suspect most places you've applied have rejected you the moment you told them where you were living, or where you received your education. You would have had more luck at Quin-owned establishments, but if Celadon speaks against you, they will not hire you, either."

"I am not sure whether I'm meant to be impressed that you are aware of the bald discrimination Quin face in your city," Dahlia bit out, "or horrified that you are so aware, and yet do nothing to alleviate the situation."

She was three steps ahead of him before she seemed to realize that he had stopped, shocked by her blunt, accusing words.

She turned, for the first time appearing chagrined. "I apologize," she said, ducking her head. "I spoke with no regard to your station, or the kindness you have offered. I have very little reliable information about any measures you have taken to ensure equality in this city or the rest of Kavet. I have only ever heard these topics discussed by people like Celadon or my father, who I now know will speak badly of you no matter what you do."

The apology did not make him feel better, because in truth Verte had done very little to address the issue of which she spoke. But what was the royal house supposed to do? Force people to employ zealots, who often caused trouble with customers or refused to carry out the portions of their jobs that forced them into contact with sorcery?

This was not the time to debate the issue. Verte started walking again, and attempted to change the subject.

"I had heard," he said, attempting to put levity into his voice, "that Quin girls were taught to be meek and placid and defer to the men in their lives. You don't fit that expectation."

Dahlia tossed her head. When she replied, it was in the modulated tone of a teacher. "A Quin lady is polite, not *meek*. She thinks before she speaks or acts, considers consequences, and accepts advice, but that does not mean she has no voice or autonomy. She is expected to respect the leadership of her father, her community leaders, and her husband when she has one—but that does not mean she must tolerate abuse. The moment Celadon slandered me and raised his voice and hand against me, he lost all right to my respect."

You need to . . . to keep her, teach her . . . protect her, Henna had said.

Oh, Henna, who is this woman you have put into my path?

CHAPTER 12

DAHLIA

"Thank you. I'll be fine." Dahlia kept her head up and her tone modulated as the stout, gray-haired woman who had guided her to one of the many guest chambers nodded politely.

"Very well," Sepia said. "I will assign a maid to assist you from now on. If you need anything, simply ring, and she will attend you promptly." Sepia gestured toward an ornate silver bell set on a small, velvet-topped table by the door. It was smaller than a duck egg, and couldn't possibly make much sound, which meant it was probably enchanted somehow.

As soon as Sepia closed the door behind herself, Dahlia felt her knees give out and she slid to the floor.

All other contemplation abruptly broke off in favor of the single, overwhelming thought, *What have I done?*

It was all well and good to tell Celadon to take his judgmental words and accusations to the Abyss and storm off, but what *now?*

The Terre was right. If Celadon spoke against her—and she had no doubt that he would—she would never be able to find employment in any of the few Quin establishments in the city, and she had already learned that the non-Quin ones were unlikely to hire her.

She looked around the luxurious guest room. *Rooms.* She was in a parlor larger than the kitchen at home. It had its own fireplace, currently unlit, ringed with marble so polished it looked like it had never seen a flake of ash. The floor was nominally stone, but covered with such a plush, luxuriously woven rug it might as well have been made of feathers. What was Dahlia doing in such a place?

What if Celadon was right?

No. She didn't believe that. Yes, she knew Terre Verte's reputation, but the same rumors made it clear he had no need to take advantage of the idiotic country fool Celadon clearly thought Dahlia was. The prince had plenty of beautiful and powerful women available to him.

So why am *I here?*

She was still on the floor when there was a polite knock on the door, and a maid brought a compress for Dahlia's cheek. It hadn't occurred to Dahlia to ask for one, which meant the bruising and swelling must be obvious enough that Sepia had seen it and taken the initiative.

Dahlia thanked the maid, who curtsied and backed out of the room as Dahlia probed the tender area below her left eye. At some point in their argument, Celadon had grabbed her wrist as if to drag her physically out of the house; pulled along, stumbling, she had tripped over a bag of candles Ginger had left in the hall and slammed her face into the doorpost. The asinine look on Celadon's face as he attempted to apologize had infuriated Dahlia so much she had responded with a slap so hard it was probably closer to a punch, a level of violence she hadn't known was inside her.

She set her jaw as she put the compress to her cheek, wondering how bad the bruising would be by the time Festival rolled around, and whether she should ask Sepia for some cosmetics to try to hide it. At that moment, it seemed more satisfying to brazenly display the injury and tell the world how it had happened.

But if she attended Festival with Terre Verte, she would be representing the Followers of the Quinacridone not only to the royal family but also to the visiting nobles from Silmat and Tamar. She would not allow the evening to focus on one awful, hypocritical example of a preacher, when the movement as a whole was still dear to her. She had to represent herself, and Eiderlee, and the Indathrone family, and the rest of the Quin community—who would have condemned Celadon for resorting to violence at all.

That meant Dahlia needed to get up, gather her composure, and figure out how to make it through the day and evening without shaming herself.

She would have liked something to write on and with while she organized her thoughts, but wasn't so desperate for it that she wanted to bother the servants. Instead she stood and paced, as if she were standing in front of a class teaching, and considered aloud what she needed to do next.

"I need to ask about etiquette. Greetings, introductions, titles," she ticked off, thinking of the trouble she had already had when introduced to the prince. Dear Numen, she would be meeting *the* Terre and Terra, wouldn't she? Almost certainly.

Her mouth was dry. Thankfully Sepia had left a decanter of cool water and a clean glass. Dahlia put the compress down to pour, and only then realized her face no longer hurt. She touched where the injury had been, but the swelling and tenderness were completely gone.

I should also find a polite way to ask the staff here to warn me if they have just handed me something magic, she thought, putting the compress down and examining it with a grimace. There was nothing on the cool, cotton-swaddled compress to indicate it had been made with sorcery, but simple ice would not have healed her so perfectly. She wouldn't necessarily have refused the aid if she *had* known, but she didn't like the precedent it set that she hadn't been warned.

"Talk to Sepia if you get a chance," she added to her verbal list, trying to refocus herself. She continued making her list, and by the time she had eaten breakfast and the Terre had returned, she had a bevvy of questions ready. They were her armor, her preparation for battle against a future that was suddenly unsure.

Verte, as he insisted she should call him, answered each one thoughtfully and patiently, only occasionally displaying amusement or chagrin.

"I'm still not sure I understand why you need me at all," she said, after Verte had reviewed the situation with her.

Terre Verte nodded, with a smile that was clearly forced. "The why is complicated," he said. "Among the Osei, a son has no status. He is a political nonentity until a queen claims him. For me to have a right to be in the room and at the bargaining table, I need a woman by my side."

"And I'm all you could get." Dahlia didn't believe that for a moment, and knew her skepticism was audible.

Verte shrugged. "Henna's right. If I can't have *her* here, I would rather be able to focus on my task with the Osei and spend my free time tonight speaking with you and trying to get a better grasp of the conflict with the Quin than politely flirting and trying to avoid giving the wrong impression to a woman who might think I'm offering her a chance at the throne."

Dahlia considered asking again why he couldn't have Henna there, but he had avoided the question earlier. He also avoided acknowledging that the idea had clearly been Henna's in the first place.

"Do you have any questions about the etiquette regarding the Osei?" Verte asked, moving on. "That part is critical."

That part was *simple*. Dahlia summarized what he had told her. "I only speak to the Osei queen. I do not approach any of the princes, make eye contact with them, or pay attention to them. I treat your father—" she managed to refer to the king of Kavet with only a slight tightening of her voice "—in the same manner, as the Osei will see him as belonging to the Terra. All the other men at the event will be unattached and therefore it is not a problem if I speak to them."

Not just one seamstress but a team of men and women interrupted at that point, bustling in to measure Dahlia and present her with an assortment of finished and half-finished gowns they promised could be ready in a few hours. Terre Verte took his leave then, but Sepia returned to answer the seamstress's questions about cut and color.

Dahlia stood mutely though the process, thinking wryly, *this is what my tax dollars go to, is it?* She understood that she would be with the prince, representing

Kavet, and that called for a certain level of formality in dress, but the casual assumption of power and wealth still dizzied her, highlighting the gap between her life and Terre Verte's. And as she considered different views, she thought of her parents, and how they would react if Celadon wrote to them about the morning's events before she had a chance.

"Do I have time to send a letter?" she asked Sepia, pulling the head servant aside as soon as the seamstresses were gone.

"Yes, you should have a few hours before you are expected to appear with the Terre. Would you like me to send a secretary?"

"No, thank you. If I have that much time, I'll go to the stationer myself." She wanted to do this on her own, and she wanted to get out of the palace for a while, and be away from all the unfamiliar finery. "If that's all right?"

"You are a guest, not a prisoner," Sepia reminded her. "You are free to go where you like. Do you need directions?"

"No, thank you," Dahlia said again. She had visited a stationer not far from the palace the day before, hoping for work, though a surly apprentice had sent her away the moment she asked about job possibilities.

As she passed through the crowded market, she caught a glimpse of Celadon surrounded by about a dozen other men and women and her breath hitched. Compared to the bright costumes of the merchants and decorators, the small Quin group appeared cold and severe.

Dahlia hurried on, hoping not to be seen.

"Someone chasing you?" the stationer asked as she stepped into his small shop too quickly. He moved up to peer out the window, then shook his head. "Cremnitz and his band give you the shivers?"

"A little," she admitted. "I need to write a letter to my father, and have it delivered to Eiderlee as soon as possible?"

"Here to Eiderlee takes four or five days," he told her. "But it being the Apple Blossom Festival, the post won't leave until tomorrow morning." He frowned, studying her face. "Did you try to send this yesterday? I saw you talking to my apprentice Grayson, but you left in a hurry. I hope he wasn't rude to you."

"Not overly," Dahlia said, distracted. Celadon wouldn't be able to get a letter out any sooner, so the delay shouldn't matter. "He was busy, and I wasn't here as a customer. If I purchase paper and ink, do you mind if I write the letter here?"

"That's fine. Just give me a minute to tidy up, then I'll help you find your materials. I had a young man in here having some trouble with a love-letter," he confided. "I had to pull everything out before he found something he liked."

He started ruffling papers together, and Dahlia drew a deep, calming breath. The familiar scents of paper and ink made her eyes sting with tears, which she quickly blinked back before the stationer could notice. *This* was her world—not palaces and magic and royal balls.

Hoping to hide her moment of sentiment Dahlia reached forward to help, tidying stacks of delicate flower-petal sheets, linen, and small bottles of inks and perfumes. "Looks like he had quite a time of it," she observed inanely. "Is Grayson not here to help you today?"

The man let out a bitter laugh. "On a festival day?" he asked incredulously. "He was supposed to come in to prepare inks this morning before I let him off for the afternoon, but I suppose the lure of the day was too much for him."

As the shopkeeper carefully wrapped the flower sheets to protect their delicate edges, Dahlia found a stack of what felt like good-quality cotton-blend correspondence paper.

"May I use this?" she asked.

The money in her pocket was all she had to her name at the moment, but the penny or two she might save by using cheaper paper wasn't worth it. This letter was too important. She wouldn't risk having her explanation to her father arrive smeared and wrinkled due to cheap stock.

"Help yourself to whatever you need. I'll put the rest of this away, then tally your items."

Dahlia took a sheet of paper, then located what

seemed to be an acceptable, basic ink, and a glass pen with a simple, elegant shape that fit nicely in her hand.

Careful not to splash the ink, she described the morning's events, what had led up to them, and the decision she had made. She did not include specifics of the insults Celadon had thrown at her, only that he had shown no respect or trust in her character or her integrity. When she tried to describe the way Celadon had dragged her down the hall, her hand shook and she had to pause.

Blue eyes wide and face flushed, Celadon had shouted his attempted apology at her in the same volume as his accusations, including a denial she would have accepted from a three-year-old—"I didn't mean to!"—but which was despicable coming from a grown man. He might not have deliberately slammed her into the wall, but it wouldn't have happened if he hadn't violently put his hands on her in the first place.

She had said enough. Let Celadon mention her "accident" and try to explain it away in *his* letter. Dahlia's parents weren't stupid, and they knew Dahlia wasn't, either.

I hope I can still make you proud, she concluded, blinking to hide tears from the shopkeeper, who was watching her write. *I will let you know when I am settled. Love, your daughter, Dahlia.*

She capped the bottle again, then blotted the letter dry.

"Eiderlee, you said?" the shopkeeper asked as she sealed the letter, and wrote her father's name on the outside.

"Yes."

"I'll see the courier gets it in the morning." He placed the letter carefully with several others. "You have a very clear hand, Miss Indathrone."

"Thank you." Her eyes lingered on the letter. Altering those words would not change recent events, but even so, she was seized by the desire to strike out what she had written, to undo it all.

"And you seem to know your way around a shop like this," the shopkeeper added.

"I've never needed to use one before coming to the city," she admitted. "My father has always kept writing tools in the house."

"He taught you about papers and inks?"

"Yes." Her throat was tight as she imagined the hours she had spent at her father's knee, learning these skills. He wouldn't believe Celadon. He *couldn't*. "He—" She stopped. She had been answering the questions out of habitual courtesy, and only now broke from her own thoughts to realize they didn't sound like idle conversation. "Yes, sir." She continued, "He believes it is important to know how to communicate, which includes undersanding which papers or inks are more likely to bleed, and which are better suited for casual notes versus those for public record."

"It sounds like he raised you to be a scribe."

She paused to consider her answer. A lie would probably serve her better, and now that she wasn't staying at the Cremnitz household, she wouldn't have her current address to betray her. Still, her tongue told the truth, as it always had. "He had hoped I would join the Quinacridone Order of monks," she said.

The shopkeeper's expression cooled, but then his gaze flickered to Celadon's group as if he were considering her expression when she first arrived. "We don't sell many enchantments in this shop, but we do have a few," he said. "How do you feel about that?"

"I can't work any magic myself, and I know almost nothing about it, but I . . ." She trailed off for a moment. "I've seen no evidence that it is harmful," she finally said.

He nodded. "I threatened to dock Grayson's pay yesterday for chasing off a customer, and he told me you were in here looking for a job. I suspect he hurried you away because he knows I've been considering letting him go. The only reason I haven't done it is because I'm too old to start entirely over with another young apprentice." As if in response to the blooming hope on her face, he added hastily, "I can't promise anything, long term—I have a contract with Grayson, and I'm bound by law to give him notice and a chance to correct his behaviors—but if you are willing to work, I will pay you a fair wage for your skills for as long as you're here." He pressed his lips together wryly. "I don't suppose you have any relevant references?"

She suspected this was a moment where giving the prince's name would instantly ensure her a place. Given how guilty Terre Verte had looked upon witnessing the end of her argument with Celadon, she was sure he would be willing to put in a word for her anywhere she wanted.

"I worked as a grammar teacher in Eiderlee for five years, and assisted the mayor there with secretarial work and event planning," she said. "If you will accept references from Followers of the Quinacridone?"

The stationer's mouth tightened. "I'll judge you on the merits I see," he said, "no matter who your family follows." He hesitated, as if considering, then admitted, "Grayson's enamored of a Tamari sailor and has been talking about wanting to follow her to sea. I suspect he might see your presence as an excuse to break his contract. If that happens, and you show well in the work you do for me as a hire-on, we might talk about more long-term options."

There was nothing certain about the offer, but the possibility was still enough to make Dahlia's throat tighten. Apprentice craftsmen made very little money during their training, but their master was expected to provide living accommodations, if only a tiny room at the back of the shop. Dahlia was far older than most apprentices, of course, but as he had said, she already had a firm groundwork in the training someone like Grayson would have received since he was ten or twelve years old.

And the possibility of a long-term position that would lead toward independence was an opportunity she wouldn't ignore.

Thank you, Numen, she prayed inwardly, *for guiding me here today.*

"I imagine you have plans for Festival tonight," the stationer said, "but if you come back first thing tomorrow morning, we'll see if you have the skills I need. Abyss knows I'm hard-pressed right now. Almost a decade training that boy . . ." He trailed off, shaking his head ruefully.

Dahlia left the stationer's shop with a giddy kind of breathlessness, caused by the rapid swing from nervous despair to careful optimism. She successfully made it past the Quin group without meeting anyone's gaze, and returned to the palace, deciding it would be best not to test her luck further.

CHAPTER 13

NAPLES

As the sun lifted into the sky, a chilly spring morning gave way to an idyllic afternoon. The cloudless sky was a perfect clear blue, and seemed endless. The still air made the city seem like it was holding its breath, and cradled all the scents of the day: the clean sea, thousands of flowers brought in from the country to decorate the market square, exotic spices baked into once-a-year treats, and of course wafts of magical paraphernalia ranging from incense sold by an A'hknet witch to Helio's fancy potions.

What made it perfect, though, was the warm, firm arm around Naples' waist.

Despite the Terra working him until he was near

to collapse repeatedly over the last three days—or past it, as she had warned him she might—he had been able to make it down to the *Blue Canary* multiple times to see Cyan.

His last solid memory of the night before had been the Terra mingling his blood and hers—more than he thought strictly healthy—with ash in a small bowl to produce a slurry kind of ink, which she then used to paint intricate runes on the gemstones set into the ensorcelled jewelry. Each stroke of her brush had made Naples' heart beat a bit harder, as if the blood in the ink was still connected to his own.

He woke in a heap on the couch at the back of the ritual room, some number of hours later, alone. After some trial-and-error, he was finally able to open the door, and found a note from the Terra saying she wouldn't need him again until evening.

As a post-script, she had suggested he eat something "that once ran on four legs" to help him replace lost blood. Naples had followed the advice, bought a meat pie in the market, and eaten most of the filling out of it before forcing himself to also down the crust. Food, along with several glasses of water, had stilled the shakes. A little more sleep had left him feeling human again.

Now he was here, Cyan's arm around his waist as they explored the market.

Several other members of the Order of Napthol were working. Helio had recently created a technique for juggling lights that was earning him grand applause, and as always Henna's fortune-telling garnered brisk business. Naples normally spent a few hours of the day performing for tourists and children as well, but at his current brink of power exhaustion, he was content to lazily stroll through the market with his date.

Date. I have a date.

For the day, Cyan had traded the plain, unostentatious fabrics he and most of his cohorts usually wore for a vivid saffron shirt in a style he claimed was popular in Frevania, a country Naples wasn't entirely sure Cyan hadn't made up. Instead of lacing at the throat or sleeves, it had a loose, informal neckline and a half-dozen tiny black buttons at each cuff. It was also made of some kind of touchably soft fabric too warm to be silk but too light to be kidskin.

"Are those actors?" Cyan asked, pointing.

Naples followed the sailor's gaze, and snorted laughter. Celadon Cremnitz and his cronies, dressed in severe black and gray, did look a little like a theater troupe preparing for some kind of tragic drama. They had taken a prominent position near the fountain, displacing the musicians who usually set up there, and were handing out flyers.

"The Followers of the Quinacridone, our local malcontents," Naples answered, trailing behind as Cyan approached the group.

"Oh, the Quin," Cyan said, without the exasperation Naples was used to hearing paired with that phrase. "The captain is considering a couple of Quin boys who are looking to hire on to the *Canary*. They're green as spring grass, but seem like hard workers."

Before it occurred to Naples that Cyan's gregarious curiosity might lead him to deliberately interact with the Quin, Cyan had reached forward with his free hand toward one of the fliers.

The Quin man holding the flier had been looking away, talking to one of his cohorts, but turned toward them with a practiced smile when he sensed a willing audience. His fingers tightened reflexively on the paper as his gaze took in Cyan's arm around Naples' waist, and the proselytizing welcome froze in his slightly open mouth.

The woman next to him noticed, and put on her own, only slightly more successful smile as she focused on Cyan with the gaze of a raptor. "Welcome to Kavet, sailor. I'm sorry to see you seem to have found by an . . . unfortunate element." She glanced at Naples briefly and dismissively. "Do you have a few minutes to talk? Perhaps we can—"

"No," Cyan answered coldly, interrupting. He glanced at the flier in his hand, then handed it to Naples with a sardonic lift of his brow. "As you say, I seem to have found an 'unfortunate element' and should remove myself from it."

He turned away without waiting for a reply, bringing Naples with him. Naples glanced at the flier, which seemed to be more propaganda warning about the "epidemic" of sorcery among younger children. Lifting his hand so the Quin would be sure to see, he funneled a burst of power into the paper, which caught flame and swiftly crumbled to ask.

"Petty," Cyan said, though his smile showed his approval. "Was that personal, or more generic bigotry?"

"Both," Naples admitted. "Quin think relations between two men are unnatural, but they also have a particular issue with me, and that one apparently thought saving you from me was more crucial than your so-called perversion. She's probably lamenting to her cohorts about how you would have been a good, sensible young man if only you hadn't been seduced into wicked ways by a nasty sorcerer."

Naples said the words jokingly, but Cyan's response was uncharacteristically solemn. "And if they hadn't already known you?"

Naples looked at the stark white of his hand twined with Cyan's dark one, and admitted, without lifting his gaze, "Then it might have been me she tried to save from the foreign sailor. I'm sorry. The Quin are assholes, a bunch of country mice who can't understand anyone different than themselves. They don't speak for the rest of the city."

He gestured to the crowd around them, which was currently made up of at least as many Silmari and Tamari as it did Kavetans. Other than this particular Quin group, people here celebrated the diversity.

"Good thing I didn't plan to visit the country," Cyan

murmured, pointing out the flaw in Naples' attempt at comfort. He turned Naples in his arms, looking at him searchingly for several moments before he declared, "Fine. Never mind them." He dragged Naples forward to kiss him, in defiance of all the stares from the Quin and the Napthol alike. "You promised me dancing. When does the music start?"

Naples pulled back, his heartbeat rapid, and looked toward the palace. Musicians had already set up on platforms nearby, and were watching in anticipation. The afternoon festivities would officially start when the royal family opened the palace doors.

"It should be any minute now."

Behind him he heard more raised voices, this time as the Quin picked a fight with Dove. Naples didn't understand why, but she seemed to actively enjoy verbally sparring with the dour preachers, and would deliberately draw them into ridiculous debates. Celadon had been distracted on the other side of the group when Naples and Cyan passed by, but Naples heard him engage with Dove. Fool.

Then the large public doors to the palace rumbled open, each pulled by two liveried guards, and the musicians—on fiddle, guitar, bass, and mandolin—strummed out the first notes of a welcoming tune as Terre Verte stepped out with his date, an unremarkable, straw-haired woman Naples didn't recognize. Since Henna had chosen not to go to the festivities, Terre Verte had probably made some kind of political match for the night.

Naples started forward, intending to greet Terre Verte, but Cyan's arm around his waist tightened, holding him in place. Cyan asked, "Isn't that the prince?"

"Yes," Naples replied, puzzled for an instant too long before it occurred to him that not everyone would be comfortable with the idea of greeting the country's monarch. "Didn't you say the Silmari royal family is informal with the people, too?" he asked.

"With *their kind* of people," Cyan clarified. "There must be a thousand royals in Silmat, once you count all the cousins and half cousins and bastards, and half the time there's no way to know who's who—but you always know who's nobility. Like sticks to like."

Naples pondered that for a minute, as he watched several others greet Terre Verte and his date in their usual jubilant way.

"I suppose we're different here," he speculated. "We don't have multiple noble families, just the Terre line."

Cyan laughed out loud, a full-bodied, unashamed sound that Naples enjoyed even if he didn't fully understand its cause.

"What did I say?"

"You," the sailor said, shaking his head with a rueful smile. "You prowl around the docks like the savviest scoundrel in a thousand dockside taverns, so I forget sometimes how suddenly naïve you can be. Kavet doesn't mark its nobility the same way as

Silmat, but you damn sure have them. The only difference is that, instead of land ownership and inherited titles, you have magic. And like, as I've said, calls to like."

He nodded toward the crowd that had gathered around the Terre, which was almost exclusively sorcerers from the Order of Napthol.

"We work closely with the Terre," Naples said defensively.

"Yes, you do," Cyan agreed, his tone just as it might have been if Naples had said, "It might rain this afternoon."

As Naples contemplated Cyan's words, Terre Verte spotted the Quin group and approached them with a resigned expression. The woman with him followed, lips pressed together in a hard line. The way the crowd nearby shifted to watch made the Quin look even more like they were putting on a play. Naples joined the audience happily.

Celadon came to the front of the group to square off with Terre Verte, who told him, "You and your people can't be here in the middle of the square."

The Quin lifted his chin and announced, "It's a public place."

"It's a public place that, this day, is dedicated to the celebration of the festival," Terre Verte explained. "Your group is in the way. You can stay, but you have to move to the edge of the plaza like any other merchant."

"I'm not a merchant," Celadon huffed.

"You're trying to sell something you claim is a religion. If I have to forcibly move you, you're going to end up much farther back, so why don't you make it simpler for all of us and cooperate for once?"

Naples watched the altercation and tried to consider it in the context of what Cyan had been saying. Sailors grumbled all the time about insufferable nobles and their blindness toward the rest of the world. Was the Order of Napthol guilty of the same where the Quin were concerned? Was that why the Quin were becoming ever more numerous, much to the confusion of the more-privileged sorcerers?

At that moment, Celadon spotted Terre Verte's date and his eyes widened with recognition. The same man who had initially handed Cyan the flier found his voice. "Dahlia. It's only been a few hours, and already you're trumped up like a royal whore."

"Oh, good," Naples murmured to Cyan. "I was in danger of feeling sympathetic for a moment there."

"I wasn't," Cyan replied.

Verte's gaze darkened with fury, but the woman, Dahlia, just tilted her head thoughtfully, examined the Quin man with an expression that could have cut glass, and said, "I know what and who I am, and I am ashamed of nothing I have done. Can you say the same?"

At the end of the question, she shifted her gaze to Celadon instead of the man who had challenged her, and Naples saw something he had never expected: Celadon looked away first.

The other Quin man bristled. "Perhaps you don't know what's shameful."

"That's enough," Terre Verte declared. Out of the corner of his eye, Naples saw the guards by the palace doors tense, watching the altercation closely. "Last warning. Move your little party, or I will send you all home."

"You are only the thousandth person to threaten me today," Celadon replied. "Sorcerers in particular seem to be intimidated by my presence. Man should not have the kind of power you try to wield, and when you use it against your citizens, you only prove my point."

"I don't need magic to move you." Terre Verte reached out to grab Celadon's arm.

Celadon jerked back, snapping, "Keep your hands off me."

At the same time, the Quin crony who had made the "royal whore" crack lifted his fist to swing a punch.

Verte ducked away, narrowly avoiding the blow. Cyan's arm dropped from around Naples' waist as Naples moved forward, instinctively moving to defend his prince even though he knew perfectly well there were a dozen guards hurrying to do the same.

"What in the Abyss are you *doing*?" Terre Verte demanded.

Naples wondered the same. This went past the Quin's usual fervor and into the realm of true fanaticism. Remembering how brazenly he had shoved past them a few days before, Naples felt a chill. If they were willing to assault the heir to the royal house in front of hundreds of people including sorcerers and soldiers, why would they hesitate to knife a hated deviant "witch" in a back alley?

Two soldiers seized the man who had raised his hand against Terre Verte, but instead of condemning their companion's behavior and stepping away, the others rallied to his defense. One woman caught at a guard's arm. Celadon himself attempted to push one of the guards away, which was apparently all the others needed to seize him as well.

At that point, the Quin lost their minds, kicking and punching at the guards who now poured out of the palace to subdue them.

Verte took a step back, staring dumbfounded at the group.

As Naples moved closer to the prince, he caught the distant look in the other man's eyes—he was reading power. Naples shifted his own awareness to try to see whatever Terre Verte had noticed, without success.

Cyan caught his arm, still gazing at the fight in front of them. "I've seen my share of drunken brawls on holidays like Masque—I've been in a few myself—but I'll admit I've never seen a fracas like this between priests and royal guards. Is this normal for Kavet?"

Verte heard the sailor, and blinked as he brought himself back to the mundane world. In clipped tones, he answered, "No, it is not." He turned to the closest guard, a woman who had found the prince's side the moment the fighting began. "Lock them all up," he told her. "They can cool their heels in jail for an evening." Grudgingly, he added, "Keep an eye on them and make sure they don't hurt themselves. I think they may have been drugged. Where's Dahlia?"

"I'm here."

Naples had lost track of Terre Verte's date until her choked voice identified her in the crowd, shielded by two soldiers who had taken the initiative to protect their prince's companion from the violence. She had held up to the insults well, but now looked stricken as she stepped forward and watched as the Quin were taken away. Every freckle on her pale face stood out like ink.

"Are you all right?" Terre Verte asked.

She nodded sharply. "What will happen to them?"

"I'll release them in the morning," Terre Verte said, sighing. "Much as I would love to charge them all with assault on the crown or at *least* creating a public disturbance, I don't think it's their fault."

His gaze swept the crowd. Guilt crawled down Naples' spine as he met the prince's gray eyes and remembered baiting the preachers just a few minutes ago by immolating one of their fliers. Naples couldn't see any magic acting on the Quin mob, but that only meant they hadn't been dosed by hot magic; as Dove had lamented many times, Naples was inept with cold and old magic. He wouldn't notice those kinds of spells unless one of them slapped him in the face with as much power as the Terra's enchanted net.

It took nearly a dozen guards to haul the Quin out of the market square. In their absence, the unnatural hush that had fallen over the crowd slowly lifted. First whispers rose, then more normal conversation. Someone laughed. The musicians started playing again.

Terre Verte looked hesitant as he offered a hand to his date for the first dance of the spring season, as if worried about how well she would perform. The woman grinned up at him defiantly, clearly noting his lack of faith, then tossed her head and whirled into the traditional jig with light and lively feet that left even Naples clapping in admiration—until Cyan snagged him around the waist and pulled him into the growing crowd of dancers so they could bump somewhat less gracefully through the energetic steps.

Despite the earlier brawl, if asked, Naples would have called it a perfect moment.

CHAPTER 14

VERTE

A few country steps, Verte thought wryly, as he watched Dahlia pair off with yet another dance partner, this one a Silmari aristocrat named Jade.

Verte had briefly worried that Dahlia might embarrass herself—or him—when asked to perform for the gathered crowd, but it had quickly become obvious that he was far more likely to fail than she was.

The day gown Sepia had commissioned for Dahlia was well suited to the dance, with petal-light, ankle-length skirts that swirled and flashed bright patchwork accents whenever she spun or kicked. The sun brought out faint strawberry highlights in her otherwise dull wheaten hair, which had been worked into an elaborate wrapped braid that couldn't hope to stand up to her rapid movements, and was as a consequence starting to shed pins and tumble around her shoulders.

As the afternoon progressed, the makeup of the crowd changed. In the country, children would go home to search for sweets hidden in the orchards and to tie ribbons on the fruit trees; here, many homes hosted afternoon carnivals that took over entire city streets. Working folk who had been given the day off returned to their employers to prepare for evening festivities, and sailors and the younger, more rebellious Kavetans moved to the docks district, where the Order of A'hknet merchants and entertainers would host salons dedicated to all-night dicing and card tournaments, more provocative types of dance, and the talents of their professional courtesans. There would also inevitably be fights—some spontaneous and some arranged—picked pockets, and at least one visiting aristocrat who decided despite all warnings to "slum it" and woke up the next morning to find himself with an empty purse and no idea how he spent the night except for the evidence left on his skin by a tattooist's needle.

None of it would be reported to the official authorities.

In the market square, that left the Order of Napthol, wealthy sons and daughters of Kavetan families who did not yet need to return to their own families' celebrations, and the visiting aristocrats from Tamar and Silmat, but also as far away as Frevania and the Forgotten Isles. If Dahlia felt uncomfortable with the rising prestige of her dance companions, it didn't show.

She's doing better than I am, Verte thought, sitting near the musicians by the fountain to catch his breath—a struggle that had nothing to do with the exuberant dancing. His skin crawled with power. His muscles twitched with it. The edges of his sight continually wavered as his peripheral vision caught glimpses of the net meant for the Osei, which hung suspended, waiting to fall on its prey.

By contrast, Dahlia's complete absence of power felt strange. Verte was a lightning-rod, while Dahlia was a clear glass sphere, unresponsive to the power crackling around her.

At the end of the song, Dahlia took leave of her most recent partner and sank down at the edge of the fountain beside him.

"We do that one a bit slower at home," she said, breathless. One of the merchants offered her a cup of cool cider, which she accepted with a grateful smile.

"You held your own," Verte observed. "Jade was out of his depth." He considered telling her the Silmari noble she had just danced with was second cousin to the reigning king of that country, but decided that information could wait for formal introductions at the ball. Jade probably hadn't considered it important enough to mention.

Dahlia tucked a stray curl away from her face. "Jade has not had to instruct aspiring debutants in these steps. Or did you forget I used to be a teacher?"

He didn't think he had ever *known* she was a teacher. Had he asked?

Dahlia didn't wait for a response; her eyes had fallen on a juggler who was performing complex illusions using foxfire orbs as props. "Is that sorcery, what he does, or chicanery?"

Verte knew the man. "What he's doing right now is a combination of sleight-of-hand and misdirection. He is a small magic user, though." At her querying look, he clarified. "Small magic is the term we use to refer to the simple spells almost anyone can learn. A lot of it is based on herb lore, pressure points, or physiology."

"And what of sorcery?" she asked. "Can anyone learn that?"

He shook his head. "People are either born with power or not."

"I've been told," Dahlia said, lifting her voice even while she avoided his gaze, "that children raised in the city are more likely to become sorcerers, because they're exposed to so much magic here by the royal family and the Order of Napthol."

He pondered the suggestion for a moment. "That may be, but we've had powerful sorcerers come from the country—Maddy, for instance, who leads the Order of Napthol right now. Or from overseas, like

Henna and my mother. So I would think it's just that children raised in the city *seem* more likely to have power, because they're more likely to be identified."

She nodded thoughtfully. "But where does that power come from? You say some people are born with magic, but is it all internal, or—when you make foxfire for example, what is the source of the actual light?"

He debated what answer to give her. He knew the Quin theorized that a sorcerer's power was stolen from the realms of the dead, the Abyss, and the Numen. "We don't know," he admitted. "Some people are born able to make fire. Some people are born able to make frost. Some people can tell the future, and others can make enchants to draw love. Or lust. We don't know where the power comes from, just as once long ago humans didn't know how rubbing two sticks together could make a spark."

"It doesn't bother you, not knowing?"

"Of course it bothers me. I've spent most of my life studying and trying to learn what I can," he answered. "But what I know for certain is that Terre and Napthol magics improve the lives of the citizens of my country. For example, do you know how many acres of Kavet are dedicated to tree-farming to meet the winter need for fuel? Worse, do you have any idea how many homes are destroyed by fire every year?" He thought of the devastating accident that had claimed the life of Madder's husband. "Imagine what other purposes that space could be put to, and how much safer people would be, if more of us were able to create the foxfire that can heat a house without smoke, without ash, and without fear of catching the neighborhood on fire."

Again, that nod. This time, he knew what she was thinking, because Celadon liked to throw the accusation Verte's way whenever he had a chance: *You say it's safer. You don't know the cost of this magic you use. You don't know how it might damage the innocent people around it.*

Before Dahlia could challenge him further, he saw one of the servants discreetly signal him through the crowd. "We need to go in now. It's time to prepare for the ball this evening."

Rather than a maid, Sepia herself appeared to escort the girl once they were back inside the palace. The housekeeper's expression and tone were always scrupulously polite, so Verte wasn't sure yet if her seeming protectiveness of Dahlia had to do with wanting to take close care of Verte's guest, or worry that the Quin girl would steal the sterling-silver-without-iron flatware.

Either way, he knew Dahlia would be taken care of.

A hot bath had already been drawn by the time Verte returned to his rooms, and he enjoyed the moment of peace, washing away the dust of the market and the lingering tension from his encounter with the Quin, before seeing which evening clothes his valet had set out. Verte was aware that his preferences for simple attire had created a trend in Kavet, but that fashion had clearly not taken root when it came to festival attire, which tended to lean more toward Tamari trends.

He shook his head when he saw the lace that spilled down the front of the turquoise shirt with opal buttons. At least the cuffs on the wrists were snug these days. Verte had put his foot down when gauzy, draping sleeves had made a brief spin into popularity, leaving gentlemen trying to manage their cuffs at the dinner table with all the care of ladies picking their long skirts out of mud.

His vanity was briefly flattered when he went to fetch Dahlia from her room, as she appeared to be dumbstruck at the sight of him. Then he realized her lips were pressed together not out of nerves but amusement.

When he raised a brow in permission, she said with a sweeping gesture to both him and herself, "This is ridiculous."

He laughed. He couldn't help it. The next few hours would be the most complicated political and magical tango of his life, and that meant dressing in a way that simultaneously denoted power, status, wealth, and respect—but that didn't make him feel any less silly as he saw himself reflected in Dahlia's practical gaze.

At least he wasn't alone in looking like a peacock. The patchwork style of Dahlia's dress for the day had been an echo of the multicolored, elaborately crafted bodice and skirt of her evening gown. The bodice was warm gray, with diagonal slashes in the same turquoise color as his shirt that created a dramatic V-shape to her upper body and gave the girl an illusion of more curves than she had. Certainly, he didn't remember her having quite so much bosom earlier in the day; the stiffness in Dahlia's posture suggested she wasn't entirely pleased about that part of the dress's cut, either.

Or perhaps she was anxious to be wearing a heavy, looping necklace of rose gold set with sparkling opals and turquoise; Verte knew it had come out of his mother's jewelry case, along with the matching earrings. Sepia must have asked to borrow something on Dahlia's behalf.

"You look lovely, and fully appropriate for the event," he assured her as he took her hand to lead her down to the great hall.

"I'm wearing the equivalent of my father's farm's yearly tax liability," she murmured in reply.

"Someday you can tell your father how you single-handedly kept us from refitting the docks with foxfire lanterns."

The exaggeration made her chuckle, which took some of the tension out of her shoulders.

"Ready?" he asked her, as they paused outside the doors of the great hall.

"Probably never," she replied, "but I can fake it for a few more hours."

She put her hand on his arm, and servants pulled the doors open. A marshal announced them: "Terre Verte, heir to the Terre of Kavet, and the Honorable Dahlia Indathrone of Eiderlee." Dahlia slanted a look his way at the courtesy title, which was in the style of Silmari honorifics and not one generally used in Kavet. He had a feeling that one of his parents—or maybe even Sepia—had made it up to avoid drawing undue attention to Dahlia's background.

As he looked around, Verte had to admit that the Order of Napthol had outdone itself. The room was lit by dozens of foxfire orbs in varying shades, adding yet more color to the mass of nobles and royals whose garments resembled the shimmering scales of tropical fish.

He had barely had a chance to reach the bottom of the stairs when the doors opened again and the marshal called, "Terre Sarcelle and Terre Jaune, Queen and King of Kavet." After a polite pause, he continued. "And Queen Nimma of the Third Noble House of the Osei."

Verte looked up, bracing himself. His mother and father entered the room together, united by common purpose tonight in a way they hadn't been united by affection for decades. Beside his mother stood another woman, this one tall and made of sharp angles and too-vivid colors. Supposedly the Osei could impersonate humans so perfectly that no one could tell the difference, but that was either a myth, or Queen Nimma hadn't bothered. She had approximated the shape of a human being, but the lines of her body were subtly wrong. It seemed like she might have attempted to mimic Sarcelle, whose skin was too fair for a native Kavetan and gave away her Ilbanese background. But while for Verte's mother the description "pearly" would have been metaphorical, the Osei's skin literally glistened like a pearl, with an iridescent sheen of green and blue hinting at the color of her scales.

Behind the three royals were five men whose ages were hard to determine, since they, too, had features and coloration that weren't quite correct. The marshal did not say their names.

The Osei hadn't approved of the idea of a marshal at all, and had particularly objected to the idea that the princes would be presented to the room as a whole, something they claimed was only ever done with immature princes when they were presented by their birth-queens to the rest of Osei society. Nimma's slave had declared that announcing them to the crowd would therefore be insulting and infantilizing—but was, of course, perfectly acceptable for the Terre men if they so chose.

Remembering the discussion still made Verte's head hurt.

No, that's the magic, he thought. The spell had reacted the moment the Osei walked in the room, pulling at him greedily. Across the room, he saw Naples, tonight dressed in the same immaculate black and gray as the serving staff, suck in a breath and stagger a bit. He ducked his head and murmured an apology to the Tamari noble he stumbled into, a remarkable bit of feigned subservience by a member of the Order of Napthol.

I wish Henna was here.

With Dahlia, he approached the marble stairs, and at the base bent a knee in a deep bow, as was appropriate for a prince greeting a visiting monarch. Beside him, Dahlia sank into a formal curtsey—at last appropriate for the situation and this time performed confidently and gracefully—and behind them, the gathered crowd did the same.

"Nimma of the Third Noble House, allow me to present Dahlia of Eiderlee and Kavet, who is escorting my son this evening," his mother said, making the introduction in the way they had—after yet more painstaking debate—finally agreed. "Dahlia, you and your prince may rise. Welcome to our home and our celebration."

As he stood, it was an effort for Verte to keep his gaze down and not look directly at Nimma, especially since he could feel her gaze on him.

Dahlia said, "Thank you, Terra, for your welcome and your introduction."

"I believe I am familiar with your territory," Nimma remarked. "You hunt the black and white seaducks near our sister court's waters."

Verte didn't understand the comment, but thankfully Dahlia did. She said, "Yes, our land is named for the eider ducks, and our shores border the waters of the Eighteenth Common House. I am honored to hear we have gained your notice."

Verte was saved more standing around like a useless ornament as one of Nimma's princes stepped forward and, in a soft voice that did not interrupt the women's continued conversation, said, "Perhaps you would join us, son-prince of Kavet?" The inflection and compound term he used to refer to Verte suggested there might be a specific word in their native language for a "son-prince" in contrast to a Queen's mate.

"I would be pleased to do so," Verte replied.

The Osei prince wrapped an arm casually around Verte's waist to guide him toward the other men, including Verte's father, who had apparently been given the same treatment. It was an overly familiar gesture Verte would have liked to object to, but didn't dare for fear of giving offense and disrupting the spell. Watching the other Osei men, who stood close to each other and often touched each other idly, he decided the gesture had been meant as friendly, not insulting.

The habit would work in his favor. Each time one of the Osei touched him, he felt a shock of power like frost melting across his body. Even though he knew the spell was designed to be hidden from the Osei, he kept expecting one of them to recoil from him in confusion when they touched his icy skin.

He met his father's gaze briefly. Terre Jaune's eyes, normally a dark, placid gray, were like polished steel, glistening with power. Verte saw him deliberately set a hand on the shoulder of the oldest-looking Osei prince under the pretense of saying something innocuous about the apple trees for whom this festival was named.

In the midst of the conversation, Verte felt eyes on his back. He saw his father tense slightly, but the other princes didn't react, so he forced himself not to turn until the hand dropped onto his shoulder and Nimma remarked, "You seem to fit in well with my princes."

CHAPTER 15

DAHLIA

If Celadon can speak to a prince of the Osei, I can speak to a queen.

Dahlia wasn't sure if that was petty or arrogant, but she couldn't help the thought as she made small talk about eider ducks and apple blossoms with the Terra and the Osei queen until some unknown-to-her signal prompted the Terra to say, "Dahlia, I hope you enjoy the festival. Please do enjoy a glass of wine and relax for a few minutes before dinner is announced. Nimma, may I introduce you to the Tamari High Lord of the Lasable, who is also our guest tonight?"

Far from being offended, Dahlia accepted the dismissal with relief. Terre Verte had promised they would do their best to avoid forcing her to feign court experience with the Osei any longer than necessary.

She curtseyed again, then backed away, her head high as she turned toward the crowd, pretending she was entirely comfortable standing before a group of aristocratic strangers dressed in a gown that was cut so low in the front she had to be grateful it was also almost uncomfortably snug—at least it wouldn't fall down.

Inquisitive eyes watched her as she looked over the crowd with feigned casualness. Terre Verte had warned her that he would probably need to spend much of the evening with the Osei princes, and would not be at her side much of the time. She was expected to *mingle*.

The irony struck her, as she considered how many times she had encouraged young wallflowers to socialize at Eiderlee socials. At that moment, she wanted nothing more than to slide away along the edge of the crowd.

"May I join you, Miss Indathrone?" She barely managed to conceal her sigh of relief as a familiar figure stepped toward her with a short, formal bow. "Jade Chanrell Mim-Silmat. We met earlier?"

The tall Silmari man had deep brown skin, darker than many of his countrymen in the room, and wide lips she had yet to see without a smile. Like her, he had changed from his earlier, less formal attire, and was now dressed in a sea-blue silk jacket above sable breeches and boots. "Yes, of course, I recall you," she said with an answering smile and as much dignity as she could muster.

"I remembered your saying you did not know many people in court, and thought you might appreciate some company while the Terre attends to business," Jade explained.

"I do, thank you." As she caught her breath, she also recalled her lessons from earlier in the day. "Mim-Silmat. You're of the royal family?" He had only used the Chanrell surname in their earlier, less-formal meeting.

"Only tangentially. If you add up all the Mim-Silmari and Mat-Silmari and Kan-Silmari, I think you'll end up with roughly the population of Kavet," Jade assured her, referring to the different surnames used to denote level of relatedness to the royal family. Dahlia couldn't remember which meant what. "Can I get you a glass of wine, or perhaps beg a dance of you before Terre Verte concludes the dreadfully dull business of being a prince among princes?"

She smiled, enjoying his casual flirtation, even if it was clearly based on the assumption she was someone more important than she was. "Wine would be lovely," she said.

As she watched him go, the words of Celadon's associate rang sharply through her head: *Trumped up like a royal whore.* She let out a slow breath, refusing to allow the ugly memory to spoil this evening. There were significantly more men than women in the crowd—which was probably the strongest point in her favor when it came to attracting the attention of someone like Jade—but there were enough women for Dahlia to confirm that her outfit was no more gaudy or revealing than most others. It was more modest than some, including the Terra's.

"That is a deeply thoughtful expression for such a light-hearted night," Jade observed as he rejoined her and handed her a glass of sweet cherry wine. More somberly, he added, "Though I suppose this gala is less frivolous than most. May I say your Terre is an excellent liar." Jade spoke so softly Dahlia would not have heard it if she had taken a single step farther away. Before she could decide whether or not to defend her country's prince, he continued. "I do not think I could stand there, in front of such creatures, and politely smile and chat as he does. He must even guard his thoughts, since the Osei are just as likely to be offended by those as his words. I suppose he believes they can be won through flattery, but . . ," He trailed off, shook his head, and repeated, "I would not be able to do it."

"I'll admit I know little of them except rumors I scarcely credit and the few things Terre Verte told me today."

"There are six Noble Osei houses in the tropical sea that bounds Silmat and Tamar to the south," Jade said. "It is almost impossible to avoid their claimed territory if one goes by water, which requires paying whatever tariffs the Osei decide are due. If a captain is short, he can willingly pay in hands—which means turning over a passenger or crew member or two—or have his whole ship seized or outright sunk."

"No one fights?"

Jade's eyes drifted to the Osei guests again. Their glittering skin and lithe shapes were lovely, but not intimidating. "They look harmless here, but there isn't much that's able to pierce the scales of an Osei in its natural form. The young king—I'm sorry, King Jasper; they call him the young king because he's younger than I am and just took the throne—has started trying to build weapons we can use to guard our borders if they try to fly over Silmari land, but they are far too large and heavy to carry casually in a ship."

The words made Dahlia glance toward Terre Verte again, where he stood with the five Osei princes. The Osei queen had joined him, and whatever she said made Terre Verte's shoulders stiffen. The queen stepped closer, too close to be polite.

Terre Verte looked up, and for just an instant, caught Dahlia's gaze. The expression was brief but deliberate, calling upon her to act. She had hoped to avoid this.

"Excuse me, Jade." Trying to look more confident than she felt, Dahlia cut through the crowd until she could hear their conversation.

"I think you've mistaken me, is all," Terre Verte

was saying. "Our ways do not allow the heir to the throne to leave this land."

The Osei queen tossed her head. "You say you seek an alliance. I am offering a scenario. I am not ignorant of human ways, so of course you would be allowed to return here, as necessary."

"'As necessary' is 'always,' unfortunately," Terre Verte replied. "Also, there is the matter of the Terre needing to have heirs, which I currently do not. So I really must—"

"You would be a queen's mate," the Osei argued. "Of course you would have . . . heirs." She spoke the last word as if not quite certain what it meant.

Dahlia's eyes widened as she realized what the topic under debate was: Verte joining the Osei queen's harem. His desire not to give offense at this event meant it was impossible for him to say, "No power in the Abyss or Numen would convince me to give up all my sovereign power to become the chattel of a queen of one of our enemies."

Dahlia hoped her heart wasn't beating as loudly as she thought it was as she stepped into the midst of the Osei and boldly wrapped an arm around Terre Verte's waist. She struggled not to flinch from the inexplicable chill seeping from his body.

With a deep breath, she lifted her gaze to meet that of the Osei queen.

The wyrm's eyes were like kaleidoscopes, containing all colors and constantly shifting. Meeting them made Dahlia feel off-balance, as if the floor turned under her feet while her mind raced, insisting this was *insane*, she was making a fool out of herself . . .

She tried to guard her thoughts, but she couldn't.

The Osei queen tilted her head thoughtfully, and took a step back as she greeted Dahlia with a nod. "He's yours, then?"

Dahlia unstuck her tongue from the roof of her mouth. "Yes."

"Pity." It was another word Dahlia wasn't sure the queen understood. "I thought humans only mated in pairs." She gestured to where Jade was waiting, Dahlia's wine in his hand and a confused expression on his face.

"Why limit oneself?" Numen-only-knew where those words came from, but they seemed to appease the Osei queen. The prince who had been standing beside Terre Verte moved away, back to his own queen's side, and Terre Verte allowed Dahlia to lead him out of the crowd.

She started to take her arm away, but he held tight, saying under his breath, "Thank you. That was getting awkward."

Jade greeted them both with a polite nod. "Terre," he said.

"Sorry to borrow Dahlia so abruptly," Terre Verte replied, as he led them all to sit at one of the high-top tables ringing the crowded hall. As they walked,

Dahlia realized the chill on him wasn't dissipating; he was generating it somehow, like an icy breeze seeping from his skin. "Among the Osei, a single prince goes with any queen who offers for him, and is honored by the invitation. He doesn't have a home or a family name unless he is given one by a queen. The queen of the Third Noble House seems to have trouble understanding that I'm happy to remain *here* . . . not to mention reluctant to give my entire country to the Osei."

He closed his eyes and rubbed his temples.

"Are you all right?" Jade asked.

"Mmhmm." Terre Verte opened his eyes, which seemed distant. "Neither of you can see power." He spoke the words as if reminding himself. "The Osei can't, either."

"What would we see if we could?" Dahlia asked.

His eyes refocused and he drew a slow, shaking breath. "Never mind," he said. He lifted his eyes to the foxfire orbs hovering in the air above them, and absently touched an intricate bracelet he was wearing made of woven metal strands. "My mother should signal everyone to move to dinner soon. That will be easier to manage. Jade, I'm afraid you've been assigned a different dinner partner, but I'm sure you will find Dahlia again for the dancing."

Dahlia was about to protest that, despite her step-dancing skills, she had negligible experience with formal ballroom dance when a babble of excitement reached her ears.

Before she could fully turn to look, something large dove past, inches from her head, making her duck away from its frantic flapping and mournful cries of *ki-ki-ki!*

"What on the blue seas—" Jade made it halfway through the exclamation, then broke off in order to dodge a foxfire orb the madly ricocheting creature had just sent careening their way. The glass shattered as it struck the ground, spattering ethereal light, which stuck to suits and gowns as a viscous, smoldering ooze for a few seconds before extinguishing.

"A bird," Dahlia said, laughing a little as her heart tried to return to its normal rhythm. She had never seen a bird like this before, though. It had the arrow-straight body and wide, rounded wings of a heron, but a long, trailing tail that sparkled as if carved from ice.

"Someone's exotic pet?" Jade suggested. "It doesn't look like something native to a cold land like this."

"Yes. A pet, no doubt," Verte said, in a dazed, distant voice. "I'll—"

"With that bit of excitement, I would like to officially welcome you all to the Apple Harvest Ball." The Terra's voice lifted across the crowd, amplified somehow, and rolling with her laughter at the awkward bird. "Normally I would give a speech and a toast before asking you to join me at our meal, but I think it best if we leave the staff to help our feathered friend outside before any of you lovely gentlemen find a mess in your hair. Please, make your way to the dining hall, find your seats, and I will speak to you there."

She spoke with a levity that put the crowd at ease, but Dahlia couldn't help but notice the way Terre Verte couldn't seem to look away from the bird.

After that, the rest of the evening passed with less excitement. Terre Jaune, Terra Sarcelle, and the Osei sat together at the high table, while Terre Verte sat at the head and Dahlia at the foot of the next one, along with the highest-ranked of the visiting dignitaries from Tamar, Silmat, and countries of which Dahlia had only vaguely heard. Jade had dismissed his own importance in Silmari hierarchy, but he had a seat at the table not far from Dahlia herself.

Dahlia's table partner was a duke from a country whose name she attempted to pronounce in its native tongue three times before the duke sighed, and said, "Your people call them the Forgotten Islands."

He spoke carefully, clearly struggling with the Castrili tongue commonly used in Kavet, Silmat, and Tamar, but Dahlia enjoyed the conversation despite the frequent hesitations and moments of confusion.

According to the duke, the Forgotten Islands had recently begun negotiating with Kavet for increased trade, since there was an open waterway between the two lands that did not cut across any Osei territories, and the Islands then had a reasonable course directly to Silmat. The Tamari objected to the proposal, which they feared would undercut their own trade, but the people of Silmat and the Forgotten Islands supported it as a way to protest and avoid Osei tariffs even if it made the eventual trade route longer than the traditional path through the tropical Rushing Sea.

When Dahlia wished aloud for a map, the duke unhesitatingly waved down a servant and asked for pen and parchment with an imperious tone that made Dahlia blush. The servants didn't hesitate, and three others nearby at the table joined the conversation once they noticed the duke's drawing.

I'm not sure this counts as fulfilling my hostess duties by maintaining pleasant conversation, she thought idly, as the duke appealed to Jade for a word he needed to describe the type of ship best suited for the trip. *But at least it's not eider ducks.*

"Why not go through here?" she asked, pointing to a portion of the map that seemed empty.

The duke shook his head, and waved his wineglass as he struggled to find a word. "The water is fast and shallow there," he said. "Prone to storms and . . . what call them?"

"Riptides," Jade supplied. "They're what the Rushing Sea is named for. The Jeskayque have detailed charts and ships designed to navigate them, but they struggle with the open, deep-ocean voyage from their country to Kavet. That's why our three nations are working together to come up with an agreement." He pronounced the tongue-twisting name for the Forgotten Islands with long familiarity. Dahlia resolved to master it herself by the end of the evening.

By the end of the dancing, she amended, as Terra Sarcelle stood and rang a small bell, drawing attention to herself so she could announce it was time to move to the next hall. Dahlia had been so engrossed in the conversation she hadn't even noticed when the final course was cleared away.

Remembering Maimeri's warnings, which seemed so long past now, Dahlia found herself considering the possibility of a job at the docks in a new light. If the apprenticeship at the stationer didn't work out, she might see if there were any employment opportunities there, where she could further feed this hunger for knowledge about the world beyond Kavet's isolated shores.

CHAPTER 16

HENNA

Henna had called herself a coward several times since she decided she would rather stay in and watch Clay than risk even glimpsing the Osei in the street, but now she felt like she had avoided a skirmish by volunteering for a war.

Why won't he stop screaming?

She had gone through every lullaby and sea shanty in her repertoire, first expecting and then *praying* that Clay would drop off to sleep any moment. She had taken him to the temple and made foxfire dance, let him play on the silver altar that was his favorite, given him frozen teething biscuits, offered food, water and milk, and tried to distract him with stuffed toys and coloring sticks. Sometimes the crying faded to whining for a short while, but nothing made him happy, and now it was hours past his bedtime.

She had often taken care of Clay when Maddy was out, so she hadn't expected trouble when she encouraged Maddy to go out to celebrate. Clay had never been a finicky child before, and he had liked Henna fine in the past. His mood had been cheerful for most of the day, but at some point around dinner his mood had shifted like the wind changing from a spring breeze to a summer tempest.

"Clay, honey, what do you *want?*" she implored, for perhaps the hundredth time that hour.

"Abibi!" Clay whined. "Mumum!"

Clay had already thrown several banana biscuits across the room, along with everything else she had tried to distract him with. "Your mumum isn't here right now. She'll be back later."

Clay returned to his wordless wailing. Henna began to ponder the old Tamari trick of putting whiskey on his gums—and then drinking the rest of the shot herself.

Instead, she stood up and bounced the child in her exhausted arms. "Honey, please. Tell Henna what's wrong."

What was *wrong* was that, soon enough, she was going to have to give up and go out to look for Maddy.

Clay's crying was straining Henna's nerves and breaking her heart, and she was so tired every muscle in her body tingled.

"I've fed you. I've changed you. I've done everything I can *think* to make you happy . . ." She sighed. "Okay. Maybe you want fresh air. Do you want to go outside? Watch the merchants do their magic? Maybe find Maddy?"

"Mumum!"

"Yes, we'll look for Mumum."

Leaving the sanctuary of the Cobalt Hall for Kavet's marketplace was about the last thing Henna wanted to do. Even though she knew the Osei would be inside, playing nice with the Terre at the ball and not mingling with commoners in the square, her heart pounded at the thought of crossing the threshold.

She had to put Clay down as she pulled on an outdoor dress and street shoes. He would normally have run off, his insatiable curiosity a menace to anyone who looked away for even an instant, but this time he merely sat and wailed.

Maybe he was sick? Some of the initiates in the Napthol order were healers, but they were all out enjoying Festival, like Maddy. Like Terre Verte and the Quin girl.

Like the Osei.

"Naba bibi gimme gaaaah!"

She picked Clay up again and wiped tears from his face before wrapping him in a blanket to keep him warm against the early spring chill.

"We're going to find Mumum," Henna promised him. "We'll have fun outside." *Please.*

She pushed open the front door of the Hall, bracing herself. Clay's hand caught a dangling strand of her hair in a viselike grip, and since it distracted him momentarily from his misery, she let him keep it despite her discomfort.

The first step she took onto the square's cobbled stones rocked her in the way that particularly powerful visions sometimes did.

She took another step forward, and had to close her eyes. Wrapping one arm protectively around Clay, Henna knelt and touched her fingertips to the cobbles, trying to read them like she would her rune stones.

Images washed over her from all the lives and destinies of those standing and sitting on the cobbled plaza. These cobbles were old, and had seen a lot of strife. Kavet had first been settled as a stronghold for pirates and escaped criminals. The Order of Napthol had been the first hint of civilization, and then finally the Terre had taken control.

And then the Quinacridone had come. And next—

"*Dear Numen,*" she whispered.

So much fear. And blood and ice and fire. And the brand searing its sigils into skin. Mice in the kitchen, but they weren't really mice. Ink on paper that was really steel in flesh—

"Henna!" Someone pulled her to her feet, but for a

few moments, she couldn't see anything around her. "Henna, are you all right?"

She couldn't answer right away. She needed to see—

"Mumum!"

"Clay . . . c'mere, honey. Henna, Henna, talk to me."

Against her will, she focused on Maddy's worried face. The older woman had Clay in her arms, but all her concern was directed at Henna.

"I'm okay," she managed to say. "I—" She squeezed her eyes shut. Why did these visions torment her if they wouldn't let her see enough to *use* them?

"Abibi," Clay said, softly now. "Abibi. Cay gimme. Go nini bibi."

"He's been crying all night," Henna said as Maddy turned her attention to her son. "I couldn't get him to calm down. I came outside to find you."

And then that vision. It had to do with . . . What? She thought there was something about the Quin in there. Maybe Dahlia, too. Was this why she was so important?

"Where are the Quin?" Henna asked, as she realized Celadon and his group weren't in the market.

"You didn't hear?" Maddy asked. "There was a scuffle earlier. Verte had the whole lot of them arrested."

Henna breathed a sigh of relief. She would talk to Verte tomorrow and tell him what she had seen. Maybe she would be able to make more sense of the visions by then.

Maddy, meanwhile, had already turned her attention to her son. "Honey, are you not feeling well? Henna, did he eat?"

"I couldn't get him to. He just kept crying."

"Maybe another tooth coming in," Maddy theorized. She started inside, and Henna followed. "I'll see if I can get him to nurse. Once he's hungry, there's no way to know if he's just grumpy because his tummy's grumbly."

"I'm sorry to pull you away from Festival . . ."

"No, no trouble," Maddy said. "He's my son."

Clay was still sniffling, and occasionally saying something in a tragic, serious tone, but being in his mother's arms seemed to help. By the time they reached the kitchen, he was calm enough that Maddy was able to sit with him and latch him on to nurse while Henna heated water for tea.

"Did you see the Osei?" Henna asked hesitatingly.

Without looking up, Maddy answered, "I saw them, briefly. They didn't spend much time out in the market. Knowing the little I do about them from you, it was all I could do not to spit at them, and I'm sure I'm not the only person in that market who had that idea."

"Do you really think the Terre will be able to make a deal with them?"

"A deal, or maybe something more. There's magic thick all around the palace, more so than usual." She frowned. "One of the soldiers told me to keep my distance, and that it would be bad if the Osei saw Jaune's other woman—oh, he didn't use those words of course. It was kind of cute, watching him try to find a politic way to put it."

Until the Osei were gone from the city, Henna had promised not to discuss the Terre's true plans for them, so she responded to the other part of Maddy's statement.

"The Osei would find your existence as intolerable as the Terra does."

"I know better than to draw attention to myself," Maddy said. "I wanted to examine the workings of the spell. If it's intended for the Osei, it probably needs to be as strong as it is, but I'm not the only magic user in the market who found it unsettling. While I was snooping about, I heard a rumor about a bird that appeared and caused chaos during the reception. I heard one of the servants say it looked like something from another realm."

The comment made Henna think of the royal gardens, with their charming otherworldly flora, whose existence meant there was a space between the realms somewhere big enough for their tendrils. Could the Terre spell to capture the Osei have further opened that rift? If so, what might be the consequences?

"Did the servant have any magical background?" she asked. "Or did you ask Naples?" If a sorcerer of the Napthol Order had said something looked like it came from another realm, Henna would have believed it without question, but most of the regular palace staff knew nothing of magic.

"No and no." Her frown was more fierce than her tone, which was soft in deference to the child that was finally starting to doze. Maddy gently unlatched Clay from her breast, then rocked him until his whimpering protests silenced and he settled in to full sleep at last. Once he was quiet, she added, "Naples warned me he might be working all night, and had been offered a place to sleep at the palace. I suspect he's involved in the spell and needs to stay near."

Henna wanted to continue the conversation, but couldn't fight the yawn that stole her breath at that moment. Maddy tsk'd. "Go to bed, honey," she said. "I'll put Clay down. You meditate, clear your head of whatever visions are putting that haunted look in your eyes, and then try to get some sleep."

Maddy never pried, and unlike Helio, she could manage a conversation without making it obvious she was reading someone's soul, but she always saw when Henna's power was disturbing her.

Henna tried to follow her advice, but no matter what she did, she couldn't keep the dreams away.

Storm clouds boiling in the sky. Waves cresting high, crashing on the planks.

Shadow of wings.

Splash of blood.

It was barely past dawn when Henna fought her

way free of nightmares and staggered downstairs. She dressed in a hurry and half stumbled to the market, less concerned now about the possibility of seeing Osei than she was about the possibility of not seeing what she needed to see. She needed to do . . . Something. *What?*

"What, damn you?" she asked her fickle power.

Few merchants were out this early, except for those who were in the middle of packing up after being awake throughout the long overnight festivities. Henna found one who would sell her a spiced apple tart, then paced the cobblestones, daring them to tell her their secrets. It was too early to tell fortunes, but she sat next to the fountain with her rune stones anyway, drawing curious glances as she trailed her fingers through them.

No use.

When Dahlia Indathrone stepped out through one of the palace's side doors and set her foot on the market's cobbles, it was like a cool breath down Henna's spine. The girl looked exhausted, as she should be; she couldn't have managed more than two or three hours' sleep between when the revelries at the palace ended and now. Nevertheless, she crossed the market with determined strides.

"Good morning!" she said when she spotted Henna. "This is early for you to be out, isn't it?"

"I could say the same of you," Henna replied.

The girl shrugged, and gave a sleepy smile. "I have an appointment about a possible job with the stationer."

"Good luck," Henna bid her, sincerely.

The girl continued on her way.

The next familiar face Henna saw was Naples'. He didn't seem to notice her. His steps were light and airy with good spirits; she suspected he hadn't slept at all. How could he? He was shimmering with power, glutted with it. He would never be able to lie down to sleep until he found a way to dissipate it.

Shadow of wings.

Several minutes after Naples left, she finally found the vision again—or thought she did. When she chased it, she realized it wasn't a vision at all. This time, it was real. She lifted her gaze with dread and saw an image from her nightmares: five Osei flying in formation. The one in the center had wide wings with shimmering white undersides—a queen. The other four must be her princes.

Maybe they are just flying over, Henna thought desperately.

The pride of Osei abruptly turned and dove. Serpentine bodies large enough to lift ships from the sea plummeted. They changed shape so close to the ground that the wind from their wings smacked the plaza like a hand, rattling or knocking over the light carts and tables the early morning merchants set up to display their wares. Henna squinted her eyes against the grit that smacked her face as the Osei landed with enough force to shatter their bodies had they been human.

People in the plaza scattered, scrambling away

to hide in the shelter of surrounding buildings, but Henna couldn't make her muscles move as the Osei queen looked around speculatively.

The creature had skin like liquid silver and eyes like barbed steel. As she crossed the plaza directly toward Henna's frozen form, Henna recognized her. She was the only Osei queen who ever left her own territory to visit another Osei House.

The Queen of the First House, the Royal House of the Osei, was standing in the Kavet marketplace.

Henna felt all the blood drain from her face. Maybe farther. Was she bleeding onto the cobbles? Into the core of the earth?

"You know us," the queen said. "That is convenient." Her voice reminded Henna of the bellflowers in the Terre's garden: beautiful, cold, and nowhere near human. Only, unlike the bellflowers, it was not soothing. Henna knew this creature well enough to recognize its moods, even though its features and tone did not shift the same way as a human's. The emotion she was seeing now was pure fury. "You will inform the rulers of this land that we require their immediate presence."

Henna struggled to talk, or to run, or do *anything*. She doubted her finding the Terre and Terra to deliver the Osei's message was necessary. Someone from the palace would have seen the wings in the sky. They were probably already on their way to demand an explanation.

The queen tossed her head and stated, "We have *no* treaties with human nations." She had read Henna's mind, and replied unapologetically to her thoughts. "As far as I'm concerned, your kind lost that privilege the moment a Silmari ballista shot down a prince of the Tenth Royal House."

"They . . . did . . . *what*?"

"Fetch your queen for me," the Osei queen demanded. "First I will confirm that the leaders of this nation were not involved in this treachery. Then we will decide what reparations must be made."

CHAPTER 17

VERTE

Despite the long night and his resulting fatigue, Verte woke early. It was unnerving to have the Osei of the Third House sleeping as guests in the palace; strange, quasi-magical dreams seeped from their minds to disturb his rest.

Waking early was for the best. He wanted to further research the strange bird that had appeared and disappeared so suddenly before dinner. To quell any anxious talk, he and his mother had allowed a few of the servants to overhear an "idle" conversation they had had about the exotic pet one of the Tamari nobles had brought as a gift. But as a sorcerer, one glimpse at the creature had been enough for Verte to know it wasn't from this world. It resonated with the same cold power that Verte and his father wielded, and the bird's glistening, crystalline form had reminded him of the way scholars spoke of the Numen, the realm in which souls were created and in which the blessed were received after death.

What if they could actually *prove* that cold magic came from the divine realm? What would that mean for the study and practice of sorcery?

On the other hand, cold magic wasn't the only power active last night. If a beautiful bird from the Numen could break through to the mortal realm, what more dangerous creatures might appear from the Abyss?

Dahlia would point out that is exactly what the Quin are afraid of.

The Quin were the other reason he was up early, and the only reason he had chosen studying the bird for his *second* task. Verte knew better than to let them wait for him too long; it would only feed their resentment. He took a handful of guards with him to help ensure the Quin went home peacefully, including Tealyn, who was irritated that she hadn't been allowed to stand guard during the ball and wouldn't be allowed to accompany him later when they took the Osei on a tour of the city.

Kavet in general, and Mars in particular, was not famous for its jails. Crime in the city was relatively low, with the majority of the cells' visitors being short-term occupants there as much for their own protections as for others'. Drunk and disorderly conduct—caused by alcohol or magic—was the most common reason for a person to see the inside of such a cell, and the stays usually ended with nothing more serious than fines to cover any damage caused. The lower-city and docks spawned more troublesome behavior, of course, but the Order of A'hknet controlled most of that area and rarely required—or accepted—support from official law enforcement to keep their own members in line, and sailors' transgressions were dealt with by a separate system involving the captains currently in port.

Celadon's group fit right in at the city lockup, both in terms of their attitudes and the sheen of power still left on them from whatever enchantment someone had used to goad them the day before. When Verte spoke to them, they were cool, not outright apologetic, but shocked at their own actions.

Though it had been mentioned in their presence the day before, no one asked to be checked for manipulative magic. Had they requested an investigation, Verte would have pursued one honestly, but Followers of the Quinacridone were not swift to ask a Terre for justice, especially if it would have required his magically searching them to try to identify the exact enchantment used.

The group's members were individually released and escorted home by guards, who had been instructed to ensure that each made it to his or her destination without further interference.

Finally, only Celadon was left.

Without his followers to back him, Celadon should have looked harmless. He was soft-featured, and though not small, he had the build of a merchant, not a sailor or a soldier. Still, Verte found the other man strangely unsettling. Raised in power and magic, any Terre knew not to lightly disregard his instincts, but unfortunately, he had no legal reason to hold Celadon.

Yet.

He had a strong suspicion that sooner or later—probably sooner—he would have to deal with Celadon Cremnitz again.

The preacher looked like he hadn't slept all night, which wasn't surprising given the hard, narrow mattress in his cell, and the buzz of magic still whipping around him.

In fact . . .

A slight shift in perception, and Verte realized what he was seeing—something he hadn't been able to distinguish in the magic-saturated market, and had never observed in his previous interactions with the preacher. He drew in a sharp breath as the realization sank in.

Celadon had power. Natural, high-magic sorcery. There had been no drug or prank; *Celadon* had raised energy, probably without realizing it, and pushed it at his followers.

How was it possible that Verte had missed any signs of magic before this? It wasn't unheard-of for a sorcerer's power to suddenly emerge well into adulthood, but Verte had never heard of anyone suddenly going from no magic at all to this level of strength. The only possible explanation he could think of was that Celadon's hatred of sorcery might have caused him to instinctively suppress his own power until now, when it had become too strong for him to control without training.

"Do you realize you're putting off power?" Verte asked, taking a seat outside Celadon's cell. While he generally preferred to avoid provoking the Quin, as Terre he had a responsibility to deal with problems like this.

Celadon stood, back rigid. "Excuse me?"

"You're putting off waves of magic," Verte said. The anger—and touch of fear—in Celadon's eyes confirmed that he still didn't understand. "It explains why your followers were willing to start a fight with professional soldiers *for you*. In fact, it explains why people find you so charismatic in the first place. You've been enchanting them."

While this might have been the first time Celadon's power manifested, sorcery would do much to explain the man's meteoric rise to popularity.

"My followers find me *charismatic*," Celadon said, "because I speak the truth, something that resonates with right-hearted—"

"You're a walking persuasion charm, Celadon."

"If I *have* been tainted," the preacher said, "then it is only because of your family's meddling with the other planes."

"Regardless the cause," Verte said between clenched teeth, "you *have* power. You can choose to study it, or you can choose to get rid of it, but you cannot choose to ignore it."

Celadon stepped up to the bars, fury in every line of his body. "*Study* it?" he hissed. "Let some Napthol witch put her spells on me, twist me? What kind of fool do you take me for? As for the other option you offer, I'll be damned before I let you brand me like some criminal."

He couldn't help thinking of Wenge, who had refused every offer to help him control his power until it had left him magically addicted, burned-out, and desperate. He was now recovering from the brand. Had he shared this same fear, that the Napthol sorcerers would somehow change and pervert him if he allowed them to help?

Celadon didn't have Wenge's freedom. His form of power was far more dangerous.

"You have to control it somehow," Verte snapped. "Do you understand that? As it is, whenever your power manifests, it will push others toward your will. If you sign terms with someone in that condition, you are guilty of magical manipulation of a contract. If you lie with a woman, you are guilty of rape. If one of your followers gives you so much as a copper coin, you can be charged with theft. Even if it is not intentional, if you are aware you are creating this enchantment—as you now *are* aware—and you do nothing to stop it, you will end up on trial for magical malevolence. Then you won't just be branded *like* a criminal, you'll *be* one.

"Please. Celadon," he sighed, running out of the energy he needed to fight this battle, which he already knew was probably hopeless. "Let someone teach you to shut it down. A few days of study is all it would take."

Eerily, Celadon started to smile.

"I will not join the Napthol's cult," the Quin pronounced, "and I will not be branded, and I will not accept responsibility for an affliction that you and your kind have set upon this city. Arrest me if you will. My followers will see my trial, and they will recognize it as further evidence that all I have warned them of is true."

That was one of the many things Verte feared.

"You don't think your followers might be a bit angry to learn they have been magically manipulated by a man claiming to hate all magic?" Verte asked as he unlocked the cell door.

If it were considered maleficence for a person to accidentally use magic he didn't know he had, half the members of the Order of Napthol would have been locked up before their fifteenth birthdays. Now that Celadon had been informed of his power's potential, any illegal use of it would be considered a crime, but Verte couldn't arrest him on the suspicion that he *might* break the law.

Celadon stepped out gracefully, careful to keep his distance from Verte and Tealyn. The guard was doing an impressive job of keeping her expression impassive despite the revelation of Celadon's power. If she felt shocked, horrified, or even amused at the irony, it didn't show. Verte made a mental note to acknowledge the discretion later.

"The Quinacridone's followers trust me. Nothing the Terre could do would turn them against me."

Verte tried to think of an excuse to hold the preacher, because he *knew* letting him go would be a disaster, but the laws were clear. Celadon was innocent—so far. Arresting him would be illegal, and sure to cause a riot when all the Quin in the city protested the unfair incarceration. On the other hand, given how unlikely the other Quin were to notice or even report sorcery, how out of hand could he get before an official report ever reached Verte?

Could he set someone among the Quin covertly to watch Celadon? Maybe one of the guards, equipped with a charm to ward them against cold magic persuasion, could feign allegiance with the sect?

Another task for this morning, as early as possible.

"You're free to go," he said grimly. "I *highly recommend* that you speak to someone at the Order of Napthol about learning to control your power before it gets you in further trouble. Or, if all you want is to get rid of your power, come to the palace and we'll do that. If you come of your own free will, the procedure will be as confidential as you like."

Celadon snickered. "Never in your life, Terre, will I come to you for help."

He stalked out of the jail. Verte gave up on any further attempt to reason with the damn Quin that day. He wouldn't listen.

Celadon would end up back in this jail soon, Verte suspected. *How* soon would depend on how clever and careful—and anxious to be a martyr—he was, and whether Verte could successfully plant someone in the Quin group without raising suspicion.

Verte followed Celadon through the doorway just in time to see the preacher intercept Naples. The sorcerer was sleepy-eyed, but an aura of power surrounded him like a bonfire's heat. What *had* he been doing since he was released from his duties at the ball? Or, perhaps, *whom*? Verte recognized the languid undercurrent of the magic, because it was similar to the one Henna's took on after they made love, as if her power was as stimulated and satiated as her body.

Naples and Celadon come to a stop inches from each other.

"Sir?" Tealyn asked softly. "Should we step in?"

"Be ready," Verte agreed.

"Have a good night?" Naples inquired with faux sweetness.

"Out of the way," Celadon barked. His power rose to his will and shoved at the wiry young sorcerer.

Naples was no null Quin. His eyes widened and he braced himself as if against a blow, his power rising in a wall around him. In a sleight-of-hand Verte couldn't quite follow, the sorcerer drew a small dagger.

Verte had only managed a single step forward before Naples, instead of turning the blade on the Quin, slid it across his own palm, drawing a fine line of blood. Verte put a hand up to halt Tealyn; he would give this another moment to play out.

"I want to apologize for yesterday," Naples said, with a subtle thread of power that flared when Celadon begrudgingly accepted the offered handshake. When the sorcerer's blood touched Celadon's skin, Celadon's eyes unfocused. He swayed a little and the tension went out of his body. "Come back to the Hall with me," Naples urged. "We should chat."

Verte knew his mother was sometimes able to replace the hours of preparation and ritual most sorcerers required for major magic with a few drops of spilled blood. He had tried unsuccessfully to learn the technique, and was surprised to see it wielded so effortlessly now, especially since he had thought the Order of Napthol disapproved of blood-magic.

Celadon jerked back, aware that something had happened, but too ignorant to recognize exactly what. "Not likely," he snapped, before shouldering the sorcerer aside.

Naples let out an incredulous snort, and watched the preacher storm off. As Verte closed the distance between them, Tealyn only two paces behind, Naples sheathed his knife, saying, "He'll come. He just needs time to decide it was his own idea."

Verte suspected it was true. Naples was ringing with power right now. His magical suggestion would echo through the Quin's head until he couldn't resist it anymore.

"That was illegal," Verte pointed out.

"Think the Quins will press charges?" Naples shrugged. "It doesn't seem like a good idea to let him walk around like that, and he'll never agree to get help willingly."

Verte pondered the words, and the situation. He settled on saying, "Don't push him into anything more than necessary. We will all be safer if he can control his magic, but if he pledges himself to the Order of Napthol overnight, I'll have to intercede."

"I'll try not to put you in a position where you have to protect the Quin," Naples said, his tone faintly teasing. "Now if you'll pardon me, Terre, I should get back to the Hall before my date arrives."

They parted ways. Verte hoped Naples would be able to do something to minimize the threat of the Quin preacher. In the meantime, Verte would still seek a volunteer among the guards who would be willing to try to infiltrate the group, and check in with Wenge, and search for a tear in the veil between this world and the divine, and—

A servant ran up to him, gasping, "Osei. Your parents are with them, but—" He broke off, struggling to catch his breath. "First Royal house," he managed to say. "In the market. Terra said to find you. Said to tell you they need to . . . expand the net?"

The last few words had a questioning lilt to them. He was repeating a phrase he had been told, but wasn't sure what it meant.

The First Royal queen was here. Now. *Why?* It was too early. She wasn't supposed to arrive until after Kavet had completed its negotiations with the Third Noble House.

It didn't matter.

No, it *mattered*, but what mattered more was that they needed to step up their plans. They had always intended to try to snare the First Royal Queen in the enchantment. It would be harder because they hadn't fully subdued the Third Noble House yet, but they could do it.

They *had* to.

When Verte reached the market, he slowed his steps to a sedate pace so that he could compose himself before entering the Osei's presence. From across the square he saw not just the First Royal Queen, but the entirety of the First and Third courts standing in front of his parents.

As he crossed the cobbles, he picked up the strands of the magical net, taking up some of the slack his parents hadn't been able to manage. The power felt rough and trembled as he seized it; he needed more sleep, food and ritual time to recharge before he could manage it with any finesse.

Thankfully, he wasn't working alone.

All around the market, members of the Order of Napthol had come out. They pretended to be busy with other tasks—helping to right booths and pick up wares that had been toppled as if from an earthquake, shopping, chatting or even reading—but their lips moved with murmured spells and their auras flared with power. They could feel the spell and were doing what they could to support it.

"Verte," Terra Sarcelle sighed in relief. She patted his shoulder; it probably looked maternal, but he knew she was linking their power so he could better support the work she was already doing to control the Osei queens. "May I present to you Queen Negasi of the First Royal House of the Osei. Queen Negasi, this is my son, Verte."

Out of the corner of his eye, Verte saw Celadon and Naples enter the market. Celadon's power buzzed along the net, threatening to break its trembling threads. Naples immediately caught the preacher's arm and urged him toward the Cobalt Hall; the sorcerer hadn't been in the market long enough to know what was going on, but he knew how delicate the spell was, and how disastrous it would be if Celadon chose this moment to be a bastard.

Verte bowed slightly to the Osei queen, in acknowledgement that she outranked him. "We are honored by your presence," he said.

The high queen of the Osei inclined her head slightly. Unlike Nimma, who seemed to have attempted somewhat to match her host's coloration, Negasi looked like something molten, her skin all shades of ruby and gold with a flowing, shifting quality to it that strained Verte's eyes when he tried to focus on her. Her hair, which was short and lifted like a bird's crest, was tropical blue and turquoise. Only her eyes, which were pure, gemstone green, seemed fixed.

Pick up the strands of the net, Verte told himself, trying to keep the thoughts to the back of his mind while focusing on inane details with the front. *Weave them tight and don't let go.*

CHAPTER 18

HENNA

We can do this, Henna thought. Prayed.

She had backed away as soon as the high queen's attention was off her, and now joined a dozen other members of the Order of Napthol as they tried to lend power. Most of them probably couldn't read the spell well enough to understand its purpose, but even the weakest among them could tell all three members of the royal family were struggling to pour their magic into *something.* They helped in any way they could.

Henna was too far away to hear what words were exchanged by the two opposing royal parties, but she didn't need to. The words were irrelevant—as were her own fears of what would happen if they failed. She knew what these creatures could do to those who crossed them.

I am not helpless anymore, and I am not alone. I am one of the most powerful sorcerers in the Order of Napthol and I have all my fellows with me.

The net of power the Terres and Terra had cast was truly a thing of beauty. It wasn't designed to be used this way—having so many practitioners clumsily throwing magic at it—but there was no other choice. It was clear the royal family didn't have the strength to wrap so many Osei so quickly, not when the high queen had landed in this place already seething with murderous intent.

But it was working.

Sweat burst from Henna's brow as she struggled with her end of the spell. She tried to visualize it as one of the nets hauled by the stinking fishing ships during the tuna migrations, a massive thing capable of wrapping and catching any wriggling prey that came its way, but ended up with an image more like a spider's web, slowly spinning into place. Until it was fully formed, it was fragile; its edges tore whenever anyone pulled too hard, and it would shred completely if the Osei noticed it and fought back.

She recognized me. What if—

No, now is not the time. Do this first, and nothing else will matter.

Do this first, or nothing else will matter.

Terre Verte put a hand on the high queen's arm,

leaning toward her as if he were one of her princes seeking her attention. Henna could see the way that contact strengthened his magical hold on her. The Osei looked at him fondly and ran a hand down his hair; he closed his eyes and allowed the touch, clearly more concerned with the spell than his dignity.

Henna had to look away, lest her revulsion carry mentally to the Osei.

By the time she had composed herself and turned back to the group, it looked like the danger was passing. The Osei of the Third Noble House nodded, then took their leave of their high queen and walked still in human form toward the docks, where they could change shape and take to the air without doing additional damage to the market. High Queen Negasi still had her hand on Terre Verte's shoulder, but the touch appeared idle. She was nodding calmly to Terra Sarcelle, and smiling.

The hot strands of the spell had settled on each Osei, and were beginning to melt around them like candle wax—soft now, but soon they would become hard and encasing.

A relieved sigh at Henna's elbow made her blink tired eyes and glance toward Helio. He slumped against the wall beside her, holding a silver disc, a focus tool he used for more complex magic. Unlike Henna's skin, where sweat had gathered, Helio's was clammy-pale, and there was frost rimming his fingernails and dusting his eyelashes.

Too much power, Henna thought, remembering the possibly otherworldly creature Maddy had heard about. *We're risking so much. Too much?*

Never too much. No, not when she knew so vividly what it meant to be claimed by the Osei.

"It looks like the danger is past," Helio breathed. "They can handle the rest."

He tried to stand, and his knees buckled. Henna caught him, and they both ended up back against the wall, too weak to support themselves.

They weren't the only sorcerers struggling to return to the mundane world. On the front steps of the Hall, Maddy squeezed her eyes shut and took deep breaths to ground herself before she tried to stand. In her arms, Clay stared in fascination at the magic suffusing the market. Other, less powerful initiates and novices gathered themselves however they could. A young novice pushed herself to her feet next to a stall selling fragrant oils, exotic herbs and spices, and hot foods warmed on a brazier.

Too fast; the girl's face grayed and she swayed in a faint. The light, wooden stand had been knocked off-balance by Osei wings, and now as the novice stumbled into it, one of the shelves collapsed.

Crash.

Glass shattered. Oil splattered into the brazier and flared into orange and yellow flame that leapt to the wooden shelves and the clothes of the dizzy novice, who shrieked as fire touched her. Others leapt forward to smother the flames and help the merchant recover his wares. Henna reached out toward the fire, intending to smother it with a blanket of power.

They weren't the only ones startled by the clamor—and distracted, too distracted, at too delicate a moment.

A shriek of rage, unlike anything that had ever come from a human throat, hit her like a slicing knife. She spun to face the royals just in time to see the First Royal queen recoil, ripping out of the still-coalescing spell.

"Witchcraft," she snarled. "I can scent it now. *How dare you?*"

Terre Verte reached toward her. Whether he planned to call his magic or beg for lenience, Henna would never know. The enchantment broken, the Osei high queen leapt into the air, returning to her natural form. The wind from the first drive of her immense wings slapped Henna to the ground. She heard the crash of more market booths toppling. Helio kept his feet, but only barely.

"She's leaving!" he gasped as he offered Henna a hand to help her up.

"I don't . . . no," Henna whispered in horror as her eyes made out the Osei queen, who was still ascending rapidly. Helio must not have seen what she held.

Queen Negasi had Terre Verte gripped in her claws.

No.

Henna had seen an Osei lift a shark, tuna or marlin into the air—then dash it against the rocks to kill them before eating. Compared to one of those thousand-pound fish, Terre Verte was small and so very frail.

"*Fight*," she whispered desperately to Verte. The Osei queen's body shuddered under the assault of his desperate magic. Her mates circled near her, voicing their concern in high, birdlike cries, but unable to fight an enemy gripped within their queen's talons.

Down on the ground, Henna heard the palace guards shouting questions and orders to each other, but what could they do? Kavetan soldiers' swords were made of steel, but what use was a sword against a predator of the air?

Queen Negasi was two hundred paces above the market before the Terra overcame her shock enough to react. With a cry she snatched up a shard of broken glass from the ground and used it to slice a long wound down her own arm.

Black power like tar flowed from the wound. The Terra flung her arm out, scattering drops of blood across the cobbles.

A creature answered the Terra's call. It flowed like smoke and fire from the pool of scarlet blood and coal-dark magic, insubstantial as mist but vicious as a whip.

"Dear Numen," Henna whispered.

"No," Helio choked out. "Not there."

Henna's eyes couldn't follow the movement of the beast as it shot into the sky, but she knew when it struck the Osei queen because she screamed, her flight faltering. Savage rents appeared, a startling crimson, in previously flawless snow-white wings.

"*Bring back my son, you thrice-damned bitch!*" the Terra shrieked.

Another cut, another splash of blood. The beast's power glowed more brightly, an indigo sun, and the Osei queen fell. Close to hitting the ground, she tossed Verte away. He fell to the cobbles, dazed but breathing. The Osei queen hit the ground gracelessly; one shoulder and outstretched wing struck the front of the palace, knocking loose a chunk of marble. She snapped at the ethereal monster the Terra had summoned.

Henna ran forward, intending to pull Verte away from the battling beasts, but a lash from the Osei queen's tail sent her sprawling backward. She smacked the cobbles hard this time, winded. Spots danced in front of her eyes.

The Osei queen opened her wide mouth to reveal multiple rows of glistening teeth, like a shark's, and hissed her fury. As if realizing the true source of her torment was not the beast but the sorceress who had summoned it, the Osei swiped at the Terra. She would have caught her if a dozen guards hadn't leapt forward, forming a wall at the same time that Jaune grabbed his wife and dragged her to the side, sending them both to the stone ground with a painful impact.

The instant the Terra was distracted, the creature she had summoned snuffed out, unable to maintain its hold on the mortal realm.

The Osei queen didn't go after them. Instead, she deliberately turned toward Terre Verte's semi-conscious form. Guards closed ranks around him, too, and Henna saw Negasi hiss as she surveyed the steel raised against her on two sides.

The princes defended their queen, diving talons-first at the plaza as if intending to catch prey. Two of them managed to snatch guards up, only to then throw them at their fellows; the others recoiled with cries of pain as swords bit at their legs and even in one case succeeded in clipping a wing on the downbeat. The prince tumbled awkwardly into the plaza, and Negasi let out another furious cry.

Downing the Osei was a bittersweet victory, as the guards were forced to flee or be crushed by his massive form. Backing away to regroup, they left space so when the downed prince rolled and shifted to human form, another prince was able to snatch him up and lift him away from the battle.

The chaos left an opening, and Negasi took it.

Once again, she snatched Terre Verte into her talons and pushed into the air.

She didn't give anyone time to fight her this time. From the height of the palace's tallest tower, she released her prey.

Henna's was not the only scream that pierced the

air as Verte fell, seemed to fall so long, though surely it was only seconds, heartbeats . . .

Then his body hit the cobbles with a wet, meaty sound she knew she would hear in her nightmares for the rest of her life.

Her hands were bleeding from hitting the cobbles, and breathing had become pain; at least one rib had been broken when the Osei queen struck her. But none of that mattered now.

As the shadow of wings left, marking the Osei queen's departure, Henna crawled to Verte's side.

She was the first one there, and her immediate thought was, *It isn't him.* The figure on the ground was in no way recognizable as the beautiful man she had known. It was a remnant, a broken thing, some child's gruesome toy that had been tossed away— not the noble and powerful prince of Kavet. Not her Terre, her lover.

Others pushed her aside. Most were healers from the Order of Napthol. Verte's father leaned heavily on a merchant as he limped to his son's side, shoving or commanding others back.

Henna withdrew so others with more useful power could get to Verte. She had no skill in healing, herself. And she didn't want to see.

She went to the Terra.

Magic rose off the queen of Kavet in wavering layers of heat and her skin was scalding to the touch when Henna reached out to search for a pulse.

"Terra?"

Her searching fingers found a rapid but steady pulse just before the Terra's eyes fluttered open. One pupil was small as a pinprick, as if she stared into the sun, but the other was wide, an onyx circle in a bloodshot eye.

"Ver—" The Terra didn't get through saying her son's name before deep, racking coughs seized her. She groped around her until Henna offered her hands, and helped her turn over. On her hands and knees, the Terra continued to hack. Drops of dark bile flew from her lips.

"I'll get a healer," Henna said.

"No." Terra Sarcelle grabbed Henna's wrist in a bruisingly tight grip. "Anyone with that power should be with my son. I—" More coughing, but this bout was shorter, and brought up clean red blood. Was that an improvement? The Terra wiped her lips with the back of her hand. "I'll be fine."

Henna wanted to ask her what she had done, what she had summoned into this world, but this wasn't the time—and besides, she already knew. She just didn't know how it was possible. She would have said that raising so much power so fast would kill a person, burn their blood and boil their organs.

Maybe it did, Henna thought, as the Terra waved away healers that came to her. She accepted assistance only from a pair of servants who came to help their mistress stand. She went to her son, but the group there waved her back with no regard for her station, focused only on minimizing distractions as they worked on Verte.

As Henna watched, one of the Order's younger healers broke off from the group around Verte. He went to the queen first, then after being sent away with an impatient wave came to Henna's side.

"I don't have the strength to help the Terre, but I know how to clean wounds and wrap bandages," he said, "and I know a little bone-mending."

"Thank you, but I'll be fine." It hurt to talk, but if anyone touched her in that moment, even to heal, she knew she would shatter like glass. She could not afford weakness in that moment, not when others might need her.

The novice looked skeptical, but he moved on, seeking others who would accept his aid.

These weren't Henna's first broken ribs. She would ask Maddy to help her wrap them later. Her other wounds—small cuts and burns—weren't severe enough for her to even feel them past her numb shock.

Instead, she surveyed the wreckage of the market.

The Osei were gone. Henna wasn't the only one who had been hurt falling, or by breaking and flying glass. At least half a dozen guards were down, being tended by their fellows and the weaker Napthol healers. Either the winds of the Osei wings or the Terra's magic had shattered nearby windows, along with many fine glass containers. Henna should probably join the other non-healers who were hurrying about, making sure none of the enchantments spilled from broken jars were dangerous.

She couldn't make her legs move.

The group around Terre Verte began to thin. Only the most powerful healers—Terre Jaune, Maddy, Helio and Dove—stayed. The Terra watched with a blank expression.

Savagely, Henna hoped that whatever creature the Terra had summoned chased the Osei queen across the seas and devoured her and all her line.

In the next moment, she regretted the thought, because what the Terra had called to her son's defense was a beast never meant to walk this world.

Maddy and Helio stepped aside now, allowing Henna a glimpse of Terre Verte, of his body. Most of the blood was gone, and his wounds had closed, but he was so still.

The sound of a crying child made Henna turn with a wince. Clay was waiting in the arms of one of the palace servants, but the moment he saw his mother look up he reached for her. Maddy stepped toward her, then swayed heavily; Helio tried to support her, and they both tumbled nearly to the ground before one of the guards jumped forward, staggered under their combined weight, and urged both over-pale sorcerers to sit.

"I'll get him," Henna mouthed to Maddy, who kept trying to get up even though it was clear her legs wouldn't support her. Any magic she hadn't used on the spell for the Osei had gone into healing Verte.

Henna took Clay from the servant, a young woman who looked gray-pale with shock. For a moment, her arms tightened on the child, as if he were her touchstone in this world gone mad.

"He knows me," Henna said.

The woman nodded, and finally released Clay into Henna's arms. "Maddy handed him to me when . . . when . . ."

"Go sit down," Henna urged her. "I have him."

"Cay!" the baby shouted. "Mumum!"

"It's okay, Clay," Henna said. *Nothing is okay right now.* It hurt to hold him against broken ribs, but it was better than leaving him with the shocked servant to wail. "I've got you, and I'm bringing you to your Mumum."

"Abibi wanna Cay. No gimme?"

Clay waved his arms, slapping against the viscous patches of oil-slick power that hung in the air and clung to Henna from when she had touched the Terra.

"Can you carry him inside?" Maddy asked, staggering to her feet only with help from another guard. Once up, she was able to walk on her own, but not easily. "I don't think I can lift him, and I don't want to touch him until I wash off the—until I wash my hands."

Her hands and arms were slick with blood.

They went through the kitchen door to the Cobalt Hall. Clay hiccupped, saying again, "No gimme."

"It's okay," Henna said again, her voice wooden. "You're safe now."

"Where's Naples?" Maddy asked as she pumped water into the sink to wash her hands. "I didn't see him."

"I'll find him," Henna promised. "You stay here with Clay."

She wanted desperately to ask about Verte, but she saved the question. What must it be like, she wondered, to be a mother, and see another woman destroy the boundaries between the worlds to try to rescue her own son? Maddy needed her children with her before they spoke of whether another woman's son was alive or dead.

"No gimme?" Clay begged one more time, as Maddy sank into a chair and Henna finally passed the child to his mother.

Maddy hugged him close and wiped a hand down his hair. "He's been saying that all morning. I don't know what he wants."

"I think I know." Henna finally understood, now and maybe too late. She had seen it come from the Terra's blood and pain, seen it rip into this world from the next. Dear Numen and cold Abyss, the Terra had summoned a demon into this world. Solemnly, she looked into Clay's eyes and said, "I won't let anyone give you to the Abyssi. I promise."

CHAPTER 19

NAPLES

Maybe Naples shouldn't have brought Celadon up to his own rooms, but he couldn't think of anywhere else he could guarantee privacy for their "talk." Now he wasn't sure whether he wanted to hit the preacher, debate with him, teach him, or throw him down on the bed.

Celadon was a bit of a crazy bastard, with some intelligent ideas but unsettlingly wild conclusions. What Naples found most curious was that some of the thoughts he expressed echoed knowledge not found in the Napthol libraries, but which had been hinted at by the Terra. How he might have come by such information was a mystery. The fanaticism with which he preached it was, well, kind of sexy.

Naples had told Terre Verte he wouldn't coerce Celadon into anything drastically out of character, which probably included pushing just enough of that delicious power back at him to drive him wild, strip him down and screw his brains out. But that really wasn't *fair*, because every time Celadon turned in his pacing, picked up a new thread in his rant, or met Naples' gaze, he threw off enough energy to make Naples shudder with the effort it took not to fling himself at him.

I'll let him wear himself out, he decided. One man could only have so much power, especially when he had never been trained to center it. Sooner or later, Celadon would exhaust himself, and then he would be easier to control. Then Naples could focus on convincing him to take the brand.

The brand was the only option. He had too much power to master it in a few quick, covert sessions with Naples.

"Terre magic is *breaking* this realm," Celadon spat. "A fizzik bird from the Numen itself appears over cocktail hour, and still *no one* questions? No one is concerned?"

"A *what?*" Naples asked. How had Celadon even heard about the strange creature that had appeared at the reception—and disappeared just as quickly— let alone known a name to call it? The Terra had assigned Naples to go find it, but though he had finally been able to track its power, the bird had been gone long before he reached it.

Celadon shot him a frosty look. Naples remembered thinking the preacher's eyes were a flat, watery blue. He had been so wrong. They were all the colors of the daytime sky, shot through with silver like moonlight. They flashed with his power.

As Celadon's gaze met his own, electricity danced along Naples skin. His breath caught and his body clenched in a way that was not entirely unpleasant.

Or maybe he'll wear me out first, Naples thought, with anticipation more than concern.

For the first time, Celadon seemed to notice the reaction. He let out a disgusted sound.

"What, did you run out of deckhands to fling yourself at?"

"Excuse me?" Debate was fine, entertaining and possibly educational, as long as Celadon stayed focused on matters of the Abyss and the Numen and the origin of magic. Any initiate of the Napthol was keen for a debate on *that* subject. Even Quin criticisms of the megalomaniacal, womanizing prince and his Abyss-worshipping mother were amusing.

But Celadon was on treacherous ground now.

"I saw you in the market yesterday," Celadon said, seeming to sense he had hit a nerve, "wrapped around that sailor. It was disgusting."

"This again?" Naples sighed.

Or so he thought. Then Celadon straightened and his voice mellowed, as if he had decided to stop fighting with anger and to use his own brand of logic instead.

"I do not approve of what the Order does, but if you're successful here, you must be an intelligent, well-educated young man. I've heard you were raised in this life. You probably don't realize you could have other prospects."

Naples only half listened to the words. Celadon's anger had been titillating. Now that he was actively *trying* to entice, it was no wonder his followers flocked around him. How many of them thought they were madly in love with him? At least Naples could recognize the spell and guard against it. He wouldn't be leaving here to take vows, or whatever the Quin did to declare their allegiance, though it took all his attention to make sure he didn't let any of that dangerously alluring power slip past his shields. Noise from outside tried to distract him once, and he consciously turned his awareness from it.

Celadon continued. "You do not need to waste your life performing tricks like a trained dog for the Terre, and turning tricks for ignorant dock scum who have no interest in you beyond using you and throwing you away."

Even with Celadon's power twisting each word into a dozen crooning, seductive purrs, those accusations stung, in a way they never had before.

Naples had had his share of meaningless flings, but

Cyan wasn't like that. Even after the last few days, Naples had no illusions of being more than a "sweetheart in port," but it was the first time he had been anyone's sweetheart at all.

And he would not tolerate Celadon maligning it.

The next time Celadon met his gaze, probably expecting to see gratitude and devotion in Naples' eyes, Naples drank down the power. Celadon's cold magic was as opposite Naples' natural tendencies as snow was from fire, but sweet Abyss it still tasted . . . *well, divine,* he thought with an amused quirk of his lips. Did Celadon realize he was seducing people into his anti-magic cult by using the grace of the Numini?

"What are you smiling about?" Celadon growled. The crooning, oh-so-reasonable tone had left his voice. He had felt something, though he didn't know what.

"This," Naples answered simply.

He took the power, shaped it, and turned it.

The preacher gasped. His knees gave out and he stumbled, catching himself on the edge of Naples' desk. Unlike Naples, Celadon had no shields up to protect him, and no training in how to recognize the distinction between his own desires and those of his power.

And you're so good at making that distinction? Naples teased himself as he reached for Celadon, helping him rise, shaking, to his feet. Even if he was only looking at the physical aspects and didn't care about personality, Celadon wasn't really his type. It was only his power that made him attractive.

I won't go too far, Naples thought. *I just want to make a point.*

With proper training, Celadon might have been magically stronger than Naples, but as he was, he had been lost even before he let Naples touch him skin-to-skin. Naples didn't need to draw on his own power. He used Celadon's, manipulating a sorcerer's natural craving for magical release, which could become a physical need if left unfulfilled.

"This," Naples murmured, his body so close to the other man's he could feel Celadon's frantically beating heart, and his lips hovering over the preacher's slightly parted ones, "is what your magic does to every one of your followers when you preach at them. It's no wonder you rail so sternly against lust and female empowerment and same-sex relations. It's the only way to keep your own flock from throwing itself against you."

Celadon's control broke first. He wrapped an arm around Naples' waist to pull their bodies snugly together, and put his other hand on the back of Naples neck to close the last distance and complete the kiss.

Not too far, Naples tried to remind himself. Celadon tasted like another world—like the sweet, clear waters of the Numen sea. *This is just a demonstration. You have to let him go.*

And you really shouldn't let him do that. Celadon was scrabbling at the buttons of Naples' shirt.

Serves him right.

He was in the process of gathering his willpower

when there was a sharp rap on the door that hardly qualified as a knock. After one bang, the door slammed open. It bounced off Naples' shoulder with a stinging impact.

"Naples, I'm sorry to intrude, but—dear Numen, are you *out of your Abyss-spawned mind?*" Henna's sheet-pale face was contorted with horror and rage as she strode into the room and beheld the situation.

"Um . . . would you mind giving me a minute?" Naples asked, drawing away from Celadon's dazed form.

This was awkward. Very awkward.

Instead, Henna grabbed Celadon's arm and threw him toward the door.

"You! Out!" she snapped. Freed from Naples' hold on him, Celadon was gone in seconds.

Naples began to prepare his explanation, but he hadn't even drawn breath to speak when Henna said, "I will refrain from blistering your hide for exactly one reason: your mother needs you."

So, it seemed Henna had learned of his plans with the Terra. Well, now was as good a time as any to have it out with her. "My mother is an independent and strong woman, who is perfectly capable of functioning without her grown son. She already knows I'm leaving the Order." Shaking off embarrassment in exchange for defensive anger, he lifted his head and met Henna's gaze without shame. "Terra Sarcelle has officially offered to take me on as her apprentice. I'm moving into the palace next week."

"Terre Verte is dead."

The words—so bluntly and flatly said, so unexpected in this conversation, so utterly impossible—at first failed to process. When they did, after a very long silence, all Naples could say was, "That's absurd."

Henna cringed. "I'm sorry. I didn't mean to tell you like that. I was—Please, Naples, just come downstairs. I don't want to leave Maddy alone."

She turned away. What Naples had at first taken for smoldering anger, he now realized was nothing but a veneer of fragile self-control. Henna's dark skin made her pallor less obvious, but now that he was looking for it, he saw the tight pinch of her mouth and the fine tremble in her body.

"Henna, are you . . ." *Okay?* Of course not. "I'll be right down."

She left. Naples tried to take a few moments to ground his power and stop his head from spinning, but he couldn't, because it wasn't just power making his body shiver and his thoughts race. It was shock. This had to be a mistake. With all the power in the royal family, there was no way Terre Verte could be *dead*.

Downstairs, he found his mother, Henna, Dove, Helio, and several other members of the Order clustered together in one of the parlors. Henna was going back and forth between the kitchen and the sitting room, making and delivering tea and cocoa with a vacant expression in her eyes. Naples hovered in the doorway, overwhelmed by the pain in that room.

"How did it happen?" one of the novices—Lassia, Naples thought her name was—asked.

Everyone looked at Henna for answers.

"My fault," she said. She didn't seem to know she was speaking out loud. "It was my fault. I knew . . . I *saw* it. That vision . . . how could I have been so wrong?"

Maddy reached an exhaustion-trembling hand toward Henna as she passed, but the seer jerked away.

"The water's boiling," she said before ducking into the kitchen.

Naples braced himself, then stepped into the room.

"Nana!" Clay asked, from their mother's lap. The toddler's eyes were as red and swollen as everyone else's, though his tears probably had more to do with the disturbance in his environment. He couldn't understand true grief yet.

"Oh, Naples," his mother cried, lifting her hand toward him while the other stayed wrapped around the sleepy, sniffling Clay. He went to her; she folded her arm around his waist to hold him close, and he put an arm across her shoulders. Her body was cold from the overuse of her magic, and she was shivering from both that and power exhaustion.

"What happened?" he asked.

"The Osei," Lassia whispered, in a voice breathy with shock.

"The *Silmari*," Dove spat. "Without them, the Terre would have—"

"I thought she might kill them all," Lassia interrupted. "I've never seen anyone pull that much power, so fast, without even ritual."

The whispering continued and Naples stood dumbly, unsure what to do. The knowledge that he had been upstairs, playing with that damned preacher, while . . .

The thought made him bolt to the door, needing fresh air. He heard his mother shout his name, but he couldn't stay there any longer. He needed to breathe.

As soon as he stepped outside, the slap of lingering power stole the air from his lungs.

His foxfire orbs in the fountain had absorbed some of the spilled magic; they were bloated and heavy, now burgundy in color and so hot the water around them simmered and steamed. The market cobbles were stained with foxfire, magic, and blood.

Some of that blood cried out with a Terre's magic. Some of it was thick and dark, spilled from an Osei in natural form.

And some of it, Naples realized with equal parts awe and horror, was violet-black, and still hissing like acid on the stone.

What in the three realms did she do?

He knelt by one of those last stains. It wasn't blood, he realized, not really. It was made of almost pure power; someone without magic might see nothing at all.

He had to check on the Terra.

"I'm sorry, she isn't receiving," a guard at the palace doors told him.

"I work for her."

"The staff has been sent home."

To the Abyss with courtesy. The Terra *would* see him.

The palace guards were normally chosen from men and women with some resistance to enchantments, but they weren't true sorcerers, and there was so much raw power in the air—and blood, and agony—that it barely took a thought to turn, *"Let me in,"* into a command no one could have disobeyed.

No one was in the front hall, not even the ever-present Sepia. There was only the miasma of pain, which had surely driven even the least magically sensitive servants out of the building. Naples needed to continually force it out of his awareness in order to search the building.

The Terra wasn't in her parlor or her library, and knocking boldly on the door to her private quarters received no response.

He had expected that. Where else would she be, after all, but in the temple?

Naples found the temple's hidden doorway, closed his eyes, cleared his mind, and focused his power to open it. The archway appeared, but the sight that met him as he stepped through made him stagger back against the wall.

Terre Verte's body, encased in a cocoon of power, lay on the table in the center of the room. The ever-present stack of books was gone; it had been swept clean of all accoutrements but a new, white silk covering, and was now surrounded by the debris of Terre Jaune's sorcery equipment: runes cast in gold and silver, herbs, crystals, and other supplies Naples didn't recognize. The king himself sat on the floor, surrounded by dozens of open, discarded texts.

"Terre?" Naples asked.

Terre Jaune didn't lift his eyes from his book, or so much as twitch to show he had noticed Naples' intrusion. He was weeping as he read.

Naples walked past Terre Jaune and put a hand on the doorway of the Terra's private sanctuary.

Naples? Her voice drifted to him on a trembling breath of power.

May I come in?

The barrier on the doorway disappeared, and Naples stepped into the thick haze of smoke and magic that filled the Terra's temple.

The queen was on a velvet love seat. She normally posed there dramatically, perhaps what she would consider seductively. Now she hunched, exhausted, and bloodied.

"You're hurt," he gasped, falling to his knees beside

her. He reached out to examine what looked like claw marks on her arms and breasts, as if something had tried to dig to her heart. The blood trailed through a fine coating of black ash. "Should I call a healer?"

He wasn't strong enough to close such deep wounds, but he did what he could with the techniques she had taught him without waiting for permission or response.

"I'll be fine."

She didn't protest as he next used a piece of scrap fabric to wipe ash, tears and blood from her face. At long last, she said only, "He fought me."

"The Osei?"

She shook her head. "Antioch."

He recognized the name from her journal, which he had assumed belonged to a midwife or healer of some kind. "Who's—" *Not who. What.* He remembered the blood that wasn't really blood in the market, and didn't dare ask the next question aloud.

The Terra met his gaze for long moments.

I will battle the Abyss itself to keep this frail child.

He, stupidly, had thought the words hyperbole.

"Jaune is with our son," she said. "He can heal him."

"I've seen . . . Verte," Naples said. He didn't say *the body,* though that was obviously what it had been. "Do you really believe the Terre can bring him back?"

"Of course he can. Now run along, Naples. I need to rest."

Her faith made Naples' heart lighten. There was

no rosy, romantic haze between the Terra and Terre. If anything, they constantly *under*estimated each other. If the Terra said her husband could do something, then he could.

When he passed by Terre Jaune again, the king had both hands pressed to the bubble of power surrounding his son. His eyes were shut, and the air around him writhed with glowing symbols and ripples of power Naples couldn't clearly read.

Maybe it would take some time to close Verte's wounds, but Terre Jaune was the greatest healer ever born to Kavet. He knew what he was doing. He would bring back his son, even if he had to storm the Numen and the Abyss both to do so, as he, perhaps, had already done once before.

CHAPTER 20

DAHLIA

There was something intrinsically satisfying about the scent and texture of fine paper and the feel of a pen sliding across it, leaving behind a trail of color nearly as magical in its appearance as the foxfire orbs that kept the stationer's shop lit. Dahlia had forgotten, in her frustration with teaching, how much she enjoyed the physical act of writing. Even more gratifying was the knowledge that this work for the stationer was something she had earned. Celadon hadn't "put in a good word" and the Terre hadn't twisted someone's arm to get her this position.

The spiritual and emotional exultation were, perhaps, caused as much by exhaustion leaving her near giddy as they were by the task itself. Her entire body *ached*. It took a monumental effort to lift her arm, and she struggled to stay on task and not stare into space. Thankfully, the stationer was understanding. When Dahlia apologized for yawning as he explained her first task, he gave an indulgent smile and admitted, "I'm impressed you showed up at all."

"I said I would."

She spoke the words before considering that they might sound arrogant.

"I know you did," he replied, "but late-night celebrations like the festival tend to ruin the best of intentions. Sit yourself down. Let's see what you can do."

Given her fatigue, copying meaningless lines about foxes and ducks using different inks, papers and pens, first in script and then in box-lettering, was soothing and hypnotic.

She looked up from her sampler as a woman entered the room in a frantic rush.

"I need to send a letter," she announced. Dear Numen, was that blood on the hem of her skirt?

"Yes, of course," Dahlia said, taking the initiative. "What do you—"

"How could this . . . ." The woman sobbed. "I can't even . . . The Osei, they . . ."

The stationer stepped forward to try to calm her.

A man entered moments later. Dahlia hadn't been sure about the stains on the woman's dress, but this man's arms were most definitely red with recently splashed blood. His hands were clean, as if he had washed them hastily, but he had the tacky fluid in streaks on his face as if he had carelessly brushed away tears with bloody hands.

"What *happened*?" Dahlia burst out.

"You don't know," the new man said, hollowly. "Of course you don't know," he added, as if to himself. "I'm a healer. I did what I could. Please believe me, I did what I could." He looked at his own hands, as if he could still see the blood Dahlia knew must have been there.

"I'm sure you did," she said, inanely, casting a desperate look to the stationer. He gave her a wave and a nod past the woman he was still trying to calm, which she interpreted as permission to act. "Sit down," she urged the man. "Take a deep breath. What can I do for you?"

The man hadn't responded before the door opened again, this time admitting a familiar member of the Silmari aristocracy. "Jade," she said, greeting him with relief, "what is going on?"

He breathed a sigh of relief. "I wasn't sure if this was the shop where you were working," he said. Dahlia had told him about her job the night before when his flirting extended to asking her to join him for lunch the next day. He deserved to know she wasn't who she seemed to be; she was a destitute shop-girl, not a fancy Kavet noble. "I didn't want you to find out through strangers."

"*Find out what?*" she nearly shrieked.

"Terre Verte is dead," the healer cried. "The Osei killed him. I think . . ."

The rest of the man's hysterical words bubbled away in a gray haze. Dahlia lost time, a bit, until she found herself sitting on a bench at the side of the room, sipping from a glass of water she couldn't remember accepting.

"He can't be dead," she said. "I just . . ." She had eaten dinner at the opposite end of a table from him the night before. She had danced with him.

Besides, he was the *prince*. How could a prince die?

"The Osei," she said, remembering what the woman earlier had said.

Another woman walked in then, looked around, saw Dahlia sitting at the desk and said, "I need to tell my sister what happened. Can you take dictation?"

"I . . . yes," Dahlia answered, mechanically reaching for the paper and inks used for standard messages. The stationer was already busy composing something for the first woman, and their shop was rapidly filling with customers.

"Dahlia, you don't have to do this," Jade said.

She shook her head. "It's my job."

She could write the words, because they were meaningless. Focusing on the flow of the ink and the formation of the letters meant she didn't need to think beyond that. It didn't matter what terrible things the words said; they were only ink, and they went away when she sealed them with wax.

Jade sat beside her for a while, and then as more people crowded into the little shop, each person needing to send a message to some loved one, he started to help. He took dictation, looking away whenever a customer's eyes suddenly brimmed with tears.

A Tamari noble entered the room. Dahlia thought they had been introduced the night before, but she couldn't recall his name. Last night, his eyes hadn't been wide with shock.

"Do you have birds?" he asked.

"Excuse me?"

"Birds. Messenger birds," he clarified.

Dahlia looked at the stationer, who took in the man's garb and replied, "None that fly as far as Tamar."

The man slumped against the wall.

"The *Silver Nightingale* will leave tomorrow for Silmat, via Tamar," Jade volunteered. "She can carry a letter for you."

It was the first time Jade had said or done much more than nod since he first arrived, and his clear Silmari accent turned heads and made the crowd around them hush, staring at him. People who had previously been too focused on their own grief to notice anyone else now took in the rich fabrics of his clothes and the jewels adorning his fingers and ears and realized he was no simple scribe.

How many times had Dahlia written the words—*the Osei say this is vengeance; they claim the Silmari killed one of their princes*—without considering what they meant?

"The *Nightingale* isn't going anywhere," the Tamari noble replied. "Except the bottom of the Kavet harbor, along with every other ship there."

Jade shot to his feet, at which point the sailor lifted his hands in a gesture of harmlessness. "Not by my hand. The Osei took them out. *Nothing* will be sailing out of Kavet for quite a while. And once they do, there's not many captains mad enough to sail through waters owned by the First Royal and Tenth Noble houses."

"But . . ." Jade looked around as if waiting for someone in the crowd to say "just kidding." "The Silmari delegation . . . half of Tamar's royal house is here!" he protested.

"They can *swim* home," someone in the crowd grumbled.

Jade spun on the speaker. "There are men here with families back home! Some of them left behind wives, just to avoid offending the Osei—"

"If you were so keen to avoid offending the Osei, maybe you should have considered not *killing* one of them!"

"You two, *out!*" The stationer stepped into the middle of the escalating argument. "If you aren't here to buy something or write a letter, you can leave."

The Tamari took the cue and left, uninterested in writing a letter if no bird could carry it. Several other people looked at Jade, who hesitated, glancing toward Dahlia.

"You're a friend of hers?" the stationer asked him.

"We only met recently," Jade admitted, "but I can escort her home."

"I don't need an escort," Dahlia protested instinctively. "And it isn't time for me to leave."

"Dahlia, please, go home," the stationer urged. "I can manage here."

"I said I would work the day," she protested, her hands moving to straighten the papers that had been tossed out of order in the chaos, and cap jars of ink. "I should—"

"You should go *home*," he said, firmly.

Jade touched her arm. "Come on, Dahlia."

"I should—"

"I'll see you tomorrow, maybe afternoon," the stationer said firmly. "I think we'll open late." He patted her on the shoulder and added in a fatherly tone, "Get some rest, and take care of yourself."

At last, she let Jade escort her outside.

"I can walk you home . . . if you would like," the Silmari said, hesitating when she tensed and pulled away.

Now that she didn't have a task to complete, a focus to keep her thoughts away from the horrible truth, she couldn't avoid facing reality: Terre Verte was dead. He had been kind to her, briefly. She hadn't known him long. And now he was gone.

On the heels of that realization, a more personal, selfish reality asserted itself.

"I don't have a home."

A home, or any belongings. She had heard people say that the palace was locked down, that even the servants and visiting nobles who had been staying there had been kicked out onto the streets. The few things she still owned were there, inside that building.

Could she go back to her father? She didn't know if he would accept her, if she did. She didn't know if she could accept him, if Numen forbid, his response to the Terre's death was "good riddance."

Eventually she might have a place to stay, if she signed on as apprentice to the stationer, but she couldn't beg help from him now. He seemed like a good man, but she didn't know how he would react to learn that she had been staying with the Terre—one didn't have to be Quin to wonder about the reputation of a girl living in the palace, with the prince as her benefactor.

"Dahlia?"

Jade touched her arm again, trying to bring her back to reality.

"I'm sorry?"

"Where have you been staying?" he asked, the words spoken in the tone of one repeating himself.

"The palace," she answered.

Jade's eyes widened a little, but he didn't question her. "You can stay at the inn tonight."

She nodded, too tired to do anything else. Jade wrapped an arm across her shoulders as they walked toward the Turquoise Inn.

"I don't have money."

"We'll see about getting your belongings tomorrow."

She was still shaking her head, unable to form words to admit her situation, when Jade ushered her into the Turquoise.

They had barely crossed the threshold when the innkeeper exclaimed, "No room! I have most of the Silmari delegation already—" He broke off as he recognized Jade. "Wait a minute. You've already got a room, number seven. You know I could have given your room away at three times the price if I weren't a man of my word."

"I will see that you are rewarded for your integrity," Jade said. "In the meantime, can you recommend somewhere my friend can stay?"

"I would, but anywhere fit for a lady alone isn't going to have space. I hear some of the nobles have given hard coin to board in private homes, since they couldn't find anywhere else."

Jade frowned.

"For, let's say two extra bits, I have some extra bedding I can send up. Sleeping on the floor of the Turquoise is better than renting a vermin-infested room with a broken lock down by the docks."

Jade looked at Dahlia, who shrugged. She had been kicked out of her guardian's home and accused of being the prince's whore. Sleeping on the floor of a Silmari aristocrat could hardly damage her reputation further.

"Could you send up a meal as well?" Jade asked.

"Right away," the innkeeper assured them.

"Thank you, but I'm not hungry," Dahlia said as she followed Jade up the elegant stairway.

"You should try to eat, anyway. And get some rest."

Dahlia started to nod, then paused, looking at the single bed that dominated much of the room. She had considered her reputation before, but her mind was churning slowly, and she hadn't worried about what Jade might consider the *reality* of the situation.

Sex was not one of the topics a Quin lady was encouraged to be frank about—beyond saying *no* until she shared a marriage bed with her husband—but she formed her words with the same clarity she would use when discussing an important piece of school policy.

"I appreciate your generosity and am grateful for a place to sleep," she began. "I hope it doesn't change your mind that I am not looking for a lover . . . or willing to, um, exchange services." Her confidence deserted her at the end, after it occurred to her that *lover* might not be the proper term if Jade was expecting a more businesslike transaction.

His brows rose with surprise, and she braced herself in case he responded with anger.

"I do not know Silmari ways well," she added, to

cover her own discomfort in the face of his silence. "This seemed like a bad time for a cultural miscommunication."

Jade shook his head, chuckling. "If all the court ladies in Silmat were as frank as you, Dahlia, there would be significantly fewer garden duels at the palace. Kavetans in general are a bit more reserved than my own people, and your—" He broke off and swallowed hard, levity abruptly gone. She realized he had almost said, *Your Terre*, or something along those lines. "I was warned at the ball that you in particular come from a sect that is more conservative even than most. I respect that, as I respect your grief. We can set up a pallet on the floor once the extra blankets arrive. You can sleep there, or on the bed, and I will accept whichever you leave empty."

"Thank you," she breathed. She didn't know where she would have gone if he had responded by throwing her out, or had insisted on "payment" for the room.

"Will you be okay if I leave you alone for a while?" he asked. "I want to go to the shipyard to see the situation there for myself."

"I'll be fine. I barely knew him," she admitted. "The Terre, I mean. We weren't close."

He looked at her skeptically, as if wondering how she had ended up on the prince's arm at the ball if they barely knew each other.

Dahlia couldn't help but wonder the same.

"Even if you weren't close, he was prince of this land."

"Thank you for letting me stay here." She was jumping around in the conversation, but there were so many things she was trying *not* to think about, her mind kept hopping from one safe subject to the next. "I hope you find welcome news at the docks."

"Me, too," he said with a sigh. "I'll be back soon. Please try to get some rest, if you can."

What else was there to do?

Dahlia pushed open the shutters on the window after he left. This side of the Turquoise offered what should have been a beautiful view of the square.

She watched Jade cross the cobbles warily, staying far away from a group of soldiers mopping blood from the stone. Near the far edge of the square, a group intercepted him: Celadon Cremnitz and his associates. Dahlia couldn't hear the words, but she could see Jade tense as he listened. Finally, he stalked away.

Were the Quin chastened at all, or were they celebrating the Terre's death?

Dahlia closed the shutters, against the sight as much as against a chill wind that was rising in defiance of earlier spring weather. She sat at the foot of the bed, in front of a faux-fireplace that held a sphere of warm amber foxfire instead of wood and flames.

She must have drifted into sleep, but thankfully, not for long enough to dream. She woke as the door opened, admitting Jade, as well as a burst of cold air from the hall.

"Does Kavet's weather always turn this quickly?"

The cloak he shrugged off his shoulders and hung near the door was rimed with snow. "I was halfway to the docks when the sky went dark and it started to snow."

He shivered, moving closer to the foxfire and finger-combing pellets of ice from the dense, corkscrew curls of his hair.

"If you don't like the weather, wait an hour," Dahlia murmured, repeating an oft-quoted mantra. She tilted her head, listening to the rasping hiss of sleet against the roof. "It sounds like quite a storm."

They both jumped at a peal of thunder so deep it made Dahlia's teeth ache.

"So it is. Do you get these often?"

"Sometimes, usually in late winter or earlier in the spring though. I hope it isn't bad enough to damage the fruit tree blossoms." A late-spring ice storm had stripped half the flowers off the fruit trees one year, leading to a terrible fall for apples.

"Happy spring. I prefer robins and daffodils, myself. Did I mention that Silmat rarely gets cold enough for ice? The rivers and lakes never freeze over."

"Sounds lovely." Dahlia stared into the foxfire globe as she spoke, her mind curiously blank.

"It's quite a place, even with the wyrm breathing down our necks." Jade paused, perhaps considering how recent events would affect that problem, then continued on a lighter topic. "My portion of the family owns a shipping business, which is where most of our livelihood comes from—not just ocean trade, but up and down river, too. I've spent half my life on ships."

Hiss, hiss, hiss. When Jade stopped speaking, Dahlia could hear only the sleet, wind, and occasional thunder.

"Go on," she said. His voice was soothing, and his words kept her from focusing on the immediate past, present, or future.

"Well . . . the port city is famous for its stone arches. The city is ancient, you see, and it ran out of space centuries ago, so they started building roads on top of roads, putting up bridges everywhere and covering the city in a lattice like the top of a pie. There's no magic, but some of the art there comes close enough to imitating it . . ."

She fell asleep to the sound of his voice mingled with the storm, and had curious dreams about dragons who came in with the snow and ate all the pink and white blossoms off the fruit trees.

CHAPTER 21

NAPLES

Naples could think of worse places to get snowed in than the palace.

He could have been trapped somewhere that relied on fire for heat, or somewhere without a fully stocked kitchen. Another home probably wouldn't have had a plethora of guest beds to choose from, each more elegant than the last.

Somewhere else, however, might have had someone to talk to instead of empty halls, empty dining rooms, and empty ballrooms.

His footsteps echoed as he paced the foyer and waited for the hail to stop, or at least let up enough that he could make it across the plaza and back to the Cobalt

Hall. He didn't mind getting cold and wet when he knew warmth and dry clothes were only a dash away, but a hailstone the size of a chicken egg had narrowly missed his head the first time he poked it out; his arm still ached from where it had crashed into his shoulder. Despite his interest in healing applications for his power, he hadn't mastered the Terra's techniques well enough to apply them on himself yet.

Hours later, he was still waiting. The hail had turned into sleet and driving snow, which would cause fewer bruises but kill him just as surely if he got turned around and lost in its blinding swirls or fell and broke an ankle on the shattered chunks of ice littering the ground.

The Terra needed to rest, and Terre Jaune shouldn't be disturbed. Naples kept telling himself that. Just because he was desperate for another voice . . .

The power rising from the ritual rooms didn't help. It swelled to fill the entire palace, pushing against the walls and windows like fermentation gas, waiting to explode the moment the cork was loosened. Naples' head swirled with it, leaving him dizzy and feverish, no matter how hard he worked to block it out.

I have to get out of here.

Maybe if he stayed near the buildings and went around the plaza instead of directly across, he could make it. The storefronts might shelter him.

Even if they didn't, freezing to death would be better than this.

He pushed at the casual side door, which he had been using since starting work for the Terra. Unlike the formal front doors, it was utilized whenever the royal family or their guests wanted to come and go without ceremony and trumpets.

The door didn't budge.

Naples checked the lock, making sure it wasn't engaged. The heavy latch lifted, but the wooden door itself stayed as solid as a mountain.

Frustrated to the point of tears, he slammed his shoulder against it, to no avail.

Iced shut. That's all it is. There's no need to panic.

Naples flattened his palm on the wood and focused his magic into it, pushing heat into the ice—

Invisible power, raw and feral, lashed back at him, sending him flying across the grand entryway until he slammed to a halt on the hand-woven wool carpet. He gasped in air to replace that which had been knocked out of his lungs and shook his head to clear it. Fine particles of ice fell from his hair to melt on the rug.

What in the Abyss had done that?

No, not in the Abyss. Cold power came from the divine realm.

Naples pushed his aching body up and approached the doorway again, warily this time.

He touched tentative fingertips to the doorframe first. No reaction. He moved to the door itself, and shivered convulsively; the wood paneling was frigid, far colder than it had been moments before.

You don't want to do that.

Naples spun about, certain he heard a voice—but he was still alone. He stalked the length of the foyer anyway, calling, "Hello?"

No answer.

Fine. There were dozens of doors in and out of the palace. He would try the one that led to the gardens. It had a stone archway over it, so might not have gathered ice.

The moment he saw that door, however, his hope of freedom died. He didn't need to touch it in order to see the fine layer of frost decorating its surface.

Could this enchantment be emanating from Terre Jaune, and whatever he was doing to heal his son? Could one sorcerer possibly raise this much power on his own?

Naples raced back up the stairs, long legs taking them two at a time until he stood outside the Terre temple. He knew he shouldn't disturb the king, but his desperation was stronger than his common sense as he slapped a palm against the wall and—

Where is it?

He looked up and down the hallway. He was in the right spot. Wasn't he?

Where was the door?

He searched frantically, trailing his hand along the wall several meters in each direction from where the door should be, but there was nothing. It was gone.

Meanwhile, the temperature in the hall plummeted. His breath started to fog. He stole a heavy wool and fur cloak from a guest room and put it on top of his own, but was still shivering as he once more stood before the door.

He should have left earlier, to the Abyss with the hail. He probably would have made it. Now here he was, preparing to battle an inanimate object.

He kicked it. It didn't help or, to his disappointment, make him feel any better.

Fine. Enough being polite.

He pulled the knife the Terra had given him across his right palm, much as he had earlier with Celadon, and slapped the bloodied hand against the door. An ache of cold ate up his arm, but that pain, too, he could focus into his power and turn into heat.

Something pushed back at him. He closed his eyes, concentrating—

The world went dark.

Very brave, idiot.

Naples tried, unsuccessfully, to open his eyes. Failing that, he attempted to lift his head. No. Could he wiggle a finger?

You would keep struggling until she crushed you, wouldn't you?

Eyes . . . It would be good to see—

And you would struggle now. Relax. I won't damage you. It has been a long time since your kind walked this realm.

He felt something, and this time it wasn't cold but searing hot, and he couldn't even flinch away as the sensation trailed down his back like needles just taken from a forge.

"**N**aples? Naples, can you hear me?"

This time he managed to open his eyes, only to shut them immediately them against the glare of light. "Uugh. Where—"

"Honey, it's me. Are.you back with us?"

The second voice was his mother's, which meant he was in the Cobalt Hall. The first voice, he recognized belatedly, had been Henna's.

He opened his eyes again, squinting. "How did I get here?"

"We found you on the doorstep, burning up with fever," Henna said. "You've been unconscious for three days."

"*Three days?*" Most disturbing was not that he had been unconscious, but the sound he could still hear: sleet and hail striking the roof and the walls. "The storm?"

"Hasn't let up. Thank Numen you weren't caught in it."

At the word, Naples shivered. He didn't feel the desire to invoke the Numini at this moment.

"This storm can't be natural," he said.

"It *can* be," his mother answered, but her hesitation suggested she was pointing out a possibility, not a probability she believed.

"Helio and I have been working together to scry the cause," Henna added, "but I'm not strong with cold magic and Helio doesn't have much control over his visions. We've also spoken to all the sorcerers in the Hall with any experience with weather control. No one here can do anything like *this*."

"Maybe the—" He tried to sit up but the effort of moving stole his breath. His muscles felt lax and the simple act made his head spin. As his mother bent down to help, he saw the dark circles under her eyes.

"I'm sorry I worried you," he said.

"What happened to you?" she asked.

"I . . ." What *had* happened? "I got in a fight. With a door." He frowned. "I don't even know how I got back to the Hall. I was in the palace when the storm began." He briefly described his altercation with the strange power. He also mentioned Celadon—though he left out most of the details of their encounter—and watched his mother's surprise as he explained, "The Quin has power. How much, I don't know, but it's cold power and it's enough for the Terre to get in his face about it." *The Terre.* Three days—"Has there been any news?"

"News?" Henna asked.

"About Terre Verte," he clarified. Henna's gaze went distant; his mother winced. "I *saw* him when I was at the palace. Terre Jaune was working on healing him."

"Honey . . ." His mother sighed.

Naples managed to struggle to his feet this time, though only by leaning against the wall. "He'll be *fine*," Naples insisted. "He'll . . ." He swayed, almost falling before his mother and Henna caught him.

"Naples, lie back down," Henna said. "You've burned your power down to the quick, so your magic is eating into your stamina. I'll bring you something to eat."

"I don't want to eat. I—"

Movement in the corner of his vision made him twist, moving too quickly. This time he *did* fall, only at the last minute guided toward the bed by his mother.

Rest. He looked around, but he couldn't locate the voice, the one that sounded almost like his own thoughts, like a bar of music stuck on repeat in one's memory. *You're weak. Rest a while, and when we stop the snows you can leave.*

"Naples?" His mother sounded even more worried now.

"I'm . . . fine," he said. Lied, he was pretty sure. He resisted the urge to reach up toward where, despite all the evidence, he could feel a hand on his shoulder. Instead, he let the phantom hands guide him back down.

"Try to stay awake long enough to eat," his mother asked. "I'll wake you if you don't."

Feed, the other voice in his mind said. *Eat now, and later I will teach you to feed.*

Was this what going crazy felt like?

His mother put a hand on his brow. "You're still feverish," she pronounced.

"The fever isn't the problem," Henna said, as she returned with what looked like a bowl of soup. "You're burning power as if you're fighting something. I tried to shut it down for you, but I'm not strong enough. Can you ground yourself?"

Naples shut his eyes, trying to focus on his magic and draw it back.

No! He jumped with a yelp as he felt phantom claws at his stomach. *It will hurt you if you stop guarding yourself. Eat, sleep, and then we hunt.*

CHAPTER 22

DAHLIA

As the storm continued, Dahlia began to actively daydream about Jade's semi-tropical Silmat.

He filled the mercilessly dull hours with tales of rushing rivers and grand ballrooms, and dispelled the deadly cold with descriptions of misty forests and tranquil lakes where snow never fell.

After the first, awkward night, during which Dahlia had slept fitfully across the room from Jade, she had been horrified by her own momentary feeling of gratitude when the innkeeper had haltingly explained that the ice had collapsed part of the shed containing the extra fuel for the rooms heated by wood furnaces. He was asking everyone in the foxfire-warmed rooms if they would be willing to share with those who had originally been in the cheaper, wood stove rooms.

"Of course I'll refund your money," the innkeeper added. "I wouldn't ask if people were able to leave and find other places to stay, but I can't send anyone out in this weather."

The captive patrons of the Turquoise doggedly grouped together in the foxfire-warmed rooms, then, as the temperature dropped even further, they crowded closer so they could bring two or three orbs into each single room to bring it to a comfortable temperature. Dahlia ended up sleeping with Jade after all, technically speaking, but she didn't think it counted when the bed also held three others, and another half-dozen men and women slept on the floor.

At least the Turquoise *had* foxfire. What were people doing who didn't have such luxuries? Out in the country they would be well prepared; her father always kept plenty of wood stocked. But she remembered the Quin neighborhood, with seashells in every windowsill. Did they have enough fuel for these seemingly endless days? Despite her feud with Celadon, Dahlia didn't despise the Followers of the Quinacridone. She didn't want them to freeze to death because they disapproved of foxfire.

At last, the sleet became fluffy snow, and then the skies cleared to reveal blinding sun that bounced off the icy landscape. The winds remained bitter cold, but that didn't stop those who had been trapped in the Turquoise from venturing forth—or trying, at least.

The first people to leave needed to go through the windows. Several strong men went to work chipping away at the sometimes foot-deep layer of snow and ice that blockaded the exits, while other Kavet natives climbed to the roof, to check the ice and cut rivets for melting water to flow down. Jade offered to help, but anyone who had listened to his stories—everyone— knew better than to trust him on the ice.

The moment the door was open, Dahlia told Jade, "I'm going to check on the stationer's shop, to see if he's around and needs any help cleaning it up after the storm." It seemed the sensible thing to do, but Dahlia admitted to herself that her real motivation had more to do with a desperate desire to stretch her legs than a need to be responsible.

"Do you want me to come with you?"

The offer made her smile. She could picture Jade sliding across the market plaza in his effort to be a gentleman.

"I'll be fine," she assured him. "Your help is needed here."

Now that the storm clouds had parted, the sun's glare was deceptively bright, making the weather seem pleasant until Dahlia stepped into the bite of the wind. Despite wearing layered clothes—the ones she'd had on her back the morning of the storm, as well as an extra vest and cloak of Jade's—the cold cut through her like a blade.

Her footsteps *crunched* beneath her. She placed her feet carefully, both to keep from slipping and so she wouldn't break an ankle if the ice crumbled beneath her and her foot plunged into softer snow beneath.

"*Sweet Numen*," she hissed, when her path took her across the market.

Most of the cobbles were slick and white, but the center fountain was still liquid, simmering from the heat of the foxfire within. Rivulets of water ran from it, only to solidify a few feet away in the frigid air. Steam, wind, and winter had created a jagged castle of ice. Some trick of the weather had swirled those blade-like stalagmites toward the palace, so they stood like soldiers' lances that threatened and pinned the main gate shut.

Members of the Order of Napthol swarmed the outside of the Cobalt Hall. As Dahlia crept past, she almost ran into someone striding back toward the Hall from the palace with unwisely swift steps.

"Sorry," she murmured, keeping her face ducked down to block the icy wind.

"Dahlia?"

She recognized Henna's voice and looked up. The sorceress was bundled as heavily as everyone else, but Dahlia could still see her eyes, which were swollen and shadowed as if from crying and sleepless nights.

"Henna, hello," she said. "I—"

Henna shook her head and waved a hand, dismissing anything Dahlia might have said in consolation. "I'm glad to see you're all right. I'm sorry I don't have time to chat. I'm working to figure out why the doors to the palace are sealed."

"Sealed?"

"The Cobalt Hall took in several guards and servants displaced when the Terre and Terra sent everyone away," Henna answered. "They've been trying to get back in, but it's more than ice and locks keeping the doors shut."

"You mean the royal family sealed it magically?" Dahlia asked. *"Why?"*

Henna stared at her in wordless disbelief. After long moments, she drew a shaking breath and said as if to herself, "You didn't see. You can't understand."

Dahlia almost protested that she did understand grief—she had never lost a child, of course, but that didn't mean she lacked all empathy—but didn't understand why the Terre and Terra would use magic to isolate themselves. Then she remembered who she was talking to, and that a girl from a Quin community couldn't assume she saw the world the same way as a powerful sorceress.

"Good luck," she said softly.

Henna nodded. "You as well."

With what? Dahlia almost asked, but didn't, because Henna was already turning back toward the

Cobalt Hall. Perhaps the reply had been automatic. If it was more prophecy, Dahlia didn't want to know.

If it hadn't been for her prophecy, where would you have been the last few days?

That thought, and imagining Ginger and Mrs. Cremnitz, spurred her to pass the stationer's shop and continue doggedly north.

In an alley two streets over from the Quin neighborhood, which had been somewhat protected from the driving wind, the snow was shallower. Dahlia's gaze flickered to that shadowed space as she walked by, but it took her mind a moment to catch up to her eyes. When it did, she turned so quickly she nearly fell.

Even coated with frost, the somber black clothing was ominously vivid against the cobble, brick, and snow.

Heart pounding, no longer aware of the cold, Dahlia hurried toward the form, which quickly revealed itself to be a man's body. She touched his shoulder, wincing at the chill, and turned the form so she could see its face.

Her stomach dropped when she recognized Celadon Cremnitz. Dahlia was not a morbid thinker by nature, but her first thought *was* not that the leader of the Quinacridone movement had simply wandered out and been caught in the storm.

This was no accident.

"Dear Numen," she whispered. Terre Verte was already dead—the most well-known and beloved sorcerer in Kavet. And now here she was looking at Celadon's body—

He gasped, and Dahlia let out a choked shriek. "*Celadon?*"

His eyelashes fluttered, but his eyes didn't quite open. "Dah . . . la?"

"Yes!" she shouted. She took his hand in hers, but didn't lift it for fear of sending cold blood cascading back to his heart. She half expected to feel the stiffness of rigor mortis in his fingers, to suddenly see the gruesome truth that she had mistaken the wail of the wind for life, but his hand twitched, then moved to grip hers. "You're awake," she said, half to him and half thinking aloud. "That's good. I . . ." There was only one place she was certain would be able to move him safely and warm him. "I'll run to the Cobalt Hall. Their healers—"

Celadon managed a surprisingly vehement, "*No.*"

"I'm not letting you die out here because you—"

"Sorcerer," Celadon mumbled. "Did . . . something to me. Why I'm out here. Can't go there." His limbs started moving, shifting aimlessly, and she realized he was trying to push himself up.

"Can you move?" she asked him. He had ice in his hair and on the exposed skin of his face and hands. How could he be this cold, yet still be *alive*, much less conscious?

"House," Celadon said. "Next street . . . green . . . number twelve. Help me to it. Please." His breath ran out on the last word, as he heaved himself onto his hands and knees. He paused there, panting.

He's not shivering, Dahlia thought. That should have been a bad sign, but if he was awake and moving around he couldn't be as bad off as he seemed.

"Here," she said. She put an arm under him to help him stand, since that was obviously his intention.

For a moment, it looked like his legs wouldn't hold him, and then he balanced and straightened his knees. He leaned on her heavily and walked with ungainly shuffles.

Dahlia helped him to within sight of the green house, but then his legs gave out and he collapsed to his knees again, panting. Dahlia ran to the door and knocked frantically, and uttered praise to the divine when it opened within seconds.

She recognized the man who answered as one of the Quin who had been protesting Festival with Celadon. Judging by his narrowed eyes, he recognized her, too.

"What in the three worlds brings Dahlia Indathrone to my door?" he scoffed.

"Celadon needs your help," she snapped. "I found him out in—" The Quin had already seen his fallen leader. He shoved past her.

"Is he—"

"Alive, or he was a moment ago," Dahlia said. "He was conscious and able to walk most of the way here."

Celadon had collapsed, and his eyes were now closed. Had he used the last of his strength to get them here?

"He was walking?" the man asked.

When Dahlia nodded, the Quin seemed to consider, then wrapped an arm behind Celadon's shoulders and lifted him. "Help me get him inside," he said, animosity toward Dahlia forgotten in the face of this crisis.

Together, they managed to settle Celadon on a pallet of blankets in front of the kitchen hearth. A quick glance around made it clear that he had spent most of the storm in this one room, in front of the fire—probably wondering if his stock of firewood would last longer than the ice.

"Can you add another log?" Dahlia asked, but he was already doing so.

She reached for Celadon again. She shook his shoulder, and when she received no response, she searched for a pulse.

It was there, achingly slow but even.

"He's alive," she said, though that didn't mean much. She knew that his being alive now was no indication of how he would come through; sudden shocks or movement could cause all their efforts to be in vain. "I need some warm towels. And scissors—his clothes are covered in ice."

"I know," her Quin host snapped.

Dahlia opened her mouth to respond with equal

hostility, but saw the fear in his eyes. It was panic making his words abrasive, not intent.

She found what she needed on her own while the Quin watched his leader like a lost boy instead of a grown man. Dahlia moved around him, distancing her mind and trying to stay clinical as she cut ice-crusted clothes from Celadon's body and wrapped him in blankets and towels warmed by the fire.

Even if Dahlia had been the type of person who could wish anyone *dead*, she would still have prayed for Celadon's recovery, for the sake of the city. He was too powerful among the Quinacridone for his death not to provoke a powerful response. And if she had understood him right, if someone from the Napthol had *done* this to him . . .

"What's your name?" Dahlia asked finally.

"Ochre." The single word was not accompanied by anything else.

Dahlia gave up the attempt at conversation, at normalcy. Ochre went out for more firewood and she stayed with Celadon, wondering if she would hear him wake or just end up being there when he died.

"Dahlia?"

She blinked as she heard his voice, realizing the angle of light through the window had suddenly shifted. Had she drifted off?

"Celadon? Are you awake?" She touched his cheek. His color was better, but his skin still felt chilled under her fingertips.

"I think so." His voice was small and tight. "I'm sorry."

"Don't try to talk," she said. "Save your strength."

He shook his head. "I hurt you."

"We don't have to discuss this now."

"I was scared for you," he said, as if determined to say these words or perish in the attempt—which she still feared he could. "Made me angry. And dumb."

So scared you tried to throw me out on the streets, she thought. They could have a proper argument on the subject if he made it through the night and still wanted to try to apologize. Fighting about it right now was more likely to kill him.

She said, "It doesn't matter right now. Just *rest.*"

"Need to . . . Dahlia, you don't understand. They—" He broke off. For an instant Dahlia feared he had given himself a heart attack, but he didn't go limp. His eyes flashed silver, then as they faded back to blue, he finally started to shiver. Sweat appeared in shining drops on his forehead. When Dahlia touched his forehead, his temperature had returned to normal.

Not just cold, she thought. *Magic.* Well, he had said someone from the Order of Napthol had done something to him.

She saw the same thought in Ochre's eyes as he asked, "Celadon, what is—"

Celadon ignored his follower and grabbed Dahlia's wrist, looking at her now with his own, frightened blue eyes. "I don't know what that sorcerer did to me, but it . . ." He struggled to turn onto his stomach and half pushed himself up before he started to cough.

Ochre pushed Dahlia aside and helped Celadon sit up, and supported him as his chest spasmed with deep, racking dry coughs.

"I've got him," Ochre told her. Sounding grudging, he added, "Thank you for helping him. We'll take care of him now."

By *we*, he meant the Followers of the Quinacridone— not including Dahlia. He looked pointedly at the door, then back at Celadon, whose coughing had started to slow. Ochre helped Celadon lean on a pile of cushions and blankets and said, "I have some cider I can warm. Wait just a minute."

Dahlia took the cue to leave. Her mind churned with questions.

She sympathized with the grief the Terra and Terre were feeling, but the palace couldn't just close its doors, draw its curtains and mourn. What if there were others affected as Celadon was? Who was protecting the citizens of Kavet from magical malevolence—or managing more mundane but equally vital work? Had anyone initiated work to fix the docks and ships damaged by the Osei and the storm? Those ships were the life blood of Kavet. Who was organizing assistance for merchants whose shops and wares needed repairs? The Turquoise's wood-shed couldn't be the only building damaged by ice. Leaking roofs could lead to the destruction of trade goods and essential supplies.

Repeatedly the last few days Dahlia had pushed away fears for her parents and friends back at Eiderlee, assuring herself that her family was cautious and well-prepared, but now the possible scope of the devastation struck her. How had Eiderlee fared, and the other farming communities? And even if *they* were all right, what about the trees, animals and fields, their livelihood—and Kavet's primary source of food?

Others will answer these questions, she told herself. *It isn't your responsibility.*

Is it?

OF THE DIVINE 33

CHAPTER 23

NAPLES

Eat now, and later I will teach you to feed.

Naples had pushed the memory of the phantom voice at the palace to the back of his mind, crediting it as a fever-driven hallucination, but hadn't he heard it *before* the fever?

And what had taken him from the palace to the Cobalt Hall, if not that strange presence?

As soon as he could walk, he did something stupid: he scaled the stairs and found his wobbly way to the temple. After days trapped inside by the ice, most of the Order's members were outside making repairs, seeking provisions, or just taking in fresh air, so he was alone for the moment.

He paused in front of the shelves of supplies, uninspired. He wanted to scry, to try to call back the disembodied voice or see who had attacked him, but while he knew several techniques for doing so he had never had Henna's knack for summoning visions.

Still, he could try.

Maybe. Normally as he stood here, his power was like an itch in his spine, driving him toward this tool or that.

Or maybe like a whisper in his head? Soft guidance from a demanding voice he had never heard clearly, until recently?

He chose a bowl made of hard steel, metal which had been poured red-hot into a rough mold, and then beaten into its final form in the embers of the hottest forge. Though the heat had long ago washed away, the power of it lingered in the folds of metal.

With the bowl and the Terra's knife, he knelt in front of the steel-and-obsidian altar where he always worked. He wasn't sure he agreed with the Terra's disdain for altars. His magic craved ancient heat, and that was what this altar represented: not just the fires of a forge, but the deepest blood of the earth, rich magma turned to black glass.

Glancing about casually once more, to make sure he was still alone, he pulled the blade across his palm.

Spilling blood lets the power flow, and lets you control that flow, the Terra had explained. *When you stop the power, the blood will stop, and the wound will heal. Our kind never bleeds except by choice.*

"Our kind." She had spoken as if they were another breed, something not altogether human. The words had unsettled him, and yet . . .

And yet he let the blood flow, and knew there was something in it that wasn't in his mother's blood, and certainly wasn't in Celadon Cremnitz's or Terre Verte's. Heat, and of that heat, power.

"Talk to me," he said to the empty room. As an afterthought, from some trickle of protective instinct, he added to the invocation, "Obey me."

Blood dripped into the bowl, an offering to a power unknown, and at last he heard, *Which would you prefer?*

A breath of hot air steamed against his face.

"Both," he said.

And if I decline?

"Can you?" he asked. It had come when he called, hadn't it?

Oh, yes, I came to your summons, to taste your sacrifice of blood and fire.

"Let me see you."

You wish that?

"Yes, I want to see who . . . or what . . . I'm talking to. Let me see you."

You command it.

"Yes, I command it!" Naples snapped, fatigue making him impatient. Fatigue or blood loss. The bowl was nearly full of his blood. It wasn't large—only the size of his hands cupped together—but he had already been weak.

As you wish, the creature said. There was an audible smile in its voice.

This was a mistake. Naples' own thoughts seemed faint compared to the reverberating, purring voice of the creature.

A smoky haze seeped into the world like ink, so black it seemed to emit darkness the way a lamp could emit light. Naples' skin prickled and he looked down to see hundred of tiny scratches appear on his arms, as if he were shoving his way through a briar patch; each came into existence and faded away again within a breath, but nevertheless he shuddered, fighting the pain of heat and blade. He pressed his free hand against the altar and clenched his teeth.

The heat increased until he knew it should burn his skin, raising blisters, as did the pulse of shimmering darkness. Though it seemed no brighter, the ethereal shadow now held impossible colors, deep rich hues for which language had no words, and a terrible beauty that nearly pushed aside the pain.

Naples' heart pounded as void began to take form. Sweat sprang to his skin, not from the heat but as a match to the hair rising on the back of his neck and all along his arms, and the coppery taste of fear at the back of his mouth.

Wait, he wanted to say, *I've changed my mind*, but he couldn't form the words. He was hypnotized, his body reacting in impossible ways, both in primal fear and deep need.

Unable to help himself, he reached out with his bleeding hand—

The world went black as the creature stepped fully into the mortal plane, summoned, invoked three times, and fed in blood and fire and pain and lust.

Naples didn't remember falling, but he must have, in the power of that last passage. Sprawled on his back on the ground, he stared up at the creature with eyes and mind incapable of fully comprehending it. One moment it was nearly a man, formed of shadow and smoke and velvety darkness, and the next it was a horror made of pure pain, claws and fangs.

Naples tried to make his body obey his commands, but his limbs were clumsy and slow to respond. As he pushed up on his elbows, the creature crouched and rubbed against him, catlike. It was as much fire as fur, and he cried out in pain—yet still reached toward it when it drew back. Had he thought he had felt attraction to anyone or anything before this? He caressed that pure darkness, undeterred even by the certainty that his skin should bubble and blacken from the heat of it.

The creature laughed, and the sound was silk trailing across Naples' skin.

"Abyssi," Naples said. His throat was tight, scalded, or just locked with fear. He was looking upon a beast from the infernal realm, a place where the damned went after death. This was the creature that had spoken to him, that had saved him? It wasn't the one who had thrown him across the palace and coated him in ice.

"A mortal, even one such as you, cannot battle the Numini," the creature said, reading his thoughts.

"They are in the mortal world, too, then?" The Numen was the place where the good hoped to go upon death, and people uttered prayers and thanks to that realm, but the denizens of the divine realm were depicted in stories as creatures of righteous fury and rigid control. Their meddling with mortal affairs couldn't bode well.

"Not fully. Not yet. But soon, now that the planes have been breached." The Abyssi lifted its gaze, eyes like two cerulean coals, to the shuttered window and the snow-encrusted world beyond. "They are creatures of ice," it said. "Your power is not cold enough to let you see them or guard yourself against them, but they can see you, and they will hurt you if they can."

"You protected me?"

"Of course."

"Why?"

Every moment in this world, the creature seemed to solidify more. Naples could see it tilt its head, the way an animal will when puzzled. "You are an Abyssumancer."

"I don't know what that means."

"You call with blade, with blood. With fire and flesh. You are ours." It added, "Your kind was destroyed by the Numini in the last war. You have not walked this plane since that day."

Naples moved closer to the creature again, unable to resist its allure, and it embraced him, pinning him to its chest and wrapping him in fur so soft it would have made him weep if its heat hadn't boiled his tears away.

"Other sorcerers in Kavet use hot magic," he said. "Henna, and the Terra—"

"Others of my kind have tried to craft a mancer," the Abyssi said. It nuzzled at his neck as it spoke. "Your Terra belongs to Antioch, and the one you call Henna belongs to Sennelier. But Sennelier started too late, and is not strong enough to complete the task, and Antioch is intimidated by how powerful his vessel has grown and refuses to make the final bond. I have spoken to you and crafted you like a blade since your earliest memories, and I have no fear of your power."

"The Terra summoned Antioch across, didn't she?"

The Abyssi scoffed. "In her fury she was able to pull him across the veil even against his wishes, but when he lost his quarry into the skies he turned on her in his hunger. Her link to him is flesh and pain only, not spirit."

"I don't understand."

The Abyssi replied by twisting its tail around his waist—no, *tails*, as many as nine of them, wrapping him in a cocoon of silken darkness.

"I will teach you," it whispered. "But first, we must

feed. We must hunt. You are weak from your fight, and from what you gave to me."

The words drew Naples' attention to the bowl, which not long ago had been filled with his own blood. Now it lay empty on the floor, shining as if never touched by that precious fluid.

"There is food here," he said, though he knew intuitively that the creature didn't mean soup or bread.

"Dirt," it said disdainfully. "We need real prey."

What was he committing himself to?

No, that was the wrong question. According to the Abyssi, he had been committed to this path by another power years ago.

He knew he *should* say no. He should use any strength he had left to drive this creature out of the world. But the Abyssi held him in its inexorable grip of fur and fire, and the touch of its body sated a need so deep there had never been a word strong enough to describe it. He was where he was supposed to be.

"Where do we hunt?"

PART 2

Summer, Year 3917 in the Age of the Realms

Inside the tall, golden walls of the Numen's high court, the arbiters and judges stood at the throne room at the highest floor of the citadel and argued with ringing voices that made cool rain fall on the mortal realm. The only one absent was Mir, the high justice, who had responded to a summons even he could not ignore.

On his knees, not from respect but from despair, the judge who had tried from the start to object to the arbiters' plan gasped, "No. No. I didn't mean this. I just wanted . . ."

"This has all gone wrong," declared the third arbiter, Veronese. "Doné, you know you have my love and my faith, but it is time for us to withdraw from the mortal realm."

"Even you, Veronese?" the second arbiter, Doné, replied incredulously. "You who have stood by me since the days of the old war, you too now doubt me?"

"My children are dead, and worse than dead!" Veronese cried. "I cannot even bring them home to the citadel to comfort them. And that beast walks the mortal plain."

"That beast is why we must not surrender now. Our children have faced so much fear and pain and loss. We must not allow it to be in vain."

"There is blood on my hands," the lesser judge said hollowly. "The death of one of my own chosen. You urged me to—"

"Veronese has the right to question me," Doné interrupted, "for he has served beside me for millennia and holds a throne in the high citadel. You, child, have the right only to obey." More gently, she said, "Mortals suffer, and mortals die. That is why we do this."

"Your child will come home to you," Veronese comforted the lesser Numini. "You will be able to embrace him again. He may already stand before our gates."

Unlike his own, whose confusion, anxiety, and desolation resonated in Veronese's heart like a festering growth. Veronese had begged to greet him at the gates, to welcome him back, but Mir had refused and gone to "deal with the situation" himself.

CHAPTER 24

DAHLIA

With ten luxurious minutes of downtime before the she was scheduled to meet with the assembly, Dahlia stretched. As her eyes traced the now-familiar gray stone ceilings of the Cobalt Hall, she heard her joints *pop* from too many hours sitting at her desk reading reports.

She lifted her braided hair off her sweaty neck, then stood and walked to the window to try to catch a breath of breeze. It was hard to imagine how city-folk *survived* this weather. The window here might have had a good view once, when the Hall had been built a thousand years ago, but now it overlooked only the backs of the buildings across the alley, which meant the air that sagged through it was stagnant and sticky with humidity.

No wonder this room was available for use, she thought wryly. Then, *Don't complain about the heat. Not when you know what ice can do.*

She sat back at the desk, deciding she would take her precious few extra minutes to start a letter to her father. He had never received the one she sent the day before the ice storm began, but she had sent him others since. A few. Not as many as she should have, *would* have, if there had been time.

> *Dear Papa,*
> *I am sorry it has been so long since my last letter, and that I must tell you again that I cannot come home yet. I*

How could she convince him that she was essential here? That she was protecting his interests? That she—

"Indathrone."

She nearly jumped out of her skin when someone politely said her name. Many people in the assembly insisted on using Dahlia's surname as a sign of respect, but she suspected Gobe, a gangly, long-legged adolescent from the Order of A'hknet, did it because he knew it made her uncomfortable. It was his way of balancing his A'hknet resistance to authority with his pride at his critical role in the assembly. Though Dahlia cringed to acknowledge that she *had* such a person, Gobe was essentially her secretary these days, and she couldn't manage without him.

"Yes, Gobe?"

"One of the visitors from the agriculture committee wants to see you privately."

She sighed, adjusting her schedule in her head. "I have a few minutes. Please send him in."

She sanded the unfinished letter and turned it over, just in time for—

"Oh!" she said, as her father entered the room. She could've strangled Gobe. *Visitor from the agriculture community indeed.* She should have known he would come. She felt herself pale and had trouble hearing her own thoughts over the pounding of her anxious heart in her ears. She choked on all the things she wanted to tell him, and managed only, "I . . . was just writing you a letter."

"I decided to come myself," he said. "I didn't expect to find you *here*."

She wished she could throw her arms around him like a small child, but she couldn't make herself move. Her stomach clenched as she remembered the disappointed tone of his last message, and saw the stern set of his mouth and eyes now.

Instead, hollowly, she explained, "The Order of Napthol was kind enough to let us use a few of the first-floor rooms when the assembly became too large for the Turquoise."

"Indathrone?" Gobe was back at the door. "Jade's

here with a note from the docks committee." He grinned cheekily, oblivious to the tension in the room. "Think he could get it in any later next time? Do you want it now?"

She held out a hand mechanically. Jade and a Tamari woman named Mikva not only represented the foreign nobles still stranded in Kavet, but were in charge of repairing and reclaiming the docks and attempting to refloat at least one ship—an effort that had seen every possible setback, from infighting to an accidental fire that had destroyed large sections of the damaged and partly repaired docks and surrounding buildings.

She only realized habit had taken over and she had started to skim the summary at the top of the report when her father cleared his throat.

"One of the Order of A'hknet workers received a bird from a cousin in the Pine Islands," Dahlia said. She had never heard of such a place until recently, but apparently, they were one of Kavet's more obscure trading partners. "It's one of the first we've received since the storm. Apparently, rumors say at least one ship tried to dock at Kavet during the storm, and had to turn away when they saw the damage and the . . . the ice."

The summary actually said, *"strangely localized ice storm, which covered Kavet but did not spread into the surrounding ocean. Are we ever going to talk about whether sorcery caused this?"*

"It explains why we haven't seen any other merchant ships since then," Dahlia continued, as if her father was remaining silent so he could hear this news, and not because he was seething with disappointment and waiting for a better explanation of why she was here, consorting not only with sorcerers but also individuals of the Order of A'hknet, whose carefree ways and frequently wanton approach to morality were well-known. "They say ships won't come to Kavet if they worry they won't be able to dock, because they need to resupply, and if they can't do it here they have to pay whatever exorbitant fees the Osei charge. That's part of why it's so important to get a ship of our own in the water as soon as possible, so we can let the rest of the world know we're still here. We need—"

"Dahlia. Stop." Her father interrupted with a calm but firm voice, one familiar to her from the talking-tos she had often received after childhood misadventures. "What are you *doing* here?"

She swallowed hard, then raised her chin and met his gaze with all the pride and self-assurance of a Quin young lady who knew she was doing her work well. "I am moderator for a mixed assembly of peoples, both native to Kavet and foreign, who are working together to make up for the absence of the royal house. What I am *doing* here," she continued, with more certainty than she felt, "is ensuring that no one starves this winter because of damaged crops, disrupted trade and an absence of royal oversight. What I am *doing* is finding situations for the dozens of servants and guards who were evicted from the palace, the scores of people who lost everything either from ice damage or in the docks fire, and the stranded nobles from Tamar and Silmat, so we don't have hundreds of homeless, destitute people simply abandoned on our streets. What I am *doing* is standing up as a representative for the country so the Osei don't decide to claim this entire damned island as their territory, and forcing the Followers of the Quinacridone, the Order of A'hknet, the Order of Napthol, and every other embattled faction to work *together* so we don't—"

"Dahlia, *stop*." This time he spoke as if overwhelmed, and waved a hand in the air, pleading for her attention in the midst of her tirade. "You've said all that in your letters. I don't doubt it's important work, but why is it *you*?"

She had attended the first meetings, which had included only Quin and had formed in Celadon's house, because she was worried what would happen when he and Ochre told his followers someone from the Order of Napthol had tried to kill him. Instead, Celadon had shown his true ability as a leader: he had refused to indulge any speculation about sorcery, and had focused on how to take care of their own kind. They worked together to check in on the elderly or other individuals who might not be able to take care of themselves, to clear ice from the roads and buildings, to repair roofs, and to reestablish ties with traders—especially farmers—who brought food into the city.

The Quin had an advantage over the rest of Kavet: they never expected help from the royal house, so they didn't wait.

Other groups did, but help never came. The palace doors remained sealed. No lights shone through the windows.

When Dahlia mentioned the meetings to Jade, he asked permission to join and get help for the other Silmari; he brought Mikva along as a representative for the Tamari soon after.

Then the fire had come. The bitter, frigid winds had sucked all the moisture from the air. No one had ever taken blame for the spark that kindled one of the shattered ships the Osei had tossed onto the shore, and spread through most of the docks, burning an entire village of homes mostly inhabited by members of the Order of A'hknet as well as several storage warehouses.

Dahlia considered and discarded a dozen replies to her father before she said simply, "I was the only one capable."

Two weeks after the storm—after Verte's death, after the royal house had gone into seclusion—Helio had approached Dahlia.

The Order of Napthol has always relied on the royal house to guide our efforts and provide for our needs in exchange for our labor, he had explained, awkward with embarrassment. *But the doors of the palace are still sealed. I've heard you've started organizing repairs and other work. Rather than operate separately and perhaps against each other, we thought it might be good to put our heads together.*

Dahlia had convinced the others to let the sorcerers join their meetings, but Celadon had still been moderator then, and his first attempt to work with the sorcerers had devolved into useless bickering and such loud shouting that the owner of the Turquoise had thrown Maddy and Celadon—the two main culprits—out of the building.

Dahlia remembered her furious words as she confronted the two in the street: *You're like children! You need to trust each other, just a little, for this to work.* She turned on Celadon then. He had used his moderator's power all night to cut off every contribution or request one of the sorcerers tried to make. *This isn't just about the Quin anymore. You need to stop being so willfully blind to everyone else's needs and run these meetings in a way that treats everyone fairly. And if you can't do that, you need to step down.*

Celadon's hostility had died then, gone as abruptly as a blown candle flame. *I have spent my life focusing on nothing but the needs of the Quin. It is my habit to take their part and advocate for them. I don't know how to do anything else.*

Dahlia had never imagined that, when they returned inside, Celadon and Maddy would come to their first agreement: They had both gestured for Dahlia to take Celadon's place as moderator.

"Come to the next assembly meeting," she urged her father. "See what it is we're doing here."

Maybe, once he realized she was doing good work—even from here inside the sorcerers' home—he would be proud, and support her as he always had before.

Crystal dreams. That's what Jade called silly hopes that distracted you from reality.

Jade was a topic she had avoided in her letters to her father. He would *never* approve of her close friendship with the Silmari noble, or the plethora of more exciting rumors that had spawned about it.

"I'm here to represent Eiderlee in the farming report," he said. "I wanted to speak to you first, but I—"

"Indathrone?" Gobe interrupted.

"Yes?"

"One of the volunteer guards wants to speak with you," Gobe said. "I told him you were in the middle of an important meeting, but he says it's urgent."

"I should get to the farming committee meeting before I'm late, anyway," her father said, before Dahlia had to send him away. "Dahlia . . ." He hesitated. She braced for a last question or disappointed sigh. "This is the first time Eiderlee's opinion has ever been sought, instead of our taxes being set by the royal house and collected without question or explanation. And I do like knowing the woman in charge of making decisions here knows a duck from an ox. I was never sure the Terre did. I just worry that, in a place like this, and a group like your assembly, a young lady from the country might be seen as an easily manipulated pawn. I know you're not. But if they don't know that yet, and they find it out later . . . Please be careful."

"Don't worry, sir," Gobe spoke up cheerfully. "I've got a pig-sticker on me. I wouldn't let anyone get to her."

Her father's warning and Gobe's casual promise of loyalty made Dahlia's throat tighten. She wasn't able to respond before her father excused himself and the guard stepped forward—one of the palace guards, Dahlia noted, a woman named Tealyn, who had taken initiative to propose and organize an expanded police force when ill-willed groups had taken to causing trouble in areas where storm and fire had left large swaths of neighborhood damaged and abandoned.

"Thank you, Gobe," Dahlia managed to say before the young man raced off again.

The youth shrugged. "You've been good to us," he said simply. "I'll let the assembly know you'll be late."

"Permission to report, Miss President?" Tealyn asked once Gobe was gone.

She winced at the title. How had *that* one made it into the rest of the population? Dahlia had thought of it as a joke when one of the Tamari had suggested a vote to make her official president of their assembly, in acknowledgement of the work she did. She had waved off the suggestion and returned them all to more important tasks.

"Permission granted," she said.

Tealyn was pale, and a bit green, and her eyes were just a bit too wide. Dahlia wanted to ask her to sit, but had already learned that such a request made guards trained for work in the palace uncomfortable.

"What's wrong?" Dahlia asked instead, anxiousness twisting through her when Tealyn didn't immediately speak.

"There's been a murder. I think it's a murder." Her voice shook.

"What?" The world spun around Dahlia, and she put a hand onto her desk to steady herself.

"I found . . . we were patrolling, and we found a body."

"And you came to me?"

"The royal house has domain over that kind of crime," Tealyn explained. "Over any crime involving magic. We've always been ordered to report any suspected sorcery to them and defer to their judgment." Tealyn spoke rapidly, as if struggling to put sense into her words while her anguished eyes made it clear she had seen something horrible. "We need someone with power to investigate in order to know for sure, but any sorcerer at the Cobalt Hall is a suspect. We haven't even been able to identify the body."

"Calm down," Dahlia said, conscious of the possibility of eavesdroppers right outside the door. "We'll . . ." They would what? "What makes you think magic was involved?"

"The body was . . . I don't know how any person

could do damage like that," Tealyn said. "I spoke to the medical examiner, and he couldn't come up with a weapon that could do it. Some of the injuries looked like they had been made by an animal of some sort, but if so it was nothing native to Kavet. We thought . . . maybe the Osei . . ."

"Where is the body now?"

Tealyn was starting to calm down now that she had passed the news up the chain of command. Dahlia, meanwhile, felt like that chain had wrapped around her stomach.

"Down dockside," Tealyn replied. "It was hidden by some crates of supplies until the workers shifted them this morning. We had to move it a little so the examiner could look, but we didn't do anything else once we realized there was probably sorcery involved. I have several others keeping workers away so they can't see the scene."

"Good." What now? "I don't see any choice but to speak to one of the followers of the Napthol. Someone with magical power needs to look at the body if sorcery was indeed involved. Meanwhile, you'll continue your investigation?"

Dahlia spoke tentatively, the last few words more a question than a statement, but the guard nodded solemnly, seeming comforted by her attempt to take charge.

One more tangle, she thought. The Osei. The ice. The fire. And now this. And they all kept looking to her to tell them what to do. Longingly, she remembered when she was just a teacher, when she had a clear answer for every question and no one ever came to her to help organize something more complicated than the harvest ball.

CHAPTER 25

HENNA

Henna sat, back rigid, in her place at the high table. Maddy was at her left, then the Order of A'hknet woman, Gemma. On the other side of the table, Celadon was looking through his notes while Jade and Mikva, representatives for the Silmari and Tamari, discussed the supplying of ship rations. Two seats at the table were currently empty: the head where Dahlia would sit, and a chair next to Mikva that was always left open as a courtesy to Kegan, though he rarely chose to attend unless he had a particular interest in that day's agenda. The Osei representative had been left behind in Kavet when Verte had been killed, seemingly abandoned by his masters; Sepia had taken him in, and when the Osei had sent new demands three weeks ago, Kegan had returned to their service and joined the assembly as their ambassador.

Between Kegan and Mikva, Henna sometimes found it difficult to look at that end of the table. Mikva returned the favor; since their first, heated meeting about three weeks before, Henna didn't think the Tamari captain had ever willingly met her gaze.

This room, with its vaulted ceiling and purple-veined stone floor, was used infrequently these days, but she still associated it with joy and light. Back when the Cobalt Hall was the royal seat of the country, there had probably been lavish balls in the great hall, but the Order of Napthol primarily used it for the celebrations of welcome when newcomers entered their midst, and ceremonies of initiation when novices declared themselves full members of their Order.

The high table, set on a raised platform and reserved for the guest of honor's closest friends and family, had never seemed uncomfortable before. But now, Henna shifted, trying to find a comfortable position without making her pain obvious.

"If you need to miss this meeting—"

Henna shook her head, trying to cut off Maddy's sympathetic words before the others at the table heard them.

Too late. Celadon asked, "Are you all right?"

His tone was more wary than solicitous, as if he worried she might have some disease he could catch.

"Just a little under the weather," she answered. "I slept poorly. I'll be fine," she added firmly to Maddy.

Maddy had wrapped the bandages. She knew Henna wasn't "fine." She also knew how deeply Henna regretted the last time she had avoided a political event due to her personal discomfort, even if her presence probably wouldn't have changed the outcome of events.

Probably.

They all looked up as Gobe mounted the platform to the table. He announced, "President Indathrone is delayed by important business. She's gone to check something con-fi-dential out."

He drew out the last word, as if it were a fancy term he was excited to have an excuse to use.

At first Henna had wondered what possessed Dahlia to take the semi-literate, orphaned scamp on as her personal secretary, but she had to concede these days that it had been a masterful stroke. In doing so, Dahlia had captured the hearts and therefore loyalty of the usually fickle members of the Order of A'hknet. When she needed critical news relayed, she turned not to the severe Quin preacher or the lofty Silmari aristocrat—both of whom were rumored to be her lovers—but to an Order of A'hknet boy. She trusted him, when so much of the world distrusted and dismissed anyone who wore A'hknet's sigil.

"*President* Indathrone?" Jade chuckled. "You know she hates that title."

Gobe gave a well-practiced, to-the-Abyss-with-it

smile. "She likes it," he insisted. "She just thinks she shouldn't, because she thinks it makes her disloyal to the royal house."

"I heard there was a farmer who went to confer with her before the agriculture meeting," Celadon said. "Is there anything we should know about that?"

Gobe shrugged. Henna recognized the overly casual posture and predicted he was about to bait Celadon, just before he said, "That was a personal meeting. They seemed very . . . friendly." As if Celadon's expression hadn't gained new lines, Gobe continued. "He's a well-regarded, influential man from her hometown. But the conversation was private."

"Of course," Celadon said, flatly.

"Oh, for Numen's sake, it was her *father*." Maddy's voice was sharpened, Henna knew, by her own concealed pain. "I met him when he came in. Is there anything else we should discuss while we're here, or should we delay this session until Dahlia returns?"

Predictably, a half-dozen members of the assembly surrounding the high table stepped forward then to bring up their own grievances and ask to have them added to the agenda. Celadon jotted them all down while Gobe listened to each question and concern with a keen expression that told Henna he was memorizing every word.

Finally, she was able to flee.

The public had been given permission to use the grand hall, a few of the smaller ground floor conference rooms and offices, and the front foyer, but they were still forbidden from the personal areas of the Cobalt Hall. Therefore, Henna found only others of her own kind in the kitchen.

"Would it be irresponsible to take a nap?" Maddy asked, joining her a few minutes later. She could have been speaking Henna's thoughts aloud.

Feigning strength when every movement tugged on hidden cuts and burns was exhausting, physically and mentally. Each twinge of pulled, damaged flesh down her back and legs reminded Henna of recovering from the debilitating lashing she had received after her first, failed attempt to escape from the Osei.

Had she thought *those* wounds, *those* scars, were bad?

Then there were the nightmares. She couldn't remember the last time she had slept soundly—before Festival, surely.

"Though I need to eat something first," Maddy continued, "and see how Clay is doing."

The rambunctious toddler spent most assembly days with Helio, Dove, or Lyssia. Maddy had tried leaving him with a mundane babysitter, one of the palace servants who had been looking for work he could do, but they had quickly discovered that Clay had just enough power to make life interesting for someone without sorcery.

Staring without interest at the loaves of fresh, nutty bread waiting on the counter, Maddy pulled off the elbow-high gloves she had taken to wearing.

Doing so revealed a series of marks up her right forearm, dark patches left behind by frostbite. There were more down her back by her left shoulder; Henna had helped her salve and bandage them a fortnight ago.

"Any better?" Henna asked.

"They still ache a little, but not so bad," Maddy replied. "Yours?"

Henna winced at the question.

"Let me see."

Henna allowed Maddy to lift the back of her shirt, to examine the blistered burns running up and down her spine and across her shoulder blades, on top of the scars and tattoo that had long ago marked that skin. In addition to those, there was a row of thin but long cuts arranged like claw marks on the right side of her rib cage. Like Maddy's, the wounds had inexplicably appeared during the night.

"I'll help you salve them," Maddy said. "Yours seem to be some of the worst."

Henna wasn't sure that was true. While her injuries extended over more of her body than anyone else's, Lyssia had lost the vision in one eye to frostbite, and Helio, whose cold magic was as powerful as Maddy's, had started walking with a pronounced limp.

"Henna?" Another of their ilk, a young man who Henna knew had burns all down his left side but thankfully no serious claw marks, poked his head in the door. "Indathrone wants to speak to you."

Henna sighed and tucked her shirt back into place.

Maddy had a wonderful salve that took most of the pain away for hours, but she would have to wait until later to use it.

At least Dahlia was doing a good job, so far. Henna had considered taking charge when Madder and Celadon had nearly come to blows in the Turquoise. She thought she could have made the Silmari and Tamari and the followers of A'hknet respect her leadership. The Quin would have been tricky to work with, but she could have managed Celadon as long as he continued to attempt to be reasonable.

But she had stepped back, and made a point in front of the other followers of the Napthol to look to Dahlia Indathrone. Because she remembered a vision, the first time she had seen the girl.

You have no power in the traditional sense, the sense of magic, but you have a strong destiny . . . You aren't meant for the Order, but you will walk its halls.

After Verte had died, Henna had railed against her power and its useless prophecy. Why had it shown her the blood if she couldn't prevent it? She had demanded answers from Helio, from Dove, from anyone who could hear spirits or had any hint of prophecy within them, but the dead held their silence and visions remained blank.

Only when Henna had seen Dahlia's rise as a leader had she understood: Her power hadn't shown her a way to save Verte, but the path to save *Kavet*. If Dahlia hadn't been with Verte that day, she wouldn't have been in a position to bridge the gap between the Quin and the Order of Napthol, or any of the other groups that had joined the fledgling government.

Henna found Dahlia in her office, her face grave and her body vibrating with tension.

"What's wrong?"

"I—" Dahlia had to visibly gather herself. "We need your assistance, in a confidential manner."

"You have it, of course."

"There's been a murder." The words, spoken so softly and calmly, seemed even more crude coming from this young woman. "The guards and a medical examiner believe magic was involved, so I need someone versed in sorcery who can inspect the scene."

Murder.

Henna had been called by the royal house to help on scores of projects, so it hadn't seemed strange to join the governing council. This was another matter, a task she wanted to call someone else's responsibility.

Whose?

If it was murder, Dove's power with the dead could help them investigate, but Henna was in a better position to initially assess whether sorcery was a factor and what kind had been involved. She wasn't overly skilled with cold or old magic, but she would be able to read either if necessary, while Dove almost entirely lacked hot magic.

"I will help," Henna said.

Even before Verte's death, she had seen her share

of horrors, some among the Osei and many in visions. One more could hardly scar her worse.

Or so she thought.

Yours seem to be some of the worst, Maddy had said just before Henna came here.

Not anymore.

The body had been found outside, but moved inside a warehouse at some point after the first report went to Dahlia because flies had started to gather in thick swarms in the summer heat. It wasn't an improvement. The flies still came, and now the stench was stifling as well, a reek of decaying blood and spilled viscera that made Henna's gorge rise even before she steeled herself to step forward and look.

The phantom beast that had slashed Henna's ribs had sliced into this poor soul's body, laying open organs blistered with frostbite marks, as if the animal's claws had been impossibly cold. One side of his face was swollen and black; the other was as pale as snow in death, but otherwise untouched except by spattered blood.

She lifted a trembling hand to shut Helio's remaining eye, once gentle brown but now flat and gray. The lid wouldn't move.

"Is that—"

Bile rose in Henna's throat. She shouldered Dahlia aside, and raced outside to vomit into the alley.

"I'm sorry," Dahlia said. "I didn't know if I could damage magical evidence, if I came on my own first. I didn't realize it was someone you—"

"No." Henna managed the weak word before she retched again. "You needed to call one of us in. You agreed to lead. You did what you needed to do."

She struggled to catch her breath and make her head stop spinning. Helio. Clever, discreet, insightful, kind Helio.

Dahlia came by her side and matter-of-factly held Henna's hair back as she lost all the food she had eaten so far that day. Vomiting pulled at burned and torn muscles, and she fought not to scream against the pain—and the fear.

Which of them would be next?

Dahlia rubbed her back in a gesture that was certainly meant to be calming, but only made a squeak of pain escape Henna. She recoiled, and declared, "I need to show you something."

"Did you see—I'm sorry I have to ask, but did you see any magic on the body?"

Henna nodded. "But it isn't what you think. Please, come with me. I don't want to be overheard."

Once they were in another empty room, Henna tried to explain in simple terms an untrained mundane would understand.

"Magic killed him," she confirmed, "but it wasn't murder."

"I'm sorry, but I don't understand," Dahlia said.

"There's something wrong." That much was obvious, with a body just upstairs, but Henna began there. As she considered her own wounds—*yours are worse than most*—and what she had just seen, she felt hysteria trying to worm its way into her again. "With the Order, I mean. Since the storms, our members have started having nightmares, fits like night terrors. Often we wake, marked as if we had been attacked. For some of us, it comes in the form of claw marks and burns. Others wake coughing, lungs convulsing. Some have lost feeling in fingers or toes due to inexplicable frostbite. We've been trying to protect ourselves, but haven't been able to stop it. Now I fear . . . no, I'm certain that whatever has been afflicting us is what killed Helio."

Helio had been involved in many of the early meetings, but had mostly preferred labor to politics. He had been working on dock repair the last few days. He must have dozed off down here, exhausted from hard work and the sleepless nights. Had he woken when the magic savaged him, or had he gone into death without ever feeling the pain?

Dahlia winced at the name, but then her eyes widened as she considered the implication. "If this is an escalation of an ongoing problem, it's likely to happen again. Randomly?"

"Not randomly," Henna said, too loudly, to cover the beating of her heart in her ears. "I haven't seen any of the Quin covering their arms, haven't seen the

Silmari or Tamari flinching when someone claps them on the shoulder. The Order of A'hknet tends to be private, but I've spoken discreetly to some of their small-magic users, and they don't seem affected, either. It only affects those of us who use hot or cold sorcery."

"Helio was one of your strongest cold magic users, wasn't he?" Dahlia asked. Henna couldn't remember when that had been mentioned in their meetings—probably sometime when they talked about how to allocate resources. Dahlia had a mind like a flytrap. "Are the most powerful of you being most strongly affected?" Before Henna had a chance to respond, Dahlia followed the generic question with a more personal one. "You, Maddy, Dove—are *you* all right? Is Clay in danger?"

"We're—" Her throat tightened, strangling back the words. Dahlia hadn't asked about one of their most powerful hot magic users, Naples, because he had disappeared from his sick bed and hadn't been seen since. She didn't know him. Now, Henna would never be able to stop herself from imagining his body, ripped to pieces and rotting in some quiet place few people ever visited—

No. She couldn't think about it, not without going mad.

"Clay hasn't shown any signs of injury or even nightmares," Henna said. "The rest of us—" Again, she couldn't find the words. *The injuries down my back look very similar to the ones that sliced across Helio's chest and stomach. Maddy's frostbite scars on her hands and arms are the same as the ones on Helio's liver and intestines.* "Those of us who use primarily old magic, like Dove, don't seem as strongly affected."

"What's causing it?"

"We've been calling it 'wild magic,' because it doesn't seem to be under anyone's control or connected to any intentional ritual. One theory is that it is emanating from the palace," Henna said. "Many of us believe we could learn more and possibly reverse the effects if only we could get inside, but so far no one has been able to breach the shields the Terre put in place."

Dahlia frowned. "It probably hasn't helped that you have all been putting your strength into other tasks. Why didn't you come to me sooner? I would never have asked you to focus your efforts elsewhere if I had known your people were being injured."

"Our alliance with the assembly in general, and the Quin in particular, was so tenuous for the first few weeks," Henna pointed out. "We felt it would be unwise to share details like this that might exacerbate the situation, and distract from more important work that needed to be done."

Dahlia set her jaw in a resigned expression Henna recognized from council meetings. It tended to precede Dahlia's cutting through an argument, calling out whichever council member's pigheaded stubbornness was causing problems, and declaring a resolution. Henna usually delighted in seeing it, since Celadon and Mikva were the most frequent targets of Dahlia's ire.

She was alone now.

"I know the Order of Napthol values its privacy," Dahlia said. "I respect that. But can you honestly tell me you wouldn't have reported these injuries to the Terre immediately?"

Henna swallowed thickly, and spoke aloud what they already knew: "You, and the council, are *not* the Terre."

"I know." Dahlia sighed. "I do not have the royal family's knowledge of sorcery, but even I can see that addressing this danger is critical. If it were just your adult members deciding to put other work ahead of their personal safety, that would be one thing, but you have minors in your care—Clay and two, or is it three, novices?"

Henna nodded, chastised. They had three novices currently who had not yet reached their majority. Two had had the nightmares, though neither had any injuries. Yet.

Dahlia continued. "I'll tell the guards to release the body to the Order of Napthol as next-of-kin. Then, I'm going to add an agenda item to the upcoming meeting explaining that the sorcerers of the Order of Napthol have been removed from all other duties. You need to focus your attention on opening the palace. Whether you share the details of your affliction with the assembly is up to you, but I expect you to report to *me* regularly."

Henna nodded again. There was one more thing

they could do, but she didn't know how Dahlia, who still openly identified as Quin, would feel about it.

After sharing her decision in an authoritative tone, Dahlia added more gently, "And please, remember, you and your order aren't alone. I can't be Terre, but that doesn't mean I can't help you, if you're honest and tell me what you need."

The words were an unwelcome barb, since Henna had just been considering whether or not to lie to her about the necessary next step.

She sighed. "If you mean that, there is one more thing we need to do before we try the palace doors."

Most of the guards that ringed the building less than an hour later were there to keep the area as private as possible. Henna had to admit, while they could have managed the same effect with sorcery given enough time and effort, Dahlia's assistance had allowed for a more rapid and efficient solution.

One of the guards was particularly familiar to Henna from numerous visits to the Cobalt Hall to see Dove. Verte had first put them together, though he had done so with the expectation that Dove would help Tealyn understand sorcery, not that they would develop a far deeper relationship after his death.

"I won't ask if this is safe for you, because I already know the answer," Henna overheard Tealyn saying to

Dove, as Dove prepared herself to look at the scene. They had covered most of the body, but Dove needed to be able to see Helio's face for her magic to work best, and there wasn't much they could do about the smell. "I will remind you that I'll be here waiting when you're done."

"I should never have taken the brand," another voice lamented, drawing Henna's attention away from the private moment. Wenge paced the warehouse vestibule, his hands crossed tightly across his chest.

Even though Wenge's power was gone, he was a fount of information about old sorcery, particularly that which dealt with the dead. Henna had brought him as an expert whose power couldn't distract Dove as she worked.

"The brand saved your life," Henna reminded him.

"Dove is powerful," Wenge admitted, "but I was more powerful. She hasn't been able to speak to Terre Verte. I was almost always able to summon any spirit I wished, even when they didn't want to come. What if she can't reach Helio? I could have—"

"You would not have learned anything because you would not have been here," Henna interrupted, less gently than she might have if this weren't such a familiar lamentation at such an anxious time. "Your power was killing you."

Wenge believed being able to force any spirit to speak to him showed his strength; Henna, like most of the Order, saw that only as a sign of his previous power addiction and willingness to burn his own life in pursuit of his sorcery. Dove probably could do the same, if she had equally little regard for her own physical and mental survival.

One reason Henna wanted Wenge to shut up was the fear that Dove might do just that: look at Helio's corpse, and let her desperation drive her to go too far. Tealyn was right. This *wasn't* safe.

But it was necessary.

The two women embraced briefly. Dove started to pull away, her power already billowing in a way Henna knew meant her mind was probably drifting into the deep, still realm of the dead. Tealyn tugged her back and kissed her firmly.

For a moment, Dove seemed confused. Her power condensed like water beading on glass—then Henna lost all awareness of it as she turned away, remembering the last time someone had held *her* that way.

Verte. Driven by her visions, she had given up her last chance to see him, dance with him, hold him, or taste his lips against hers.

"Something to remind you you're alive," she heard Tealyn said firmly. "You always tell me that's the greatest danger in this kind of work."

The others stayed behind as Henna and Wenge followed Dove to the alcove. Henna heard Dove swallow thickly, but she didn't gag at the stench, and her face remained calm as she knelt next to the body and touched Helio's cheek, avoiding the blood and seeking clear skin.

As Dove reached out with her power, her skin paled, going as gray and waxen as Helio's. Henna couldn't see her eyes, which were closed, but knew from past experience that they, too, would have the flat dullness of death.

Dove's breath rattled out. Then in. When she spoke, it was with a voice other than her own.

"I'm sorry." The rapid, weeping words resonated like the copper bells at the tops of country town halls, some of which could be heard even here in the distant city when the wind was right. "I'm so sorry. It is against all we believe to shed blood. We only want to protect you. You are my chosen. You named your Order in my honor and I—"

The words cut off abruptly. Dove gasped, a wheezing, labored sound that made Henna step forward, concerned she might be choking before another voice stole her lips, this one more familiar.

"They speak of the old war here," Helio said through Dove. "It ended thousands of years ago, but will never be over. They call us the protected, but we are the pawns and the prizes to be won. They are fighting over what they must do now. They—"

Another gasp, and the voices fell silent. Dove collapsed forward, onto Helio's body, which *squelched* and released another wave of noxious odor; Henna and

Wenge hastened to help her up before the congealed blood soaked through the blankets covering Helio's wounds and reached Dove's clothing and skin.

As they passed through the doorway, half carrying her, Dove's body jerked and went rigid. On one last rush of air, a new voice spoke with a command that made the glass windows ring: *"Find the Terre."*

CHAPTER 26

NAPLES

Question one: Where was he?

Naples opened his eyes and tried to assess this situation.

It was dark. That was all he could tell without moving. In theory he *could* move, but he didn't want to until he had answered question two: Who was he with?

He tried to remember what had happened before he fell asleep. It was getting harder and harder to do.

For the moment, he was lucid. That was good.

Though, a few hours ago, when he had been lost in the haze of flesh and sweat, that had been good, too—

No, he had to keep focused. He wasn't Abyssi, no

matter what the creature seemed to think would be best. He couldn't spend the rest of his life feeding, gorging on power until he was bloated like a tick, and then collapsing like a sated lion to sleep the day away.

Why not?

That voice did not belong to the sleeping man half on top of Naples, but to the Abyssi curled against his other side. It had one hand on his chest and was kneading like a kitten that had been badly weaned. Its claws drew spots of blood with each clench.

Feed, fuck, sleep, it said. *What's missing?*

At some point I should eat, Naples thought as he rolled over, upsetting the other man in bed with him, who let out a semi-conscious grumble before falling back asleep.

He drew the distinction between *feeding* and *eating.*

Why? the Abyssi asked.

Naples had learned how to talk with the beast silently some time ago, but he had also learned that it was nearly impossible to communicate with. Its range of understanding was too limited.

Because this isn't all I am.

The Abyssi leaned down and licked the beading blood from Naples' chest. The sensation, as always, sent a wave of heat through him and shot shivers across his skin, unfocused his eyes and curled his toes.

Stop that.

You were being boring, it said. *You try to draw lines like a Numini.*

I try to draw lines like a human being. Naples tried to sit up, and on one side the Abyssi pinned him, and on the other his bed partner—who in the three realms was he, anyway?—lazily looped an arm across his waist to hold him in place.

"Get off me," he said to both of them.

The other man shifted a little, enough to suggest he was starting to wake up, and asked, "Hmm?"

"Off!" Naples snapped.

The man edged away. "You're a grumpy bastard in the morning."

Off! he repeated to the Abyssi, who pulled back with a hiss. At last, Naples managed to sit up, saying, "Yeah," to the man beside him and trying his damnedest to remember who he was, or where they had met, or for that matter when, or where they were. He looked around, squinting to make out shapes in the darkness.

Finally, he had to turn toward the other man, who was still lounging in bed. "Where are we, who are you, and where in the Abyss are my clothes?"

"Excuse me?"

"Sorry for being blunt," Naples grumbled, but he was tired of this. "Can't remember how we got here."

"Aaa . . . fuck." The other man stood, fumbling for a lamp. "Look, if someone slipped you something, it wasn't me. I would never—I mean, you seemed—"

"Oh, shut up. I'm not going to try to get you arrested. I just want to know where I *am*."

"Western outskirts of Brockridge."

"Western what of where?"

"What *do* you remember?"

Naples could hear the other man struggling to get an oil lamp to spark, and realized he had not only shacked up in a town he'd never heard of, he was with someone who wasn't equipped with foxfire. Talk about slumming.

He moved forward impatiently, navigating in the dark, and needed only to brush fingertips over the lamp's glass in order to focus enough power to light the wick. The flame burst into life, violet-white for an instant before it settled into a more normal orange-yellow.

In its light, he could see the other man's eyes widen. He shifted back a bit.

"Don't tell me you're a Numen-damned *Quin*," Naples blurted out before he thought better of it.

"Not *quite*," the other man replied, with a very blatant once-over of Naples' still nude body, reminding him that the Quin frowned on such relations. "But I'm not an Abyss-damned sorcerer, either," he said, copying Naples' inflection.

The Abyssi started laughing. The Quin remained oblivious, blind to the demon in his presence. He drew a steadying breath and said, "Look. I noticed you at the town inn. You seemed pretty obviously on the prowl. You noticed my looking and struck up a conversation. You said you hadn't paid for a room yet, so we came back to my place. You don't remember any of that?"

Naples shook his head.

"And you don't remember getting to Brockridge?"

Naples frowned, trying to recall. "How far are we from the city?"

"About twenty miles. My name's Argent, by the way."

"Yeah, sure. Naples." Names weren't at the top of his priorities. "Clothes?"

"Somewhere around here."

They didn't talk for the next few minutes as they pulled on clothing that had obviously been pulled off in a hurry.

How long had he blacked out for? A day? Two? Longer?

I'm bored now, the Abyssi complained.

"Are you going to be all right?" Argent asked. "Do you need help to get back to the city?"

The city . . . yes, he should get back there. He should see how his mother was doing, and make sure she knew he was—

Had he had this conversation before? These thoughts? Naples was suddenly sure he had, at which point the question became, how many times had he woken like this?

"If you're going to faint—"

"I'm okay." He waved off the solicitous mostly Quin.

Argent hesitated a moment, then finally offered, "How about breakfast? We meant to have dinner last night, but it didn't happen."

Naples nodded. He had just been saying that he

needed to eat, hadn't he? His stomach wasn't making any complaints, but maybe it needed something to remind it of its purpose.

Maybe *he* needed something to remind him he was human.

As they left the bedroom, however, Naples received his next surprise. The shutters in the bedroom had been drawn, blocking the dawning light. Here they were open, revealing a pink and gold sky above sprawling fields.

Brockridge was apparently a farming community. Naples was no expert when it came to soil and plants, but he was bright enough to tell that there was no ice on these fields, no snow. The ground had been turned and planted. A haze of green suggested the tiny tips of new plants sprouting.

Naples stared in shock as Argent built up the fire in the wood stove—without asking for any help, though Naples could have accomplished the goal in an instant.

"What do you grow?" Naples asked, fishing for hints of how long had passed since the ice storm.

"Potatoes and wheat," Argent answered. "We also have turkeys. There are some fruit trees and vines on the property, but they're mostly supplemental, growing where there's room for them."

Naples took a moment to be impressed as his gaze skimmed over the fields and collection of other houses. "Do you own this land?"

Argent shrugged. "To an extent. It takes more than

one man to plant and maintain it all. The land's in my name, and I oversee the work, but at the end of the season, the crops are shared by everyone who works."

"Hmm." Trying to sound casual, Naples asked, "Did that ice storm do any damage out here?"

"Don't *remind* me," Argent replied as he came to stand beside Naples. He set a hand on the sill, looking out at the fields with obvious pride. "Thankfully we hadn't planted yet, but we spent weeks clearing debris and fixing fencing. Three tenants' roofs caved in. We were lucky enough not to lose much in the way of seed—a lot of other farms ended up with flooded root cellars or seed stores—but the winter wheat was hit hard, and the fruit trees—" He glanced at Naples and whatever he saw in his face made him cut off abruptly.

"*Weeks?*" Naples echoed.

Argent looked at him nervously.

"*What did you do to me?*" The Abyssi had temporarily disappeared, but Naples spun about, reaching out with his magic and demanding its return. "*Damn you, get in here!*" There was no immediate reply, except from Argent, who had backed in the general direction of the knife rack.

"I'm not crazy," Naples snapped.

"Of course," Argent replied. "On second thought, would you mind leaving before breakfast?"

Naples shook his head. "I'll go. I just—" He broke off, realizing suddenly that he wasn't wearing his knife.

"Fuck," he whispered, returning to the bedroom in long strides. Though, given the amount of time that had passed, he had no reason to believe he had only just misplaced it.

Lifting a hand, he summoned magic as simply as snapping his fingers, and immediately a globe of ruby-colored foxfire hung above him.

Well, the Abyssi had promised him power, hadn't it?

It hadn't mentioned a clause about losing weeks of his life.

"What are you looking for?" Argent asked.

"Knife," Naples replied bluntly, which made the Quin's eyes widen. "It's not a weapon, it's a tool. And it was a gift from the Terra."

"Black handle?" Argent asked as Naples proceeded to ransack the room in his search. When Naples nodded, Argent added, "You were wearing it at the inn, and when we got back here. A lot of travelers carry some kind of work knife, so I didn't think much of it. I'm sure it's around here somewhere."

He was speaking in the smooth, even tone of a man trying to calm a wild animal.

Close enough.

They searched together, Argent frequently glancing warily to the foxfire Naples had summoned. They turned the entire house upside-down, even rooms Argent swore they hadn't been anywhere near.

Looking for this?

Naples spun about as he heard the Abyssi's voice, to find the creature standing there, holding up the Terra's knife in a loop of one of its many tails.

"Naples?" Argent asked, seeing Naples' attention turn.

"*Hand it over,*" Naples said, holding out a hand to the Abyssi and trying to feel as confident as he made himself look and sound.

You were upset. It seemed wise to disarm you, the creature said, spinning the knife around his nine tails the way Naples had seen sailors spin blades around their fingers. *Are you ready to come play now?* It looked up at Argent, who was standing by in a remarkably protective fashion, as if prepared to come to Naples' aid if necessary. *Or do you really prefer the Quin?*

"Give me back the knife. Then we're going back to the city."

"Naples, who are you talking to?" Argent asked again. When Naples didn't reply, he added, "*What* are you talking to?"

The Abyssi moved forward, and though Naples stepped to the side to stay between it and Argent, it managed to move past him like smoke, as impossible to block as the air.

If you prefer, we can play here. Naples reached out to grab the Abyssi, forgetting the danger in such a move. The moment his hand closed on the creature's arm it pulled him close, wrapping him in darkness and fire.

He struggled to pull away and it placed a hand on his chest, setting claws to flesh not quite hard enough to draw blood.

It trailed those claws down his chest, ever so carefully. Naples tried to stay focused, but felt his back bow and his legs start to weaken.

He was only barely aware of Argent moving forward, stupidly trying to come to his defense against an enemy he couldn't see, until the Abyssi slashed out. The claws that had so carefully not pierced Naples' flesh turned Argent's chest to red ruin in a second.

The man fell backward with a scream, terror in his eyes.

Naples struggled against the Abyssi's grip, intending to go to the other man, but the creature's hold didn't lessen.

Abruptly, he realized why it was being so gentle with him. It wasn't threatening to bleed him, to hurt him—it was being very careful *not* to. It also didn't worry Naples would stab it; that wasn't why it had taken the Terra's knife away.

Blood was power, and while a good blade was indispensable, there were other ways to bring that crimson magic to the surface.

Naples spun in the Abyssi's arms and turned its own techniques against it. He pressed himself against its chest and let nature—if anyone could argue that such lust was natural—take its course. He let himself shiver at the feel of that silken fur sliding across his still bare chest.

Kissing an Abyssi was a sensation not easily described. Its mouth was shaped mostly like a man's, but the short fur that covered its face was softer than any beard or stubble, and Naples was very aware of the needle-sharp teeth that would probably take off his tongue if it dared to venture forth. That was fine, since once the kiss had begun, the Abyssi preferred to be the aggressor. It tightened its grip on him, and its heat became scalding.

Lust is as strong a power as blood. It had told him that when they first left the Cobalt Hall. It was one of his last clear memories. *If you won't hunt with claws, you can hunt with flesh instead.*

Naples rubbed a hand along the Abyssi's cheek, feeling the tiny spines that lined the top of its cheekbones, just under the fur. Those spines weren't quite sharp enough for his purposes, but as he broke the kiss, maneuvering so the Abyssi turned its head, his arm was close enough that its instincts took over.

Teeth sank into the meat of Naples' arm. He bit back a shriek as the pain hit him, just before blood cascaded down his skin and the Abyssi's smoke-black fur.

Blood was good. He could use it, and he did, to shove his power forward. *"Give me the knife."*

The Abyssi went rigid, fighting him. It didn't turn the blade over, but it couldn't stop him from taking it.

"*Now go.*" Again it fought, pushing Naples' own power back toward him, sending him stumbling a pace away. It didn't matter if Naples wasn't touching it directly anymore. His blood still coated its fur, and that was enough to force it to obey. "*Go! Leave me!*"

It disappeared.

Naples collapsed, too exhausted to do any more than clutch his injured arm to his chest. The bleeding had stopped, but the meat the Abyssi had bitten off would take longer to heal, and the wound still throbbed with pain. He was lucky the Abyssi hadn't stripped it to the bone.

He didn't dare stand up, certain he would faint. Instead he crawled on knees and one arm to where Argent lay, hyperventilating. The taint of the Abyssi clung to him.

"I saw it," the farmer said in a choked voice. "I saw it."

"It's gone," Naples replied. *For now*, he thought. He didn't delude himself into thinking he was strong enough to keep such a creature at bay for long.

CHAPTER 27

HENNA

It had been one day since Henna had stood by Helio's corpse and listened to the words from beyond the veil, words she was no closer to fully understanding. Who had that mourning, apologetic voice been? Who were the "we" who wished them no harm? All the souls of the dead? Or something more powerful—the creatures of the Numen and Abyss? What did it mean if *they* were fighting?

She didn't understand, but she stood before the palace doors, this time with a satchel of tools and almost every cold magic user from the Order of Napthol, including Dove, who insisted she had recovered well enough to help. Dahlia waited just behind, trying to be present, supportive, but unobtrusive.

Find the Terre. Those words, at least, had been clear enough that even Clay, back in the Cobalt Hall, had woken from his nap shouting them aloud. For the next day, he had repeatedly babbled portions of the conversation Dove had with the spirits in garbled toddler-tones that reminded Henna eerily of his pleas before not to be given to the Abyssi before Terre Verte's death.

Now, standing before the palace, they could all only hope the command had come from an entity that meant them well.

Every report since Naples' first fight with the door had made it clear that the power blocking it was cold. Henna doubted her hot magic sorcery would be helpful, but hoped her visions might be able to guide the others' actions.

She settled in front of the doorway with her rune stones in front of her and the other members of her order behind her, so she could use their power to enhance her own. She tried to clear her mind, the way she used to when sitting in the market, telling fortunes—before. Before it all began. Before she had seen wings in the sky and blood on the cobbles.

As she trailed her fingers through the stones, she could feel all those things: the Osei; Terre Verte's death; the blood of the Queen of the First house splashing across this door as the Terra summoned a demon to destroy the creature that had taken her child—

No!

Henna would not relive that.

Such pain. Cold seeped up her arm, an echo of so many years of loneliness, of deep aching sorrow.

Then, suddenly—

"Terre?" she whispered, her eyes shooting open.

There was just the door.

For an instant, she had been so certain that Verte was there, that he was standing in front of her. She looked back at Dove, wondering if that woman's power had allowed Henna to briefly hear the prince's ghost. But Dove was undisturbed, her eyes shut in concentration.

Henna put her mind back on the door, trying to let her thoughts skip idly to allow room for the visions. Between memories of the past and anxiety for the future, it was a struggle, but if she wanted any chance of protecting her people and stopping the dream assaults before another sorcerer was ripped apart in the night, she *had* to get into the palace.

She took a deep breath, shoving away the image of Helio's ravaged body. She stood, leaving the rune stones behind, and pressed both palms flat against the door.

Cold. The pain came from the door, so she let her thoughts rest on it. And yes, there was someone inside, but he was so far away. The barrier between them was thick, and set to keep out . . . the Terra? Had he set these walls against his *wife*, to restrain her?

To restrain what she had summoned?

That had to be it. These were cold walls, but they had been designed to keep out power like Naples' or Henna's. Most members of the Order of Napthol used hot power to some extent; even those of them most inclined toward ice, like Helio and Maddy, usually had some affinity for hot power as well. That explained why none of them could pass. They had been trying to use force. What they needed wasn't a battering ram, but a key—someone with the right flavor of power, unmuddied by experiments with other forms.

She happened to know just such a person.

"Someone get Celadon Cremnitz."

"*Who?*" Dahlia asked.

"Celadon," Henna repeated. It was possible Celadon had disclosed his power to Dahlia, but Henna wasn't certain. The Order of Napthol's alliance with the Followers of the Quinacridone was so tentative, they had all agreed it would be best to let Celadon keep his secret—as long as he wasn't actively endangering anyone. As long as the council included sorcerers, they could keep him from using his power unintentionally to manipulate anything.

"I think the shields set on the palace door might completely ignore him," she told Dahlia, hoping the Quin's ignorance of sorcery would keep her from asking too many questions. "He may be able to get inside, and if he does, doing so may breach the wards sufficiently to let the rest of us in. Do you think you can convince him to try?"

Dahlia frowned thoughtfully. She cast a look around at the crowd, possibly considering what she would ask without an audience, and deciding the same thing Henna had: less said here was better.

She nodded. "I will try."

She did better than try. She returned with a skeptical-looking Celadon in less time than Henna would have thought possible. At Henna's urging, he sighed, then put a hand on the palace's front door.

Only then did he hesitate. "If the Terre blocked this door, it was probably for a reason, wasn't it?"

Helio's lifeless eyes flashed in Henna's memory.

"It could be dangerous to open it, but I think it's *more* dangerous to leave it closed," she said. "Will you try? Please."

"We've been functioning without the Terre and Terra for weeks," Celadon argued. "Even assuming they're still *alive* in there, which seems unlikely, why do we need them, and why *now*?"

"The magic blocking this door is leaking into the rest of the city," Henna explained, struggling to keep her voice level as she said aloud what she knew perfectly well was exactly what most Quin feared about sorcery. "It's hurting people, only members of the Order who are sensitive to power so far, but there's no saying it won't be dangerous to your people, too.

So yes, the Terre probably put this shield in place for a reason, but it's *dangerous*."

Celadon nodded, slowly.

"And why am *I* the only one who can do this?" he asked.

Henna glanced pointedly to the mixed group of onlookers. "We can discuss that later." Too softly to carry beyond their group, she added, "Privately."

He still looked as though he might balk, for good reason. Celadon didn't understand his magic, or *want* to understand his magic; most days, he acted like it didn't exist, even though Maddy, Dove, and even Wenge had all urged him to accept help managing it.

"Please," Dahlia said.

That was all, but it seemed to be enough for Celadon. He put his hand back on the wide wooden latch of the palace's main double doors and tugged at it. Henna held her breath, waiting for him to strain against the impossibly locked door—or be thrown back, as Naples had been.

Instead, the heavy door, which had remained motionless for a month and a half, shifted.

Celadon, unaware he had already done something trained sorcerers had found impossible, set his shoulder to the door to use his whole body for leverage. It still seemed massively heavy, but it *moved*.

Celadon paused, He was breathing heavily, but instead of sweat, he had a fine layer of frost across his brow and upper lip. He reached up to brush it away, and Henna saw the flash of fear in his eyes as his fingers first touched the ice, before he swept it clear of his skin.

"It's open," he said.

Henna rushed forward.

Stupidly.

A blast of frigid air swept from the doorway and pummeled her like a shell slammed to the sand by storm waves. She was aware of nothing until her head struck the cobbles with a sickening *thunk* that brought a slew of violent afterimages:

Terre Verte, striking the ground.

The lash, ripping into flesh.

Osei claws, sinking deep into a ship's sides.

The old war, a battle so fierce it tore the worlds—

"Henna?" Maddy's voice interrupted the dazed visions. "Henna, can you hear me?"

Henna opened her eyes, then shut them against the glare of sunlight. The visions were fading like dreams.

"You hit hard," Maddy said. "Don't try to move yet." Her fingers worked along the back of Henna's head, painful at first but then cool and soothing as her magic sought and mended swelling and fracture.

Henna didn't try to stand, but she did speak. "I didn't think," she gasped. "I just wanted—" *to find Terre Verte, who we all know is dead.* "I acted on impulse. But I felt the doorway. It's *open* now, finally, just warded against hot power. Celadon shouldn't have a problem. I think your hot power is minimal enough that you could go, too," she added. "It wouldn't see you as a threat. Find the Terre." She reached up and touched Maddy's hand.

"You—"

"We have other healers. I'll be all right."

"I should go, too," Dove said, stepping forward, "if it will let me." She didn't need to add why; if Terre Jaune and Terra Sarcelle were dead, Dove was best equipped to learn what had happened and why. "And Dahlia should try."

"Me?" Dahlia had bravely conquered many difficult tasks in the last weeks, but in this moment she stared in horror at Dove. Given the amount of blood on the back of Henna's head, even after Maddy's quick ministrations, it was hard to blame Dahlia for her hesitation.

"I would rather not go back to the council with only Celadon and two sorcerers to report whatever we find," Dove said logically. "The others will trust you more than us." She slid a glance at Celadon that suggested she didn't want *his* report to be the only one the other Quin heard, either. Henna agreed.

"Be careful, all of you," Henna whispered.

Maddy grasped her hand, then stood. "We will be."

Henna nodded, then winced and gagged hard as her stomach rolled, warning her that she still had a concussion even if Maddy had healed the skull-fracture she had probably also suffered.

There were no further dramatics as each of the

chosen four stepped forward: Celadon first, with a level of bravado Henna had to assume was feigned, then Dahlia with considerably more hesitation.

Maddy stopped short as she tried to follow, as if she had encountered an invisible barrier, but nothing threw her back. She pressed a hand against empty air and whispered a quiet plea Henna couldn't quite make out, then drew a deep breath and said more loudly, "Terre Jaune, I am your child's mother, and you will *let me pass!*"

The barrier gave way so abruptly Maddy stumbled, nearly falling. Dove hurried behind her.

Then they were gone.

Lassia, Helio's last student, offered Henna a hand to help her stand slowly up. The woman's initiation had been only the week before, but she was a fair healer already, so Henna was grateful for her help.

They had made it only halfway across the plaza when Mikva emerged from the Cobalt Hall and hurried toward them. As usual, her gaze skipped over Henna as she searched the crowd, probably looking for Dahlia.

Eventually, she asked as if of the air slightly to Henna's left, "Where is Indathrone?"

Henna ignored her. Her head ached, and her skin felt wind burned and tingled with residual magic.

"Henna?" Mikva said, apparently resigned to the fact that Henna was the only council member available. "I need Indathrone."

Henna turned, a motion that made her head swim and forced her to lean harder on Lassia, and watched Mikva's gaze avert, as if she suddenly found the purple sparkles in the Cobalt Hall's exterior walls mesmerizing.

After all the nightmares and pain, after weeks sitting at a table with this woman almost daily, after identifying Helio's ravaged form, after otherworldly voices and a hostile door, Henna did not have the patience to coddle this Tamari sea captain.

"If you cannot be bothered to *acknowledge my existence*," Henna snapped, "I am not inclined to respect *yours*."

"I've offered to take you with us when the ship sails," Mikva said, as if that solved everything.

"And I have declined."

"Henna, you really should sit down," Lassia urged. "Let's go inside."

"You're one of the sea travelers!" Mikva exclaimed, switching to the native Tamari tongue as if that would make her point more effectively. "It is the worst kind of luck for a boucan to be land-locked."

"I'm *Kavetan*," Henna snarled back.

"Some of the other Tamari say your relationship with Terre Verte was why the Osei fought against him. You know they speak for the sea."

"The Osei killed Verte because he dared stand up to them," Henna responded, her fury so cold it made her body shake in a way that had nothing to do with her injury, "which is something the Tamari have *never* done."

"But—"

"Tell Dahlia Indathrone your theories about bad luck," Henna challenged. "See if she believes I am an asset at the council table, or a threat."

Dahlia won't believe it, Henna told herself. *She is wiser than that.*

Henna hoped.

"If you tell me where she is, I might do that," Mikva said coolly.

"She isn't available right now," Henna said shortly. "Is there something *else* I can help with?"

"The Osei," Mikva said. "Kegan received a message from the Third House—he says Dahlia has been waiting for it?"

After everything else, Henna didn't have any concern to spare for this latest news. The Osei slave always insisted that everything he had to say must be the council's top priority.

"I couldn't go after her if I wanted to," Henna admitted.

"And you *don't* want to," Lassia added, chastising. "You need to sit, and accept some healing."

That, too.

After all, it wouldn't do to be injured when she slipped into nightmares and her magic filleted her like a fish. Or when the Osei came back and finished the job they had started.

CHAPTER 28

DAHLIA

Where, Dahlia wondered, was old-fashioned misogynistic Quin paternalism when it might have *benefited* her? When had Celadon become someone who would willingly guide her with a pair of sorcerers into the clearly enchanted and possibly cursed palace?

Whenever he learned to respect you, she told herself. *Stop whining.*

Dahlia looked around the foyer, which was dimly lit by sunlight filtering through foggy windows, and a chill breeze passed over her; she shivered, wrapping her arms across her chest. It was summer outside, but in here it felt like the dead of winter. She wished she had worn a cloak, but didn't dare suggest going to get one for fear they wouldn't make it back inside.

"Does anyone know their way around here?" Celadon asked. "I only know the way to the prison and the petitioners' hall."

"I know the general layout," Maddy answered. "I think I can find the private wing and the ritual rooms. Those seem the logical place to start."

"We need light," Celadon suggested.

The palace, which had been bright and lively during the festival, was now cavernous with shadow. Lamps and foxfire orbs alike had gone dark, their glass stained with smoke. Maddy showed the way to the central hearth, but though Celadon found flint and tinder there, along with fresh lamp oil in a storage closet and a handful of candles, they couldn't seem to make a spark.

At last, Maddy pulled a coin-sized sphere of foxfire out of her pocket, and they groped their way forward by its faint, flickering illumination, which turned the rich carpets and paintings to dull shades of gray.

The more they walked, the more Dahlia felt as though she was exploring a tomb. Even their footsteps were muffled by the stale air as they ascended the stairs and entered a wing of the building Dahlia had never seen.

"It's getting colder," Celadon observed.

"The door to the temple should be somewhere

around here," Maddy said. Her voice was husky, as if her throat were tight and dry. She put a hand to the wall and Dahlia saw her shiver. "It's normally hidden, though we might be able to—"

"This?" Celadon asked, looking at what appeared to be a blank wall.

Maddy crowded closer, peering at the space in the dim light. "Where?"

"Here," Celadon said. "It's right . . . you don't see it." He looked at Maddy, and then at Dahlia, who shook her head. "Why can I see it?"

Maddy sighed heavily. "It's hidden from those without magic, and Jaune has set up some kind of barrier against those with a certain *type* of magic. Your power is closer to his."

"It is not," Celadon protested, an indignant reflex.

Dahlia expected him to add more, to argue against the suggestion he might have *any* kind of magic, but he didn't.

Stunned, she reached out a hand to pause them all. "What magic?" she asked.

Celadon's expression dropped as if she had slapped him, and he averted his eyes. "Nothing I chose, I assure you," he mumbled. "I'm not even convinced it's true." His words sounded more desperate than defiant, and his downcast gaze betrayed that he *did* believe it, much to his shame.

"This isn't the time to argue. You have power," Maddy said. "Specifically, you have what we call cold magic sorcery. That's the same kind I use, but yours is . . . *purer*, I suppose, because you've never worked with old magic or hot magic. That's why you could open the front door, and it must be why you can see *this* door when Dove and I can't. Now, can you see how to open it?"

"With the knob?" Celadon suggested sardonically.

He reached out, and as he motioned as if turning a knob, Dahlia finally saw the outline of a doorframe, so faint she might have assumed it was a trick of her eyes if it hadn't been pointed out to her.

"It's stuck," Celadon complained.

"Locked?" Maddy asked.

Celadon shoved with all his strength at the invisible door with an *Umph*, before reporting, "I don't know. The knob turns, but it feels jammed."

Maddy stood beside him. She leaned against the wall and crooned, "Jaune? Are you in there? Can you hear me?" She looked back. "Dove, do you sense anything?"

Dove shook her head. "I've been listening," she said. "I should be able to hear echoes of the Terre ancestors who spent their lives and deaths in this building, but there's only a ringing in my ears. *Something* is here, but whatever I'm hearing isn't a ghost."

"I'm tired of fighting doors." Celadon pushed Maddy out of the way, then flung his body against the supposed doorway and demanded, "Open, you Numen-cursed thing!"

As his shoulder struck what appeared to be solid stone, the archway shimmered. Celadon flew through the stone as if through water. Dahlia darted after him without thinking, and though she flinched when she should have struck the wall, she passed through without injury.

She emerged on the other side regretting the valiant act, however; it was so cold here that her breath hung heavy and white before her. She crossed her arms snugly across her chest, but couldn't stop from shivering. Maddy and Dove, when they followed a moment later, did the same.

Celadon, who had fallen into a pile of frost-covered books, pushed himself up. Unlike the rest of them, he seemed unaffected by the cold. He looked around with consternation, stopping his scan of the room when his gaze reached another door, this one seeming etched in ice and snow on the wall. It cast a pure, silvery light that made Dahlia blink, blinded momentarily by its glory.

"I suppose *that* door is next?" she asked.

Maddy nodded. "It must be his private sanctuary. The Terra and the prince should have them, too—"

"Here's the Terra's," Dove said in a tight voice. She was standing in front of an archway beyond which Dahlia could see only faint shadows. "I still can't hear Terre Verte or Terre Jaune, but I can hear *her* now. She's—*oh*." Dove's voice cut off with a strangled cry. "You work on *that* door," Dove said, gesturing toward the ice-encrusted door. "I'm going to help the Terra." She stepped through the dark doorway.

Dahlia briefly considered following, then immediately decided no power in the mortal realm could induce her to step through those shadows, which seemed to have devoured Dove.

Responding to Dove's directions with a brusque nod, Celadon brushed snow from his clothing and strode up to the icy door. Upon closer inspection, it didn't look like a real door—there was no knob or latch, just ornate paneling painted by frost—but then again, Dahlia hadn't even been able to *see* the last one.

The instant Celadon's fingertips touched the surface, he jumped back with a startled hiss.

"What happened?" Dahlia asked.

Celadon shook himself, stepping forward again. "It felt like something stung me."

Celadon and Maddy both jumped then, Celadon whipping his head around, looking about as if he had heard something. "What was that?"

Dahlia looked around, too, even though she knew it was stupid. Why had she come here? She wasn't a sorcerer; she was a *liability*. She had seen what this power had done to Henna when she tried to walk through the door. Worse, she had seen what it did to *Helio*.

"Jaune?" Maddy asked, moving toward the door. "Oh, sweet Numen, he's trapped in there. I hear you, honey." She reached for the door, pressed a hand to it, closed her eyes, and leaned forward as if listening.

"How in the three realms did he get *trapped?*" Celadon demanded, shaking his arm and flexing his fingers.

"Maybe when he warded the palace to contain . . . something else." There was a hitch in Maddy's voice, as if she had changed what she was about to say at the last minute. "But that's gone now. We need to help him."

"Are you all right?" Dahlia asked Celadon.

"Pins and needles," he answered. "It feels like I stuck my arm into a bundle of jellyfish."

Dahlia wanted to ask about more than his physical state, about his apparent magic and how he felt about being forced to use it, but now wasn't the time.

"Jaune, honey, you have to help me," Maddy was saying. "I can hear you . . . I want to help you . . . please . . ."

"A desperate woman can be a dangerous creature," Celadon said softly. "I'm not quite sure I trust her." He looked to the opposite doorway, where Dove had gone.

"Neither would I," Dahlia said truthfully, "but Henna was the one who sent us here, not Maddy. She has valid reasons to think we can't ignore this any longer, and I agree with her."

"What do you know that I don't?"

Maddy let out a frustrated cry. "It's no use. It's blocking me. Celadon—"

"I'll try," Celadon said reluctantly. "Move aside."

Maddy moved enough to let him press a hand to the door. He winced, but this time he didn't draw back. Dahlia saw Celadon's body tense as he pushed, with no visible result.

"Push with your power, not just your hands," Maddy advised.

Celadon gave her a look as if she had just suggested he swallow hemlock.

"It's not going to kill you," Maddy snapped.

"Let's assume I'm willing to do this," Celadon bit out. "How would I go about it?"

"Oh." Maddy seemed to deflate a little. "Just . . ." Maddy chewed her bottom lip thoughtfully. "You have power. You've used it already, plenty of times, intuitively. Your will can direct it. Many people who use cold power find it helps to chant, or otherwise use words to focus their intent."

"You want me to *talk* to the door?"

Maddy shrugged. "Try it?"

Celadon shut his eyes as if trying to compose himself. "This is absurd," he muttered, but the words had the sound of surrender in them.

This time he put both palms against the door without flinching. He closed his eyes and Dahlia saw his lips quirk, as if he were struggling to take this exercise seriously.

When after a period of silence there was no response, Celadon opened his eyes. He cast Dahlia a look she thought was supposed to appear amused, but which revealed anxiety and disquiet simmering beneath Celadon's confidant façade.

He turned back to the door.

"Hello, door," he said. "This is a little uncomfortable. If you would spit the Terre out already, we could leave you alone."

"Celadon," Maddy sighed.

Celadon cleared his throat.

"Open. Open, open," he said under his breath, his gaze fixed on the icy patterns of the closed doorway. "Open for the Napthol lady, would—*shit*." The curse came as the doorway shifted, patterns becoming brighter.

"That's it," Maddy breathed.

"His arms," Dahlia whispered to Maddy, as blooms of frost first covered Celadon's hands and then started crawling over his wrists.

"It's an expression of the power," Maddy answered. "It won't harm him."

"Okay, door," Celadon continued, voice tight. "This hurts like a son of a bitch, so let's finish this, all right? Open. Now. The Terre made you, so *open* and let him pass."

The doorway brightened further, until Dahlia had to avert her gaze. From the corner of her eye, she saw Dove emerge from the other room, gray-faced and panting.

Dahlia hastened to help the other woman to a chair.

"She's dead," Dove said. "I don't know where her body is, but I could feel her death in the room. She went peacefully . . . somehow. Peacefully, in blood and pain and—I don't understand. I tried to speak to her, but it was even less coherent than what I could get from Helio."

Celadon let out a deep, shuddering growl, drawing Dahlia's attention back to him.

"It's going to hurt him." Dahlia couldn't help but remember the blackened wounds like frostbite that had marred Helio's corpse.

Maddy shook her head. "He'll be fine. Celadon, it's responding when you invoke the powers it knows. The Napthol, the Terre. Try—"

Celadon either wasn't listening, or didn't need to be told. "Open, damn you!" he shouted. "Open in the name of . . . in the name of the Numen and the Numini. Open in the name of Madder of the Order of Napthol. Open in the name of Clay, the child of Terre Jaune."

Each name made the doorway glow, but Dahlia forced herself to return to Celadon's side despite the blinding glare. If it seemed like the doorway was harming him, she could shove him away from the door, and hope that broke the connection.

Dove pushed to her feet as well and drifted next to Dahlia as if in a trance. She whispered, "I hear them now. They have been trapped so long."

Instead of weakening, Celadon appeared to be gaining strength as frost wrapped his body and the doorway pulsed with silver light. His voice echoed, ringing like rain striking bells. "Open in the name of Celadon Cremnitz. Open in the name of Dahlia Indathrone. Open in the name of the Quinacridone and give me the Abyss-damned Terre or I swear I'll—"

Lightning struck.

Dahlia cried out as she fell, the stench of ozone assaulting her nostrils. Somewhere in the aftermath of the blast, she thought she heard someone calling her name, but she couldn't make out anything past the ringing in her ears and the spots in her vision. Then the darkness came.

CHAPTER 29

NAPLES

Again, Naples woke somewhere dark.

This time, though, there was pain. His joints felt full of hot sand when he shifted, his chest ached with each breath, and muscles in his back and shoulders twitched when he tried to push himself up.

Only the Terra's training allowed him to push past the sensations and struggle to his feet, then lift a trembling hand to summon foxfire.

He managed only a sickly yellow glow, but it was enough to reveal Argent's bedroom again. He was wearing pants this time, and someone had bandaged his arm where the Abyssi had taken a chunk out of him.

The door opened. "I thought I heard you moving

around in here," Argent said as he stepped through. With a pointed look to the foxfire, he added, "Hasn't that gotten you in enough trouble already?"

"What am—" Naples started to cough and had to try again. "What am I doing here?"

Argent sighed. "What do you remember?"

"I'm not—I didn't *forget*," Naples said, too sharply, considering it was a perfectly valid concern after their previous conversation. "The Abyssi tried to kill you, and I'm responsible for its being here, so why am I not out on my ass?"

"You fought it, you healed me, you passed out," Argent said. "I wasn't going to toss you unconscious on the street."

"I'm a danger to you."

"You're a danger to yourself it seems," Argent replied. "There's stew on the table, if you can eat."

Naples' head spun. Eat. He should try to eat. But not here. "I should leave before it comes back."

"If you can walk without falling, you can leave," Argent compromised.

Of course he could *walk*. He was standing, wasn't he?

Naples took a step forward and his legs trembled. They gave out and his knees hit the ground hard. "Damn it," he hissed. He shouldn't be this weak.

Argent came to his side and hooked an arm around his waist to help him up, careful of his injured arm.

Despite his state, the touch of flesh to flesh provoked

a response. Argent raised one eyebrow. "Your libido and your sanity aren't even remotely linked, are they?"

Naples tried to shrug, but it was a sorry effort. This weakness wasn't just blood loss, but lack of power. He had used everything he had to send the Abyssi away. And there was a source of power right here . . .

Argent dumped him in a chair at the kitchen table and shoved a bowl in front of him. "Rabbit stew," he announced. "Eat. Then maybe you can explain to me what is going on."

Eat. He had to eat. Food could also supply his body with energy, not the same kind of rich energy and not as fast, but it would work. He picked up the spoon with his left hand, regretting that he hadn't thought to offer his non-dominant arm to the Abyssi.

He had to force the first bite into his mouth, force himself to chew and swallow something that tasted like dust and ash, but then his body remembered what *food* was. The scent of the stew reached him at last. His mouth watered, his stomach grumbled, and he began shoveling broth and chunks of meat and delicious vegetables down his throat as if he hadn't eaten in—well, over a month, probably.

Dirt, the Abyssi called food like this, but Naples' body had finally remembered that it was human. At some point Argent put bread in front of him and he downed it instantly, using the last bit to mop the remnants of stew from the bowl.

"More?" Argent asked when Naples paused, staring at the bowl like a dog at an empty dish.

Instead, Naples leaned back, shaking his head. His stomach was so full it was painful, but this was a good pain, not magic and fire, but a stomach stuffed with nourishment.

"So," Argent said as Naples basked in the return of humanity. "You're a sorcerer. I'm guessing Order of Napthol, not one of the smaller sects. Obviously powerful. I'm no witch myself but I know what a foxfire orb like the one you summoned last time sells for, and I know that's because they're rare, but you snapped it up like it was nothing. Also, you're close enough to the Terra to have received a gift from her. You've lost time, a lot of it if I'm judging your reactions right. And—" At this, he drew a deep breath. "If I'm not mistaken, you got into a fight with a demon. I'm not sure you *won*, but I don't think you lost, either."

"That's about the gist of it," Naples answered. "You sound remarkably calm about all this."

"I've had some time to mull it over," Argent said. "You've been in and out for two days. I'll admit I spent the first day mostly in shock. I might still be in it. But I had the sense to send someone to the city to bring one of your own people to help you. I know I am in way over my head."

"One of . . . my people. You sent someone to the Cobalt Hall?"

Argent nodded.

Naples wasn't certain how he felt about that. "Did you tell them my name?"

"Is that a problem?"

Quite likely, his mother was now racing toward this place full-tilt. He had been missing for—"Exactly how long *has* it been since the ice storm?"

"A little over six weeks."

He had known, yet even so, the information rocked him. Six weeks; a month and a half. Just gone. And he knew if the Abyssi came back now, with him this weak, it could easily dispose of Argent—and anyone from the Cobalt Hall who showed up—before pulling Naples back into its web.

After that stunt you pulled, I'm not sure you deserve me.

Naples stood, drawing the knife from his waist and turning toward the Abyssi.

It stepped back, its tails lashing angrily.

"Argent, you should leave," Naples said, keeping his eyes on the Abyssi as he spoke. "Right now."

Argent didn't question him; he was gone through the door in seconds.

The Abyssi meanwhile crossed to the stove, where it sniffed disdainfully at the last of the stew. *You're more than this*, it said.

"Maybe I don't want to be."

It smirked. "You can't help it." When the Abyssi spoke in Naples' mind, it felt like warm breath on the back of his neck. When it spoke aloud, the words resonated in his bones. "You are your power and your power is you. If you try to turn away from it, it will devour you. Or the Numini will. Or maybe I will."

It moved with impossible speed. The knife went skittering across the room and Naples was briefly airborne, until he slammed sprawled on the table. Crockery fell to the floor and shattered.

The Abyssi followed. Its eyes literally flashed, blue flame flickering in their depths, with anger and amusement.

"I gave you power," it crooned. "I turned Kavet into your personal playground. And what did you do? You turned that power against me!"

"You stole a month and a half of my life!"

"Stole." It snickered. "Listen to yourself, like time can be stolen. You have spent the time hunting, gaining power, learning your magic. You have spent the nights in lust and gluttony and the days sleeping deeply. I have taken nothing from you. Or do you think you could have fought me, as you did over the Quin, when first you called me?"

Naples remembered fighting the Abyssi. He also remembered the foxfire on which Argent had remarked. And he knew that no, he never could have done those things before, even after the Terra's instruction.

"Argent was good to me. I don't want him hurt."

"I have no reason to hurt him. He's barely better than dirt, anyway. I prefer richer fare." Very deliberately, it let its claws pierce the skin of Naples' chest. As always, with the pain and the beading of new blood came a rush of magic that made Naples' breath catch. He had lost power earlier, fighting the beast, but now as it leaned down to lick blood off his skin, its power—pure dark Abyssal magic—wrapped around him.

No. He wouldn't let himself be lost like this again.

He pushed against the demon. In response, it encircled his wrist with one of its tails.

"I believe you made an offer," it said.

"I did *what*?"

It licked his lower lip, and then ran its cheek along his like a cat. Lips close enough for Naples to feel smoky breath on his ear, it said, "You made an offer. And you're strong enough now you might even survive the follow-through. You probably will."

"I didn't—" Naples broke off with a yelp as its claws pierced his pants, and the thigh beneath.

"You pressed your body and your lips and your power against mine. And then you ordered me away. Did you think I was going to forget that?"

"You know I was just trying to—aah." It bit him, not hard enough this time to take flesh, but enough to steal his breath. It left a near-perfect circle of tiny dots from its pointed teeth, low on his stomach just above the waist of his pants. It licked the new blood away as it had the last, and this time the rasp of its tongue brought different blood in a rush. Hard, breathless, and sweating and shivering simultaneously, Naples nevertheless tried to push himself up.

The creature caught his other wrist, and then slapped his shoulders back down on the table.

He tried to push back with any power he could summon, but the Abyssi only shivered and rubbed its body against his. It moved upward and covered Naples' mouth with its own, while its fingers wrapped around the back of his neck to hold him in place. With the tips of the Abyssi's claws at his throat, Naples had no choice but to let it part his lips and turn the kiss into something full of possession and hunger.

When it pulled back, Naples sucked in droughts of air, filling desperate lungs.

"You do not," the Abyssi said, very clearly, very deliberately, "tease the Abyssi. You make an offer, you keep it. Now . . ." Its claws cut through the waist of his pants, slicing cleanly through the fabric down to his knee. "Let's see what a mortal body can take."

CHAPTER 30

HENNA

Henna accepted Lassia's ministrations, but despite the healer's admonitions, she couldn't keep still. She spoke with Gobe, who had custody of the letter from the Osei, had already ordered the fretting Kegan out until Dahlia returned, and threatened to do the same to Henna if she asked him questions he couldn't possibly answer because, "I'm not Dahlia Indathrone—or hadn't you noticed? I don't discuss her business when she's not around."

Henna pointed out this was Kavet business, and therefore *council* business, but Gobe maintained his loyalty to Dahlia above anyone else.

Another messenger arrived, a woman young enough

that her face didn't show the exhausted wear Henna would have expected given the quantity of travel-dust staining her rumpled clothing and tanned skin.

"I'm supposed to deliver this to one of the leaders of the Order of Napthol, and see you open it before I go," the messenger said. "It's urgent."

Actual Cobalt Hall business? Henna wondered, accepting the letter. "From where?" she asked, pressing a coin into the messenger's hand as she broke the seal. This kind of urgent message was usually a plea for help after a young person suddenly discovered a talent for sorcery in a disastrous way.

"Brockridge Farms. I rode most of the night to get here."

"Make sure you get some . . ." Henna was in the middle of offering food and a place to rest for the exhausted messenger, but she lost all coherent thought as she recognized the name in the first sentence of the scrawled, hasty handwriting: *Naples*.

> *I have a young man named Naples in my care. I believe he is a member of your order. His injuries are not life-threatening but I fear he may be in a more mystical danger, which I am not capable of assessing or protecting him from. I've enclosed directions. Please send someone immediately.*

Henna didn't hesitate.

If Maddy and the others found the king, queen,

or prince, alive or dead, Henna trusted them to deal with it without her help. As much as she wanted to be there, for closure if nothing else, Naples was alive—for now, anyway—and he *did* need her.

Henna left a note for Gobe telling him she had to attend to urgent business, and left the letter from Brockridge Farms with Lassia as further explanation. Then she packed a bag with some basic tools, took two horses from the stables at the edge of town, and rode as hard and fast as she could.

The trip took her a good part of the day. As she finally approached the long dirt driveway leading up to the main farmhouse, the lingering power buzzed around her like a swarm of gnats. Some of it felt like Naples' magic, but there was also another, more foreign power—a power she knew immediately did not come from the mortal realm. She had felt it only once before, when the Terra had summoned a demon to protect her son.

This much hot power should have been enticing, like a fine wine, but something in Henna quailed to accept it. Instead, as she pushed forward, she instinctively put up her shields, strengthening them with what cold magic she could evoke.

The front door was ajar, so she stepped inside, then followed the viscous ropes of magic through to the kitchen.

Henna almost screamed as she stepped into the room. *I'm too late.*

There was blood everywhere, the worst of it sprayed across the table like some obscene sacrifice, the congealing fluid nearly black with Abyssal magic.

Naples' power was like Henna's, magic of fire and blood—and that was what it had wrought.

Looking at it made the burns and slashes across her back sting anew.

She scanned the room desperately, searching for Naples, but almost missed him at first. He glowed with power, so intensely it was hard to focus her eyes and look past the magic to the man beneath.

He was curled on his side in a fetal position, blood slicking his skin. Claw marks dragged down his back and across his chest, and Henna could see trails of savage bites made by something sharper than human teeth across the meat of his shoulders. They were the same kind of wounds she and the other hot magic users at the Cobalt Hall had suffered, but more extensive than any she had seen.

She jumped with a yelp as the door banged open behind her, admitting a man she didn't know. He took one look at Naples and went pale, clutching at the doorway to steady himself.

"Who are you?" Henna demanded.

"Argent. I live here. I—you're from the Order? Is he . . ."

"He's alive." It seemed a miracle, but the steady pulse of his power was proof. "Can you get water? I need to clean him up before I can tell if anything is still bleeding." Henna had learned from personal experience the mystical wounds didn't bleed as long or as much as they should, but the deeper ones could still be dangerous if not attended.

Stay with me, Naples, she prayed. While waiting for Argent to return with water, she tried to examine him with her magic, but the power in the air was too thick for her to make out any details. All she could tell for sure was that Naples had not been alone here.

Again, her mind flashed to the beast the Terra had summoned. Was it a coincidence that she could feel the remnants of the Abyssal realm here so soon after forcing open the palace doors?

Argent retuned with a bucket of well-water and a handful of cloths. "Do you want me to warm it?" he asked.

"I'll do it." There was so much power in the air she didn't need tools; she put a hand to the tin bucket and focused her will on *heat*; it took only seconds to warm it to body temperature.

"How did he end up with you?" Henna asked Argent, as she knelt and began to carefully wash the blood from Naples' skin. The claw marks across his chest looked the deepest, but his power seemed to have successfully stopped most of the bleeding, and the skin around them showed no burns or blisters.

"We met a few nights ago," Argent answered. "He seemed fine the night we met. The next morning, he said he had lost time. He couldn't remember our meeting or coming back here, or coming to this town. Or anything, back as far as the ice storm." He started to shake as he continued, his gaze going distant. "And then . . . then . . ." He trailed off, locking his jaws shut around a whimper. "I didn't know what to do, except send that message."

Henna tried to imagine what Argent must have seen. Most of the Order's members had been struck while sleeping; given what Henna knew of Naples, it wasn't a stretch to imagine Naples in bed with Argent, and waking in a panic when the blood began to flow.

"I think he'll be all right," she told him gently. At least, he would live. How he would cope with the scars was another matter. "Do you have a blanket, something I can wrap him in?"

Argent nodded and went to fulfill her request without further question.

Naples woke as they were transferring him to the couch in the next room, wrapped in the softest blanket Argent could find. He gasped and his eyes opened, the pupils so dilated with pain that the copper was nearly hidden, giving him a look like one of the blind.

"You're okay," Henna said. "I'm here. You're hurt, but you'll heal."

"Henna," he gasped.

"I'm here."

"You should get out of here," he bit out. "It could come back. It could—"

"I'm not leaving you. Once you're strong enough to travel we'll bring you back to the Cobalt Hall, but until then—"

He pushed her away, and shoved himself to a sitting position.

"Don't try to stand," Argent advised. "You're hurt and weak."

Naples shook his head, black hair still matted with blood falling in his face. "Hurt, yes," he said. "Not weak." He closed his eyes, and as Henna watched, the bite marks along his shoulders faded to scars. The scars then softened to new pink flesh. The claw marks along his chest went next.

"Don't burn more power than you need to," Henna warned.

Naples ignored her.

The cuts down his chest and back didn't fade as completely as the shallower bite marks, but they closed. Did Naples realize he was doing something none of the rest of the Order could do at all? Injuries that deep even from a non-mystical source would have been nearly impossible to heal for most of the Order's healers. And there was no magic in the city of Mars that had been able to touch the nightmare-induced burns and slashes.

When had Naples become that much more powerful than the rest of them? Had the Terra's instruction made the difference? Or had something else happened in the last six weeks?

"If you're okay to ride," she said once Naples opened his eyes, "we should get back to the Hall."

He shook his head. "I won't stay here, but I shouldn't go with you. I don't want to put anyone else in danger."

"We're already all in danger," Henna said. "You're not the only one who's been injured like this. One of us has lost his life already. I was terrified I was going to find you the same way, and I swear I am *not* going to let you disappear again."

"It *killed* someone?" Naples went impossibly paler. "Who?"

"Helio." It was the second time she had bluntly informed him of a death he should have learned of in a gentler fashion, but it it was the only way she could convince him to come home with her, she felt no guilt. "You *need* to come *home*."

He nodded slowly, his eyes closed. "Then I'll come."

"I'll tell you everything that has happened while you've been gone," Henna said. "And I want you to tell me what you've been doing, too."

"Of course I will."

Henna never would have been able to say what tipped her off, since there was no change in his expression, but she had known Naples too long not to recognize that he had just lied to her. For whatever reason, he had no intention of telling her what he had gone though in the last six weeks.

This was not the moment to push the issue. "Your mother has been mad with worry over you."

At that, she saw genuine distress. "I'm sorry. I didn't mean to disappear the way I did."

Henna looked up at Argent, who had been standing out of the way, awkwardly looking between Naples and Henna. "I've got something you can borrow to wear," he said to Naples. "It'll be big, but it's better than nothing."

Naples nodded, eyes widening a little, as if just noticing that he was naked except for a blanket. "Thank you. You've been really decent."

Argent's lips quirked in a half smile. "You weren't bad yourself. Maybe after you're better you can come visit sometime—if you remember me, that is."

"You're memorable."

Henna's mind was somewhere so far away—the recent disasters, horror at Naples' earlier condition and relief that he was alive, fear and anticipation—that it took her a moment to recognize the verbal byplay as flirting. *Now?*

Such was the resilience of youth!

CHAPTER 31

DAHLIA

Dahlia?

Dahlia walked along an endless white beach, disoriented and confused. How had she come here? Where was *here*?

"Dahlia?"

A voice called her name and she turned, but there was just more crystalline sand. Her head spun. No matter what she did, she was always walking down a strip of beach, gently lapping waves presumably on her left and rolling white dunes equally likely on her right, but no matter which way she turned she wasn't able to face them.

It is not safe for you to see our majesty, little one. You still have work to do in the mortal realm. When that is complete, we will welcome you with open arms.

"Dahlia!"

Go, with our love.

This time when she turned, the world didn't just rotate with her. Vertigo struck, fierce and undeniable; all sense of up and down disappeared. She wasn't standing; she was lying on her back.

Opening her eyes took an effort. Her lashes felt gummed shut. How long had she slept?

Had she been dreaming? She thought she had.

"Oh, thank Numen," a voice breathed. Dahlia blinked furiously, struggling to focus her eyes. There were still spots in her vision, as if she had stared into something too bright.

Lightning.

At last, the afterimages started to fade and Maddy blinked into focus.

"Did the door open?" Dahlia asked. She was surprised to discover that her voice sounded normal, not raw. She had expected her throat to hurt. It seemed like a lot of things should hurt, but nothing did.

She wasn't numb, though. She could feel the sheets over her and the—

"Where am I?"

They weren't in the palace ritual room anymore, but in a small room with gray stone walls warmed by woolen tapestries depicting pastoral scenes of goats grazing in a rocky pasture. It wasn't a style Dahlia had seen anywhere in the palace, which tended toward more vivid colors and images of splendor and . . .

And white sand. Had she seen a beautiful white beach, somewhere? Maybe on a picture in the ritual room . . .

"Stay with me, Dahlia," Maddy said. "You've been in and out for over a day. You're in the Cobalt Hall now, in one of the unused rooms in the second floor living areas. We thought it best to bring you here to rest where no one would bother you."

"Thank you." Dahlia knew it was an honor that she'd been allowed into this sacrosanct area of the Cobalt Hall. "How badly injured am I?" There was no pain, but perhaps magic was subsuming it.

Maddy shook her head. "You have a few bumps and bruises from when you fell, but nothing serious. There was a blast of power when Celadon opened the door to Jaune's private ritual room. You have no experience managing magic or defending yourself from it, so it overwhelmed you. We had to spend the last day clearing the remnants of it from your body. Carefully," Maddy added hastily, seeing Dahlia's expression.

Dahlia tried to conceal her shiver of horror. She accepted that magic was not the all-consuming evil that many Quin believed it was, but she was also one of the few who knew exactly how dangerous it could be when uncontrolled.

"The others?" she asked, pushing herself up. "Is Dove all right? And Celadon?"

"Dove was dazed for a while, but she has enough experience to clear the excess power from herself on her own. Celadon and I both have enough cold magic that we weren't affected."

"What of the palace?" Having shaken off the last remnants of her dreams, Dahlia wanted answers. "Did you learn anything that can help you with the wild power that's been harming sorcerers?"

Maddy touched Dahlia's brow, then her cheek, like a mother checking for a child's fever. Whatever she found must have satisfied her, because she took a deep breath and answered the questions. "The seals on the palace are broken. The doors are all now open, and the other strange phenomenon—like the inability to make a spark—have stopped. It seems safe, so Sepia is putting together a proposal to make use of palace space to house some of the stranded Tamari and Silmari."

That sounded like Sepia, organized and efficient as always.

"We don't know for sure what effect this will have on the wild power that's been harming us, but there were no problems last night. And we—" Maddy's voice broke, revealing for the first time the emotion beneath the calm composure of a healer and a member of the council. "We found Jaune's body. We believe he died from power exhaustion." She shook her head, as if she couldn't quite believe it. "It's rare, at least among well-trained sorcerers, but it happens if a magic user is too focused on their work and doesn't maintain their body in other ways. They burn all their physical resources to support their magic." She swallowed thickly, and cleared her throat. "It may be what killed the Terra, too, but we never found her body."

"Are you—"

Maddy interrupted Dahlia's inquiry, saying swiftly, "But we found Terre Verte. He's alive. Just barely, but it's enough, we think. His father must have spent all his power to heal him, but afterwards Verte didn't have enough strength to free himself of the shields Jaune put up to protect him."

"How is—" No, that question could wait two more minutes. "How are *you?*"

Maddy sighed, her body sagging as if the question had finally given her permission to abandon her stoic professionalism and let herself be a human being. "I knew he was probably dead. I've been telling myself that, that I need to accept it and let myself grieve, for weeks now. But seeing it . . ." Dahlia took Maddy's hand, and Maddy squeezed it tightly in response. "I feel like I've made a trade, one heart for another. We received word of Naples while we were in the palace. Numen willing, Henna's gone to find him."

For a guilt-stricken moment, Dahlia couldn't remember who Naples was. Then she recalled an overheard, worried conversation early in the council's collaboration with the Order of Napthol.

"Your older son," she said aloud, confirming. No

one had officially reported him missing, but Maddy's relief made it clear she had been worried in ways she had not disclosed to the council. Dahlia couldn't think of a follow-up question that didn't sound accusatory— *Surely he hasn't been missing all this time? Why did no one mention it?*—so she said only, "I am sure Henna will be able to bring him home."

What did she know of the matter?

"Gobe has a stack of notes for you, whenever you're ready," Maddy said, changing the subject, as if uncomfortable discussing her own fears and hopes. "And Celadon wants to see you as soon as you're up to it. He has been frantic with worry, blaming himself, even though we've assured him a thousand times that you will be fine. He also stayed here last night, to stay near to you."

"You let him do that?" Despite the extraordinary circumstances, Dahlia was shocked to hear the Quin preacher had been allowed to sleep in the Order of Napthol's private halls.

"He has a right to be here, if he chooses," Maddy said. "His power is indisputable, and despite his personal reservations, he willingly used it to help us open the palace and find the royal family. He could have sat back on the high ground, and reminded us he's been warning us sorcery is dangerous for years. And it's good for him, too, that he is here. He has been asking questions. He pretends they're casual, but he's clearly desperate to understand his power even if it frightens him. I hope he will eventually accept formal training. Do you want me to let him know you're up?"

"I'll find him," Dahlia said, swinging her feet to the floor. "If that's all right with you? I feel like I need to stretch my legs."

"You're no sorcerer," Maddy said, "but we owe you much. I feel you, too, have a right to be here. If anyone bothers you, tell them to bring their complaints to me."

They found Celadon not in the room he had been given, but on the first floor in what Maddy called the medical wing—specifically, at the bedside of the still-unconscious Terre Verte.

Celadon looked up with a dazed expression as they entered, as if his mind had been far away. Then he jumped out of the chair he had previously occupied and rushed forward.

"You're all right," he breathed. "They told me you would be, but I couldn't believe it, not . . . the way you looked when we carried you out . . ." In contrast to Maddy, who still maintained a neutral expression despite all the emotions Dahlia was certain must be roiling inside her, Celadon wore every raw emotion on his face for the world to see: relief, guilt, fear.

"I'll leave you two alone. I'll let Gobe know you're awake, too, Dahlia. He's been threatening to assault the Cobalt Hall if we don't produce you soon, and I don't think Jade is far behind."

Dahlia nodded, but all her attention was on the still figure across the room, stretched out on an austere oak-framed bed. She stepped up beside Terre Verte, and a sense of wrongness washed over her.

Maddy said he was alive. It was hard to believe that was true. His skin was the gray-white color of unwashed eider down, mottled in places, and his cheeks were sunken and shadowed. Someone had brushed out his hair such that it shone in chestnut splendor around him, an obscene contrast to the rest of his features.

"Someone should have warned you," Celadon said as Dahlia reeled at her first sight of the prince. He caught her arm to steady her.

"Words wouldn't have been enough."

Dahlia had grieved for his passing. She had, like everyone else, cried that it wasn't fair, and had wanted him back. But just then, he looked like someone who should be allowed to die.

"What's keeping him here?" she whispered.

She didn't realize she had spoken aloud until Celadon replied, "Nothing that should be." He paused. "I didn't like him. I disagreed with him on many points, and I didn't trust him. But I didn't hate him and I never wanted . . ."

He trailed off, looking at Dahlia.

"I believe you," she said.

He had changed in the last six weeks. They all had, but Celadon perhaps most of all. His flashfire temper and instant judgment and disdain were gone, his streak of arrogance tempered into a quiet confidence mixed with moments of honest uncertainty.

"I worry about the magic keeping him here," Celadon said. "I worry that . . . *look* at him. If magic could have healed him in the market square when the Osei attacked him, I never would have argued with it, but this—"

"It doesn't seem natural," Dahlia agreed when he stopped again. "But if there is a way to save him, don't we have to try?"

"Not *we*. Me," Celadon answered. "*I'm* the one who opened that door—those doors. Maybe it would have been better to leave them sealed. I just, I don't know."

Dahlia remembered what Henna had told her about what the members of her Order were going through. "Have you been having nightmares?"

Celadon looked at her as if she were mad. "Haven't we all been?" he asked at last. He let out a frustrated sound. "I don't know where I stand anymore. I'm inside the Numen-damned Cobalt Hall, by the sickbed of a man I have opposed most of my life. A man I pulled back into this world through sorcery. And I—" He swallowed hard. "It nearly killed you, you know. That blast. I wanted to stay beside you, the way you once stayed with me, but I couldn't, because the magic . . . *my* magic . . . made me even colder than you were. I couldn't push it back the way Maddy and Dove could, so I would have frozen you to death. I carried *him* out, and let them take you." He finished the tirade with his eyes closed, leaning against the wall. "I'm sorry," he said. "You don't need this."

She put a hand on his shoulder. Celadon Cremnitz having an existential crisis was less terrifying than Terre Verte looking like he had been dragged bodily from the Abyss.

He had been so noble, fighting the Osei. This wasn't the way he should go, wasting away in bed.

Celadon followed her gaze to the prince. "I wish I knew what I was seeing, when I look at him. Ever since the palace, the magic has been . . . worse, more vivid." She had the sense that Celadon continued to look at Terre Verte as he spoke partly because he could not stand to meet her gaze while saying such things. "I can't make myself stop seeing it. It's strongest around Clay, which I guess makes sense, since he's Terre Jaune's son. But I can see it on Maddy and some of the others, too. Most of the time it's peaceful, just a kind of haze. I can ignore it."

The words were a confession. They would have brought opposite reactions from any follower of either the Quinacridone or the Napthol. One would hate him for something he never wanted, and one would praise him for something he had always reviled.

"And when you look at Terre Verte?" Dahlia asked.

"Whatever I'm seeing, it's all tangled." He frowned. "During the fire down at the docks, I was with the others, hauling water. All of a sudden a cat streaked out of the burning building, screaming like a child, its fur on fire. None of us could reach it at first, and by the time we managed to corner it and pour water on it, it was just this charred *thing*. Impossibly alive. Finally, one of the men with me had the courage to step forward and break its neck to put it out of its misery. That's what the power around Verte reminds me of.

"I'm no expert at magic. But every instinct I have tells me that what I'm seeing is every bit as cruel as that fire. Letting him lie here, watching him, it's like all of us staring in shock at that cat, soaking wet, with its fur gone and its skin rolling with blisters and blood where it wasn't just—" He gagged, and turned away from the Terre and Dahlia both. "It's like the magic is fighting itself and he's just lying there in the middle, defenseless, seemingly quiet, but *screaming* in my head to let him go. And I don't know what to do," he concluded. "I don't know if the followers of the Napthol can see it, or if it's like that door in the palace, invisible except to me. If they can see, they're ignoring it. If they can't, I know they'll never believe me when I tell them. They want him back so badly I don't think they care what it takes. And I worry they'll ask me to help him, like I did in the palace."

"And you won't." Dahlia tried to keep judgment

from her voice as she spoke the words. Was she in the crowd Celadon referred to, the ones who cared more for Terre Verte's return than the cost?

"I don't know," Celadon replied. "That's what frightens me. When I first reached for the palace door, I had that same sense, like there was a voice in my head telling me *no*. I let them convince me it was the right thing to do because they know more about magic than I do. Now that voice is ten times stronger and I still don't trust myself."

She couldn't see what Celadon could see, so she fell back on the same method she had used over the past six weeks, when others asked for her leadership on a matter she knew others were better equipped to handle. She asked, "What do you think is the right thing to do?"

He didn't answer at first.

Dahlia pressed. "You've told me all this. Maybe because there's no one else you *can* tell, but I like to think it's because you have some trust in my judgment."

He nodded. "You've led Kavet this last month and a half. Yes, I trust your judgment. And your strength."

"So tell me: without fearing what other people will push you to do, or how the others in your order will respond—or those of the Napthol—what do you feel is the right course of action?"

Again, he was quiet for long moments. His gaze traveled back to Terre Verte.

"Celadon?"

"There isn't an inch of me that doesn't believe I should put a pillow over his face and send him back to that other world," Celadon replied. His voice was so soft Dahlia could barely hear him—but it was absolutely sure.

CHAPTER 32

HENNA

Henna brought Naples to the kitchen entrance so they could avoid the constant crowd. She had briefly mentioned that the front areas of the Cobalt Hall had been used for the council's work the last few weeks, but she doubted Naples fully understood the scope. Naples was used to the Cobalt Hall being an inviolate sanctuary to members of the Order of Napthol. This political incursion would take some getting used to.

Her goal was to find Maddy first. Maddy would want to see her son, and Henna desperately wanted to know the results of their search of the palace.

Fortunately, Maddy was in the kitchen, bouncing Clay on her knee as he whimpered in toddler-unhappiness. Her eyes were cast down to her son, heavy with exhaustion, but she glanced up at the opening door and her face lit with joy and relief.

"You found him," she breathed, coming to her feet and lifting Clay into her arms with barely a wince. "Naples!"

Maddy threw her arms around her son, though Clay attempted to wriggle back with uncharacteristic shyness toward his big brother. Henna saw Naples flinch, as so many of their order did lately, but he returned the embrace fully.

"I'm sorry I frightened you," he said. "I didn't mean to be gone so long." He touched Clay's head affectionately, then pulled back when the toddler's gray Terre eyes widened and his lips started to quiver in a way they all knew could be prelude to a tantrum. Six weeks of separation was a long time in an almost-two-year-old's life. "I'll explain all I can once—"

Naples broke off, looking past his mother. Henna automatically turned to see what he was looking at.

Across the room, Celadon stood at the hearth, frozen in the act of spooning porridge into a bowl. Dahlia had a hand on his arm, as if she had been about to urge him from the room.

Naples shrugged off his mother's hug and observed dryly, "This is an interesting happy family."

"We never would have made it into the palace without them," Maddy defended hastily, while the two men looked daggers at each other.

Henna could see on Naples' face the battle between his desire to say something nasty to drive the outsiders away and his desperate need for answers. At last he swallowed and said, "You got into the palace. Did you find the Terre? The Terra, is she—What did you find?"

"I'm sorry to confirm that Terre Jaune and Terra Sarcelle are both dead," Maddy said, only the faintest hitch in her voice. "From the looks of it, they have been dead for weeks, since the time the palace was sealed." In the silence that followed, Maddy added in a small voice, "The spell is too old for me to make out, and Celadon doesn't have the training. But if I had to guess, I would say he gave his life for his son's."

Henna felt the floor shift, like a ship deck during stormy seas. "Verte?" she whispered.

"He's alive?" Naples said, his voice hollow. He clutched at the doorframe to steady himself. *"He's alive?"*

Maddy nodded. "Dreadfully weak and still injured. I think Jaune—" Her voice hitched on the name. "I think Verte's father must have put up those shields to keep his son's soul from escaping. To keep him from dying, and to keep scavengers from the other planes away. Only it took all his energy, and when it was done, Verte didn't have the strength to break the shields, so he's just . . . been there . . ."

Henna gasped in horror as the truth struck her.

"We left him there. We left him trapped there for *weeks*, hurt and starving and—"

"None of you knew," Celadon asserted. "You had no reason to think he could possibly be alive, or that Terre Jaune could have created such a trap."

"Since when do you defend members of the Napthol?" Naples said sharply.

"Shut your Abyss-damned mouth," Celadon snapped back. "I may not approve of sorcery, but at least I've *been* here, helping, while you've been fucking around and—"

As Henna's mind went to the wash of blood she had found at Argent's farm and her instant certainty that no one could have survived it, Naples crossed the room in a bound and slammed both hands against Celadon's chest to shove him against the wall. "You have no *idea* what I—"

Before anyone else could intervene, Celadon struck out, not physically, but with a burst of power that echoed in Henna's head, eerily familiar to the one that had pushed her away from the palace doors. This time it was Naples who went flying, white streaks of ice forming across his skin.

"Never again do you get to put your hands on me," Celadon spat.

"Why?" Naples growled, pushing himself up and stalking back toward the Quin. There was a knife in his hand now. Where had it come from? "You seemed to be having fun before we were interrupted last time."

"Stop it!" Dahlia shrieked. Everyone in the room jumped, and Naples and Celadon both looked at her.

Dahlia stepped boldly between the two men, eyes flashing with the same irritation Henna remembered seeing when she had followed Celadon and Maddy out of the Turquoise and berated them about their petty arguments.

"Naples, put away the knife," Dahlia said, in the same soft but inarguable voice she used to give instructions at assembly meetings.

Naples glared at her. Celadon shifted his body, clearly not wanting to undermine Dahlia's attempt to end the conflict, but fighting the instinct to put himself protectively between her and the hostile sorcerer.

Dahlia didn't know what she was facing.

Henna had assumed Naples' knife was some kind of work tool when she saw him strap it on, so hadn't given it a second thought. But now, having seen it better—an elegant, waved steel blade, clearly designed for ritual—she could only imagine what Naples planned to do with it in this situation. He didn't intend to throw punches.

"Naples," Henna said, adding her voice to Dahlia's command, "put it away."

Naples hesitated, too long. Then, thank the wind and sea and all the powers beyond, he tucked the knife back into the sheath at his waist before disdainfully brushing frost from his arms and the folds of his shirt.

"You're becoming remarkably adept for a Quin

who swears magic is the bane of civilization," he remarked to Celadon.

"And you haven't changed at all," Celadon replied.

"Naples, maybe you should get some rest," Henna suggested firmly. She had to get these two men out of the same room.

"I've had plenty of rest," Naples spat. "It's a shock finding rats in the kitchen, is all." He deliberately moved past Celadon; the preacher held his ground as Naples examined the food on the hearth, then served himself a heaping bowl of porridge.

Maddy handed Clay to Dahlia, who instinctively moved to cradle the toddler protectively, then stepped between her older son and the preacher. They weren't actively fighting anymore, but Henna could understand why Maddy wanted to add a barrier between them—and why she didn't want to be holding Clay while she did it. "If it weren't for Celadon, we never would have broken through the shields on the palace," Maddy repeated, adding, "All your power wasn't enough. Neither was mine, or Henna's."

"A mortal can't fight the Numini," Naples murmured thoughtfully.

"What?" Maddy asked.

Naples shook his head. "Never mind. I'm going to eat upstairs, and then maybe take that nap." He turned to go, only turning back at the last minute to say, "Mother . . . I did miss you."

Maddy nodded, her expression torn between gratitude for her son's return, and distress over his behavior.

Naples didn't stay long enough to hear her say, "Welcome home, son. Welcome home."

As soon as Naples walked out, Clay began to weep. Dahlia held him closer, rocking him and whispering to him, unmindful of the tears and snot that marred her shoulder.

"Don't wanna go away," Clay whimpered.

"You're not going anywhere," Dahlia said.

"Kwicwone said go away."

At first the word sounded like nonsense, but then Henna ran the sounds through her mind again, slowly. "Quinacridone?" she asked.

Clay's apparent power, combined with his inability to communicate his thoughts, continued to be both frustrating and ominous. He was as likely as any toddler to babble randomly, but he had also, somehow, been afraid of the Abyssi for hours before the Terra had summoned it. Henna and Maddy had both been driving themselves mad since then, trying to decode the child's words, which tended to be as inscrutable as rune stones in mundane hands.

This time, Clay nodded, seeming excited she had understood the word.

"Do you mean *Celadon*?" Henna asked. Celadon was the person most likely to be referred to as some variant of "Quin" around Clay, but Henna couldn't see him threatening a small child, even before he had gained his recent measure of calm cooperation.

"No!" Clay shouted, his favorite word these days. "Cel'don pretty."

A dry chuckle drew Henna's attention to where the subject of their conversation was still standing, leaning against the doorframe.

"Thanks," he said, sounding tired. He looked up at Maddy and added, "I'm sorry about that. I didn't mean to do anything so . . . extreme."

Henna had never told Maddy how she had found Celadon and Naples together that day, and to her knowledge Celadon had never shared it with anyone, either. Given the limited situations in which she could imagine the reserved, socially staid preacher ending up body-pressed against a male Order of Napthol sorcerer ten years his junior, she suspected his response wasn't extreme at all.

"I didn't realize you knew how to do anything like that." Dahlia tried to keep her tone carefully neutral, but couldn't quite manage it.

"I . . ." Celadon looked at the two sorcerers in the room with the wariness of a cornered dog. "I *don't* know how. It just happened."

"When you're ready," Maddy said, "I can help you understand how it happened, and stop it from happening unexpectedly. You're safe enough in the Cobalt Hall, since any of us can step in if needed, but I don't think you would want one of your Quin followers to see you do something like that in the middle of an argument."

Clay hiccupped again, then said, "Brek'st? Pease?"

Celadon accepted the distraction with obvious relief, looking away from Maddy and scanning the kitchen for Clay's food. Soon, Henna thought, he might decide that accepting help to control his power was worth it, but he wasn't ready yet.

He spotted the toddler's plate on the counter and asked Maddy, "Is this his?"

"Is it cool now?" Maddy asked. "He's extremely sensitive to anything hot."

"Brek'st!" Clay said again. "Brek'st!"

"Looks like an omelet, little guy." Celadon quickly checked the temperature, moving as confidently as if they were in his own kitchen. "That's related to the power, isn't it?" he asked, his tone overly casual. "People with cold power don't mind the cold, but are sensitive to heat. People with hot power can stand a lot of heat, but not the cold. And his power is like the Terre's." As he spoke he placed Clay's breakfast and spoon in front of Maddy's chair.

"Thank you," Maddy said, sinking into the chair with Clay on her lap. "Yes, that's right. There's no way for us to test his strength when he's this young, but Jaune said . . . he said Verte was like that, too."

Celadon nodded and his questions stopped, though Henna could see the thoughts continuing to percolate behind his eyes.

Henna wanted to stay, to tell Maddy more about what she had seen when she found Naples, but she didn't want to share the story in front of Celadon and Dahlia. Instead she leaned down and embraced Maddy lightly. "Be gentle with Naples when you talk to him. I'm not sure he *knows* what's happened to him."

Argent had said Naples had "lost time." Henna suspected that was an understatement.

"I will," Maddy said. "Verte is in the second room in the recovery hall," she added, referring to a handful of rooms kept for guests with serious illnesses or injuries who required more than a few minutes of time from the Cobalt Hall's healers.

Straightening, Henna nodded. "How . . . how is he?" she asked. She couldn't help remembering the blood splashed around Naples' body, or the wounds that had killed Helio. Could she stand to see her lover like that?

"He isn't well," Maddy answered with gentle honesty. "We haven't been able to get him to wake yet, or respond to us at all. He was trapped for weeks in the palace, without anything to sustain him but the magic. But Jaune kept him alive. If he could do that much, I have to believe we have the power to do the rest."

Henna nodded, her heart racing. Maddy hadn't said "I *do* believe," but "I *have to* believe." Henna too found she needed to believe that. Otherwise, she didn't know how she would face the guilt of having left him behind, or the terrible, anxious hope for his return.

Faith was all she had. She hurried to his side.

CHAPTER 33

NAPLES

Did it kill Helio?

That thought, above *almost* all others, left Naples unable to close his eyes to sleep. Henna had kept her description of Helio's death vague, either to protect Naples' sensibilities or to avoid reliving it herself, but the fact that she believed Helio had been killed by the same power that left Naples bloodied and unconscious in Argent's house told him all he needed to know. Henna and the rest of the Order thought some kind of "wild magic" was responsible for the death, but they didn't know an Abyssi was walking free in the mortal realm.

He stood up, dressed, and climbed the stairs to the

temple. Later he would go see Terre Verte, but he had work to do before he could bear to stand before his prince. Also later, he would go to the Terra's private ritual room, since almost everything he knew about Abyssi and their realm had come from her. But he didn't have the nerve for that yet, either.

The Terra is dead. She was probably dying when I saw her last. "I need to rest" was the last thing she said to me. Maybe the last thing she said to anyone. I walked away from her.

Terre Jaune is dead. He put everything into trying to heal his son.

Helio is dead.

He hadn't known Helio well; their powers had been too diametrically opposite, so Naples had never studied with him. But he was a familiar face now lost, in a time when too many touchstones had gone missing.

Did I kill Helio? Would I remember if I had?

He hadn't been in the city. He had been twenty miles away in Brockridge.

Why would the Abyssi have killed Helio?

What else could have killed him?

He was alone in the temple, which seemed odd at this hour, but lucky, since the methods the Terra had taught him were often at odds with the ones the Order advocated. He needed to find a way to protect himself against the Abyssi. Eventually he needed to find a way to throw it out of the mortal realm entirely, but for now, he would settle for some way to keep it from overwhelming and overpowering him.

He thought back to the charm he had made Cyan to ward against the Osei. Could he use similar magic against the Abyssi?

Would it have helped Verte if he had been wearing a charm against the Osei?

Why did I waste my efforts on a sailor, when I knew the royal family was—No, they knew what they were doing. It would have been presumptive . . .

"Damn," he whispered. Too many stupid and terrible things had happened without his having time to process them. He knew they only *seemed* so close together because he had lost time, the time the others had used to mourn and recover from the shock.

He forced his mind back to the problem at hand. He had used iron against the Osei. What was an Abyssi's weakness?

He paced the temple before the shelves of tools. He knew what nourished an Abyssi: blood, heat, pain, and lust. He knew it couldn't eat anything but newly killed flesh and blood, and that once a carcass was cold it was what the Abyssi called "dirt" once again.

Cold. Was that the key? The Abyssi was a creature of shadow and flame. It devoured heat.

Of course, Naples too was a creature of fire. He had always used hot magic. Cold magic couldn't even *see* the Abyssi, just as Naples' magic had been blind to the Numini that guarded the palace doors. No, if the Abyssi could be hurt by the cold, then the Numini should be sensitive to heat. Naples' hot magic attack the day he had been trapped in the palace would have damaged the Numini there.

A mortal can't fight the Numini, the Abyssi had said.

He froze as the thought struck him.

A mortal *had*, hadn't he? Celadon had breached the palace doors.

Henna's theory had been that Celadon could get past the shields because they had been designed to hold back hot power. Naples knew those guards hadn't been put in place by the Terre at all, but by a creature of the cold, either guarding the Terre or trying to contain him.

It made no sense that a shield made of cold power would be blind to its own kind, which meant it had either allowed Celadon inside, or the preacher had forced it to let him in. Celadon wouldn't have known the difference.

Or would he?

Naples frowned, his gaze still on the shelves, but his mind no longer seeing the tools.

Did the preacher know more than he let on?

A theory entered Naples' mind. He left the temple. Earlier he had been horrified to come home and find the Quin in the kitchen, but now he prayed Celadon was still nearby.

There was one person aside from Celadon that

Naples knew who had recently demonstrated a shocking increase in power, and that was Naples himself. He knew exactly what he had done to gain that strength. The question was, what had Celadon done?

Naples checked the kitchen first, but it was empty. As the scent of food struck him, his mouth watered and his stomach clenched, reminding him of the blood he had lost and the energy he had spent since Argent's rabbit stew. He took a generous slice of sweet apple bread. It didn't look appetizing, but he could eat it quickly. He reached for the jar of honey, but regarding its contents made his stomach do a slow, nauseated roll.

He left the kitchen, doggedly shoveling the bread—*dirt*—into his mouth as he continued his search.

He spotted Celadon, still beside Dahlia, in the front hall. Unfortunately, fifty or so other people had joined them, mobbing the preacher and the country woman as if they were celebrities.

Naples gawked at the crowd. He recognized austere Quin mingling with not only other members of the Order of Napthol but also foreigners, men and women Naples knew for a fact were A'hknet prostitutes, and peddlers, tradesmen, and sailors. What were they all *doing* here?

Henna had said some groups held "meetings" in the Cobalt Hall these days, but Naples had pictured small, carefully supervised units that came when summoned and left when instructed to do so. These people seemed to have been loitering and chatting.

Naples wanted to scream at them to leave, to go, to clear out of this space that was supposed to be his home and sanctuary. In that moment, the fact he had planned to leave for an apprenticeship with the Terra was irrelevant. This was like moving back to one's childhood home to discover squatters using old photos for kindling and throwing refuse on the floor.

He had turned to flee the chaos when someone hesitantly called, "Naples?"

His spine went rigid and he turned as if braced for battle, lifting his chin to peer through the crowd. It took too many moments to recognize Cyan's face in the group.

The naked joy and relief in the sailor's expression were a balm against the crowd's invasion. Naples felt an answering smile on his own face.

Henna said the docks had been destroyed, and no one had sailed the morning after the Apple Blossom Festival, or in the weeks since. It hadn't occurred to Naples that Cyan would, of course, have been among those trapped. He searched for something more gracious to say than, "It's been a while, or so I hear. I don't remember most of it, since I was busy being seduced by a demon and getting into a fight with a door that left me in a three-day coma, but I've got a room upstairs if you're interested."

He had a few moments to decide, since Cyan needed to shoulder past several people to reach him. Once the sailor was close enough, Naples settled on saying, "I'm glad to see you're safe, but I'm sorry you're stuck here."

"Sorry, are you?" Cyan asked, with a raised brow and a strange shadow of doubt in his expression.

"I was being polite," Naples admitted. "I'm happy to see you."

Cyan chuckled, but the sound had a forced edge to it. Tone weighty with relief, he added more seriously, "You say you're glad to see *me* safe. I was half-convinced you were dead. I kept asking about you and being put off. No one would tell me where you were. I decided . . . I hoped . . . you just didn't want to see me anymore, but I feared worse every time I saw your mother's face."

"I was out of town," Naples said vaguely. He didn't want Cyan to think he had been avoiding him, but also didn't want to tell him the truth. "I didn't think you would look for me, so I didn't think to tell anyone it was okay to let you know where I was. My Order guards its members' privacy." He looked around the room. "Or, it used to."

The excuse didn't explain his mother's anxiety, but he could brush that off as being related to other recent events. These hadn't been easy times for anyone.

Cyan laughed again, and this time the sound was more sincere. "They still do. We're allowed in a few of these front rooms, but I know people who've been sternly and painfully reprimanded for straying beyond the bounds of our fences."

What about Dahlia and Celadon in the kitchen, then? Naples dared to hope that had been an anomaly. He still didn't like it, but he could grudgingly accept that unusual times called for unusual bending of the rules.

He was debating whether he should try the line about the room upstairs when Cyan said, "I have a question about your art, if you have a few minutes."

"Oh?"

Cyan had always idly acknowledged Naples' connection to the Order of Napthol and the magic it implied without seeming overly impressed by it, and he rarely asked questions. Now he held up his left hand, where he was wearing the anti-Osei ring.

"I haven't had a chance to test this yet—I'm not complaining about that—but having it has made me think: Could you create a charm like this on a bigger scale?"

"How much bigger?"

"A ship." The interjection came from another sailor waiting a few paces behind Cyan, who had apparently taken the conversational turn as a cue to intrude. "Or better yet, a weapon."

Cyan gave Naples an amused smirk and said under his breath, "I had planned to wine-and-dine you a little before springing the whole plan on you."

"I'll happily agree to wining and dining another time," Naples assured him. He looked briefly across the hall to where Celadon and Dahlia were still surrounded by their adoring masses. He wouldn't be able to catch the preacher alone any time soon. In fact, given Celadon's dislike and distrust of him—both admittedly deserved—Naples would probably have to be a bit crafty to pin him down. "Tell me more about your plan."

"It isn't a firm plan," Cyan said, "just an idea. We came to talk to members of the Order about it, but no one seems to know how you made the Osei charm. Do you want to come with us down to the docks? I'll show you what we've been working on, and you can tell us if there's any chance of mixing magic with our designs."

"I still hold that trying to bring magic into this is asking for trouble," a third Silmari, a man Naples didn't know whose clothes and poise suggested an aristocrat more than a sailor, interjected. "We don't need—"

"So says the man sleeping with Indathrone," someone else interrupted. "I for one would like to get home someday."

"And speaking for those of us from here," a Kavet native added, "we'd like to get the trade routes open before we starve this winter."

How had Naples' tête-à-tête with Cyan become the center of a raised-voices argument? He tried to back up, only to realize the crowd had closed behind him.

"Isn't magic part of what got us into this trouble in the first place?" the first objector asked. "Dahlia is working on an agreement to—"

"No," the Kavet native interrupted, "the *Silmari* are what got us into this trouble in the first place, by attacking the Osei."

Now that he had been referred to as Dahlia's lover, Naples knew who the Silmari aristocrat was—Jade. Henna had mentioned him, and the fact that she didn't think he and Dahlia were sleeping together, despite what rumors said. He was nominally the leader of the Silmari, but given the argument Naples was witnessing, his authority was not absolute.

Cyan caught Naples' arm and pulled him in the direction of the door, using his wider frame to muscle others aside as necessary. "They can argue for hours," he said. "Let's go."

They escaped the press of arguing bodies and found their way to the docks. Once there, Cyan continued to explain. "We've been told the Silmari back home took down an Osei prince. Supposedly they had been working on some large weapon they could mount on towers on the shore, but even Jade can't imagine what madness prompted them to actually *use* it. I personally don't think it's a good idea to try to repeat that kind of violence, given the consequences of success. I'd rather find a way to make them avoid us, or just not notice us as we sail, so we don't need to try to fight." He shrugged. "But I don't know a damn thing about magic, so it's hard to figure what's possible."

"I know as little about ships," Naples admitted. He had spent plenty of time here at the docks or even on-board a variety of vessels, but he hadn't been paying attention to the ships themselves. "Show me around so I can see what I have to work with."

"We've only got the one functioning ship in the water so far," Jade said. "It's taken all our time and most of our supplies to get her outfitted. We're hoping if we get one vessel to do a run and spread the word that the danger is past and the docks are open again, we'll get Kavet-native ships and merchants from other countries to return."

He strode proudly onto the decks and Naples followed at a slower pace, considering the materials he saw around him.

Wood and rope and cloth were worse than useless unless he planned to set them on fire. There was metal on the ship, but the proportion was low, of course. A ship made of metal couldn't float.

Cold magic could sometimes be imbued in something like fabric or rope, but even if Naples could use that kind of power or help someone else work the aversion charm, cold magic was sensitive to material value, use, and respect. It would fray in the face of a rough sea voyage.

It might be possible to mount something on the top of the masts, or weave something more compatible with his power into the sails. He looked up at the sailors scampering about the rigging. As he considered the height of the masts against the blue sky, his stomach and mouth tried to change positions. He put his head down, fighting vertigo. On second thought, no power in the three realms would convince him to climb up to look more closely.

"Are you all right?" Cyan asked.

Naples nodded, taking a deep breath. "How in the Abyss do people go *up* there?" he asked weakly.

"Mmm, there goes my fantasy of having you in the crow's nest," Cyan murmured, and Naples' stomach flipped again, for entirely different reasons. "Do you need to get up there?"

Naples shook his head vigorously. Maybe, instead of tying the spell to the ship, he could attach it to a person. "Who's the captain?"

"That hasn't been decided yet," Cyan answered. "She was put together with salvage from three different ships. I was first mate of one of the vessels, and I'm on the list of candidates now." He paused a moment, but it was a heartbeat too long before Naples realized he was probably expecting a congratulatory or impressed reply. "Jade's in the running, too. Some people are trying to argue that she should have a native captain, since she was built here, but she's mostly made of Silmari materials. Most Kavetan ships either spend winter in more tropical waters and return to Kavet in late spring, or overwinter here and leave as soon as the harbor's clear of ice, so there weren't many in port when the attack happened."

"Would it help if I said I can do more if you captain her than if a stranger does?"

"It might help with the vote—can you believe they're *voting* on the position?" Cyan interrupted himself. "How is that the way to choose the captain of a respectable vessel? It's what pirates do." He shook his head. "But—the ship and her safety are most important to me, so yes, it probably would help with the vote, but it only matters to me if it's true."

"It's true," Naples said. "It's even more true if one of the possible captains is opposed to the idea of magic in the first place. Magic is responsive to will. No matter how strongly I tie my intention into it, if the man in charge of this ship disagrees with its presence, that will influence the spell's effect." What he didn't add was that, since his magic was tied to sex, it would be easier to make a powerful link with someone he had bedded. And hopefully would bed again.

Cyan nodded. "Then I'll put that word out." He paused, his gaze skimming the ship. "Do you want to continue the tour? We can conclude with the captain's quarters. They're not particularly lavish, but there's a bunk. And a door. And a lock."

Finally.

"I thought you'd never ask."

CHAPTER 34

HENNA

Henna froze in the middle of the sickroom, resisting the impulse to recoil from the . . . Was it an odor? No, not quite. The miasma, like a lingering stench on a breeze or a discordant song in the distance, wasn't perceived by any of her natural senses.

Then, just like a fleeting smell or a sound, it was gone from her awareness before she could grasp it.

She closed her eyes to try to identify the repulsive magical taint, but couldn't find it again. It might not have been in the room at all; perhaps it had drifted from faulty spellwork upstairs. Or maybe it really *had* been a lingering smell, perhaps the remnants of some healing ointment, so subtle now it seemed like a magical afterimage.

Maybe she had been smelling her own fear. While her eyes were closed like this, she didn't need to look at the form on the bed and see what ruin might be left of the beautiful, vivacious man she loved.

But closing her eyes was dangerous, too. Behind her lids, Helio's body appeared. Then Naples, torn apart, his blood splashed across the room.

Henna opened her eyes and crossed stiffly to the bed. Between the wounds on her flesh and the pulled muscles from her desperate ride to retrieve Naples, every fiber of her being ached—but none of it was as bad as the feeling in her heart when she saw her beautiful prince, who now lay as still as a corpse.

She tried to hearten herself by considering that, in some ways, Verte looked more alive than Naples had. There might be wounds hidden by the sleep-shirt and loose cotton trousers someone had dressed Verte in, but what she could see of his body was whole. His skin was pale, stripped of any tan by his weeks away from the sun, but his mother's Ilbanese blood made the fairness like porcelain instead of the rotten mushroom color many Kavetans turned when they spent too much time inside.

There was no blood, and no scars to indicate where the blood had once been. Bones must have broken when he struck the cobbles, but the planes of his face and body were flawless now. Such was the work his father had done to heal him.

But where is his soul?

Mikva's accusations rose unwelcome to Henna's mind. Many seagoing Tamari believed a boucan's soul was eternally tied to the waves, so if one stepped onto land as Henna had done, the body would become a savage husk while the spirit lingered as a vengeful ghost. If that were so, Henna's ghost haunted the shores of the Ninth House of the Osei.

Was Verte's ghost somewhere? His spirit wasn't in his body. Looking at him, sensing the wrongness in him, she was sure of that much.

A scuff behind her made her jump, twisting, heart in her throat—but it was only Dove.

What did you expect, you silly goose? Henna chastised herself. That figure on the bed had put her in mind of wraiths and fiends.

"I'm sorry," Dove said, hesitating in the doorway. "I didn't realize you were in here. I can come back later if you want to be alone."

"No, no, it's all right," Henna said hastily. She swallowed the lump in her throat. "He isn't really alive, is he?"

Dove hesitated. "He isn't really dead, either. I've been able to glimpse his spirit, but I'm not strong enough to grasp it or communicate with it. My hope is that, if we can tend to his body so it regains its strength, his spirit will be drawn back of its own accord."

Hope. Henna held tight to that word, though it felt hollow in her heart.

She moved out of the way as Dove touched Verte's brow and his cheek, and sent her magic through his body to examine him. Henna couldn't follow the nuance of the mostly old magic work, but she could tell part of Dove's efforts involved funneling raw power into Verte to strengthen him.

"Is that safe for you?" Henna asked, concerned, when Dove pulled back.

The other woman nodded absently. "I know my limits," she said. "By this afternoon, we should be able to get some broth into him. Food will speed up the healing if we can get him to take it." She rubbed her eyes and blinked, betraying the fatigue she usually tried to conceal. "Have you seen anything in your—no, you haven't had a chance to scry since getting home, have you?"

"Not yet."

"There are things we should probably know," Dove said softly. "We believe Terre Jaune died of power exhaustion, but we don't fully understand what killed the Terra, or even what happened to her body. We don't know why the king set those shields around the palace, what he was trying to contain, or what breaking them may have released. The answer isn't in the realm of the dead, but might be available to your sight."

Henna looked at Verte again, but it wasn't his deathly visage that made her shiver. Dove was right.

"I'll scry," Henna said. "Maybe I can see something about how to help Verte as well. You should probably rest."

Dove nodded tiredly. "I will. Please let me know if you learn anything."

Henna went to the temple to get her tools, then returned to Verte's room to work by his side. It was only as she spread the fabric across an ottoman to create a makeshift altar that she noticed the fabric was white silk, very different from her usual altar cloths. It made sense to choose tools associated with cold power to investigate cold power, she supposed, but she hadn't done it intentionally.

"I'm scared," she said, partly to herself, partly to Verte, and partly to the power she hoped would answer her call. She set out her rune stones as she spoke, arranging them in a circle. "I'm frightened of the way things are changing. The idea of putting a new ship into the water and possibly bringing the Osei back here terrifies me, but I also know what it's like to live in a place where you stare at someone else's food and your stomach grumbles and you start wondering whether you're strong enough to fight them for it. Kavet could turn into such a place, if we don't reestablish trade."

She recalled the darkest days with the Osei, the ones that had turned a child of the water into a land-dwelling sorceress and fortune-teller.

"I don't want to lose Kavet." That was one of the few things she knew for certain. "After I escaped the

Osei, I stopped on the first dry land that would take me. I never thought it would become home the way it has."

She knocked tears from her cheek with an angry hand.

"So I need guidance," she said. "I need to understand what has happened these last two months, to know what to do next. I need to know what the danger is and how we can face it. Speak to me. Please."

She realized she was doing more than using her second sight. She was raising power—cold power, which responded to invocation. Fine. She didn't fight the instincts driving her as she felt the fragile bubble of cold magic develop in the room. Would it tell her what she needed to know?

We can help you. Words on the wind, echoing with gratitude and longing. Henna looked around, wondering if she had heard them aloud or if they were part of some vision. *Thank you for reaching for us. I thought I had lost you when the beast claimed you.*

Henna closed her eyes, and focused on the voice. This was more than instinct guiding her power. Someone was *talking* to her.

"Who are you?" she asked tentatively.

The image in her head was familiar: Crystal waves lapping against a sea of brilliant white sand. She had seen it before, whenever she spoke to Helio.

Sadness from the being in her mind washed over her as she thought of her fellow sorcerer, and she knew this was the voice that had spoken through Helio to apologize.

He was dear to us, as you all are, the voice sighed, heavy with grief. *Veronese has spent the centuries guiding the Terre line, but I am the one who took the children of the Cobalt Hall and taught them to use divine power. They renamed their order in my honor, Napthol, and—*

NO!

Henna gasped as another being screamed into her mind and vision. Perfectly clear waters darkened, swirling with red and black as the other power intruded.

She is mine and you will NOT steal her!

Cold wrapped Henna as the being of the white sands gripped her more tightly, stealing her breath like a winter wind. *She called to me. I will not abandon—*

MINE! The beautiful white beach was being replaced with an image of a bog where gray tussocks decorated with swamp-fire in a dozen impossible colors rose above opaque water whose surface shone like an oil slick.

Henna gasped. The Abyssal creature's grip cut and burned, not just in vision but in reality.

"Let go!" she tried to shout, but her voice was strangled.

Mine, the Abyssal voice snarled again, a challenge not to Henna but to the softer, gentler voice.

You will kill her if you do not release her, the Numini warned.

Lost to the icy realm or dead—they're the same to me, the Abyssi replied indolently.

"They're *not* the same to me!" Henna snapped back. This time she found her voice. She focused her power, or tried to focus the power. Her gifts of vision were separate from her sorcery, and these were creatures of magic, who didn't truly exist on this realm to begin with. How to fight them?

They existed fully enough to kill her. Somewhere in the physical world, she could feel fresh blood sliding down her skin. This, she understood, was how they had killed Helio.

Nor are they the same to me, the Numini granted. Its calm, comforting presence suffused her, promising her wordlessly that all would be well. It would take care of her. Then it added, *It is better to be dead than to become a monster's tool.*

The Numini tightened its magical grip on her, trying to pull her away from the beast, and it was cold, oh so cold, freezing the breath in her lungs. The Abyssi responded to the struggle with glee and amoral abandon.

With impossible effort, Henna wrenched her eyes open, freeing herself from competing visions. As soon as she did, she saw the blood pooling on the white silk.

There was blood on her hands. On her arms. In her hair. How badly was she hurt?

She tried to stand but fell as her back seized, spasms

running down her spine and her thighs as damaged muscles shrieked in protest.

In her own blood, she traced runes of protection and sanctuary that she had learned not in the Cobalt Hall but as a child on Tamari ships. Instead of the infernal or divine realms from which she now fully believed her sorcery came, she invoked Azayalee, god of the sea and the wind, to protect her.

Slowly, she felt the battling powers recede. New lines of frost and fire stopped appearing on her skin. But was it too late already? How much damage had been done?

She struggled to breathe, knowing she had to move, or at least find enough breath to scream. If she didn't get to a healer soon, she would bleed to death here.

No. Henna had survived the Osei. She would not die now. Inch by inch, she managed to drag herself to the door, and there she paused again, gasping for air. The doorknob seemed to be miles away, too high for her to reach. Her reserves were gone. She couldn't go any farther.

She crumpled.

*"**H**elp her!" The plea came from the lesser judge, Napthol. The Abyssi had successfully pushed him away from the mortal child it had claimed, but a beast of the infernal realm had no power to heal. She would still die, and then she would belong to the Abyss after death.*

Doné looked down at the mortal realm with disdain. "Why should I help a creature as riddled by the Abyss as a dog with mange?"

"Because you did not help before. Because your child is strong and healthy, while mine——"

"You waste your time arguing with Doné," Veronese interrupted. "She will never bend to help a mortal she feels is already lost to the infernal realm. But I will. I have put off doing this. I hate hurting him so. But I swore a vow, and it must be done."

Verte knew he was dreaming, but he couldn't wake up.

He was falling, and all of existence was void blackness as he passed through it, forever and ever. It could have been terrifying, but he knew he was dreaming, and dreams couldn't hurt him. He just fell.

Then he was kneeling. In another lifetime, the concept of kneeling anywhere to anyone would have kindled his indignation. But he wasn't himself now. He was an actor in a role, living a scene written by another.

His knees did not hurt. Nothing hurt. He had never known pain. He had never been cold, and he had never been hungry.

To many voices arguing, arbiters and judges shouting, their voices raw enough that the high justice of the Numini needed to step in.

"*Step aside.*"

"*You are young, and you are rash.*"

"*Don't you understand what I am trying to do?*"

"*I understand what you have done.*"

"*Which of us was it that allowed Modigliani to sink his teeth into that realm?*"

"*Modigliani is only satisfying an appetite that was already there.*"

"*How dare you raise your voice in this place?*"

"*Aren't you forgetting something?*"

Verte looked back. Had something been forgotten?

"*You have to get up now.*"

Oh, no. He was happy being asleep. Sleep was good. It was easy. Waking would end all that. Falling wasn't so bad, because he knew that in dreams, nothing could hurt him. Awake, he could be hurt.

"I don't want to get up. You promised—"

"*Others made other promises. Vows are in conflict.*"

"Can't I stay a little longer?"

It wrapped a silver wing around him. "*Not much longer, I'm afraid.*"

Verte was walking on white sand. It was cool beneath his feet, especially where waves lapped his toes, but he was not cold. The ocean was clear, not just like the turquoise tropical seas of Silmat and Tamar, but like diamond. He could make out fish, like amethyst and emerald gemstones, darting between streaks of light.

He couldn't remember what he was doing here. He had been told to wait, hadn't he?

He walked up the beach to where the dunes were covered in bellflowers, among which the tiny nectar-drinking birds flew. That field gave way to silver trees with tear-shaped fruits that shimmered in the light, more red than any apple or exotic bird had ever been.

Finally he came to a wall of beaten gold. He put a hand on it. His fingers left no oil on the surface as he walked, trailing them along the smooth metal until he reached a gate.

The path was set with gold and green amber cobbles, and blocked by a massive gate of wrought copper and gold, shut fast.

"You know I can't let you in," said the being just beyond. *"Why do you keep coming here?"*

Why? He couldn't remember that, either. "I'm leaving soon," he said. "I want to come inside once before I go."

She shook her head.

"Let me in, please."

"You haven't earned it."

"Let me in!"

"No!"

He struck a hand to the gate. They had given him back his name when they had told him he had to leave, and he used it now. "I am Terre Verte, and I demand you open this gate!"

The gate started to quiver, making a sound like thousands of bells.

"Three times I conjure you, invoke you, command you. Open. This. Gate."

The gate dissolved into a fine mist.

The mist shattered in a rain of fire, which flung him backward.

Falling—

Falling, and now he *wasn't* dreaming, and when he hit the ground it was going to hurt.

What makes an infant cry is not the shock of the cold, or the pain of birth, but the impact of the spirit colliding with flesh at the moment of first breath.

That first intake of air scalded Verte. He turned over, coughing and screaming. His skin felt covered in burning pitch, but his core was ice.

I'm sorry, someone whispered. *You still have work to do.*

No. I don't want to—

Hush. You'll be all right. The pain will . . . pass.

He knew why it hesitated. It didn't understand pain.

As the tremors subsided, he reached for the memories. He thought he remembered an ocean—

Someone whimpered. The sound was soft, but it was the first sound Verte had heard in the mortal world and so it resonated through him.

It took an unreasonable effort to untangle his limbs.

By the time he had, he was panting and exhausted. Why had he bothered? Oh, yes. That sound. Now he just had to remember how to put his legs to the floor, how to balance his body above them, so awkward, so uncomfortable. At last he stopped in front of the door and reached for the knob.

There was blood on the frame, a crimson streak, still wet, near the bottom. Was it his? He looked back and saw blood on the floor, the wall, the door.

There was someone on the ground. It was her blood he had seen.

Above her hunched the beast.

"Modigliani," Verte said aloud.

The Abyssi looked up and tilted its head with curiosity. Nine tails waving behind it, eyes glowing blue, it watched him intently. *"You're in the wrong world,"* it said.

"So are you," Verte replied. He thought he remembered an argument of some sort. He couldn't recall, except that it had been about this Abyssi. Verte looked at the woman. "Did you do this?"

"No," the demon replied. *"I just found her."* He put a clawed hand in the pooled blood and announced, *"It's still hot."*

The door pushed open, making them both fall back, startled. It was another woman. She spoke, but Verte couldn't make out the words. She came to his side, but barely even looked at him before she went to the fallen woman.

The demon moved past the two women and one

of its tails brushed Verte. It hissed and pulled away with a whimper, the fur on that tail frost-singed.

"*You shouldn't be on this plane,*" it announced. "*Go away.*"

Deliberately, it set its hands to Verte's shoulders. The air around them sizzled like lightning, but the demon didn't draw back. Instead, it shoved.

Falling again.

Verte could hear voices, but couldn't seem to reply.

"He was up. I came in because I heard him screaming, and he was up and—"

"You didn't even—"

"I was focused on Henna," the first voice snapped. "I love the Terre as much as any citizen of this country, but Henna is like my sister. So yes, I looked away from the prince to save her life."

Henna. Verte knew that name. It didn't belong to either of the voices, though. He turned it over in his mind, trying to make connections. *Henna.*

"His color looks better," the second voice said, the words like an apology. "If he came out of it once, that's a good sign that he will come out of it again."

You must wake, a voice said. *All the way this time, fully into the mortal realm. Trying to hold onto a different plane will drive you mad, and it will drive mad the Abyssi who stalk around you seeking flesh. I can protect you from them, but you must . . .*

Wake . . .

Up.

CHAPTER 35

DAHLIA

Dahlia hesitated with the nib of her pen a hair's breadth above the creamy paper. The ecru cotton stationery taunted her, awaiting her response.

The Osei had proposed several tentative arrangements they would consider acceptable, many of which Dahlia had rejected out of hand—such as demands for yearly tribute, paid in slaves—and all of which were predicated on the assumption that all members of the royal house were dead.

Queen Negasi of the First Royal House,
By way of Queen Nimma of the Third Noble House,

By way of Prince Aelric of the Third Noble House,
By way of Kegan, servant of the Third Noble House,

It was, she thought, a ridiculous way to address a letter, but Kegan had been most exact in the proper wording.

> *Your servant has relayed your most recent message to us.*

The Osei referred to Kegan as "chattel" instead of a servant, but Dahlia's flesh crawled whenever she saw that word. Her altering the word in her own speech and writing did nothing to change Kegan's position, but needing to consciously make the decision each time to defy the Osei on this small matter meant she couldn't become complacent about it, either.

Each country dealt with the Osei in their own way. Kavet didn't have the power to fight them outright, but if Dahlia had any say in the matter, they wouldn't become mindless pawns, either. She had refused any proposal from the Osei that forced Kavet to provide slaves, and in a fit of pique had gone so far as to counter-demand that the Osei give Kavet the right to an itemized listing of all human slaves claimed in forfeit for outstanding debts, and the related right to free any of its citizens claimed as slaves by paying the liability against them.

Apparently her audacity had impressed Queen Nimma. The Osei's message in response was brief:

If as you say the foolish Terre Queen and princes who assaulted us are already dead, and you are now the reigning Queen of this land, we are willing to consider this point.

What was she supposed to say in response?

Dahlia was not queen.

And Terre Verte was not dead.

Once the Osei learned a member of the royal house still lived, they would surely go back to their original demands for retribution. Would it be enough for them that Queen Sarcelle, who had used magic against their high queen, was dead? Perhaps Dahlia could convince them that—

Perhaps Verte can convince them. Not you. If he is alive, it is no longer your responsibility.

Except that the Osei would not negotiate with an unattached prince, even if they were willing to overlook his attempt to bespell them.

Dahlia pushed the barely started note aside, admitting to herself it was useless to reply until they knew more about Terre Verte's condition.

Instead, she asked Gobe to bring in her other messages, and flipped through them quickly. Now that the seals had been broken, the palace was apparently open to anyone who wanted to go inside; the power that had stifled flames and frozen the air had dissipated. Sepia had taken a crew of servants inside to check for storm damage and report what repairs needed to be made.

"She had your belongings from the palace moved

to your room at the Turquoise," Gobe added, when he saw her studying the notes from Sepia about the palace.

Dahlia looked up, surprised. "Please give her my thanks when you see her."

Funny, the things a person can forget. Dahlia had grown so used to wearing others' clothing that she had almost forgotten about her own. Her own hairbrush. Her own shoes.

"Dahlia." Her name again, but she recognized the voice—and his warmth—before she had turned toward Jade. He always stood a little closer than most Kavet natives considered proper, though when she asked more worldy women if she should be flattered or offended, they had told her that was simply the Silmari way. Covertly observing the other Silmari nobles had confirmed the assurances as true. "I'm glad to see you up and about."

"Thank you. I'm glad to *be* up." Though she would be even gladder to lie down. She didn't ache as badly as she should, but her body felt heavy and tired despite her long sleep.

"I'm sorry to add one more thing to your docket, but the shipbuilders are going to need some time at the next meeting."

"Is there a problem?" The last time that committee had spoken at the general meeting, it had sounded like progress was being made.

"There has been . . . an idea. One I personally am opposed to, but which several of the others seem to have gotten behind. I think we might want to speed up the debates over who's going to captain her, so we can start to establish a firm authority with regards to such matters."

Dahlia nodded, trying not to show her reservations on her face.

The shipbuilders' committee had finally decided that since this ship was so important, the entire voting body should decide on her captain. More than one individual had mentioned to Dahlia that they thought the vote was a horrible idea, that a good captain was not necessarily the man or woman who was best *liked*, but the motion had passed.

Since then, it had been made clear to Dahlia by much of the assembly that her opinion would guide many others'. Jade knew that as well as she did. But she wasn't certain he understood that he wasn't assured her vote.

She knew of the rumors, but Dahlia was still far too Quin to tumble into bed with a man she knew had every intention of taking the first ship back to Silmat. He continued to flirt casually, but was never pushy enough for her to feel uncomfortable.

Granted, she suspected that his infinite, gentlemanly patience with her refusal to sleep with him had more to do with his having at least one other lover in Kavet than it did his being that perfectly accepting of their platonic friendship. That was, as she understood it, the Silmari way.

But it wasn't her way.

She glanced at Celadon, her other rumored lover, who was now also waiting by the doorway. She remembered the way he had touched her hand for comfort earlier in the kitchen. Unlike Jade, who tended to do things like give an impromptu shoulder rub or to wrap an arm around Dahlia's waist when they walked side by side, Celadon was always formal and reserved. The rumors about him came from the sheer amount of time she spent in his company, as if it were impossible for a woman to be friends with a man *without* sleeping with him.

"We'll bring the captain decision up tomorrow, and establish some kind of . . . expedited campaign schedule." She frowned again, or would have if she hadn't discovered instead that she was already frowning. She would have to make sure runners were sent down to the docks so all the candidates would come to the meeting, and a potentially good captain wouldn't lose by default because he was busy doing his job.

"**W**hy did I agree to do this?" she grumbled as she and Celadon finally managed to get outside. They were stopped twice more crossing the plaza, but that was fine; at least they were in the open air.

"Someone needed to," Celadon reminded her, "and you were the only person capable."

Dahlia sat beside the fountain. Three of the four foxfire orbs had cracked from the heat; members of the Order of Napthol had removed them, leaving only one, which sputtered like a dying candle flame. They would need to be replaced before winter or the fountain would freeze.

"Dahlia!"

She turned with a grimace she tried to hide behind a more appropriate expression. It was easier to smile when she recognized the young lady coming toward her, up the path that led to and from the docks.

"Ginger, what brings you down here?"

"Yes," Celadon echoed, more gravely, "what *does* bring you to the market—from *that* direction?"

Ginger tossed her head defiantly. "You only said I wasn't supposed to go to the docks on my own," she said. "I had Serves with me. He escorted me all the way to the market street, then needed to report back to his ship." The frown she gave her brother turned into a smile as she turned to Dahlia. When Dahlia had first come to the city, the girl had embraced her as if she were a sister. The last few weeks, they had become close once more, despite Celadon's attempts to keep Ginger away from the city's political scuffles. "Will you come to dinner with us tonight?" she asked. "I want to celebrate. We've been hired to make the lamps for the new ship. And I'd like you to meet Serves."

Celadon asked, "Did you ask Aunt Willow—"

"Of *course*," Ginger interrupted. "*She* has been asking to have Serves over for weeks. *You* are the one being a grouch."

Dahlia watched Celadon grit his teeth as his sister flounced her hair again, and then reached up to brush it back off her face.

She was on the verge of laughing at Celadon's protective instincts when she noticed the mark on Ginger's wrist. It looked terrifyingly like it was a frostbite scar, wrapped halfway around Ginger's wrist. The gray-black mark was ugly on the girl's skin—twice as much so because it reminded Dahlia of the wounds she had seen in a devastatingly severe form on Helio.

"What is this?" Dahlia asked, pulling Ginger's arm toward her to examine the mark.

"Oh." Ginger pulled away and tugged her sleeve down. "I don't know. I'm absent-minded sometimes. Aunty says I probably leaned on something. I don't remember doing it, I just noticed it there one day. Anyway, I should get the order back to Aunt Willow." She patted her pocket. "I'll see you tonight, Dahlia."

She kissed Celadon on the cheek, and then hugged Dahlia before hurrying off.

"I'd like to kill that sailor of hers," Celadon observed, tone resigned.

"Ginger mentioned a beau, back . . . before," Dahlia said. "I didn't realize it was so serious."

"It probably wouldn't have been, but a lot of sailors

have been stranded here," Celadon replied. "Ginger waited until a week ago to tell us about him."

"Scandal," Dahlia breathed.

Celadon nodded sharply before noticing the teasing glint in her eye. "I didn't yell at her for seeing him, or forbid him from coming to dinner, did I?" Under his breath, he added, "Little sisters should *never* be allowed to date."

Back to the more concerning subject, Dahlia asked, "How long has she had that mark on her wrist?"

"I don't know. I didn't notice it until the same moment you did." He sounded disappointed in himself.

"I know it's not . . . ." She struggled with how to phrase the request. "Would you be willing to let someone from the Cobalt Hall look at it, just to make sure it is what it looks like?"

"What *else* would it be?"

"Some of the members of the Order have had odd injuries like that just appear recently." She didn't want to disclose all the Order's secrets, but Celadon needed some information. "Sometimes they're serious. It seems to be related to their magic."

"My sister doesn't have magic," Celadon snapped, instinctively, before shutting his eyes and drawing a deep breath. "*Please*, Numen, don't let her have magic."

"Someone at the Hall would be able to tell for sure," Dahlia said. "It's not something I want for her, either, but it would be best to know."

"Is it, really? Knowing hasn't helped me any."

"If she has magic, and it's possible it might *hurt* her, she needs to know," Dahlia pointed out. "And if she doesn't have magic, and the affliction attacking the Order is spreading to non-magical people, we need to know that."

He let out an exasperated sigh. "Why do they have to *hide* things like this?" he demanded. "I have spent the last month and a half arguing with the other Followers of the Quinacridone, and convincing people that we have to co-operate with the orders of Napthol and A'hknet. We have to be open with each other and we have to work together, or we won't last the winter. But the damn sorcerers won't let anyone in, won't let anyone help, won't share any kind of information that might be helpful to us . . ."

Dahlia had done no more than lift an eyebrow, reminding him who he was talking to and that she had been on his side throughout, and he broke off.

"I'm sorry," he said. "It frustrates me, that my people are compromising all they believe in order to help this city, while it feels like no one else is willing to bend an inch. The idea that it might have put my sister in danger now makes my blood boil."

"Hopefully it's nothing," Dahlia said. "There's a chance it might have nothing to do with magic."

"Hopefully," Celadon echoed. He started to cross the market in long strides, trusting Dahlia to keep up with him. "Let's try to catch up with her. I'll feel better if we can get this sorted out quickly."

CHAPTER 36

NAPLES

Naples and Cyan slammed into the captain's quarters with little pretense, already pulling at each other's clothes, a task made more difficult by the fact that neither of them wanted to break the kiss locking their bodies together.

Yes, Naples had work to do. He needed to find a way to corner and interrogate Celadon Cremnitz, and he had to find a way to bind back the Abyssi. Those were important things, and part of his mind was adamant that he should be working on them. But this was important, too.

I need the power to do my work, he thought, but he knew that was only an excuse.

Cyan made him feel *good*. Unsullied. Fear and pain faded away in his presence.

Naples wasn't in a strange town with a man he couldn't remember meeting. He was with someone who looked for him whenever the ship came in the spring, and thought of him while in distant ports.

He wasn't with the Abyssi.

The thought made him freeze for just long enough for Cyan to notice. The sailor raised his head, saying past his rapid breath, "You okay?"

Naples nodded, unable to speak, and dragged Cyan's head back down.

He tasted like the cold mint tea volunteers brought for the men and women working to repair the shipyard, and of the huskvine root many Silmari sailors chewed to help them focus. Not of smoke and fire. His lips were hard, aggressive, but the little nibbles of his teeth on Naples' lips were human and did no damage. The hands that roamed over Naples' skin, even when they clenched in passion, did not burn or draw blood.

Naples pushed Cyan back against the wall, and the sailor laughed.

"Aggressive today," he observed, pulling Naples closer without moving away from the wall.

"Complaining?" Normally Naples preferred dominant partners, but just then he felt the need for control.

Cyan shook his head and smiled. "Nope."

He let Naples strip off his shirt and undo his belt, revealing deep brown skin marked with the signs of a rough and hard-working life: a scar left by the lash of an ill-tempered and impatient ship's mate, early in Cyan's career as a sailor; a smaller scar on his ribs from when he had fallen from a low section of rigging directly onto the ship's slop bucket in a failed attempt to impress an adolescent crush; and a shallow slice on his belly that was the result of a bar-room brawl in another distant port.

Naples traced these marks of humanity with his hands, and then with his mouth, remembering the way Cyan had shared the stories during a post-coital half-dozing conversation.

Modigliani. The Abyssi had told Naples its name, finally, as it entered him. *His* name. Naples kept thinking "it," but the demon was most certainly male. He claimed to be a prince of the lowest level of the Abyss, and Naples knew he had spoken the truth when he said his power alone would have burned most men's blood away, had he tried to take them.

Modigliani hadn't been entirely certain Naples was strong enough.

For a while, Naples hadn't been, either.

Being with the Abyssi was ecstasy. And it was pain. And it was magic. And it was terror. And Naples had been too lost in all of that to even notice that every time the Abyssi's hands crossed his skin, they drew blood—blood that, once raised, only heightened the power until it should have blackened his flesh.

"Naples?" Cyan asked.

"*What?*" Too sharp, too loud.

The sailor was looking at him with frowning concern. "Are you all right?"

"I told you—"

"I know what you told me." His voice was soft, but firm. He urged Naples back on his feet and pulled him close, but gently, not passionately. "What's wrong?"

"Hard few weeks," Naples admitted, giving the sailor as much honesty as he could stand.

"Do you want to . . . talk?" the sailor suggested, despite the fact that his body was clearly voting in favor of other pastimes.

Naples shook his head. "I want *you*," he said. "Distract me from my thoughts. If you think you're up to it?" He tried to make the desperate plea into a teasing challenge, but wasn't sure he succeeded.

Regardless, Cyan took him at his word. He lifted Naples onto the empty chart table, and finished the work of unbuttoning and removing his shirt.

This time it was Cyan's turn to freeze, his gaze locking on the last of the wounds left by the Abyssi. Naples hadn't had the power to heal all the Abyssi's "love marks" right away, so the deepest ones remained as pearly scars.

"Not important," he said. "Spell gone bad."

Cyan nodded, but slowly.

It was only moments later, though, as soon as the rest of Naples' clothes were gone, that Cyan stepped back and demanded, "What the *fuck*, Naples?"

Gooseflesh raised on Naples' skin where Cyan's warmth disappeared. "I could say the same."

The sailor's eyes were wide, and his gaze was not focused anywhere Naples wanted it to be. Watching Cyan's eyes dart place to place, staring at the scars, Naples let out a frustrated snarl.

"I've seen a man who survived a leopard attack," Cyan said, slowly, "but it didn't look like this. And Kavet doesn't have leopards."

"It wasn't a leopard attack," Naples spat. "Can we just—"

Cyan pulled him close again, a hand on each side of Naples' hips, and at first Naples thought the sailor had decided to ignore the obviously closed wounds and trust him that they were nothing but the consequences of magic Cyan couldn't possibly understand. One of his hands slid down Naples' back, and then he reached around Naples' leg as if to lift him onto the table again.

Then he dropped him, pulling back with a hiss of horror, and Naples realized what he had been doing.

Each place Cyan had just touched was scarred. Claws not quite like a cat's had traced the exact lines the sailor's hands had followed. Cyan was too smart to miss the connection.

The silence stretched into eternity, it seemed, before the sailor said, "Rumor has it Kavet's sorcerers have dealings with the Abyss."

Naples stood, lust now intermixed with anger. "You've always known what I am."

The sailor scooped Naples' pants off the floor and tossed them at him. "I knew you were a follower of the Napthol. I ignored the rumors because I know better than to trust the kind of gossip a man hears in port."

"What does it *matter*?" Naples demanded.

"*It matters if you are fucking a demon!*" Cyan seemed to want to shout but was struggling to keep his voice down, so it came out as a strangled cry. "It matters because if you're doing that, I have no idea what other rumors are true."

"You're not my *father* and you're certainly not my *wife*," Naples said. "Since when do I owe you explanations?"

He pulled on his pants, then reached for the rest of his clothes. To the Abyss with Cyan, with the ship, with everything. All of Kavet could burn for all he cared.

"Since I haven't been able to get you out of my head!" Cyan shouted. "*I jumped ship for you, Naples.* If the storm hadn't locked all ships back in here, if I hadn't had the horror of that morning as an excuse, I would have lost *everything*. At the time, it seemed like a reasonable idea to give up my entire *life* for a chance to touch you again."

Naples recoiled. "I never—"

"I wrote it off as the effects of the festival, all the magic in the air, and general restlessness. But if you hadn't disappeared—"

"I didn't do a damn thing to you."

Probably. Naples was no ignorant novice who might accidentally use his power to seduce and entrance, but that night he had been tied tightly into the Terra's spell for the Osei. Could that have—

"It wouldn't have been the first time, would it?" Cyan challenged.

"I don't know what you're—"

"They say you raped Celadon Cremnitz, and that you tried to kill him."

Naples let out a sound that was half laugh and half growl. Dressed now, he shoved past Cyan, and started toward the door. If Cyan wanted to blame his stupid decisions on Naples, that was his own issue.

Cyan grabbed his arm.

"Get your hands off me," Naples growled.

"Deny it. Deny *something.*"

"Fuck. You."

He pushed at Cyan, but the other man held on. "Naples, *please.* Tell me I'm wrong, or tell me I don't understand. Because no matter what else might be true, those scars on your body make me think you're in trouble."

Naples spun on him with the rage of a wounded badger. He spoke each word clearly, concisely. "I'll tell you this about me, and about how my power works. I've had you. I'll have you again any time I want you. I've had my power so deep inside you that, if you don't take your hand off me *right now*, I'm pretty sure I can melt your body into tar before you can scream."

Cyan pulled back. Not immediately, but with the wary horror of a man confronting a dangerous animal.

Fine. That was good.

Naples stalked out of the room. Cyan did not follow.

"We don't need him."

Naples spotted Modigliani lounging on the deck like a cat basking in the sun. Scrambling deckhands were moving past and around him, instinctively avoiding the smoky figure without consciously noticing him.

"I don't need *you*, either."

The demon just stretched. "What else do you have, Mancer?"

The words stung. In that moment, the only answer Naples could come up with was, *Not a damn thing*.

He started to descend the ramp to the docks and the demon moved, catching him by the shoulders and holding him tight.

"He was tasty," it crooned. "You said yourself, we could have him again if we wanted him. So why are you upset?"

"Go away," Naples sighed.

To his surprise, the demon obeyed.

Alone, Naples walked with heavy steps back to the center of the city. He had every intention of returning to the Cobalt Hall, but instead his feet took him into the palace. Now that the seals on the door had been broken, the place had a dusty feel to it, like a once-living beast now mummifying in the summer heat.

He climbed the stairs two at a time, and when he reached it, the palace temple let him in.

He passed through the outer temple without paying any attention to it, and when he touched the next door, the Terra's private sanctuary admitted him with a sigh of magic like coming home.

The blood wasn't visible and didn't hang in the air as an odor, but Naples could still sense it. Spilled power. Spilled life. He would have known the Terra was dead even if no one had told him.

He collapsed in a chair and laid his cheek on the old table, his tears flowing freely and staining its scarred surface.

What am I becoming?

He remembered his words to Cyan. He had felt himself turn in his head from sex to a different kind of lust, one for blood and pain. All the fear and hurt had twisted into anger, and he had wanted nothing more than to strike out and injure the one who had injured him.

You could have lied, his common sense was telling him. *You could have laughed off the accusations, and convinced him his suspicions about those marks were silly. You could have defended yourself against his other accusations.*

He hadn't wanted to lie—or even tell the truth, in the case of Cyan's accusations about Celadon. He had wanted Cyan to just *trust* him. Stupid.

No matter what else might be true, those scars on your body make me think you're in trouble.

Trouble, yes.

Sex with Cyan had been good. That was *it*. That was all. And it was over now, so there was no use dwelling on it.

Naples needed to fix the problem. To protect himself. Tell some pretty lies and mop up the mess.

He closed his eyes.

"Terra," he sighed. "Where did you go? You *taught* me this. You started me on this path. Now I've lost you . . . and I'm losing myself. It's not the blood that's the problem, it's the Abyss in my *brain*."

No answer. Of course not. She was gone.

Moving away from the altar, he perused the books Sarcelle had brought to Kavet from her homeland and added to in the decades since. She hadn't been much of a book-teacher.

He found a slim volume by a Tamari scholar titled *Creatures of Blood*. He flipped through it, giving a self-deprecating snort when he found a warning he knew Terra Sarcelle would have brushed off as tripe written by old magic users afraid of the newer forms.

Abyssi are creatures of immediacy and instinct. They are pleasure-centered, and rarely able to focus on anything beyond immediate gratification. Though they are capable of childlike joy or temper, and may switch from one to the other given even a slight distraction or provocation, the deeper emotions are beyond their grasp. That which pleases them one moment may be devoured the instant it bores them, without any lingering sentiment, and as the most intent Abyssi can usually be distracted by the prospect of food or entertainment, they are incapable of focusing on long-term goals or consequences.

Those who work with fire and blood—those which come from the Abyssi—must be careful that they control their tempers and their whims, both of which can be devastating if left unchecked.

Naples threw the book toward the vanity across the room, where it smashed into the Terra's cosmetics and perfumes. Several shattered on the ground, and the reek of talc and lilacs filled the room.

"Why?" he demanded the dead air. "Why *teach* me this?"

He swiped at one of the shelves of ritual supplies, sending priceless materials flying across the room. A knife-blade bit into his hand, but out of habit he drank the power inside and closed the wound before a single drop of crimson fluid touched the floor. He let out the scream of a trapped animal, and it trailed off into a sob.

He had seen his mother's horror, and Henna's, when he had drawn a blade during his fight with Celadon. He shouldn't have let them see that, but damn it, hadn't they felt the power the Quin wielded? How could he have ignored it?

And now he was alone in this room and—

Or not.

Modigliani wrapped him in his arms and tails, fur like night caressing his skin. "They're afraid of you," the demon whispered, "but they'll come around. Humans are naturally wary of those with power. Once they get used to your strength, and understand our purpose here, they will not fear you so much and you will not have to feel such . . ." It trailed off. Shame was not a concept the Abyssi could understand. "Such hurt."

Naples didn't have the strength of will to pull away from the demon.

He leaned back against it.

Just for a little while, he told himself. *Just until this feeling passes.*

"I don't want to disappear again," he said. "It frightened me."

"Then I'll make sure you stay here," the Abyssi said. "Right here." It nipped at the nape of his neck, just enough to draw tiny beads of blood to the surface. "And I'll be . . . gentle . . . with you this time."

Gentle, too, was not a concept the Abyssi truly understood.

CHAPTER 37

DAHLIA

As Dahlia, Celadon, and Ginger entered the kitchen and found it empty, Ginger's shoulders slumped with draining tension. Dahlia saw her look around, taking in the plain surroundings, and wondered what she had expected. Cat entrails hanging from the ceiling?

Dahlia hesitated. She knew outsiders were rarely allowed here. Their earlier access had been an exception. But this was an emergency—or could be. She needed to find someone who could help them.

She led the way up the hall that allowed access to the private quarters, because it was the only area of the Hall she knew her way around.

"Hello?" she called.

A woman she didn't know stepped out of one of the rooms. She frowned at their presence, but asked in a carefully neutral voice, "Can I help you, Dahlia?"

"I'm sorry to intrude," Dahlia said, "but I need to speak to Henna or Maddy. Are they available?"

There was a heartbeat of hesitation before the woman replied, "Henna isn't available right now. I might be able to find Maddy."

"Maddy would be better to talk to, anyway," Celadon said. "We want someone who uses cold power."

Ginger's eyes widened as her brother made such a knowledgeable statement about sorcery, but the normally verbose girl didn't speak.

"What do you need her for?" the woman from the Order asked. "We're very busy."

"Please, just let her know that Dahlia wants to speak to her as soon as possible," Dahlia said, trying to cut past the woman's obvious hostility toward Celadon.

Reluctantly, the woman nodded. "I will speak to Maddy," she said. "Would you wait in the kitchen?"

The kitchen wasn't as much an exile as the front hall would have been, but the wait was still fraught. By the time Maddy entered the room, both Celadon and Ginger were so tense Dahlia worried they might shatter if startled.

Maddy looked exhausted. Dahlia had expected to see her at least a little refreshed since the return of her son, but instead the circles under her eyes were even more pronounced than usual and her steps listless.

"Is everything all right?" Dahlia asked, now almost more concerned about what was going on with the other woman than she was about Ginger.

Maddy shook her head, but didn't explain. "Who's this?" she asked, looking at Ginger.

"Maddy, this is Ginger Cremnitz, my little sister," Celadon said. "Ginger, this is Madder. She's a member of the Order, and she's going to help us."

"Hi," Ginger said, barely a squeak.

"Hello," Maddy replied, with an obvious attempt to gather herself and be kind. "I think I've heard your brother mention you. How old are you now?"

"Seventeen," Ginger answered.

"Seventeen . . . I have a son not much older than you."

Clearly nervous and desperately seeking any kind of response, Ginger blurted out, "Is he cute?"

Maddy and Dahlia both let out a burst of surprised laughter; Celadon grimaced.

"Sorry," Ginger said. "I've never been introduced to a sorcerer before." She seemed to think that was impolite, too. She colored more deeply, and said again, "Sorry."

"It's all right," Maddy said. "What brings you to the Cobalt Hall today, Ginger?"

Ginger hesitated, looking to Celadon for guidance.

"Show her your wrist," Dahlia said. "It's okay."

Ginger pushed up her sleeve to reveal the unsettling mark. Defiantly, she said, "I'm just here because my stupid brother is paranoid and thinks I . . . What?"

She stopped, her moment of bravery reduced to a

quiver of fear again as Maddy took her hand to examine the injury.

"*What?*" Ginger repeated, when she didn't get an immediate reply.

"Ginger, would you be willing to do a test of two for me?" Maddy asked. At Ginger's wary expression, she added, "It will be a little like playing a game."

"You want to test me for magic?" Ginger guessed.

"What do you want her to do, and why?" Celadon interrupted. "No one ever talked to me about any kind of test."

"We didn't need to test you," Maddy replied. "Your power is very aggressive, and hard to miss even for someone who doesn't use cold magic."

"Your *what?*" Ginger squeaked. "Celadon!"

He put his arm back around her shoulders. "So you can't see any on her?"

"I can't, no, but the wound *is* magical," Maddy replied. "It's possible she has just a little power, very tightly repressed."

"If it's repressed, I think we would all rather it *stay* that way," Celadon asserted. Ginger nodded violently enough Dahlia worried for her neck.

"If this mark is made by her own power," Maddy said, enunciating her words as if speaking for a small child, "then obviously, her magic isn't repressed completely, which means it *will* come out, just as yours did. And if this *isn't* made by her own power, then we have an even worse problem than we thought, and it isn't just members of the Order in danger." To Dahlia, she added, "I'm assuming, since you got him to bring his little sister into our corrupted halls, that you told him about our troubles?"

Dahlia nodded.

"And we should have been told when they started!" Celadon said. "Your secrets put my little sister in danger. If Dahlia hadn't seen—"

"*Shut up!*" Maddy snapped, surprising them all with her deviation from her normal poise. "You do *not* get to lecture me on the dangers of what is happening, not when every morning I have to treat my people for these injuries. Not after I spent weeks wondering whether it had killed my son. Not when I'm down here trying to care for your sister while the woman I think of as my family is upstairs so badly hurt she may not last the night. Not when—"

Dahlia stepped between them, putting a hand on each of their arms. "Henna's hurt?"

Maddy drew a deep breath. "She is. It's the same kind of injury many of our members have experienced. We found her quickly and were able to bandage the wounds and stop the bleeding, but the magic that creates the wounds is beyond the abilities of our healers." She scrubbed at her weary eyes. "We thought opening the palace would help. If anything, it's made the situation worse."

"If you need to be with Henna, we can wait," Dahlia said.

Celadon stiffened as if he might disagree, but held his tongue.

Maddy shook her head. "There's nothing more I can do for her right now." She looked at Ginger, who had gone even paler and was biting her lip with anxiety. "Oh, honey, I'm sorry. I'm so sorry. I should never have . . ." She held out a hand to the girl. "You'll be okay."

"If I have magic," Ginger said, "I can get rid of it, right? I can take a brand. Can't I just do that right away? Do I have to be tested? I mean, it's just a little mark."

"If you have magic, the brand is an option." Maddy had to force the words out. "But if you don't, giving you the brand can hurt you. It looks for magic, and if it doesn't find any, it keeps looking."

Celadon drew a deep breath and spoke formally. "Madder, I am sorry I snapped at you. While I do wish your people and mine could communicate more freely, Dahlia's right that this isn't the time or place for the argument. I know you will do anything you can to help my sister, even though you have your own burdens, and I appreciate that."

"I need to bring her to the temple," Maddy said. "There's no danger in the tests, and they won't hurt in any way." She hesitated for a long moment before adding, "She's a minor, so if you want to stay with her, you can."

"I would prefer that."

Resolutely, Maddy led them into the bowels of the Cobalt Hall and up a wide spiraling staircase. At the third floor, she stopped by an ornate doorway decorated with runes in inlaid gold and silver.

"Dahlia and Celadon, you can follow us in, but I must ask that you remain by the door and *not* speak or attempt to influence Ginger's answers. If you have questions, you may ask afterwards. Any distractions—especially from you, Celadon, since your own power is so strong—could lead to a mistake in my reading of her power, which as I've mentioned could be very dangerous if she chooses to take the brand."

Both Dahlia and Celadon nodded solemnly. Dahlia's heart went out to Ginger, who was trembling as Madder pushed open the doorway and escorted her inside.

Dahlia looked without comprehension around the room, taking in sights she had never seen before and likely would never see again. Almost every wall was lined with shelves, many occupied by books, but others weighed down by an assortment of paraphernalia ranging from sparkling crystal or finely worked metal to what looked like bits and pieces of junk. Small, mismatched tables of various heights, sizes and materials were placed around the room in no obvious arrangement.

She glanced at Celadon; he had crossed his arms across his chest and leaned back against the door, but the posture didn't look entirely hostile. It was almost as if he were fighting the impulse to reach out.

Dahlia edged closer to him and he took her hand. She could feel a fine vibration in him, and his palm was cool against hers.

"Sit down," Maddy said to Ginger.

"Where?" the girl asked, looking from table to table. None were high enough for chairs, though several had brightly colored cushions next to them for sitting.

"Wherever you would like," Maddy answered. "You can look around first if you want."

Though she was obviously still nervous, Ginger's natural curiosity had apparently returned. She walked through the room, eyes wide as she examined the tables and the shelves. She started to reach out once, then jerked her hand back.

"It's okay," Maddy said. "You can look at things, touch them or pick them up. You won't damage anything and nothing here is going to hurt you."

Celadon closed his eyes, as if he understood better than Dahlia what any of this meant and hated it.

"Is this part of the test?" Ginger asked.

"I want you to be comfortable before we begin," Maddy replied, "and not distracted wondering what something is."

Ginger let out a snort. "Comfortable and not distracted. *Here.* Sure." She idly picked up a small crystal bowl, then set it back down carefully, as if afraid it would break. Her fingertips trembled as she continued to explore.

Though Maddy had implied this was not part of

the test, Dahlia could tell she was paying attention to what Ginger reached for, and keeping a mental list.

"Can we get on with this?" Ginger finally asked, putting down a jar of what appeared to be honey with an audible *thunk*.

"Take a seat," Maddy said again.

Ginger sighed. With one last glance around the room, she sank down in front of a small glass table with a square of white silk embroidered in silver thread covering most of its surface.

As she knelt, Dahlia saw Celadon let out a silent sigh. He closed his eyes.

Madder went to one of the bookshelves and pulled down a simple box the size of a loaf of bread. It was smooth wood, silver-gray, without ornamentation. She put it on the floor next to the table Ginger had chosen and took out a large stack of glossy cards.

"These cards have symbols on them," Maddy said, fanning several out so Ginger could see. "I want you to sort them into piles, according to which symbol is on them."

Ginger watched doubtfully as Maddy put three large stacks of cards face down on the table.

"Do I need to know what the symbols mean?" Ginger asked.

Maddy shook her head. "No. If it matters to you, they're letters in the old Dursay alphabet. Just sort them according to how they look. If you find a blank card, set it aside."

Ginger reached for the first card, turned it face up, then paused to look at Maddy. "Just put them into piles?"

Maddy nodded. "Yes, as many as you need."

Ginger looked at the first card a few moments longer, then shrugged, put it down face up in front of her. She glanced at Maddy again, but the sorceress gave no further instructions.

The task seemed simple to Dahlia, but as she watched, Ginger's expression made it seem less so. She sorted the first three cards into separate piles with apparent ease, then hesitated at the next one. She frowned at it, started to move it toward one pile, then stopped and chose another. She continued to look at the errant card as if it had somehow tricked her and she wasn't sure of its position. She picked it up, then put it back down, in the process revealing its face to Dahlia.

The card, as far as Dahlia could tell, was a perfect, glossy white. Blank.

CHAPTER 38

NAPLES

Naples limped into the temple, hoping to find it empty, and was shocked to recognize its occupants. He was only a breath away from demanding that Dahlia and Celadon explain their presence in this sacred place when he noticed his mother and the girl sitting across the altar from her.

He didn't recognize the girl, but her features gave her away as a Cremnitz, even if Celadon's intense, protective gaze hadn't made it clear that she was kin to him. She was sitting at one of the altars almost exclusively used by cold magic sorcerers and was apparently being tested.

Celadon glared at Naples when he entered, but didn't attempt to stop him. Maddy would have warned him that distracting Ginger could influence the test though Naples was surprised the Quin cared enough to be able to stay so silent.

It might test Celadon's self-control too much if Naples lingered there in the doorway, just a breath away from the preacher, but Naples couldn't resist seeing how the girl was doing. The testing was always exciting, not just for an individual who came to the Hall but to everyone. He stepped into the room, careful to keep his footfalls soft and quiet.

He probably could have done a song and dance routine without fear. The girl was completely fixated on the task before her, and paid him no attention.

The "game" Madder was playing with the Cremnitz girl was simple. There was a collection of cards. Each one bore a symbol.

To Dahlia Indathrone, some of those cards would appear blank. On some, she would see a completely different symbol than what a magic user would see; on others, Celadon and Naples would see different symbols, as some lines were drawn with cold power, and some with hot. There were some cards Naples could see but a weaker member of the Order could not. So the test, in addition to determining the presence of power and the type, could also estimate power level.

The girl hadn't put aside any blank cards. That

meant she had power—maybe not a lot, but enough that she had come this far in the testing.

His mother would have let her explore earlier and watched what tools she was drawn to. Did her eyes trace runes and symbols as she walked, or did she run her fingers over the edges of crystals? Did she rub a bit of ash between her fingers, or walk by it, oblivious to its presence? All those little hints could tell so much about a person's eventual tendencies.

Naples wished he could have seen it.

For a while, as he watched the test continue, he let himself be pulled into the excitement of the moment—and then felt the crash of disappointment as he recalled that this was Celadon Cremnitz's kin. She couldn't possibly understand. She didn't realize how many people came to the Cobalt Hall desperate to pass this test, only to fail.

She would never know that Naples' mother had to work to keep the smile from her face, because a smile might influence the girl's choices or affect her instinctive use of her power. The Cremnitz girl, undoubtedly raised Quin, couldn't know that she would deserve a celebration, that she need only accept this gift she had, and she would be welcomed into the Napthol family with pride and joy.

Times were hard; Naples understood that. But no matter how hard, if she walked out of the temple and allowed Maddy to announce her as a member of their Order, people would *cheer* for her.

But she wouldn't. He knew that as surely as he knew Celadon was standing beside him, the grinding of his teeth audible.

The girl put the last of the cards in its place and then looked up with a sleepy, dazed smile. Naples let himself grin. Even with his whole body aching as if he had taken a beating, he wanted to pick the girl up and spin her in his arms and congratulate her.

He might have, if he hadn't been sure that Celadon would murder him on the spot.

Naples' mother did it for him. She pulled the girl to her feet and hugged her tightly, saying, "That was wonderful!"

"Did I do well?" the girl asked. "When you told me what to do, I thought it would be easy, but it was really difficult."

"You did great," Maddy replied, finally allowing herself a wide smile. "I'll need to go through them carefully so I can get more of an exact idea of how you did, but—" As she spoke, her gaze moved up. She was still smiling when she first turned to Celadon, and then Naples saw her hit the same mental wall he had moments before, as she realized who she was talking to. She quirked a half smile at her son in greeting before saying to Celadon, "You should be very proud of your sister."

Celadon flinched from the words. "I take it that means she has power."

"I do?" the girl asked. "I thought . . . I was sure I . . ." Wide-eyed, she asked, "I really do?"

Maddy nodded. "You really do."

"You know what you need to do, then, to prepare the brand?" Celadon asked.

Naples' already fragile self-control snapped as a wave of revulsion rolled through him. *What?*

"She wants to take the brand," Celadon replied. "My sister does not need this—"

"How old is she?" Naples demanded.

"Seventeen, and old enough to know what she wants."

"Gentlemen." The Indathrone girl stepped between them with a nervous, forced smile on her face. Didn't this woman know how stupid it was to stand between angry sorcerers? "That's enough. This is about Ginger, not you."

Naples looked at the girl, who was staring at the seven piles of cards she had put on the table. "Ginger?" he asked.

She looked up with an expression of amazement on her face, but tears in her eyes. "Hi," she said softly.

He moved closer. Celadon actually *growled*, but Dahlia prevented him from stepping farther into the temple.

"Naples—"

He touched his mother's arm, shaking his head to interrupt when she tried to stop him.

"*Someone* needs to tell her," he said. "She deserves it."

She let him pass.

"Nice to meet you, Ginger," he said. "My name is Naples."

"You're Maddy's son?" she asked. Then she blushed.

He nodded. "I'm Maddy's son, yes. I was raised here in the Hall."

"And you're a sorcerer."

"And I'm a sorcerer," he agreed. Were they really only two years apart in age? She seemed so *young*. Of course, that's how the Quin liked their women, soft and subservient to their men. "Ginger, I know your brother doesn't like magic, but even he knows it can be used in good ways. Otherwise he would have taken the brand himself, right?"

Ginger's eyes widened.

Celadon growled, "You bastard, you leave her alone."

Naples spun about. "It's true, isn't it? You're going to allow your little sister to *mutilate* herself, when you have been willfully and knowingly using your power since the Apple Blossom Festival. That's to say nothing of the fact that it is *illegal* in the country of Kavet to brand a minor. For a reason!"

"Naples—"

"No!" He broke off his mother's protest. "I don't care that she's a Cremnitz. She should be allowed the same rights and privileges of anyone who has ever passed that test! She should be celebrated. She should have a party given in her honor in a hall lit by foxfire orbs in every color of the rainbow and decorated with roses on every table. She should be able to study, to know what it feels like to turn ash into crystal. She should absolutely *not* be told that something the Numen graced her with at birth is shameful and dirty, and she should never be forced to lie down on that table and bite down on a strip of leather to keep from screaming while they brand her and burn her power away like a criminal!"

Why were there tears in his eyes? He didn't even know this girl.

"Her power could be dangerous to her," Dahlia said firmly.

"Sailors face death every day on the seas," Naples said. "Farming accidents claim lives every year. *Life* is dangerous, but we make of it what we will with the tools we are given. A person should not have to be ashamed of what they *are*." He glanced down at the piles Ginger had made, and then looked back to the girl herself, who was visibly shaking with emotion.

He started to reach out, to put a comforting hand on her arm, and stopped himself just in time to keep from having Celadon leap across the room to stop him.

"You have what is known as cold power," he said. "It's the kind your brother uses. People with cold power are often very good healers. Some can take crystals and coax them to make music. Some can turn ice into beautiful sculptures. You can have a place here, if you want it."

Ginger Cremnitz had the most incredibly wide doe-eyes. No wonder her brother was so protective of her; Naples had never once been interested in a girl or woman, but he imagined, looking at her, that she probably couldn't go far without young men panting after her.

"Look," he said, recognizing how overwhelmed she had to be feeling, "it will take a little time to sort through the cards, and after that, it will take a couple days to make a brand specific to your power—one that will scar the least, and hurt the least. In that time, I want you to consider your choices. If you have any questions, you can ask anyone in our Order, and we'll answer you. And if you decide that you don't want to take the brand, and your family disagrees with you, you have a place to go."

"Maddy, Dahlia, would you please escort my sister downstairs?" Celadon asked through clenched teeth. "I need to talk to Naples alone."

"Alone, oh?" Naples teased. He wished he could get away with hitting the man, but knew he couldn't.

"Naples," his mother said, the tone heavy with warning.

"I'll play nice," he promised. "I need to talk to him, anyway."

The ladies left, Dahlia and Ginger each with a last nervous look back, and then Celadon and Naples were alone in the temple.

"How *dare* you," Celadon growled, "try to influence my sister? Try to convince her to keep her magic, when you know what it could do to her?"

"The wild power's effects vary with the strength of the user. Ginger has power, but even if she dedicated herself to her magic today, she wouldn't develop her abilities fast enough for them to endanger her before we can sort this out."

"She already has one frostbite scar," Celadon said.

"*One*," Naples replied. "One scar, which didn't seem to bother her at all today. Do you have any idea how much pain and trauma is associated with taking the brand? It looks like a small mark, but its effect on the body isn't minor." He shook his head. "She has a couple days. Hopefully she'll come to a reasonable decision. If she doesn't, I *will* step forward and assert the law which protects minors from guardians like *you*."

"Times have changed," Celadon asserted. "The Terre aren't here for you to—"

"Whether or not you and Indathrone think your council is the new king and court, I will fight to protect that girl."

"Protect her from *what*? I will protect her from *you*. All that crap you fed her about magic, I notice you didn't mention—"

"She has time. She'll make a decision," Naples said, trying to change the subject. Hearing Celadon speak of branding that girl had raised a kind of righteous fury in him, but he knew he had important things to say to the preacher, and that this was likely to be the only chance he had to speak to him alone. "If you really want to protect her, you can help us figure out what's going on with the magic in Kavet."

"I don't know a damn thing about your magic," Celadon growled, moving toward the door.

Naples stepped in his way. "Your power is a different type, but in its own field, it may be as strong as mine. But I have been studying here since before I was old enough to talk, while you only just recently realized you had yours. How?"

"How, *what*?"

"You are one of the most powerful cold magic practitioners in Kavet and you don't have a single frostbite burn on your body, do you? Because you aren't just a sorcerer. Who have you made your deals with?"

"I don't know what you're talking about."

"Damn it, Celadon!" He almost caught the other man's arm before he thought better of it. As amusing as it would be to nudge Celadon into replicating that shocking display of raw power he had shown in the kitchen, Naples didn't have time to get thrown across the room again.

"The only thing I know about sorcery," Celadon spat, "is that it is *killing* your kind. I know it is why Terre Jaune and Terra Sarcelle are dead. I know it murdered the potion-maker, Helio. And I know it has gravely injured and possibly killed Henna. So how can you—"

Naples felt his world spin. "What do you mean? What happened to Henna?"

How he hated Celadon for the look of triumph in his eyes right then. "Maddy told us before we came up. Go look at her. I gather she'll live or die in less time than it will take to make the brand. Wait for *that*, then come back and tell me whether I should let my sister join your cursed ranks."

CHAPTER 39

DAHLIA

Dahlia hesitated in the hallway with Maddy and Ginger. "I'm not sure we should leave those two alone together."

"They can take care of themselves," Maddy answered, shaking her head sadly. "And Naples wouldn't get into a fight in the temple. There's too much of value that could be damaged."

Ginger spoke up. "Celadon really has magic?"

Maddy nodded. "He only realized it recently. He doesn't like it, but he decided not to take the brand, and has been able to use it to help us at times."

"Hmm."

Dahlia could see the girl reevaluating her entire

life in much the same way Dahlia had upon reaching the city. Dahlia watched the conversation, intent on making sure Maddy gave the girl honest answers and didn't try to bully or manipulate her into anything while Celadon was distracted.

As Maddy led them back downstairs, Ginger asked, "Is magic really dangerous, or is that my brother being Quin?"

Maddy paused to consider, then spoke carefully. "It can be dangerous, especially lately," she admitted. "But if I thought your life was in danger, I wouldn't have let Naples argue with you against taking the brand. Most members of our Order have relatively little power, as you seem to, and the wild magic hasn't bothered them much."

"But it is what hurt your friend Henna?"

The girl was bright, though at that exact moment, it looked as though Maddy wished she were less so.

"Yes, it's what hurt Henna," Maddy said. "She is nearly the strongest of the hot magic users here."

Ginger tilted her head. "Who is the strongest?"

With a wince, Maddy admitted, "Naples."

"I'm sorry," Ginger said softly. "I know you're worried about people you care for, and probably don't like being pestered like this, but I think I need to ask these questions."

"I know. I will answer any questions you put to me."

"Then . . ." Ginger drew a breath. "Naples is your son, and you said Henna is like a sister to you. They're in more danger than I am. If taking the brand could keep them safe, why haven't they? And do you wish they would?"

Maddy leaned back against the wall and shut her eyes as she took several slow, steadying breaths.

"You saw Naples' reaction when Celadon mentioned the brand. Sorcery isn't a tool to him, something that can be picked up and put down when it's convenient. It is part of who he is, and it is a part he cherishes. Taking the brand would kill part of him." Maddy opened her eyes then, but stared at the ceiling as she spoke. "As he mentioned, branding is also painful, and often has long-term consequences. There have been only a few cases in Kavet's history where powerful sorcerers were convicted of repeated crimes of magical maleficence and branded in consequence, but we share them among ourselves as cautionary tales, because such sorcerers rarely live full lives after. They report phantom sensations like people sometimes do when they lose limbs, and often suffer chronic pain or illness. It isn't as bad among those who take the brand before their power fully manifests, as you are considering, but I still do not think it is healthy. And anyway . . ."

She sighed again. As she reached the more critical part of her explanation, she turned her gaze back on Ginger.

"I know I could lose Naples to his power, but even

if he took the brand, what then? Would he become a
sailor? A soldier? He isn't the type to take any kind of
'safe' profession. Times are hard for magic users, but
they're hard for everyone in Kavet right now. At least
this way, he's true to what he is. I wouldn't steal that
from him, even if it were my choice to make."

Maddy had been frank and, as far as Dahlia could
tell, honest. The longer their conversation in the hall
went, the less concerned Dahlia was about leaving
Ginger alone with Maddy and the more worried she
became about Celadon and Naples being alone together in the temple.

"Maddy, do you want to show Ginger around and
let her know what options she has if she doesn't take
the brand?" Dahlia suggested. Maddy wouldn't want
to give such a tour with an outsider in tow, and Ginger
might have questions she would feel more comfortable asking without Dahlia present.

"Would you like that?" Maddy asked.

Ginger's eyes lit up, the curiosity Dahlia loved about
her clearly reacting to the offer to see more of a place
that had always been so mysterious and forbidden.

"Yes, please," she said.

Dahlia left the two of them together and back-
tracked to the temple. She apparently shouldn't have
worried; she encountered Celadon, unharmed and
alone, before she had gone up an entire flight of stairs.

As he saw her, he demanded, "Where's Ginger?"

"Talking with Maddy," Dahlia said evenly.

"*Damn.*" He sighed heavily, then started walking again, leading them back toward the public areas of the Cobalt Hall.

Dahlia had expected more than the one whispered curse. "That's it?"

"She's seventeen," he grumbled. "I can't make her decisions for her, and she would be a fool to make a decision like this without thinking it over and getting all the information she feels she needs. And Ginger isn't stupid." He frowned. "She still has lousy taste in men, though. She's too sweet to realize a man can have a pretty face and say pretty things and be a snake inside. I don't care what kind of power Naples has. If he takes advantage of her, I'll kill him."

Dahlia didn't intend to discuss Celadon's hatred of the young sorcerer, so she turned the conversation. "How will her beau respond to her considering the Order? He's Quin, isn't he? Or close to it?"

Celadon paused, contemplative. Started to smile. Stopped. Mock-frowned. "That isn't a fair tactic to take at all. Now I must choose between wanting her to get rid of Abyss-spawned magic, or wondering if the magic could get rid of that damn sailor. And if he breaks her heart because he learns she has magic, I'm going to end up *defending* the Order and beating the tar out of him."

Dahlia laughed and Celadon gave a self-deprecating smile and a shrug. He was no sailor, used to hard labor and dockside brawling. He wasn't likely to make good on any of his physical threats.

They returned to the assembly room, which was quieter now that it was after the dinner hour, but not empty. A lively group in the corner was debating something having to do with fruit trees, a topic of which Dahlia was heartily tired.

The first time she overheard Terre Verte's name, she turned toward it just in time to hear a man say in a hushed murmur, "*No, really, I saw them bring him out of the palace.*"

Recognizing him as one of the Quin, she nodded toward Celadon, who drifted as if aimless toward the group.

The gossip about the prince had started.

Dahlia left Celadon to get the news from his people as she walked the length of the sideboard, wishing there were something more appetizing on it than a few shreds of bread that had been put out many hours ago.

Dinner. In her worry about Ginger, she had entirely forgotten about dinner with Willow Cremnitz. She hoped Celadon had thought to send someone to the house to let her know they wouldn't be there, since they were far too late now.

"Forget to eat again?" a teasing voice behind her asked.

"I suppose I did," she said. "I was . . . busy."

"You always are." Jade turned her gently and put his hands on her shoulders, then applied gentle pressure with his fingertips, trying to release the tension that turned the muscles of her neck and back to steel.

She shut her eyes, leaning into the massage with a sigh. The first week or so after the ice storm, her heart had given a little lurch every time she saw Jade. The handsome aristocrat had been her savior, and his tales of his native land had been romantic, an escape from the Turquoise and the bitter, extended weekend. In the time since, that dazzled infatuation had faded to a more gentle fondness. She valued his friendship and was glad she had been too focused on political conflicts to fall for his casual flirtation.

Not that she never wondered what would have happened if she had been the kind of girl who could have given herself over to an ill-advised whirlwind romance.

"Can I interest you in a bowl of fisherman's stew down at the Crawdiddy?" he asked.

"They're open already?" Dahlia recognized the name of the tavern a group from the Order of A'hknet had proposed opening. Mentally, Dahlia reviewed the most recent update she had received about the dockside market.

"Oh, stop that," Jade chastised gently. "I've come to recognize the crease that forms on your brow when you're picturing reports. Yes, they started taking in supplies this afternoon and are open for the first time tonight. They've specifically asked for the honor of your attendance."

The amused lilt in his tone took the pressure off the otherwise lofty invitation.

"I would love to," she answered, just as Celadon returned to interrupt their conversation with a disapproving frown. He had pulled her aside once to let her know it "looked bad" when she let Jade touch her so familiarly; Dahlia had been too tired at the time to care about anyone's approval, and had stared him down wordlessly until he backed off and mumbled an apology. He hadn't brought it up again.

"I can make sure all the captains have received word about tomorrow's debate and election while I'm there," she mused.

"*Or*," Jade suggested, "you can relax and have a nice meal."

"Do you really think the docks after dark are the best place to bring a lady?" Celadon asked.

"You mean with all the foreign sailors getting laced, whoring about, and starting brawls?" Jade shook his head, exasperated, in response to Celadon's scandalized expression. Dahlia understood the Silmari's point, but also knew he had chosen to be crude to irritate Celadon.

"The docks are almost as staid as the central market at the moment, and will probably stay that way until ship-trade opens again," Jade continued. "Besides, I don't think there's a man or woman in this city who wouldn't jump into the fray if someone tried to threaten Dahlia."

Dahlia did what she usually did when the two of them squared off, traditional Quin values coming into conflict with Silmari disdain for fussy delicacy— she walked away. If the Crawdiddy had managed to open early, she wanted to support that establishment. She could decide whether to be angry with Jade or Celadon later.

As expected, both men stopped bickering and hurried to catch up to her before she reached the door.

She addressed Celadon first. "You'll keep me updated?" she asked, referring to Ginger without saying her name.

He pressed his lips together, but nodded. "I'm going to stay here until she comes out."

"And if she chooses to stay the night?"

Dahlia tried to keep the question quiet, but knew Jade overheard. Thankfully, the Silmari had the sense to recognize the private conversation and say, "Dahlia, I'll meet you outside."

She nodded grateful acknowledgement. Once Jade was gone, Celadon said, "If she chooses to stay with the Order, I'll have to tolerate that, but I won't have it while she's still my responsibility. If I don't see her by a reasonable hour, I'll go looking for her."

Dahlia winced. "I'll come back after dinner. Please don't go storming the Cobalt Hall without me."

If someone needed to fetch Ginger, Dahlia knew

she could manage it with far less conflict than Celadon could.

She was about to leave when Celadon asked, "What exactly *is* your relationship with Jade?"

"Is it any of your business?"

Quite simply, Celadon replied, "I'd like it to be." As Dahlia tried to puzzle out what those artless words meant, she noticed the pink flush creeping up Celadon's cheeks. He drew a deep breath. "I know I've been a beast to you at times in the past, and it won't surprise me if you tell me to find a hole in the Abyss to crawl into, but . . . well, I was hoping to have a conversation with your father. And I was hoping you could give me some hint as to whether you would like that."

She stared at him for a moment. Her father? Did he have questions about farming? Or—

Oh. Now she understood.

And she couldn't help her response. In the face of Celadon's nervous, rambling words, contrasted with all the stress and horror and uncertainty of the last few days, she laughed out loud.

"You are . . . such a Quin." The Followers of the Quinacridone believed in those old-fashioned manners, of declaring intentions for courtship to lady and father, of permission and ritual and romance. But Dahlia had pictured the actual conversation so much differently.

"Well . . . yes," Celadon managed to answer, confusion, hope, and nervousness showing equally on his face.

Dahlia wasn't certain how she felt about the proposal. As he had admitted, he had treated her terribly, and even if he had apologized for that, even if she had seen him change, did she trust him not to revert to his previous ways as soon as the crisis passed? On the other hand, saying yes wasn't a commitment to accept any future proposal. What he was asking was, did she want to give him a chance?

Celadon drew a shaking breath. "I don't want to pressure you, but saying *something* would be nice."

"I think . . ." She considered his very earnest—now bordering on terrified—expression, resisted the urge to start laughing again, and said, "You should speak to my father."

Celadon nodded, his anxiety shifting to elation. It was a new kind of expression for him, one that was quite endearing. "I'll do that, then."

"Let me know when you hear back, if you have a question for me."

"I assure you, I will."

She felt a kind of giddy joy that made her steps buoyant as she walked down to the docks and flavored the food at the Crawdiddy better than any fish and spices ever could.

It wasn't Celadon specifically that made her feel so good, she realized. Courtship and marriage had never been her ultimate goal in life, and though Celadon had become a close friend, she didn't get lovesick and sigh at his name or feel butterflies in her stomach when she gazed into his blue eyes. Instead, it was *hope* that had brightened her gaze and lightened her steps. It was the assumption that there would be a future, and happiness in that future. It was the thought that, someday, things would return to normal.

CHAPTER 40

NAPLES

Why hadn't his mother even *mentioned* that Henna was hurt?

No, no. Much as he wanted to be angry about the oversight, Naples knew the answer. She hadn't been his mother when he had seen her; she had been Madder, leader of the Order of Napthol, and she had been with a potential new student. She had also been in front of Celadon and Dahlia.

Knowing that, Naples still hated that it could have been hours before he learned what had happened if Celadon hadn't mentioned it.

He didn't know if he believed the Quin's protests that he had no idea what Naples meant about his power. Unfortunately, if the Quin had somehow bound himself to one of the divine others in the way that Naples had bound himself to one of the infernal, he didn't intend to admit it.

It's like he doesn't trust me, Naples thought wryly.

Naples shook his head, trying to clear the short confrontation from his mind.

He sent away the novice that had been watching Henna, shut the door to the sickroom behind himself, then rounded on the Abyssi he saw crouched at the foot of Henna's bed.

"I didn't do it," Modigliani said with a yawn before Naples opened his mouth. "I was just waiting to see if she died so I could eat her."

"Then what did do this to her?"

"Power," the demon answered.

"In the form of one of your kind?"

It leaned over Henna, close enough that Naples moved forward, ready to intervene if it tried to touch her.

Celadon had said she would "live or die," as if he didn't know or care which one. It took only a quick glance for Naples to know the latter was more likely. The novice Maddy had assigned to watch her had been a healer, but she hadn't been working when he entered; she had been using her power only to keep track of Henna's vital energies, waiting for the moment when others should be summoned to say their final farewells.

"No, not like me," the Abyssi said. "I'm the only

one like me. She isn't strong enough to bring one of us into this world."

Henna also wasn't stupid enough to try. "Then what made these injuries?"

"Power. Your body accepts power. Hers fights it."

"Why?"

"Because you are Abyssumancer. And she is human." The Abyssi was getting impatient, which meant trying to question him further would be useless. It didn't matter anyway; Naples would find out more about the injuries' origins by trying to heal them than by trying to understand the demon's words.

He put a hand over Henna's and shut his eyes to focus, only to be distracted when the door opened behind him to admit Maddy and the Quin girl, Ginger.

"What's she doing here?" Hearing his own accusative tone, he said directly to Ginger, "You have every right to be here. I just don't see why you would *want* to be. Do you know her?"

Ginger shook her head. "I wanted to see. That sounds terrible, I know. It's hard to believe a sorcerer is afraid of anything."

"None of our healers have been able to do anything about these kinds of wounds," his mother warned him, taking in the situation. "The power that made them pushes our magic away."

"I was able to heal similar wounds on myself," Naples said. "I don't know for sure that I can do anything, but I'm planning to try." To Ginger, he added,

"You can watch if you would like. It might look a little strange or even scary to you, and my power doesn't work the same way yours will, but maybe it will interest you."

Ginger nodded, eyes wide. "I would like to see, if I won't be in the way."

"You don't have enough active power yet to interfere," he said. "Mother, would you mind stepping out and giving me a little room?"

Madder nodded. "I should go check on Clay, anyway. You'll look out for Ginger? And Ginger, is that all right with you?"

They both nodded, so she stepped back through the door and closed it behind herself.

Though his mother mostly used cold power, Naples had studied with her long enough that he could sometimes feel her when he worked. That was not, however, the real reason he wanted her gone. She wouldn't approve of his methods. That disapproval was far more distracting than her power ever could be.

"Is there anything I should do?" Ginger asked.

"Make yourself comfortable," he replied. "I'll answer any questions you have after."

She nodded and leaned back against the wall, watching him.

Modigliani yawned widely. "We aren't going to go anywhere fun until this is done, are we?"

"Nope," Naples answered, softly so Ginger wouldn't hear.

He knelt beside the bed again and put one hand on top of Henna's. He had studied with her extensively as well. He knew the way her magic was supposed to feel, which was what made it easy to recognize the wrongness in it. *Power*, Modigliani had said, and he was right. There was so much extra magic twined in with Henna's, it was no wonder it was burning her. Once Naples had healed her, maybe there would be a way to siphon some of that extra power away, to keep it at a level her body could handle.

First, though, she was bleeding inside. *That* was easy to sense; his magic was drawn to blood. While it had been easy to heal his own wounds, though, he wasn't familiar enough with hers to act with the same level of instinct. He also had to be careful not to push any extra magic into her when her body was already overwhelmed.

"Would you like help?" the Abyssi finally offered.

"Why would you help?"

This time Ginger heard him. She tilted her head, curious, but seemed to understand that he wasn't talking to her. She didn't ask, at least.

"I'm bored. It will go quicker if I help." He crossed to stand behind Naples, embracing him almost in his usual fashion, but leaving his arms free. "Besides, you plan to drink the extra power from her."

"Only to help her."

Modigliani shrugged, dismissing the importance of the distinction. Naples returned his attention to Henna.

For an instant, with the demon so close, he couldn't help but see Henna as the Abyssi did: blood, meat, and power, something more worth devouring than repairing. A creature too weak to be of use.

He shut his eyes and bit his lip, fighting the demon's influence on his mind. This was Henna. *Henna*.

"Henna," he said aloud, before putting a hand on her chest over her heart.

Modigliani put his slightly larger hand on top of Naples'. He flexed once and his claws drew pinpoints of blood from Henna's skin in four places, just above the tips of Naples' fingers.

It was enough to form the connection. Suddenly Naples could see Henna's injuries as if he were looking at a detailed mural by the clear light of day. The wounds on her skin, though deep, were superficial compared to the damage done inside. Her *heart* was bleeding, the veins supplying it with blood broken. There was blood pooling in her lungs. If not for her magic, she would have been dead already.

Naples worked like a surgeon, using his magic in the most effective way he knew. He absorbed the spilled blood, and used the power from that to knit together the ruptured veins and arteries. The Abyssi did what the Abyssi did best: it fed. It worked deftly, helping Naples sever the foreign magic from Henna's. When that power fought back, the Abyssi subdued it and consumed it happily.

And the alien power *did* fight. Naples recognized

the stain of the Abyss clutching at Henna's flesh, but Modigliani had been honest; it wasn't his power corrupting her. Another Abyssi had set its hooks into her—when? When the Terra had opened a tear to that realm, trying to save her son? Or earlier, perhaps the moment she had first stepped on Kavetan soil?

Naples felt his body tremble with fatigue as he turned his attention to the cuts and burns up and down Henna's skin. With the power that had made them gone, they were easier to heal, but Naples was nearing the end of his strength. Maybe he could borrow just a little . . .

He threw himself back with a growl, and then fell, panting, to his knees. The Abyssi stood above him, disappointed.

"Naples?"

He looked up toward the voice with eyes that were nearly blinded by hunger. Meat. That was all the figure was at first as it moved closer.

Naples clenched a fist, trying not to reach for her. He had needed the Abyssi in order to heal Henna, but he would not let it have him again.

Ginger knelt beside him. "Are you all right?"

"Give me some space?" he managed to gasp.

She scuttled backward. With her farther away, it was easier to breathe and to remember that he was human.

"She would be tasty," the demon said. "Not for your normal feeding method, though."

"And then Celadon would fucking kill me," Naples

grumbled. "Get out of here. Go have your fun without me for a while. I'll meet you later." The Abyssi obeyed, and Naples pushed himself up. His legs wobbled, but that was just fatigue; food would fix that. Now that he was capable of looking at Ginger and thinking like a human being, he lifted his gaze. "Sorry. That took a lot out of me."

His voice was breathy. He could feel his racing heart not just in his chest but across his skin and even in his eyes.

"She looks better," Ginger said hesitantly. "Pale, though."

"She *is* better. But she lost a lot of blood. She will be weak awhile," Naples said, "but she'll be all right. And I think I managed to disconnect the wild power that hurt her in the first place."

Ginger's eyes widened. "That's wonderful!" Naples stumbled and she caught his arm, which nearly made him laugh—he had to have at least six inches on her, and here she was practically holding him up. "Are you all right?"

"Tired," he admitted. He looked at Henna and satisfaction suffused him. She would sleep a while longer, but once she woke and they got some food into her, she would be fine.

He was mostly walking on his own power by the time they reached the hallway.

"How long was I working?" Naples asked.

"A little over an hour maybe," Ginger answered.

"Someone looked in once. The cuts on her skin had started to disappear by then, and I didn't want them to distract you, so I told them you were working and shooed them out."

"Good thinking. Thank you. You stayed the whole time?"

Ginger nodded. "Like you said, I couldn't see anything except when the marks started to disappear, but it was still interesting. And after that other person tried to barge in I thought it would be good for you to have someone watching over you."

He heard her stomach grumble and remembered that the testing probably would have used much of her energy, just as working on Henna had taken his.

"Do you want to head down to the kitchen with me to get something to eat?" he suggested.

"Is it okay to leave her?" Ginger asked, frowning at Henna's still-unconscious form.

"We'll pass my mother's room along the way. I'll let her know Henna is healed but resting, and she'll make sure someone is assigned to watch her." More likely, Maddy would go sit by Henna's side, perhaps even sleep in the bedside chair with Clay snuggled on her chest for the night.

"All right," Ginger said. Then, "Wait. No. I should probably get home."

"You should eat something before you go," he urged her. "You don't have the training yet to real-ize how much power you burned during the testing.

Putting out power without taking anything back in is asking for trouble, and a bad habit to get into." Truth, every word. What he didn't mention was that he also wanted to have some time to talk to her before she returned to Celadon's clutches. "Come on. Let's raid the kitchen."

She smiled shyly, and for the first time it occurred to him that she was almost his age, and a girl, and to anyone who didn't know him, his protectiveness could easily be misconstrued as flirting.

Of course, what he had in mind was more like outright seduction—not for sex, but for her *life*. She deserved to be in the Order whether she knew it or not, and even if she didn't want to join them, Naples was horrified by the idea of her taking the brand. If a little flirtation could help coax her away from a lifetime of Quin brainwashing, it was worth it.

CHAPTER 41

HENNA

Henna opened her eyes to see dawning sun through the window of one of the healer's rooms.

She seemed to remember passing out, certain she would never know anything but the realms beyond again, so opening her eyes was a pleasant surprise. She turned her head and found Maddy next to her with Clay clambering up her body from her lap.

"Enna!" the toddler exclaimed, diving from his mother to Henna. "Enna all better? No boo-boo? No more abibi?"

His earnest concern and outpouring of words brought tears to her eyes. She braced herself to catch him, anticipating pain that never came. Remembering phantom claws ripping though her skin, Henna gingerly lifted her shirt and touched her stomach. Clay echoed her movement, patting her whole, unmarked, unburnt, uncut skin.

No more abibi, Clay had said. It was the first time she remembered hearing that word from him since the day Terre Verte had died.

Had she dreamed about an Abyssi?

"Naples did it," Maddy said, anticipating Henna's next question. "Even with all his strength, I didn't think he could."

Henna sat up. Though she was weak, for the first time in weeks she was not in any pain. Steadying the toddler against her chest and moving didn't make her body ache, which meant the burns and cuts that had marred her back were also better.

"And you're not the only one who's up," Maddy added. She stepped aside and there behind her, sitting in a bedside chair, was . . .

"Verte." The word came out as a whisper as Henna sprang out of bed. Her legs failed to support her. Verte moved to catch her, and Maddy moved to catch them both, with all of them reaching to make sure Clay didn't fall; soon the four of them were on the floor, laughing. Clay let out a squeal of delight, thinking it all a great game.

"We're quite a set, aren't we?" Maddy asked, but she was smiling. "None of us strong enough to fight a kitten."

That didn't matter. Butt still on the floor, Henna grasped Verte's hand, which was cool and trembled slightly as it squeezed hers weakly. "You're alive."

He was still pale, but it was the pallor of sun-deprivation and fatigue now, not the flat grayness of death.

"So it seems," he replied. He sounded dazed and his expression was unfocused, but that was understandable given what he had gone through. Henna felt a bit overwhelmed herself, and her brush with death had been far briefer than his.

Maddy managed to stand first, and offered a hand to Clay, who nearly pulled her back over when he tugged himself up. "Both of you, if you can walk, you can come down to the kitchen with me. If you can't walk, I'll bring something up. Either way, moving around and eating are what you need."

Henna and Verte helped each other stand. "I can walk," Henna asserted. She *wanted* to walk. She had been so sure she would never walk again.

Verte nodded quietly.

"This way," Maddy suggested. She moved slowly, allowing Clay to set an ambling pace as he walked with his hand in hers, leading them through back halls. "Indathrone is holding one of her meetings. I don't think we should get in the way."

"Indathrone?" Verte asked. "The farm girl?"

Sheer relief and gratitude had put Henna in a

good enough mood that she almost grinned, imagining what most people in the assembly would think if they heard their beloved Dahlia referred to as "the farm girl." Then her elation struck a wall, and reality cascaded down on her. How would Verte feel, to see such a woman running his country in his absence? How would the people feel, to see him returned after all this time?

All desire to smile gone, Henna considered everything they were going to need to tell Verte, starting with the demise of his parents and the devastation that had struck his country in his absence, and concluding with Dahlia's rise to power and the complicit role the Order in general, and Henna in particular, had played.

"We'll explain once you're sitting down," Maddy said.

There seemed to be a thousand miles between Henna's sickroom and the kitchen. By the time they reached it, she was winded and breathing heavily, and Verte's movements had become slow and lethargic. He paused as they passed through the hallway, near enough to hear bickering voices from the grand hall.

Clay settled into the corner to play with a set of painted wooden stacking cups as they spoke, occasionally interrupting their conversation as he *clacked* one against another with an unpredictable percussive rhythm.

"What is the meeting about?" Verte asked.

Henna and Maddy exchanged a glance. "There is a *lot* we need to tell you," Henna admitted, "but you should eat first and regain some of your strength."

"How long was I gone?"

Henna hesitated, torn between wanting to keep him calm long enough to see him get some sustenance into his body and the surety that she needed to be honest with him.

"Six weeks," she admitted. "And a lot has happened. But you need to—"

"That is the third time you've put me off." He wobbled once, caught himself on the wall, and turned toward the front hall. "I'm going to see what's happened in my city."

"Verte—"

He pulled away from her and strode down the hall with steps that gradually gained confidence as he neared the grand entry chamber, as if he drew strength from his determination. Henna followed closely, but short of putting hands on him and wrestling him back, she couldn't stop him. By the time they reached the great hall, Henna's heart was pounding so hard she could hardly hear the debating assembly.

She *could* hear the first whisper of, *Terre.*

"Terre?" someone repeated. And then another, and another, until it became a wave of sound. At the head of the high table, Dahlia's face blanched. She looked at the assembly—and they looked not to the prince for guidance, but to *her*.

At last, after too long, Dahlia stood and dipped into an awkward curtsey at the edge of the raised platform. Gobe, seated next to her, stood when Dahlia stood but lingered protectively by his beloved leader, glaring at Verte. Celadon and Jade, who had been with her at the table, both seemed frozen in place.

Dahlia stepped down and crossed through the crowd to stand in front of Terre Verte. Her lips were pinched and her hands were clasped tightly in front of her.

Celadon, Jade, and Gobe followed a few paces behind and flanked her as she reached the prince. Respectful, or protective?

"Terre," Dahlia greeted, with another deep curtsey.

Henna saw several people in the crowd make abortive moves to follow her example, then hesitate as they realized the three men hadn't. The ambivalence with which they all looked at Terre Verte was unmasked.

"Terre," Jade said at last, acknowledging Kavet's monarch with a nod of his head. Celadon's eyes were wide with shock, and Gobe's narrowed with dislike; neither spoke.

The crowd started murmuring again, a buzz that rose in volume as Dahlia and Verte stared at each other across the few feet of charged air. After too many moments when Verte only stared at her, Dahlia rose to her feet and lifted her head, expression mostly deferential—except her eyes, which flashed with unspoken irritation at his failure to acknowledge her.

"Truly, extraordinary things have occurred in my absence," Verte said, looking at the Silmari, the leader of the Quinacridone, and the Order of A'hknet youth in turn before his attention returned to Dahlia. Henna could hardly hear him over the crowd.

Dahlia lifted an impatient hand, a gesture Henna had seen her make countless times before, and silence fell again. "Terre, perhaps we could meet in private for a few minutes?" Dahlia suggested. "And Gobe, could you—"

"No." Verte interrupted her, which brought a rumble of disapproval from the crowd. "Finish your meeting. I am obviously not needed."

Dahlia went, if possible, paler. Celadon reached for her as if to stabilize her, but she waved him back.

"Terre—"

"Carry on," Verte said, firmly, before turning. With stiff movements, he strode through the crowd, which parted before him like a school of fish before a shark.

Dahlia and Henna exchanged a desperate look, and then Henna dashed after her prince.

Her love.

The monarch of a country that had, in his absence, quite obviously held a silent revolution.

He kept walking, out the front door and across the cobbled market square, as if oblivious to the stares and whispers that followed him. By the time Henna caught up to him in the royal gardens, her muscles burned and her head ached. Naples had healed her wounds, but her body was too weak to go racing about the city.

"Terre . . . Verte . . . please," she gasped. "I can't keep chasing you. And I need to explain."

Verte's strength gave out and he collapsed to his knees in front of the blackened, thorny stalks that were the only remains of the snow roses.

"Six weeks," he whispered, on his knees with his shoulders hunched and his hands pressed against the fallow dirt. "Six weeks, and the Quinacridone are meeting in the Cobalt Hall? Six weeks, and I walk into that place, and a Quin country farmer stands in front of me and holds up a hand for silence before she summons me into a private meeting? *What in the Abyss has happened to my country?*" he demanded. "Where are my parents? How can they condone—"

His expression fell, undoubtedly in response to Henna's own.

"Tell me," he said. "Tell me everything that has happened."

So she did. She started at the beginning, with seeing him fall. The Terra summoning the Abyssi to defend him. The palace being sealed off. The storm. Naples' fight with the door. The weeks of hardship, of turmoil, of suppressing riots. The meetings. The shipyard.

Dahlia's rise to power.

Henna did not dash away the tears that ran down her cheeks as she told him of the wild power, of the affliction upon the members of the Order of Napthol. Of Helio's death. Of her own fears. Of seeing Naples on the floor, his body barely more than meat left over after the claws had savaged him.

Verte did not cry. Instead, his expression turned cold and blank. When she tried to stop, though, and urge him to return to the Cobalt Hall to rest, he commanded her to continue.

She explained how Celadon had helped them break into the palace at last, and how they had discovered his parents' deaths, and then, against all expectations, found him.

And she told him of sitting beside him to scry, to try to find some answers to all these horrible things. As she described those last few moments before her wounds had appeared, she had to press her hands against the graveled ground to keep her body and breath steady. Only as she spoke did she remember the argument she thought she had overheard. Had it been a nightmare, or had it been real?

Were the Numini and Abyssi really fighting each other, using sorcerers' bodies as their battleground? She didn't describe that part because she didn't think she could put it into words yet.

She did tell him how she had opened her eyes to

find blood all around. She told him of falling, of being sure she would never get up again.

Verte stared at the dead roses almost the entire time. When Henna fell silent, wishing he would say *something*—selfishly wishing he would comfort *her*, when she knew it should be the other way around—he stood instead.

"Please don't make me chase you again," she pleaded.

"I'm not going far."

His footsteps took him behind the palace, past the edge of the gardens to the Terre mausoleum. He knelt in front of that crypt, reverently this time.

"There is a grave in there," he said, "that belonged to a prince, years ago, who was lost at sea. The coffin is empty except for silk and jewels."

"Verte—"

He shook his head. "My mother, my father. Where are they?"

Henna blinked. She didn't know the answer. "I was away when the palace was opened. I assume your father's body was brought to the mortuary for internment. The service hasn't been held yet." Dear Numen, had it even made it onto the *agenda*? Surely someone had remembered to arrange a memorial?

Dove would have remembered. If not her, Sepia, or . . . *someone* would have at least tended to death rites for the king of Kavet. Wouldn't they?

"We never found your mother's body, but Dove

confirmed her death," Henna added, keeping her moment of panic to herself, to discreetly follow up on as soon as Verte wasn't looking. She wouldn't let him see how cruelly his family had been neglected. Forgotten, even by her.

"You said she summoned an Abyssi," Verte murmured, sounding distant. "The beasts of the Abyss can devour a human faster than you can draw breath, and leave no trace behind." He shared the grisly fact without apparent emotion.

A chill breeze whipped around them, making Henna shiver. She looked up and saw that the sky was heavy with dark clouds.

"Maybe we should go back inside?" she suggested.

Verte looked up at her with an empty expression. "Inside *where*? Inside the Cobalt Hall, where the Quinacridone seems to rule now? Or inside the palace, which has been given as a home to foreigners and the dispossessed?"

"We will make this right," Henna promised. "But for now, what is important is that you get your strength back. Kavet still needs you. Please, come back to the Cobalt Hall with me."

"I'll stay here a little longer first."

"Verte—"

"Damn it, Henna!" he cried. "I was willing to give my life for Kavet. That's what I was raised to do, and it's what I did. But I never thought my father would give *his* life to take away those wounds, never expected to have *Celadon Cremnitz* of all people drag me back into this realm. Never expected to crawl my way back to consciousness and look up only to realize I *am not wanted here.* So let me lie here and be at peace a little while. Alone."

"I'm sorry," she whispered.

"Please, Henna."

"May I sit with you?" she asked.

He looked up at her at last, his gray eyes shining with tears. "I would appreciate that."

She sat and leaned against his side. If it rained, they would get wet, but a summer rain never harmed anyone. If this was what he needed, she would let him have it.

I never expected Celadon Cremnitz of all people to drag me back into this realm.

Verte probably didn't realize it, but he had confirmed one of Henna's worst fears. There was only one reason he would need to be brought *back* into the mortal realm: if he had already passed beyond it.

I was willing to give my life for Kavet. That's what I was raised to do, and it's what I did.

He had been dead. Henna wanted to think it had only been for a few moments, until his father healed him, but knew that was naïve. He had been in the realms beyond for weeks, until they bullied Celadon into bringing him back.

"I've told you about how the weeks have passed here," Henna said. "Do you want to talk about . . . about anything?"

His body answered the question for her as he started to shake, and his breath hitched in a muffled sob. She wrapped her arms around him and leaned against his shoulder, trying to comfort with her nearness, knowing there was nothing she could say.

"I don't remember it well," he whispered, his voice hoarse as he spoke around his tears. "But I . . ."

He trailed off. Aside from his gasping, hitching breaths, he was silent for several minutes.

"The Numini see us as infants, young and foolish and in need of authority figures so we . . . so we don't soil ourselves and choke on our toys." His bitterness gave way to awe as he continued. "But to be with them is to be like a child wrapped in a mother's perfect love and protection. They welcomed me and said I could stay forever, but then they locked me out, an unwanted child desperately pressing his face against the window until they chased me away."

"When your father called you back?"

He glanced at her, tears making his lashes darker and emphasizing his startled expression, as if he hadn't realized he was speaking aloud or that she would hear him.

He shook his head, lifting his face and closing his eyes as the first drops started to fall, blood-warm in the summer air. His eyes closed, Verte didn't flinch as the skies opened, and the cascade of rain turned his body to a glistening silver statue.

Henna instinctively hunched against the water, then shook herself, remembering once again the little girl who had laughed through a summer shipboard squall.

Let this rain be cleansing, she thought. *Let it give us strength.*

They would need it.

DAHLIA

CHAPTER 42

DAHLIA

Dahlia took a deep breath and gripped the edge of the table to keep from swaying as a wave of dizziness swept over her.

It had been like seeing a ghost. She had heard the whispered word, *Terre*, spread through the crowd, and then she had looked up and into his eyes and the horror had seeped over her.

And guilt, of course. How many petitions had crossed her desk, suggesting a vote to officially renounce the Terre line and vote Dahlia Indathrone into power as official President? She had refused to acknowledge them or ever bring the subject up at the assembly, because she knew what would have happened. They would have approved the measure in a landslide.

Fool, she cursed herself.

She should have stayed down in her curtsey. If only she could have found the words she needed, she could have expressed gratitude for Verte's return and asked him to step to the high table in her place. She could have escorted him back into power.

Instead, she let her pride get the better of her. When he had ignored her, she had stood, met his gaze as an equal, and then made that damning movement, which had become so natural to her in the last month. She had taken authority in the moment she might have passed it to him.

"Can we please get back to the topic at hand?" she implored the chaotic group for perhaps the fourth time.

She had considered walking away after the Terre left, but feared without leadership the crowd would become a mob, answerable only to its own whims. So she had climbed once more into her chair at the high table, and called the meeting back to order.

"I think the topic at hand should be the Terre being alive," someone shouted back. "And what we intend to do when he comes back in."

"He *left*," someone else said. Too many people were talking too loudly for Dahlia to pick out the owner of each voice. "He obviously didn't have any respect for this assembly. He'll just—"

"He's the *Terre*," someone, one of the members

of the Order of Napthol Dahlia thought, interrupted. "He was nearly killed in his attempt to protect this country from the Osei, and the king and queen *were* killed. They didn't abandon us; they were taken from us. Terre Verte is back now, and I think we should remember that—"

"Remember that we don't need a prince," one of the Silmari objected. Their presence, which had seemed so natural until now, suddenly chafed. What right did Silmari and Tamari nobles have, to weigh in on the subject of Kavet's government?

"Whether or not Kavet needs a prince," Dahlia said, "we do need a *ship*. I think we are all in agreement on that. That ship, and who will captain her, is supposed to be the first order of business today."

And what am I going to say to the Osei? She still hadn't written that damned letter. It had seemed natural the day before to think she would know more if Terre Verte woke. She knew *nothing* more.

"Where is Cyan, anyway?" someone asked.

Dahlia skimmed the crowd. Cyan *still* wasn't here? She had sent a message to his ship the night before, and another one early that morning. She had hoped he was just running a little late, since as far as she could tell, he was widely regarded as the best prospect for the position.

She looked at Gobe, who was always a fount of gossip. He shrugged. "Last I saw Cyan, 'e was walking off with some of his crew, and that sorcerer with the black hair and funny eyes. That was yesterday though."

The sorcerer in question had to be Naples, whose coppery-brown eyes were indeed notable.

"Celadon!" That was one of the sailors. "Have you seen Ginger's new sorcerer boyfriend anywhere about?"

Oh . . . *fuck*. When had *that* rumor started?

Celadon shot to his feet, murder in his eyes.

Putting all the authority she had unwillingly gained in the last weeks into her voice, Dahlia snapped, "Celadon!" He looked up at her and his expression turned sheepish. "Go get some air." She made sure the words were *not* phrased as a suggestion. "Gobe, run to the docks and find Cyan, or someone who can tell you where he is." The A'hknet youth nodded, and obediently scampered from the room.

Dahlia searched the crowd, and spotted Maddy near the back.

"Maddy, would you try to find Naples?" The woman nodded, and stepped out. "To the rest of you, we're going to take a brief recess. When we get back, we will decide on the ship captain, and then and only then will I open the floor to *respectful* discussion of the Terre's return. Suitable topics will *not* include Celadon's sister's love-life—"

"Or magic?" someone called out. He ducked back into the crowd before Dahlia could recognize him.

"Ginger Cremnitz is *not* a topic for *debate*," Dahlia

insisted, "and anyone who drags her reputation into this room will be immediately thrown out. Do I make myself clear?"

There were muted sounds of assent.

"Then we break until lunchtime. I will hold individual meetings in case anyone wants to add to the afternoon's agenda, but please remember I have a hard time holding more than a dozen conversations simultaneously."

She stepped down from the dais and, as expected, was mobbed instantly. She fell back on her calm smile, an expression she had learned to hold during the last six weeks no matter what was going on behind it. She nodded and smiled and spoke softly, until those around her reflexively lowered their voices to match hers, and once they had done that she said, "Would one of you mind bringing me a glass of water?"

The patient, blasé request stymied all of those who had worked themselves up to argue about the Terre.

Someone brought the requested water. Dahlia took a sip, and cleared her throat.

"I have heard the thoughts that many people have raised over the past six weeks," she said to the men and women standing before her, "but most of those comments and suggestions were in answer to what we believed to be abandonment and negligence by the royal house. The Terre has been *sick*, recovering from wounds taken in defense of Kavet, and I think we must—"

"The Terre," one of the men pronounced, "was

dead. I was one of the doctors there the day the Osei—" He swallowed thickly, cleared his throat, and continued. "I was there. So were more than a dozen healers from the Order of Napthol and every doctor in the city of Mars. The strongest healers in the Order pronounced that there was nothing they could do."

"What . . . exactly . . . are you implying?" Dahlia asked. She inwardly cursed herself for sending Maddy away just when her input was needed most. She and Dove were best equipped to respond to these kinds of accusations and explain the magic that had brought Verte back.

"I'm not *implying.* I'm saying it right out," the doctor replied. "We have no idea who that man is, but I for one doubt he is who he looks like."

"If not the Terre—"

The doctor spoke over the objections of those around him.

"The wyrm can change their forms," he pointed out. "It's common enough in Silmat for them to try to sneak into the population by masquerading as humans. The Queen of the Third House tried to take Terre Verte as her prince. They want control of Kavet. Who is to say this isn't how they plan to take it?"

"We would recognize an Osei," one of the members of the Order said, a novice whose name Dahlia didn't know off the top of her head. He often attended meetings, but tended to hang near the back and not participate.

"Would you?" the doctor replied.

"Then we test him with iron," one of the Silmari suggested. "That's what is done back in our country."

The young sorcerer gasped. "You do not seriously mean to ask the prince of Kavet to prove his identity!"

"You're a magic user," the doctor said, turning on the sorcerer. "Were you there the day the Osei attacked? Did you see the wounds?"

"*I* saw them." *Thank Numen*, Dahlia thought, as she heard Naples' sardonic voice in the crowd. She was doubly grateful that Celadon was still out of the room. "I am the only person who followed the Terra and Terre into the palace, and spoke to them both, and saw the measures the king had taken to revive his son."

"Measures that would have taken six weeks?" the doctor scoffed.

"Possibly," Naples replied. "Terre Jaune was the best healer in this land. He had wrapped his son in some kind of shell, doubtless to hold him in stasis and keep him alive while he—"

"Not *alive*," the doctor said, softly. "Say the truth. Hundreds of us, everyone in the market that day, saw him die. If Terre Jaune was keeping his son anywhere, he was keeping him from crossing over to the world after. For how long? And if you believe Terre Verte is who he says he is, I would argue we have something even more dangerous in our midst than an Osei. We have a soul trapped on this plane. Or maybe just a body without its soul."

"Spoken like a Numen-damned *Quin*," Naples spat. "Terre Verte is *alive*, and here you stand and slander him, because you haven't the faintest idea how our power works."

"I haven't used your magic, but I have heard the rumors. I know that since Terre Verte fell, your people have been afflicted by 'wild power.' I know it has killed at least one of you. I know it has struck even Ginger Cremnitz, who never meddled with your works in the entirety of her life. I may not be a magic user, but in my time as a doctor I've cut an arm off a man to keep it from poisoning the rest of his body. I can recognize the signs of an infection."

"Serves." The sharp, unexpected chastisement came from Ochre, one of Celadon's Quin followers with whom Dahlia had intermittently clashed since their first interaction at the Apple Blossom Festival. "This isn't the best time or place or manner for this discussion."

Serves; Ginger's beau. Ginger hadn't mentioned he had been a ship's doctor, but it made sense given the rest of the conversation.

Letting Ochre's words be the final say on the matter of Ginger—and speaking over Serves' attempt to make them otherwise—Dahlia asked, "Naples, do you know Cyan's whereabouts?"

The sorcerer tensed as if stung and answered too sharply, "Why would I?"

Not helpful. Hopefully Gobe would be able to find him quickly.

Dahlia spotted Celadon coming back inside, skin and hair slick from the rain Dahlia hadn't even noticed falling. She nodded toward one of the back conference rooms, then turned to Naples.

"Would you be willing to tell me more about what you saw when the prince was hurt?" she asked the young sorcerer. She needed to talk to him, Maddy, and Dove, she decided, and come up with a plan before she let the council reconvene.

She spoke the words "would you be willing" as a matter of courtesy. She didn't expect him to practically snarl, "No, I would not be willing, because it's none of *your* business. Verte is back—and someone needs to point out that he is not prince anymore, but with his father's death, he is *king*. It isn't up to country farmers or Silmari sailors or A'hknet courtesans or even Napthol sorcerers to make that decision. He is the only legitimate heir to the line that founded Kavet from a bed of volcanic rock a thousand years ago!"

Without waiting for a reply, he turned sharply and stormed off toward the private areas of the Cobalt Hall.

Dahlia sighed. "Jade, would you try to find Maddy, and Dove if you can?" She had expected Maddy to come right back, but something must have delayed her. "I want to consult with them before we reconvene this afternoon."

Jade nodded. "I'll find Gemma as well," he offered, referring to the Order of A'hknet leader, who generally chose whether to attend meetings based on how she felt the topic would specifically affect her people. Otherwise, she spent meeting times supervising work rebuilding the docks. "Should I plan to sit out, and hear your thoughts this afternoon?"

"Yes. Thank you." Naples' words hadn't fallen on deaf ears. He was right that this wasn't a matter for the foreigners to decide.

As they entered the conference room, Celadon said, "This is going to get ugly. Do you have a plan?"

"Do you believe the accusations about the Osei?" she asked, keeping her tone neutral to hide her own skepticism.

Celadon scoffed. "I wish it were so simple. At least that would be an easy accusation to prove or disprove," he said. "I believe he is Terre Verte. But I do fear what magic brought him back into this world, and I think anyone who thinks the rising of the wild power is coincidental is an idiot. But maybe that's a price the Napthol is willing to pay."

"They say they don't know what is causing the injuries."

"The magic they use does not come from this plane," Celadon asserted. "Naples all but admitted that to me. After all, it is hard to doubt where he believes his power comes from, after he accused me of making deals with the Numini to get mine."

"He did not!" Dahlia exclaimed, just as the door opened to admit Maddy, who was even more sodden than Celadon.

"Sorry for the delay," Maddy said. "I went to check on Terre Verte. He and Henna might both drown in this rain, but otherwise he's all right . . . as all right as we can expect, anyway. Dove won't be able to join us. She's working with Sepia and Tealyn to plan the memorial services for Jaune and the Terra, now that their deaths have been officially confirmed."

"Of course," Dahlia said hollowly. It hadn't even crossed her mind to plan such a thing, perhaps because she had thought of the king and queen as having been dead for a month and a half. She had mourned them long ago. She cleared her throat, thinking about how she would confront Maddy about the fact that Terre Verte clearly *had* been dead, and what did that mean now? "What are we going to say when people ask about Terre Verte this afternoon? They deserve to know the truth about their prince, but—" She corrected herself. "King, I mean. Naples is right about that. If we acknowledge him, he is king."

She couldn't miss the way Maddy tensed in response to her words.

"We're not considering *not* acknowledging him, are we?" the sorcerer asked with unconcealed horror.

"I'm not officially considering or not considering *anything*," Dahlia sighed, looking toward the door. Once Gemma arrived, she feared they were going to need to discuss just that—how to support Terre Verte's return as king, and how to respond if the citizens of

Kavet were truly insistent that the time of kings in Kavet was over.

It's too big a decision, she thought. This one council in this one city couldn't possibly speak for the entirety of Kavet, but they had no choice. What happened in the Cobalt Hall in the next few hours, she feared, would define the future of the entire country.

CHAPTER 43

NAPLES

Naples stormed away from the argument, feeling foolish for engaging in it at all. These people were too ignorant to listen to reason, and anyone ungrateful enough to sit there and whine about the sacrifices the Terre had made for them wasn't worth his breath.

And Cyan! It wasn't Naples' responsibility to know where every old lover was, and Cyan had made it clear that's all he intended to be.

Or so Naples thought.

It was hard to clearly remember his last few, biting moments of argument with the sailor. The wave of fury had been like a drug-haze, an Abyssal dream. He had been impressed with Dahlia once, when she had stood up to the Quin who tried to harass her at the Apple Blossom Festival, but what gave her the right to interrogate him?

She wasn't interrogating you, you fool. It was a simple question.

With the Abyss pounding in his brain, his own common sense sounded like an alien voice, distant and unfamiliar.

He needed to hunt. No, he needed to *eat*. He was showing all the signs of power addiction, which wasn't surprising since he suspected he had gone weeks without ever properly grounding his power and reaffirming his tie to the mortal world. The edgy hostility would pare back if he could pull his power in.

You need help.

He couldn't ask for help.

Finding Ginger poking about in the kitchen lifted some of his simmering irritation. When she had trudged home late the night before, he had worried he would only ever see her again when she came to take the brand. Now he smiled to see her.

"Morning," he said, using a yawn to hide his grin and putting a pleasant tone into his voice with less effort than he feared it would take. It helped that his relationship with Ginger was neither antagonistic nor sexual. His power had no interest in her, so he was able to more easily view her as a human being would. "It's chaos in the next room, if you hadn't noticed."

"Probably my brother, with more of his high-handed holier-than-thou big-brother-knows-best-so-bow-down-and-worship propaganda," Ginger spat, with enough venom to take him aback.

"I take it your conversation with him last night went . . . badly."

Ginger nodded to the corner, where a battered travel bag sat. "I can stay here, right?"

The last word was soft and desperate, and made his heart ache for her. His irrational rage at Cyan's rejection had been amplified by his magic, but it had originally been caused by genuine pain. The look in the sailor's eyes when he turned from solicitous lover to skeptical accuser had been worse than a knife. What would it have been like to face that from his own family?

"You can stay here. I'm sorry about—"

"People don't choose to have magic, right?" Ginger demanded. "I mean, I could choose to take the brand, and be rid of it that way, but there's nothing I did that *gave* it to me."

He shook his head. "Some people just have it."

I have spoken to you and crafted you like a blade since your earliest memories.

"Celadon says being around magic users can cause it."

Naples shrugged. "That might be true. There do seem to be more sorcerers born in areas where they gather and study. But we don't know anything for sure." Modigliani would probably know, but Naples never had the sense to ask any such scholarly questions when in the Abyssi's intoxicating presence.

Ginger sat down hard in one of the chairs. "Well if that's the case, it's *Celadon's* fault, isn't it? *He* has magic. And he's got Serves on his side, now, too." At Naples' confused look, she explained. "Serves was courting me. He was worried I was so late getting home last night, so my aunt said he could wait with her for me to come home. I told him where I had been, and he and Celadon both started *yelling* at each other, and it was like when Dahlia left." She bit her lip, and added in a soft voice, "Celadon *really* doesn't like you."

"I know." There was an understatement.

"Serves said a lot of nasty things about you, too."

"He's a sailor?" Naples asked, assuming the ignorant fool in the next room and Ginger's Serves were the same man.

"Sailor and doctor," Ginger answered, with what looked like a habitual smile, which quickly faded.

"There are a lot of true things he might have said, and a few nasty not-true things," Naples admitted, remembering Cyan's accusation that he had raped and tried to kill Celadon. Given Serves' occupation and the fact that he'd been in the Cremnitz home at the time, the accusations he had slung about probably had less to do with Celadon and more to do with Naples having fucked half the sailors in Kavet. The Followers of the Quinacridone frowned on such libidinous behavior, especially when it included two men. "But whatever he said, it looks like you decided to come back here."

"Yeah, well . . ." Ginger paused, and had thankfully turned back to the cabinets when she said, "Whatever. It's not like you're having sex with my brother."

The expression she missed on his face was paired with a sudden bout of coughing from the doorway. Naples turned, with an over-solicitous, "Mother. That cough sounds . . . terrible . . ."

Maddy drew a wheezing breath, coughed once more, and cleared her throat. How much had Henna told her about what she had seen? Enough, apparently, that she had tried to smother an inappropriate laugh.

"Yes, came on me very suddenly. Just then."

When she sat, though, the wince that crossed her face was genuine.

"Are you all right?" Naples asked. Damn it, Henna had said many of the others were afflicted with these power-driven wounds, but it had never occurred to him to worry about his own mother.

She nodded. Naples saw the lie in it, but she was his mother. If she felt the need to hide her pain at that moment, to appear strong to Ginger and perhaps to him, he couldn't force her to do otherwise.

"Ginger, it's good to see you here again," she said instead. "Are you hiding from the foolish debates in the next room, too?"

"The shipyard debates aren't foolish," Ginger retorted. "Jade is a good captain, but he's an aristocrat, and a lot of sailors object that he was given his position and didn't earn it. If the vote goes with him, a lot of people will wonder if that's just because Dahlia was behind him, and that will damage his authority even more. Cyan's considered one of the best prospects. His interest in sorcery makes a lot of the Silmari nervous, but those who have served with him say he is stern but fair." Her gaze slid to Naples. "Mikva is also vying for the position, but there are rumors that she sailed pirate when she was younger. Some of those rumors work for her, since she knows how to handle herself in a sea fight, but Kavetan and Silmari sailors are mostly men, so her sex works against her, too." Noticing that both Naples and Maddy were looking at her with surprise, she shrugged and blushed. "Serves talks about the captainship campaigns a lot. I listen. It's interesting."

"Would you rather be out there following the debates, then?" Maddy asked. "Or participating? You're not of age to vote yet, but Gobe forced them to pass a measure saying everyone over the age of twelve has a right to speak."

Ginger shook her head. "They're going to elect Jade, especially once the rumor gets out that he's asked Mikva to serve as his first mate if he wins, or has offered to serve as hers if she does. Whether or not he is the better captain, there's one thing he can offer that Cyan can't ever match." She held up her hand and rubbed three fingers together in a familiar sign for "money." "He'll be able to draw credit from the first Silmari-allied port the ship stops in, to repay Kavetan merchants who are providing supplies, and pay for any trade goods we manage to get aboard. That's probably why Cyan didn't bother to show."

It's not my fault, Naples thought with relief.

"I wonder—" Maddy didn't finish before she started to cough, for real this time. The racking coughs doubled her over, and when they ended, she left dots of scarlet on the handkerchief she used to blot her lips. "How bad is it?" Naples asked.

Maddy stared at the crimson smear on the handkerchief, then carefully folded it and tucked it away again. "Not as bad as it looks," she said.

"Let me see?"

She shook her head. "Healers haven't been able to do anything."

"He healed Henna," Ginger reminded her. "Maybe you should let him try."

"Henna's wounds were made with hot power," Maddy pointed out, with the gentle tones of a teacher correcting a student's misconceptions.

But when Naples reached to roll up her sleeve, to further reveal the wound he could just barely see past the cuff of her shirt, she didn't stop him.

Thick bands of ruined flesh twisted their way up her arm, sunken like scars but ashen and chalky-black like frostbite. Naples had met sailors whose fingertips looked like that, but he had never seen such extensive damage so high up a limb. It wasn't in patches, as if the skin had been exposed to the cold by a gap in clothing, but in twisting lines as if caused by ropes colder than ice.

There had to be *something* Naples could do.

He had to swallow twice to control his revulsion and force himself to gently touch his fingertips to the worst of the injuries he could see. Then he closed his eyes, trying to visualize the extent of the damage the way he had with Henna. The blood on her lips meant something inside was hurt.

With anyone else, it would have been impossible without the help of similar magic, but this was his *mother*. He had been born of this body.

He had barely touched the edge of the silver power he could feel deep within her before a jolt like lightning went through him.

He heard a *crash*. The *thump* of something heavy hitting the ground. People calling his name.

When he opened his eyes, he was on the floor. Modigliani was licking his cheek, and Ginger was grasping his hand. Only a heartbeat had passed; his mother was still laboring to push her sore body out of her chair to come to his side.

"Stupid," the Abyssi said.

"Naples, Naples, talk to me!" his mother said, as she knelt stiffly beside him.

He raised the hand Ginger wasn't squashing. "I'm okay. That was unexpected."

"Because you're stupid," Modigliani provided.

"I wouldn't let the Numini touch you. Why do you think they would let you touch one of theirs?"

Naples waved away Ginger's and his mother's help, wary of touching anyone with cold power at that moment, and stumbled to a chair on his own. Modigliani stayed behind him, wrapping him in his tails to warm him from the chill of divine magic.

"I'm sorry," Naples said.

"Don't you dare apologize to me!" his mother snapped, fear making her voice shrill. "And don't ever try that again or I swear to Numen I will set you over my knee like—"

"Don't." His eyes widened. Just for an instant, he had seen her power flare, silver and gold like a halo, visible even to his usually cold-blind eyes.

"Don't . . . what?" she asked, aware that he wasn't objecting to her frightened threat.

"Swear to Numen," he said. He understood a little, suddenly. "One of the Numini is what has its claws in your power. When you invoke them, you make it stronger, and it hurts you more."

"That doesn't make any sense," Maddy objected, but Naples saw Ginger nod thoughtfully. What he was saying wasn't far from what the Quin had been warning them all of for years.

"Just . . . don't," he said. Everything hurt.

"We should feed," the Abyssi suggested.

Yes, that would be a good idea.

No. He was going to eat.

He needed to move, though. The kitchen was thick with cold power, like a rising field of static electricity that would shock him if he dared touch anything. He needed to get away from it.

"I'm going to go out for a while," he announced, pushing himself up. "Maybe I'll . . ." He trailed off. If this had been a simple case of power exhaustion or addiction, he would have gone to Henna. Could she help him against an Abyssi? "I'm going to the market." He could find something to eat there. *Something that once ran on four legs.*

That was his plan, but it wasn't the central market his feet took him to. Despite the rain, which was no longer cascading down in sheets but still maintained a steady fall, he took familiar streets down to the dockside fishing market.

His once-usual haunts were strange and bleak, a strange juxtaposition of rubble and new construction. The fire had gone out long ago, but his magic responded to the memory of heat trapped in the charred debris that hadn't been fully removed, and the shadow of soot that remained on buildings that had been near the blaze but hadn't burned.

One of the few buildings that appeared complete and open was a wharf tavern whose sign read *Crawdiddy*. The symbol of A'hknet was proudly displayed via a stained-glass panel in the front window that Naples thought he remembered seeing on another building previously; it must have been salvaged from the fire.

Inside, Naples ordered a plate of salmon and a hard cider he barely tasted as he sat alone, listening to a nearby bard singing "The Seduction of Knet," which described how a "creature of fire" had been wooed and won by a "creature of ice" and transformed into the entity from which the Order of A'hknet took its name. The original Tamari versions of the song never used the words Abyssi or Numini, but Naples had heard translations that did. He shook his head now to hear it, considering all the things Modigliani had said, and trying to imagine what mad circumstance would lead to an Abyssi and a Numini even speaking to each other in reasonable tones, much less bedding each other.

"Naples?"

Lost in thought, Naples hadn't noticed Cyan's approach until the sailor stood across the small table, hands on the back of the chair on the other side.

Naples felt himself hunch like a cornered animal, and tried to force his body to relax. "Cyan," he managed to say, before his throat tightened and he could say no more. It probably sounded curt.

"Can we talk?" Cyan asked.

Naples shrugged, and gestured toward the empty chair.

"You know they're looking for you at the captain-ship vote?" Naples asked as Cyan sat down.

"Gobe found me and I sent him back with a message. The vote's a sham at this point, anyway. It was decided the moment Mikva said her family has a letter of marque that will earn them safe passage through the territory of the Twelfth House, and Jade said the Chanrell fortunes could safely secure any debt the ship incurs before she leaves here. I can't compete with blood, not for this voyage, so I figured I'd save myself a walk in the pouring rain."

Naples winced, taking the words many ways. He hadn't forgotten their conversation about Kavet's version of nobility, or that Naples was part of it.

"I'm sorry."

"I am what I am. I'm *proud* of what I am. I worked my way up to second mate on the *Blue Canary* on my own merits. I'll be third on this vessel, for now, but I don't think Jade will last long as captain. He'll want solid land under his feet before the year is out." Cyan shrugged, then sighed. "And you are what you are. I spent a lot of time since I saw you last consulting with A'hknet witches about sorcery. None of them practice your kind of magic, but they knew enough to give me some perspective."

"And what did you learn?" Naples asked guardedly.

"That men can be assholes when you blue-ball them." Cyan's blunt words startled a laugh from Naples. He added with more seriousness, "But I knew that already. I *didn't* understand how dangerous your power can be. There have been rumors lately about sorcerers being mauled or even killed by their magic. And I spoke to a guy named Wenge who went into pretty grisly detail about the balancing act your people must perform, between using your power and being used by it. When I asked you about a charm for the ship, I didn't realize that kind of spell might be as risky for you as my running the rigging in a storm."

Naples drew a breath, but instead of speaking, took another sip of his cider. He wanted to apologize, but how could he explain the terror that came from lost time, the fight with the Abyssi, or the way it had returned to claim his supposed "offer"? How could he possibly describe the way being in Cyan's arms had made him feel safe and cared for and *clean* again—or the agony of having that taken away abruptly, replaced by a reflection in Cyan's eyes of everything Naples felt about himself?

On the second attempt, his voice worked.

"I'll tell you the whole story," he said, "if you want to hear it. But not here." He didn't want these words overheard.

"We could go back to the Cobalt Hall?" Cyan suggested. "It's slowed to a drizzle out there, and Gobe said they would hold the vote after the lunch break, so it's about time for me to go show my support for the future captain. Afterwards, you and I can find somewhere private to talk."

Talk. Right.

Naples shook himself. They would have to find somewhere not *too* private, if Naples wanted to get through the whole story. Maybe he would be brave enough to ask Henna to join them, not only as a chaperone but to help him explain and maybe just to *help* him, once she, too, understood what was happening to him.

Or maybe not yet. He didn't think Modigliani would see Cyan as a threat, but he might see Henna as one.

He walked beside Cyan to the grand hall, and considered whether he would be able to stay long enough to watch the vote and be supportive without picking a fight. He had no intention of taking this sham of an assembly seriously unless Terre Verte deigned to join them, but many others clearly felt differently. Even his mother, though she wasn't currently in the room; maybe she was still working with Ginger.

"We were going to hunt," Modigliani purred, appearing after Cyan had given Naples a kiss on the cheek and stepped forward to join the others voting on the ship captainship. "That is better than wasting our time listening to talk."

The refrain was old and tired, but there was a new note in the Abyssi's voice. Anxiety? What could the demon have to be anxious about?

"Maybe later," Naples said.

"We should *go*," it urged, and this time it was definitely worried. Naples stretched out his awareness, trying to catch whatever power was unnerving the Abyssi, since he couldn't imagine anything else it feared.

Finally, the smell reached him, like ozone. The hairs on his body lifted and a cool breeze licked the back of his neck.

"It's not our concern," Modigliani said when Naples turned toward the private area of the Hall, the source of the errant power.

"My mother is back there," Naples argued. "That makes it my concern."

Henna had tried to glaze over her description of Helio, and what his body had looked like, but she hadn't been able to control her expression, and Naples had seen the horror there. If this inexplicable spike in cold power was about to claim a victim, it would probably be the most powerful magic user left in the Cobalt Hall: his mother.

He had to do *something*. He couldn't idly sit by while the Numini tore her apart.

CHAPTER 44

DAHLIA

As she crossed through the crowd back toward the dais, Dahlia wondered if it was too early to start drinking. Heavily. Or whether it was too late to pick up the habit.

Should she have sent someone for Verte? Or gone after him herself? Invited him to join the captainship vote, or lead it?

Her stomach clenched as she imagined handing her assembly to him, and having him take royal, unilateral control.

That's not your decision to make.

She wouldn't send for him, but if he came in, she resolved to recognize him immediately and ask him to take the stage to speak for himself. She hadn't decided yet whether it would be better if she then took a seat in the audience, to demonstrate she was willing to return to being his subject, or to leave the hall entirely so no one could appeal to her as leader.

She, Maddy, Gemma, and Celadon hadn't come to any conclusions or made any resolutions. Dahlia shouldn't have expected it; no matter how well those disparate groups had come to work together, they still had irreconcilably different opinions of the royal house. Eventually they had returned to the main room, bowing to the inevitable need to run the meeting before the crowd became a mob.

"It will be good to see home again, even if it will take a long trip to avoid Osei territory," Jade said, sighing as he stepped up beside her. Dahlia been considering the crowd, and had almost forgotten he was there. "I've enjoyed your company these last weeks, but I doubt it'll surprise you that I hope to keep to tropical waters as soon as this voyage is done. So, I suppose this is goodbye."

He touched her arm and she paused, lifting her gaze to his. When he was sure he had her attention, Jade touched gentle fingertips to her chin to tilt it up a notch higher. As he leaned down, there was a moment when she could have turned her head aside, but she didn't. Nor did she have time to consider the situation in detail before she felt his lips on hers. She felt her blood heat at the kiss, light as it was.

She didn't jerk away, but she put a hand on Jade's cheek to gently ease him backward. Like their entire flirtatious friendship, the kiss was nice, but ultimately she allowed it because they both knew it could never become anything more.

Next to Dahlia, Celadon cleared his throat, loudly. Dahlia heard assorted other reactions from the crowd around them, ranging from snickers to sighs, but ignored them to the best of her ability.

"Relax, Cremnitz," Jade said with a grin. "I'm just saying goodbye."

"A mighty forward goodbye," Celadon muttered.

"Celadon," Dahlia said, putting a hand on his shoulder.

Jade turned back to Dahlia, ignoring the other man. "Dahlia, it has been an honor to know you these last few weeks. You have become an incredible woman." With one of his quirky smiles, he added, "But even if I meant to stay, you're right that we would never work out." He glanced briefly to Celadon. "I don't have it in me to stand in the background and play second fiddle, even for a lady I admire."

He bowed, then mounted the dais where Mikva already waited. Looking over the crowd, he waved to someone in the back of the room—Cyan, Dahlia realized with relief. Even if it seemed unlikely that sailor would win the captainship, she had been worried about his absence.

"Am I asking you to 'play second fiddle?'" Dahlia

asked Celadon, pondering the words as she and Celadon slipped through the crowd to the refreshment table. The would-be captains could hold their court a few minutes longer, and then she would call the assembly to an official vote.

Celadon shrugged. "You don't *ask*; you require it. That's something I accepted before bringing up the subject of a courtship. You're all but running Kavet these days. Any man who wants to stand beside you is going to have to stand a little behind."

"What about when Terre Verte comes back? Will you be happy courting a duck farmer?" She spoke in a teasing tone, but the question was serious. The scribe who had offered her an apprenticeship had understood why she couldn't continue her work there as her assembly leadership position took more and more of her time, so there was no bad blood between them, but he had also filled the job long ago. Once Verte was back, Dahlia would once again be a penniless girl trying to make her way in the city.

"Will you be happy *being* a duck farmer?" Celadon returned.

"I'm hardly going to hold a coup because I'm sick of the farm," she mumbled, avoiding his gaze. Through the crowd, she saw another familiar face: Celadon's sister had just crept into the room with Maddy. She looked up, saw Dahlia and Celadon, and pointedly turned her attention toward the captaincy candidates.

"She's furious at me because I told her to shut up about that damn sorcerer," Celadon explained. "She wouldn't stop going on about him last night after she got home. Naples this, Naples that. My sister," he concluded, "has *lousy* taste in men."

"At least that's a relationship that won't go anywhere. I don't think she's Naples' type."

Celadon let out a sound that was almost a growl and the room became colder, enough so that Dahlia saw several people look around as if to identify the source of the sudden draft. Maddy shot a look at Celadon, warning in her gaze. She started to cross toward them, and Ginger followed reluctantly.

The instant they were close enough to be heard without shouting, Ginger announced, "I get to start my studies here today."

Celadon flinched visibly, as if she had slapped him. "Ginger, what Serves said last night—"

"Oh, Naples and I talked it out," Ginger answered, with a defiant toss of her head. "I was a little disappointed that he's into men, but maybe we can go down to the shipyard and look at boys together. I have a feeling we're going to be *great* friends."

Over Ginger's shoulder, Maddy mouthed the words *I'm sorry* to Celadon.

"Now excuse me, but I'd like to focus on something *important*." Ginger turned back toward the dais, giving the movement an extra flounce.

The girlish strut turned into a stumble; Ginger's

breath hissed in, and her hand went to the back of her neck as if something had stung her.

Celadon hastened to his sister's side, and reached her just in time for her to clutch at Maddy as her leg collapsed under her. Celadon lunged forward and lifted her off her feet, then turned to carry her, despite her protests, toward the private rooms at the back of the Cobalt Hall. As he did, Dahlia saw the blood seeping through the back of Ginger's dress.

"Put me *down!*" Ginger snarled. "Dahlia, tell him to—"

"You're bleeding!" Dahlia told her. "We need to see how bad it is."

"I don't—*aaah-eh.*" Ginger's protest cut off with a moan as the red stain spread.

The moment they reached one of the private sitting rooms, Celadon half threw Ginger onto a couch, and ripped open the back of her dress in one frantic motion. Ginger squealed in dismay, but Dahlia caught the girl's hand to stop her from pushing her brother away. They needed to know where the blood was coming from.

Ginger's back, once pale and smooth, was crosshatched as if she had been brutally flogged. As Dahlia watched, more injuries appeared, blood-blisters rising, bursting, and then falling into black-gray burns.

"Dear Nu—" Maddy cut herself off, clenching her teeth against the words. "Celadon, back off. You're leaking power all over her."

"I don't—"

"Get *back*!" Maddy shouted, shoving Celadon. He stumbled back several steps, and then hung in the doorway, gaze lost.

Ginger's whimper pulled Dahlia's attention back to her.

"It's okay," Dahlia said. She looked at Maddy, pleading with her to give the same assurance, with the strength of honesty.

"We're going to take care of you," Maddy murmured. "Celadon, run to the kitchen and bring back the red bag from the corner. It has all my supplies to treat these injuries. Ginger, try to breathe. You're going to be okay." She lifted the back of Ginger's shift to reveal another wound, this one livid red blisters in nearly the shape of a handprint, on the outside of her right thigh. "Celadon, go!"

Celadon jumped, and ran from the room.

"Can I do anything?" Dahlia asked.

"This shouldn't be happening." Maddy's voice wavered with her denial. "I never would have agreed to let her study here if I had thought this would happen. Dahlia, keep Celadon out. Ginger's power isn't strong enough to do this on its own."

"Celadon would never hurt her."

"Not intentionally," Maddy answered. "But that fool Quin has too much power, and he refuses to take a brand or study to control it. Who knows what he's doing accidentally? Convince him to keep out of here, then bring back that kit and some water. I need to dress these wounds."

Ginger mumbled something too soft to understand. Dahlia could hear the squeak of pain in her voice. She dashed off in the direction Celadon had gone, which caused her to collide full-body with Naples, who had been coming the other way. "What's happening?" he demanded.

"Ginger," Dahlia gasped out. "Help me find—" He had already shoved past her. Dahlia heard another yelp from Ginger as he pushed through the doorway, but this one sounded more like a complaint of modesty rather than pain.

Celadon had already found the medical kit, a basin of water, and towels by the time Dahlia located him.

"I'll take it," she said. He handed her the kit and the towels, but it was clear that she wouldn't be able to hold all three things without spilling the water everywhere. "Help me carry this, but then you have to go. Maddy thinks your power is making this happen. Not intentionally," she added hastily, "but because you can't control it."

They returned to find Naples sitting in front of Ginger's sprawled form. He hadn't reached for her, but was talking to her softly. The instant Celadon entered the room, Naples' head whipped around and he growled, "Get out of here."

"You." Dahlia thought Celadon was going to follow the guttural word with something more foul, but instead he fell next to Naples. "Can you heal her? She said you healed Henna."

Naples shook his head. "I can't do anything with cold power."

"Celadon, you have to *leave*," Maddy and Dahlia said almost simultaneously.

Naples shook his head. "It doesn't matter at this point. Your power has already done its damage by opening a gateway." He started to reach out as if to take Ginger's hand, then stopped, balling his hand into a fist in his lap. "You're going to be okay, Ginger. You'll get through this."

Maddy snatched the supplies from Dahlia and Celadon and began gently cleaning the wounds. "Naples?" she asked.

She didn't need to clarify her request. Without looking away from Ginger, Naples touched the metal edge of the basin of water. Moments later, Dahlia saw steam waft across its surface.

Ginger coughed, but managed a half smile. "This is embarrassing," she groaned, with what Dahlia couldn't help but think of as the composure of a Quin lady in the face of personal fear. It was the same inner steel Dahlia had summoned to help her cope with being thrown from Celadon's aunt's house at the beginning of all these misadventures.

Naples shook his head, the light expression on his face more obviously forced than Ginger's. "This is nothing," he said. "When my power did this, I ended up stark naked in front of Henna. *That* was embarrassing. You've still got most of your shift."

Ginger laughed a little, then winced.

"Also," Naples said, continuing soft banter to keep Ginger distracted as Maddy cleaned and dressed the wounds, "it really upset this guy I had just met. Nice fellow. Not my normal type—he's kind of Quin, actually—but a sweetheart."

Ginger smiled as he continued to speak. Celadon scowled, and Dahlia readied herself to step between the men if he tried to pull Naples away from Ginger. Thankfully, no matter how Celadon felt about Naples, he seemed to recognize that the sorcerer was helping her keep calm.

"Almost done," Maddy said. "You should stay as still as possible until the blisters go down, but you'll be okay. I don't think the wounds are deep."

Speaking to Naples, Ginger asked, "Would you hate me if I said I think maybe I've decided to take the brand after all?"

Naples swallowed heavily. "I think you and your brother should both take it." He looked up with a black glare, as if responding to a voice Dahlia hadn't heard. "No," he said angrily. Then he added, "Fine, then fix it!"

"Naples?" Ginger asked, her brow wrinkled in confusion.

Naples stood, and continued his argument with thin air. "No. No, don't *give* me that rubbish. I don't care."

"Who are you talking to?" Dahlia asked, uneasily staring at the spot where Naples' words seemed to be directed.

"*What* are you talking to?" Celadon amended, edging closer to Naples and Ginger while visually sweeping the area around them.

Naples turned back to Ginger. "Come on, hon," he crooned. "We should go. The brand—"

He reached for the girl, and the concussion in the air made Dahlia's vision cross with spots and her ears ring. When she looked up from where she had fallen, the only person still standing was Celadon.

"Naples!" Maddy's cry turned all of their attentions to where the young sorcerer was kneeling, gasping. He had been thrown into the wall with so much force he had left a crack in it. "Naples, are you all right? What—"

"I'm fine," Naples said. As he struggled to his feet, he was clearly leaning on something Dahlia saw only as open air. "Ginger, go with my mother. To the palace. She knows how to give you the brand, against pure cold power. Even if it's done in haste, it can't do more damage than not doing it now can. Dahlia, help them."

Ginger drew herself painfully to her feet, pulling her shift into place as well as she could. When she tried to put weight on her injured leg it buckled beneath her, so Dahlia took her arm to support her.

"*Later*," she snapped, at the first person who tried to get in her way. Then at the second. As a half-dozen "concerned" citizens—nosy would be more accurate—blocked their way, she shouted, "Gobe! I need to get through."

The Order of A'hknet boy didn't bother with niceties. He started stomping feet and whacking at the crowd with a fireplace poker. After a few shins were bruised, people started backing up and pushing others out of the way.

They raced across the market plaza. Maddy's ministrations had partly closed Ginger's wounds, but her swift bandaging couldn't keep them from opening again in response to their frantic movement; Ginger's blood trickled over Dahlia's arm as they followed Maddy through the palace doors, and then along increasingly narrow side halls until they found an ominous, steel-gray door carved with symbols that made Dahlia's vision swim and her head pound when she tried to make them out.

Maddy yanked it open and gestured for them to go ahead, down narrow stairs.

They left Kavet's humid, sea-salt air behind, and entered a place where every breath seemed flat and not quite sufficient.

Maddy's face was gray and she held her lower lip tightly between her lips as she peered into the rooms they passed, looking for something.

"Here," she said, her voice colorless as she pulled

them into a nondescript room. "Lie down, Ginger." She gestured toward a couch whose utilitarian lines made it appear angular and cold instead of simplistic and elegant, then held up a leather strap. "Dahlia, help her hold this between her teeth."

CHAPTER 45

NAPLES

As his mother, Dahlia, and Ginger hurried to obey his frantic commands, Naples accepted the Abyssi's help to stand. He had a feeling he had separated a rib from his spine when he hit the wall; he could feel it shifting inside him, cutting him. A few months ago, the pain would have been debilitating, and the injury possibly fatal.

Learning how to harness the Abyssi's power had made him no stranger to pain; he could move past it, and use both the pain and the internally pooling blood as fuel not just to heal the injury but to prepare for the upcoming confrontation.

Celadon turned slowly, as if his body were unfamiliar to him. He flexed his hand, staring at the way those digits moved under the fine layer of frost blooming across them.

"Celadon?" Naples asked.

"We should not be here," Modigliani warned.

"I don't fully understand what's going on," Naples said, "but this is my *home*. I'm not going to let him . . ."

The preacher looked up finally, and the eyes he lifted to the room looked blind. The pupils had constricted to tiny dots, and the normally blue irises were silver-white.

"We. Cannot. Fight. Numini." The Abyssi said the words as if he had said them a thousand times before—and maybe he had. Naples knew he was sick of being thrown across the room. "He belongs to Numini. You belong to Abyssi. So long as he has the Numen's grace he's no good to eat and no good to fuck and—"

"Since when?" Naples interrupted. Celadon had been powerful before, but Naples had been able to do more than touch him. Whatever had given Celadon all this extra strength, it had happened recently.

Of course, so had the Numini trying to crawl into the world through Ginger.

"When he opened the rift to bring the dead one back, the one you call Verte, he broke the veil between the mortal realm and the divine one. One of the princes of that realm rode him through the open door. Naughty Numini—but it's not our business."

"Celadon, listen to me," Naples said, ignoring the

Abyssi's warnings. "Can you hear me? I know I'm the last person you want to listen to, but whatever you're doing right now, you need to stop. You need to call that power back. Ground and bury it."

Celadon looked at him. Stepped forward. Modigliani swept between them, crouching protectively between its Abyssumancer and the Quinacridone preacher.

"Call it back, Celadon," Naples pleaded.

The preacher trembled and collapsed to his knees. His head bowed and his chest heaved as he fought to pull back the power he had unwittingly summoned.

"That's it," Naples whispered as Celadon struggled. "You'll be okay."

The next time Celadon looked up, his eyes were once again human blue, but they were still filled with a desperate kind of pain. "Something's wrong."

That much was obvious.

"We'll take you to get the brand," Naples said. "This is just—"

"No!" Celadon recoiled with a cry, until he stood with his back pressed to the wall. "I can't. I don't know why, but I know I can't take the brand. I know . . . I think they told me, when I passed the gate to bring back Verte." He whispered, seeming lost in memory, "They didn't want me to do that. It wasn't time. They tried to warn me, but I didn't listen. It isn't time, but time . . . they don't understand time."

Naples looked at Modigliani. "What is he talking about?"

The demon shrugged and rolled onto its back like a cat wanting to play, now seeming unconcerned. "Numini are very big on rules and right and wrong and how things should be, so they are always debating and saying this and that. It's tiring. Feed, fuck, play. That's what matters. Abyssi know."

There was too much residual magic in the Cobalt Hall; it had to be making this situation worse. Why had no one insisted Celadon either be branded or trained before this? Someone with this much power should never have been allowed to walk about ignorant. "Let's go outside, Celadon. It will help you clear your head."

And maybe, once outside, Naples could calm Celadon down and coerce him across the plaza and to the room in the palace where the brands were made.

Celadon nodded. Naples shook off the concerned questions from the ever-present collection of bureaucrats and would-be politicians and policy-makers in the hall as he herded Celadon out into the damp afternoon air. Having an audience seemed to do the preacher good; aware that he was being watched, he instinctively drew in his power to conceal it from others.

That was good.

Celadon stopped by the fountain, staring into the water and its one last foxfire orb. Modigliani slunk after them; when Celadon stopped, the Abyssi splashed a hand in the fountain, making Celadon flinch from the spray of water.

They had to get into the palace. Out of public. Out of danger.

Away from people—like the one approaching them right now.

At any other moment, *any* other, Naples would have been overjoyed to see Terre Verte. Now, he knelt anyway—it was the thing to do when greeting one's prince for the first time in weeks, and when so much of the country was uncertain as to whether it planned to do the same—but he itched to move on.

"Terre," he said respectfully.

"You found the right plane," Modigliani said, jumping up to greet Kavet's prince.

The Terre looked directly at the Abyssi. He frowned, as if struggling to remember, and at last said, "You pushed me."

Modigliani nodded.

"You can see him?" Naples asked, a wave of joy sweeping through him, and almost making him forget about Celadon. Terre Verte could see the Abyssi. That meant . . .

Naples had no idea what that meant. Even Henna, whose power was closest to Naples', hadn't responded to the Abyssi's presence earlier. He never would have expected Terre Verte, who mostly used cold power, to see it.

He didn't know what the dazed look in the Terre's eye meant, either, or why there was such a long hesitation before he said, "And you're Naples. Madder's son."

"Yes, sir." The Terre could use cold power. If he was strong enough to see the Abyssi, could he heal Ginger, and close her off to the parasitic power the way Naples had closed off Henna? "Terre, we're in trouble, and—"

"So I can see." Verte looked past Naples to Celadon as he said it.

Celadon struggled to his feet, looking at Terre Verte with a wounded expression. Naples resisted the impulse to curse. This was not the time for a Quin-Terre conflict.

"Celadon, keep calm," he urged. "Terre, could you give us a moment?"

Instead, Terre Verte's expression mirrored Celadon's—disappointment and sorrow.

As the blue of Celadon's eyes started to fade to silver, Modigliani yawned. "We might as well move on."

"Shut up," Naples hissed.

"You poor, abused child," Celadon crooned, in a musical voice that was more than human. It should have been beautiful, but it made Naples' guts writhe. "You aren't supposed to be here."

Frost appeared on the preacher's skin, as if he were made of glass instead of flesh and blood.

"Neither are you," Verte replied. "Celadon, Celadon," Verte said, his voice barely a whisper as he invoked the power of naming. "You don't understand the entities speaking through you. You have to control them before they do more damage."

Naples expected Celadon to shout back, but instead his eyes widened in an expression of pure panic. "Help me," he whispered.

Verte nodded. He stepped forward and touched Celadon's hand. "Stay with me," he said. "Focus. Don't let the Numini use you like this."

"A mortal can't fight the Numini," Naples recalled aloud.

"No," Verte said, "but a Numenmancer can. Celadon should be able to command them just like you can command your Modigliani." To the Quin preacher, Verte said, "Push her back. I can't do that for you. You opened the door in the palace against her will. You can push her away the same way. You remember how."

Celadon shut his eyes and Naples saw his lips move in silent prayer.

Terre Verte sat at the edge of the fountain, and Celadon knelt before him as he struggled against the divine force riding him.

"Good," Verte said, softly. "Almost."

The frost on Celadon's skin melted, and his flesh returned to a heathy, human color.

Naples looked up, and couldn't resist a smirk as he saw how large their audience had grown. How would the Followers of the Quinacridone react to seeing their leader in such a position?

Modigliani leaned against Naples' back, purring. "Can we *go* now? We still haven't fed, and I can't touch either of them."

"We'll go hunt in just a minute," Naples promised.

He wanted to make sure Terre Verte could get Celadon to take the brand, first. Ginger should be done by now.

Celadon smiled and gazed up at Terre Verte like a small, triumphant child showing off a new trick. His brow glistened with sweat from his exertions. He didn't seem distressed to find himself kneeling on the ground in front of a Terre.

"Celadon?" Naples asked. The preacher nodded. "Terre, he needs to take the brand. Celadon, you understand that, right?"

This time instead of panicking, Celadon nodded again. "I understand."

"I can do it," Verte said. "Naples, may I have my mother's blade?"

Naples drew the knife with a frown. "What for?"

"We should do this as fast as possible. I don't need all the tools we normally use."

Celadon looked at the blade nervously, but didn't flee. "What do you need me to do?" he asked. "And do we have to do it here?"

"Is the Numini still pushing at your thoughts, trying to come back out?" Verte asked in reply.

Celadon shut his eyes and drew a deep breath. "Yes."

"Then we must work quickly. It won't hurt." Verte held out his hand for the knife.

Naples handed the precious tool over reluctantly. That knife had become a part of him. It was twined with his magic, and—

In the instant Terre Verte's hand closed around the handle, Naples' awareness of the other man's power swelled. The shock of cold lasted only an instant, but it was enough. He could see behind the prince's eyes another entity, with talons and wings and righteous fury. The Numini wasn't riding him the way it was Celadon, but its essence suffused him like a drug, or a poison.

"Wait—"

There was no *wait*.

As promised, it surely didn't hurt. With the Numini subsumed and for the moment powerless, Celadon's body was defenseless to a blade driven with muscle and magic, straight between his ribs, and into his heart.

It was over in an instant. Celadon fell, a hand going to the hilt with shock.

The screaming began around them.

"I'm sorry," Terre Verte whispered. "It was the only way I knew to—" He staggered, and Naples shuddered against the flash of icy wrath. Whatever the Numini had intended for Terre Verte to do, this wasn't it. "I'm sorry," Terre Verte gasped. "I know you disapprove of bloodshed, but how else could I send her back to you?"

"Terre!" Naples was only barely aware of others running toward them. "What have you *done*?"

"A truly mortal act," Modigliani said, his body going taut, his eyes sparkling and his tail lashing. "Mancer, you have made your allies cross." The Abyssi deliberately moved closer and put a hand on Verte's shoulder. No flash of lightning challenged him; no icy blast threw him away. "Very cross."

Terre Verte dragged the blade out of Celadon's body and turned toward the Abyssi, biting out the words, "This is *my* world." He pulled the knife across his palm, mingling his own blood and the preacher's.

"You don't have the strength," Modigliani said, his eyes flashing with challenge.

Terre Verte concluded, "And you are *not* welcome here."

Naples recognized what the Terre was about to do only the moment before he slapped a palm to Modigliani's chest. The Abyssi shrieked, and Naples stumbled at the backlash of searing power, an instant before he would have pulled the two apart. They struggled.

And Modigliani was right—Terre Verte was not strong enough.

More screaming. It seemed like his ears rang with the cries of hundreds, even before the heat of blood surrounded him. Someone's hands were on Naples' shoulders, trying to pull him back, but he was aware only of the Abyssi and the fact that it had just, in a single move, rendered Naples' Terre to a wash of red that spattered across the plaza, sizzling and burning wherever it touched flesh.

Naples threw himself at the beast.

He was still weak; he hadn't hunted since healing Henna. He didn't have the strength to go hand-to-hand, or more rightly power-to-claw, against a prince of the lowest level of the Abyss.

It turned on him with a hiss and a slash of claws.

The blood was enough. Naples put a bloodied palm, not against flesh or stone, but to the veil between the worlds.

CHAPTER 46

HENNA

All at once, it was over, leaving behind the stench of sulfur and burned flesh.

Henna wiped blood from her eyes, but opening them only revealed more of the same: a red stain, nothing more. Celadon, Verte, and Naples were all gone, into that crimson wash. So too was the demon, which had only become visible the moment Terre Verte had set his hand to it.

Clay, huddled in Henna's arms, stared with his wide, innocent eyes at the bloodstains.

She and Verte had been almost dozing, still morbidly near the Terre crypts, when the burst of wild power from the Cobalt Hall had washed over them like a storm wave. Verte had urged her ahead, saying he needed to go more slowly, so she had reached the Hall alone, only to find novices and initiates alike bleeding and gasping. She didn't see Maddy, but she heard Clay's cries and dashed up the stairs to find Lassia curled protectively around the child as if to protect him from the phantom beast that had cut claw marks into her ribs.

Henna had taken Clay, thrown a pillowcase at the bleeding sorceress to use as a makeshift compress on the cuts—the wounds were ugly, but not life-threatening—and then hurried to find the others. She had been so relieved to find Naples with Terre Verte, and then, and then . . .

"What happened?" Maddy raced from the palace in a shambling, ungraceful lope that was the best she could manage with her own injuries. She hadn't seen . . . Thank Numen she hadn't *seen*.

For once, Henna would like to not be there, to not see . . .

Ginger, leaning heavily on Dahlia, limped to catch up to Maddy. Her skin had the flushed, sweat-slicked sheen of someone recovering from fever—or of a cold magic user whose power was just branded away.

"What happened?" Ginger echoed. "Where are Celadon and Naples?"

"Dead," someone whispered.

Henna's awareness extended like a bubble given

more breath. There were so many people around, staring. She had heard them scream when they saw the demon, but her mind hadn't grasped them as more than a disembodied shriek.

"No. No!" Ginger's objection was the useless protest of the helpless. "I was only gone a minute!"

Maddy's face lost all color and expression. She didn't speak, just stared at the splattered blood and power that had once been her oldest son.

Then everyone seemed to be shouting at once. Ginger, shouting for Celadon, as if he might just be hiding somewhere. Clay, shouting for his mama, who took him from Henna's arms and held him to her chest as the tears began. And of course, all the voices calling for Dahlia.

Dahlia, what's going on? Indathrone, please explain. Tell us what happened, tell us we're safe, tell us . . .

Dahlia must have heard her name as a dozen people called it, but the young woman never looked up from the carnage. She had no power. Even with decades of study, Henna wasn't sure she fully comprehended what had just happened—so how could Dahlia?

"What was that thing?" so many voices demanded.

Other cries reached Henna's ears. Words like *murder.* And *monster.* And worst, *deserved it.*

"We have to get inside," she managed to whisper. "Away from—" *the blood* "—the crowd."

She grabbed Dahlia's arm in one hand and Maddy's in another. Ginger stumbled after them, gripping Maddy's other side.

"I will call a meeting as soon as I have something to say," Dahlia managed to choke out, when someone from the crowd boldly broke away from the others and stepped in her way. "First *I* need to understand what just happened."

"Healers," Henna managed to say. "We need mundane healers, as many as are available."

Dahlia glared at the crowd when no one replied, and snapped, "You heard her. Gobe, Gemma," she said, spotting those individuals nearby, "I know there are herbal healers and apothecaries among your people. Can you get them?"

"Yes," Gemma answered simply. "Gobe, you run to Graham Street. I'll go to the docks."

"You can have free access to the Hall," Maddy said as they reached the entrance. "Please, help anyone you can."

In the meantime, they needed to come up with a plan to stop this, *now*.

"We don't *know*," Dahlia snapped at last, when one last sailor demanded an explanation just before they escaped the crowd. She slammed the hallway door on the continued noise from the crowd, and then closed and bolted the kitchen door as well.

"But we do know, don't we?" Maddy broke her silence with a quavering voice. "Naples explained it. He said . . ." She drew a breath, but it seemed to hurt her more than give her strength. "He said one of the Numini was what was causing the injuries, and that invoking it gave it more power."

"Not just Numini," Dahlia said. "I think he told Celadon he—" She hesitated, looking around as if worried how Naples' mother and friends would react to her words. "I think Naples was working with an Abyssi. It's what gave him *his* power."

Henna wanted to deny that, but how could she?

"This is my world," Henna muttered, "and you are not welcome here."

The blood on her skin had made the old injuries, the ones Naples had healed, ache afresh.

"Do we think the Terre was acting on his own?" Dahlia asked. "He spoke as if Celadon was being manipulated by the . . . the Numini. Do we know if Verte was acting under his own will?"

She stumbled over the name of the divine others, but that was all. She did not flinch to name the dead.

"I don't think we have any way of knowing," Henna said.

"It matters less," Maddy said, "than stopping it from happening again."

"How do we stop it?" Ginger asked. The girl sat awkwardly at the edge of her seat, cautious of the wounds both from the wild power, and from the brand at the center of her back. She kept fidgeting and scratching at the back of her hands, trying to relieve an itch Henna doubted would ever be soothed.

But she was alive, at least.

"How do we fight the denizens of the other realms?" Dahlia asked. "What does it take to weaken a *demon*?"

Silence fell.

Maddy stood, but only long enough to get a banana cookie for Clay. Henna watched crumbs fall to the floor.

"You'll get mice," Ginger warned as no one moved to sweep up the fragments.

Maddy shrugged and sat back at the table. Clay munched on his biscuit.

"There was a spell made," Dahlia said, "to protect against the Osei. Could something like that be used to guard against the Abyssi and Numini?"

"Aren't the Numini supposed to be *good*?" Ginger asked. "Why did they . . ." She choked off. Stood and got a glass of water.

They were all refusing to think about what had happened. Henna embraced the numbness of shock. Once it was gone she would start to feel again, and she couldn't afford that, not until they had come to a decision.

"The Numini aren't good or bad," Dove said. Her hands were clasped firmly in her lap, and covered by a shawl. Henna didn't want to know how bad the damage was. "They're creatures of absolutes, without knowledge of compromise or any acknowledgement of situation or moral relativity."

"Killing Helio was an accident, I think," Henna said, remembering what the creature who had spoken through Dove had said, and forcing herself to recall the terrifying moments when she had been certain she was about to die. "When I was hurt . . . I don't remember it well, but I think an Abyssi and a Numini were fighting over me. They both knew what they were doing could kill me, but they didn't mind that cost."

"So . . . we don't know what they want, ultimately," Dahlia said, "but it killed Helio, and Verte, and Celadon. It nearly killed Henna and Ginger, and others are still being tended by physicians. It seems clear that whatever they want, it isn't in our best interest."

"No doubt *they* think it is," Maddy grumbled.

"Is there a spell that might protect against them?" Dahlia asked.

"No," Henna snapped, frustrated. Maddy had already addressed that; Dahlia just hadn't understood because she didn't use sorcery herself. "The Others feed on power. Any spell we're strong enough to weave will only assist them."

Silence, again.

Ginger moved, painfully, to sweep up the crumbs.

"You don't have to do that, honey," Maddy objected, watching the girl make small, careful movements.

"I need to do *something*," Ginger said. "Sitting drives me crazy."

An idea seeped into Henna's mind. It was a horrible idea—but it was a horrible situation.

"How do you get rid of mice?" she asked.

Ginger looked at her like she was crazy, and then looked pointedly at the hand-broom she had picked up. "You don't get rid of mice, not unless you've got a cat. You stop leaving food out and they stop coming." She shook her head, and muttered a disdainful, "*Sorcerers. Don't know the simplest things.*"

"Henna?" Maddy asked.

"What's the best way to keep stray cats out of the garden?" she asked, wondering if the same memory she had just recalled would come to Maddy's mind.

Maddy stared blankly at her for a moment, frowning, then seemed to realize what Henna was talking about. A few years back, they'd had a terrible time with feral cats in the neighborhood. It had turned out that a nearby butcher had been deliberately leaving out scraps for them.

Maddy sounded puzzled as she answered, "Get your neighbor to stop feeding them."

Henna stood and paced as she spoke, thinking aloud. "Naples said invoking the Numini made them stronger. So we stop doing that. We stop feeding them, and make it so there's nothing here they want. Just like any other pest. Right?"

"We can't change the way people talk," Ginger said.

"That isn't true," Henna argued. "And I was thinking about more than that, anyway. For a little while, we *starve* the Others. We make the cupboard barren, so to speak."

Dahlia's brow crinkled. "I don't follow. What, exactly, are you proposing?"

"I'm proposing . . ." Henna drew a deep breath, arranged her scattered thoughts, and started again. "I've lost too many people I love, and come close to losing others—not to mention almost dying myself. I'm willing to make a sacrifice, if doing so means I don't lie awake listening in the night, wondering if the next time Clay screams it's because his magic is ripping him apart. I'm proposing that I take the brand."

She had seen what the brand did to a magic user, but it was nothing compared to the devastation the wild power had wrought in the last days. "As well as everyone else in the Order who is of age and willing. Those who refuse, we ask to refrain from using their power until it seems the danger has passed—small-magics as well as high sorcery, since we don't really know the effect of one over the other. I propose we shut down the temple. In short, I propose that we be very . . . very . . . careful to clean up all our crumbs."

"Not everyone will agree with you," Maddy said softly.

"Not everyone has had the blood of the dead splashed over them, not once but twice," Henna said flatly. "We'll convince them."

Dahlia rubbed her eyes as if they pained her. "I need to go back out there and answer the assembly's questions. If I try to put them off by saying the Order of Napthol is 'dealing with the problem,' they will riot."

Henna's heart was pounding so fiercely with the sweeping finality of her own suggestions that it dizzied her. She gripped the back of a chair to steady herself. "Tell them the truth," she said. "Tell them everything. Tell them the royal house served them loyally, but reached too far and damaged the veils between this realm and the next. Tell them that monsters from the Abyss and the Numen have walked the mortal world in the last few weeks, that their battling probably caused the ice storm and has caused death and injury since then. Tell them the sorcerers of the Napthol Order are going to do whatever we must to seal the rift and protect this world again."

"Ask the Followers of the Quinacridone for help, in Celadon's name," Ginger suggested, "before they can decide the Napthol sorcerers deserve what they get." She looked around before concluding with apologetic haughtiness. "You will need them. They know how to survive without magic."

Dahlia pulled her ever-present sheaf of paper from her pocket and made shorthand notes as she spoke.

"I'll address the assembly, tell them what has happened, and ask for volunteers to join a high-priority committee to draft a series of recommendations for how to eliminate all unnecessary magic from Kavet until such time as it seems the threat is passed." She frowned as she considered how people would respond to suggestions that they police their language, and whatever else the committee came up with. "We may have trouble with members of the Order of A'hknet. They don't like to be regulated."

Henna shook her head. "They don't like to be dead, either. We'll make it work."

Dahlia stood, straightened her back, and schooled her tired expression into one of determination. Henna's heart went out to the young woman.

You have no power in the traditional sense, the sense of magic, but you have a strong destiny.

Destiny was unfolding before Henna's eyes.

Dahlia was following her suggestion, but even so, seeing her square her shoulders sent a shiver down Henna's spine.

A whisper in the back of her mind asked, *What have I created?*

EPILOGUE

Choking and coughing in a futile effort to clear blood and ash from his lungs, Naples lifted his head.

He spat a gob of sooty crimson phlegm onto black sand that glistened like oil, reflecting every color in the world.

The instant his blood touched the sand, a swarm of long-legged white creatures, like some horrid combination between rats and spiders, scuttled over. Naples slapped one off his hand and shoved himself up and back with a cry, kicking another away as it tried to bite his ankle. He tripped over a rock jutting up from the sand, and barely managed to avoid falling on a jagged edge of what looked like obsidian, standing up like a blade.

He stood again, more carefully this time. The

white swarm watched him with gray eyes bobbing on gently swaying stalks.

Where . . .

He lifted his gaze to the horizon.

In one direction was a vast desert formed of black caves and rock formations. The darkness was broken by multicolored lights, and bleached-white bones. In the other direction, he saw jagged cliffs hosting what looked like the remains of ancient trees, fossilized eons ago. Where the cliffs met the beach there was a narrow rim of sand, which could be traversed if he watched his step. If he picked a direction.

Some kind of tar-like substance dripped down the cliff and ran in sluggish rivulets over the sand nearby, forming a lazy, ominous stream. It didn't look like a good thing to touch, and Naples didn't fancy his chances of jumping over it and maintaining his footing on the other side, so he put it behind him. And he started to walk.

And to walk.

Night fell, and he shuddered in the cold. Finally, his exhausted, battered body succumbed to sleep. He woke to find a creature like a giant green tick latched on to his leg. Naples had to use a shard of bone to cut each leg off before he could pry the creature's maw from his flesh. After, his entire leg ached. He wondered if he had been poisoned.

Could poison kill him if he was already dead?

He didn't feel dead.

Another night came. This time the darkness revealed a swarm of luminescent creatures. When he touched one, it exploded into a scalding wash of mercurial sludge that raised burn-blisters on his arms, shoulder, and face. He didn't sleep that night, just waited.

The next morning, he moved on.

Or, he tried.

With thirst and hunger clawing at him, he didn't get much farther before he fell. Maybe he could rest a little while . . .

Could the damned die a second time in this place? Or would he just lie here eternally?

A new kind of creature sniffed at him. Naples tried to lift his arm to shoo it away, but someone else did so first, kicking at it roughly.

When the woman knelt in front of him, Naples was sure he was hallucinating. Her eyes shone the way an Abyssi's did, but her wine-red skin was smooth, not furred. And she looked familiar.

She touched his shoulder where an ungraceful stumble into the cliff walls had drawn blood. "Not many people cross the realms with flesh intact," she said, before lapping his blood from her fingertips in short, catlike strokes of her tongue. "And you taste like power."

"Help me." His throat was dry as the sea beyond him, but he forced out the words.

"Why?" she asked, tilting her head. Again, she seemed so familiar.

"Please."

She smiled, and it was that smile at last that allowed Naples to recognize her—or, more accurately, her lineage. He was sure this was the Terra's child, most likely with the Abyssi Antioch. Given her apparent age, he suspected she had been conceived not long after Terre Verte was born.

"I always wanted a pet," she said, reaching out one slender hand. "Well, come along."

Verte opened his eyes. This wasn't right. This wasn't where he was supposed to be. Where was the crystal sea, with the sand like diamonds? Where was the gate, which should have opened for him?

I did what they told me to do.

Why had they forsaken him?

"Terre Verte." The low, rumbling voice was Modigliani's. The prince of the lowest level of the Abyss stalked around his prize. "You lost the Numini's grace when you slew another mortal, or else I wouldn't have been able to touch you."

Verte tried to stand, and only then realized his body was wrapped in chains.

"You have power," the Abyssi said, "and have done us a service by slaying the Numenmancer and driving his Numini out of the mortal realm. My sire wishes to make you a deal, if you will hear it."

The king of the Abyss was a sight no mortal could

see and survive. Only the dead and damned could look upon the darkest demons.

Verte stared long at a creature made of pure acid smoke, of claws and fangs but mostly just of *sharp* and *hot* and *pain*.

"I don't want to make a deal," he said.

He had that much pride left.

Too much pride, maybe.

Henna clenched her teeth firmly on the leather strip.

They called it *hot* power for a reason: it burned. As Maddy set the sigil against Henna's flesh, the magic screamed, and seared, and tried to tear its way into friendlier territory. Henna bit down harder to keep from shrieking, and more so, to keep from crying out, *"I've changed my mind!"*

Or worse, *"Dear Numen, make it stop."*

She was more powerful than Ginger had been, more powerful than any hot magic user still surviving within their Order. The brand had never been meant for someone like her. The human body wasn't made to take this kind of severing.

In the aftermath, her flesh felt cold and numb. There was no heat left in the world.

As soon as she was steady, she lifted herself from the chair. The brand, though barely the size of a coin, seemed to pull worse than any of the scarred burns and claw marks had.

"Ready?" she asked Maddy, as she prepared a different sigil with trembling hands.

Maddy did scream, the leather strip falling from her mouth to the ground. But it was a wordless scream, without a prayer.

Dahlia stood at the podium in front of the assembly . . . *her* podium, and *her* assembly. They had elected her President, but the Constitution they had intended to draft had fallen by the wayside, to be completed once other more important tasks were done.

At the council's suggestion, the memorial services for the royal family—Terre Jaune, Terra Sarcelle, and Terre Verte—had been brief and in the Quin style, with no mention of the realms beyond and none of the magical pageantry that would normally accompany such a lofty event. The funeral was scarcely attended, as many of the Order of Napthol sorcerers who would have been there were still recovering from the brand. Adding to the strangeness was the end, when there was only one body to inter.

Even Henna had opted to avoid that service, instead choosing to light dozens of candles and send them out to sea on a wooden raft. Mikva had helped her with the Tamari ritual, which Henna assured Dahlia invoked no divine or infernal powers, but only the sea and sky.

Around the same time, the final agreement with the Osei was sealed with what felt like anticlimactic fanfare, Terre Verte's sudden and violent death having removed the last obstacle to a disgustingly amicable arrangement. Like the rest of Kavet, the Osei recognized Dahlia as the leader of the land, though they called her queen instead of president. She had the impression they believed she had forcibly overthrown the monarchy in retribution for their crimes against the Osei, and wanted to reward her for that "service"; regardless of the reason, she was able to negotiate for safe passage and significantly lowered tariffs for Kavetan ships, favorable trading rights on several key goods, a right to purchase the freedom of any Kavetan claimed in payment for a defaulted debt, and a continued ban on any Osei flight over Kavetan land. After so much anxiety and time and power and blood had been sacrificed to that cause, Dahlia couldn't help but note how odd it felt that she signed the final treaty with a frustrated sigh, irritated that it was taking her from more important tasks.

The most critical work was drafting the document which held all the directives intended to lessen the grasp of the Abyssi and the Numini on the mortal realm. Creating it had taken weeks of debate, research, and preparation.

"Using the knowledge and suggestions given to us by the Order of Napthol and the Followers of the Quinacridone, and taking into account all of the revisions, requests, amendments and provisos this assembly has brought up, we have created what I believe will be a tolerable document for all. It's a little long, so we've printed several dozen copies of the final version so everyone can have a chance to read it. We'll hold the vote in one week's time."

Argent, the head of the farmers' coalition, looked up with a frown from where he had been flipping through the pages. His testimony about what he had seen when Naples battled the Abyssi—winning once, and losing once—had gone a long way in the debates about how dire the threat to Kavet was.

"'A little long' is an understatement," he said. "How much of this applies to those of us who don't use magic?"

"Quite a lot of it," Dahlia replied. She, too, had been surprised to learn how many little things even non-sorcerers could do to help. "I know it's long," she said again when she saw the restlessness in the crowd, "but I'm going to encourage everyone to read *all* parts. We need to be very careful."

Ginger flipped to the end, skimming the text there. "All one hundred . . . and . . ."

"One hundred twenty-six."

"Why do they do these things?" the arbiter demanded. "I could have helped them, but everything became so twisted so quickly. Time does not pass the same there as it does here. It is all so . . . confusing."

Veronese wanted to comfort his companion. They had

been together through the millennia. They had grown up together in the Age of Tears and had worked together through the Age of Mending, as they struggled to turn the mortal realm into something where their children could prosper and not know endless suffering. He could not find the words.

Deep in the Abyss, his own chosen child, the heir of a bloodline he had nurtured for generations, screamed as Abyssi savaged him in what they considered "play." Veronese had meant only to chastise the mortal for his rash actions, with forgiveness surely to come after proper repentance, but Modigliani had acted swiftly and stolen him. Now Verte was nothing more than a bone torn between dogs as the Abyssal beasts battled for supremacy.

On his knees in the deep drifts of snow that covered the highest level of the Numen, Veronese wept tears that turned to crystal upon impact with the frozen ground.

"All is not lost," Doné insisted. "I swear I will—"

"You will do nothing. Our king has commanded us to leave the mortal realm alone. Swear to me only that you will obey."

"I swear," she replied, "that I will make this right."

—END BOOK TWO—

ACKNOWLEDGMENTS

For its first draft, *Divine* owes particular thanks to the Office of Letters and Light for hosting National Novel Writing Month, and Bri Maresh for leading my virtual writing group (and providing valuable insights into toddlers, years before I ever had my own).

Revising *Divine* involved massive amounts of research, consults with sensitivity readers (thank you Ollie Lavelle in particular), feedback from longtime readers (Mason and Zim, looking at you), fresh eyes (thank you Chris Duryea), and a great deal of encouragement from my local writing group led by Remy Flagg. Even with all that support, I never could have managed without the many hours of babysitting provided by my sister Rachel, my parents, and my friend Karl so I could attend those writing group meetings.

Finally, this book never would have reached you, my readers, without the support of my agent Beth Phelan and the team at HarperCollins, including my editor Priyanka Krishnan.

ABOUT THE AUTHOR

AMELIA ATWATER-RHODES wrote her first novel, *In the Forests of the Night*, when she was 13 years old. Other books in the Den of Shadows series are *Demon in My View*, *Shattered Mirror*, *Midnight Predator*, all ALA Quick Picks for Young Adults. She has also published the five-volume series The Kiesha'ra: *Hawksong*, a School Library Journal Best Book of the Year and VOYA Best Science Fiction, Fantasy, and Horror List Selection; *Snakecharm*; *Falcondance*; *Wolfcry*; and *Wyvernhail*.

www.atwaterrhodes.com
www.harpervoyagerbooks.com

Discover great authors, exclusive offers, and more at hc.com.